The Executor

Jesse Kellerman

W F HOWES LTD

This large print edition published in 2010 by
W F Howes Ltd
Unit 4, Rearsby Business Park, Gaddesby Lane,
Rearsby, Leicester LE7 4YH

1 3 5 7 9 10 8 6 4 2

First published in the United Kingdom in 2010
by Sphere

Epigraph from *Faust* by Johann Wolfgang Goethe, translated
by Walter Kaufmann, translation copyright © 1961
by Walter Kaufmann.
Used by permission of Doubleday, a division of Random
House, Inc.

A CIP catalogue record for this book is available
from the British Library

ISBN 978-1-40745-935-6

Typeset by Palimpsest Book Production Limited,
Falkirk, Stirlingshire
Printed and bound in Great Britain
by MPG Books Ltd, Bodmin, Cornwall

FSC
Mixed Sources
Product group from well-managed
forests, controlled sources and
recycled wood or fiber
SA-COC-1565
www.fsc.org
© 1996 Forest Stewardship Council

To Gavri

The philosopher comes with analysis
And proves it had to be like this:
The first was so, the second so,
And hence the third and fourth was so,
And were not the first and second here,
Then the third and fourth could never
    appear.
That is what all the students believe,
But they have never learned to weave.
– Goethe, Faust

Choose, said the Fool.
– The Book of Odd Thoughts, 17:19

CHAPTER 1

I used to own half of Nietzsche's head. It was the only thing I truly considered mine, and on the night Yasmina threw me out, it was the last item I retrieved before going to the door and turning around to offer my concluding thoughts.

She spoke first.

'I've always hated that.'

I said nothing.

'I'm sorry,' she said. 'I know you love it. But it's really creepy.'

I told her I didn't want to argue anymore.

She asked if I would be okay. I told her it didn't matter. She insisted that it did, so I told her yes, I would be fine. This was false. I said it so she wouldn't feel guilty. You cannot live with someone for two years without developing a kind of reflexive sympathy, and I knew that if I didn't reassure her, she would spend the whole night awake, worrying about me. Not without cause: she was putting me out in the middle of a blizzard. She ought to've felt guilty. But pride forbade me from exploiting that.

'I'll be fine,' I said again.

'The more you say it, the less I believe it.'

Still, she didn't seem inclined to let me back in, her body blocking the doorway. Behind her was the apartment where we had lived and worked, where we had slept and talked, where we had made love. Observe the bulletin board, pinned with photographs and paper memorabilia, evidence of a shared history. Dinners with friends. Weekends in Salem and Newport. Remember the coffee table, a battered leather trunk unearthed at an estate sale. Adjacent to the front door, a nail juts out of the wall. Sometimes something hangs there, its absence a conspicuous reminder of all that has gone wrong.

I'm not a man easily lost for words, but standing there on the verge of expulsion, I couldn't think of a thing to say. Tears periodically rolled down her expressionless face, as though out of obligation. The contrast between us could not have been greater than at that moment. She was small and dark, bejeweled, glittering, and elegant. And I? Six-foot-three, ruddy, thick-limbed, capable of holding all my possessions – the entire physical evidence of my existence – in two hands without breaking a sweat.

This speaks primarily to how little I owned. Packing had been a depressingly brief process, everything fitting into a medium-sized duffel bag – which I'd had to borrow from Yasmina. Half the bag belonged to my laptop, my books, and six inches' worth of unfinished dissertation. The other half contained my shirts, fraying at the cuffs; my jackets, mangy at the elbows; my wrinkled khakis and jeans. Jammed into the bag's side pocket was one pair of brown loafers, scuffed beyond repair. All told, a thoroughly wretched wardrobe, one that reflected a self-image cultivated over years: rumpled scholar. Clothes belonged to the world of things. I belonged to the world of ideas. Fretting over my appearance would have meant acknowledging the importance of how others perceived me. Back then I found this idea repellent. To some extent I still do. Despite everything, part of me cannot relinquish the notion that I stand outside society, above its judgments.

It is a part of me that grows smaller every day.

Last, there was Nietzsche's head. Half-head. The left half, to be precise. I'd found it in an East Berlin flea market. For the life of me I can't say what I was doing there. (In the flea market, that is. I know what I was doing in Berlin: spending yet another travel grant doing yet more research for yet more of my never-ending dissertation.) I've never been one to make frivolous purchases, and everything one finds in such places is, essentially, frivolous. If memory serves, I was coming from the *Staatsbibliothek*, headed back to my tiny studio in Prenzlauer Berg, mulling over what I'd read that day. I must have strayed from my usual route, because when I stopped moving I found myself standing in a noisy aisle I could not remember entering, in front of a booth I could not remember approaching, holding an object I could not remember picking up.

Cold and heavy, it was made of cast iron, with a

square base that sprouted into a half-bust, a human head split sagittally: one ear, one eye, the left half of a nose. The crudeness of the workmanship testified to clumsy hands wielding inferior tools: the proportions were off, the surfaces uneven, and the eye in particular had an unreal quality to it, set alarmingly far back in its socket, as though staring out from the void, the surrounding flesh seamed and trenched. Somehow, though, this lack of refinement contributed to the overall effect, and anyway, the moustache, even one half, gave it away. Really, who else could it be?

'*Sehr lusting, ja?*'

I looked up at the vendor. He bore a distinct resemblance to Joseph Stalin, which was surreal, because among the Soviet-era kitsch strewn across his table was a teakettle adorned with hammers and sickles and emblazoned with Stalin's own face.

I nodded and turned the object over, revealing a bottom lined with peeling green velvet.

It was a bookend, the vendor said. Its friend – that was the word he used, *Freund* – was missing. He didn't know where it had come from, although he theorized that it had once belonged to a professor. '*Ein Genie,* ' he said, *a genius,* adding that the world would not be the same without him. Coming from someone who appeared to have neither shaved nor showered since perestroika, this seemed a wonderfully intellectual sentiment, and as a philosopher, I was moved to see how Nietzsche's ideas,

4

so often misunderstood, could still inspire the common man.

'$E=mc^2$,' he said. '*Ja?*'

I think I did a good job of hiding my dismay, although at that point I felt it my responsibility to take the bookend into custody. Anyone who mistook Nietzsche for Einstein could not be trusted. I asked the price. He took a second to size me up, weighing my desire against my shoddy sportcoat, before asking for thirty euros. I offered ten, we split the difference, and I left elated, my bag fifteen pounds heavier.

Over the last few years, the bookend had become something of a totem, a reminder of happier times, when I could still get travel grants. By the night Yasmina threw me out, of course, all that had changed. My funding had dried up, with no more forthcoming. My teaching positions had been given away to others in greater need, those who still held promise, those in their third and fourth years of graduate school rather than their eighth and counting. My so-called advisor had not spoken to me in months. Around Emerson Hall I had become, if not persona non grata, then a white elephant.

I therefore cherished the bookend, keeping it atop the stereo cabinet in the living room, where I could see it from my desk in the corner. It offered encouragement. Moreover, it was my sole contribution to the décor. Yasmina had never objected, and to hear her true feelings took me aback.

As I stood there, trying to conjure up an appropriately clever parting shot, I cradled it against my chest, protecting it from her.

'It looks like he has a badger on his face,' Yasmina said.

'Half-badger,' I said, vaguely.

I will assume the best of her and say that I don't think her behavior was calculated to inflict maximum damage. She was self-absorbed, but I knew that about her and loved her all the same. Even when I began to sense us circling the drain, I'd always told myself she'd never be so thoughtless as to put me out without notice. I'd been wrong.

Though I wanted to go out on a zinger, in the end all I could muster was an attempt at irony.

'The life of the mind,' I said, holding up my meager stuff.

'Enjoy it,' she said and closed the door in my face.

Downstairs, Drew was waiting in his car. He put down his Sudoku, popped the trunk, and got out. Then, seeing how little I was carrying, he shut the trunk and opened the back door instead.

We had gone most of the way toward Somerville when he cut the volume on the radio and said, 'I hope you know you can stay as long as you like.'

It was then that I knew I needed to get out as quickly as possible.

Lying atop a creaking sofabed – Nietzsche's one

lunatic eye gazing down at me from the windowsill, the snow behind him swarming like a cloud of ideas – I began making a list of avenues to explore: job websites, Craigslist. Briefly, it occurred to me that I ought to get a copy of the classifieds. The idea of finding my destiny in a newspaper seemed quaint – indeed, ridiculous – and despite the abject circumstances, I smiled to myself in the dark. Now I look back and understand that getting ahold of that paper was, if not the first significant decision of my life, at least a necessary step toward all that followed, every one of my catastrophes.

CHAPTER 2

The next three weeks found me bounced miserably from one couch to the next. Soon enough I learned that the price of a few nights' hospitality was that I retell my sob story from the beginning, usually to the woman of the house but sometimes to him, too, the two of them sitting opposite me, brows knit concernedly, holding hands as though to shield themselves from my virulent bachelorhood. Given my druthers, I would have stayed with other bachelors. Aside from Drew, though, I didn't know any. That's what happens when you've been coupled for two years: you know only other couples. And I couldn't go back to living with him, not because he wouldn't let me but because his apartment was an atrocious sty. It was just as unbearable as being forced to explain yet again how Yasmina could have possibly punted me when we'd always seemed so happy.

I needed my own place. That much was obvious. Less obvious was how to go about obtaining it, given that my bank account held a hair over two hundred dollars. I was no closer to finding work, having failed to submit a single application. My standards were high, cripplingly so. Whatever I did, it would have to be at least minimally intellectual, while still leaving plenty of time for my dissertation. Some friends thought I ought to be open to the idea of working at, say, a bookstore: a job with an aura of scholarliness, and unlike the visiting lectureships I spent my time ogling on academic networking sites, one I might conceivably get.

'Or you could tutor,' they said.

I told them I'd rather starve.

At that point I saw no cause for panic. Sooner or later, Yasmina would call, begging me to return. It made no sense to get comfortable elsewhere if I was just going to have to pick up and move back in with her. So I kept ringing up one friend after another, calling in favors, burning through all the goodwill banked over my dozen years in Cambridge. Every morning I'd rise up from whatever junky couch I'd slept on and take my laptop over to the Yard.

Emerson Hall, which houses the philosophy department, has its own dedicated library. It is proof of the extent of my alienation from colleagues and teachers that I avoided the place unless absolutely necessary, preferring to sequester myself in an abandoned corner of the sixth floor at Widener, where I sulked and pretended to write.

It was on one such afternoon that I found myself half-heartedly skimming through the *Crimson*, picked up more for diversion than anything else. The writing always made me smile – bumptious undergraduates proclaiming home-brewed solutions to global problems – until I realized that, five years hence, those same undergraduates would be editing the opinion page for the *New York Times*.

Classifieds in Ivy League newspapers cater to the young, the smart, and the desperate. Several ads solicited attractive, non-smoking women between the ages of twenty and twenty-nine as egg donors. Infertile couples would pay up to twenty-five thousand dollars plus expenses, a figure that made my head spin. My yearly stipend – back when I had a stipend – had been less than that. All for a single cell. I made a mental note to call a sperm bank and investigate the going rate.

One ad offered custom tote bags for your sorority; another a ten-year-old Volkswagen Jetta in good condition, below Blue Book. A third appeared to promote a self-published book about the history of the universe, for sale through the author's website. I say 'appeared to' because the copy was nigh on unintelligible and the person who'd written it quite plainly delusional. Anyone can advertise in the *Crimson*. All you need are no fewer than fifteen words at sixty-five cents apiece.

So, actually, I could not have advertised in the *Crimson*. The eighth and final ad came in just over the minimum.

CONVERSATIONALIST SOUGHT.
SERIOUS APPLICANTS ONLY.
PLEASE CALL 617-XXX-XXXX
BETWEEN SEVEN A.M. AND TWO P.M.
NO SOLICITORS.

Contemporary philosophy's primary activity is the hard scrutiny of language. I reread the text several times, understanding it and yet not. What kind of conversationalist? Sought by whom? Merely 'sought,' in the sense of being necessary, the way a cheap source of alternative energy is 'sought'? Can something be sought without there being a seeker? Of course not; that's not the way the verb works. Presumably the seeker in this case was the person who had placed the ad. As the sentence stood, however, lacking an agent, I felt as though I was reading the description of a state of being, rather than a job offer.

How could an applicant determine his serious-ness without knowing what the job entailed? Did 'serious' mean that I had to be serious, or that my application had to be capable of being taken seri-ously by my prospective employer? For instance, I might seriously desire to become a fire-breathing lesbian astronaut, but one could not reasonably describe my chances as serious.

The ad's tone warned as it invited, one hand outstretched, the other up in defense. Who said anything about solicitors? Perhaps the seeker was concerned about identity theft. In that case, why

11

publish a phone number? Why not an email address or, for the truly old-fashioned, a P.O. box? Something here did not jibe, and I had the feeling that I was staring into the mouth of a scam. These days it's hard to be too suspicious, paranoia no longer a patholgy but a mark of savvy.

Still. It sounded so strange, so enticingly strange.

I could have called from inside the library – there was nobody around – but I have always considered Widener a temple, disturbing its dusty silence a sacrilege. I packed up and left, crossing the Tercentenary Theater in the direction of Canaday Hall, the hideous dormitory known as 'The Projects,' where I'd lived as a freshman. Outside the Science Center, the snow was soiled, compacted by hundreds of feet, and I paused to watch a group of students putting the finishing touches on a giant, Daliesque snow-ear. Once indoors, I breathed on my hands, took out my cell phone, and dialed. A recorded voice told me that this account had been deactivated, message one-one-four-seven.

I tried again and got the same voice, and after it happened a third time, I realized that this was actually happening. Yasmina had cut me off. That she footed the entire bill seemed irrelevant just then; she had once again stranded me without a word of warning, and I was livid. I almost threw the phone against the wall. My need for a source of income grown even more pressing, I went downstairs in search of a pay phone.

★ ★ ★

12

She sounded elderly. I thought I detected an accent, although I needed to hear more than a single hello.

'Yes, hi, I'm calling about the ad in the *Crimson*.'

'Ah. And with whom am I speaking?'

'My name is Joseph Geist.'

'A pleasure to meet you, Mr Geist.'

'Thank you. Same to you, Ms . . .' I paused to let her introduce herself. She didn't, so I said, 'I'm intrigued. What sort of conversationalist are you after?'

'A catholic one. Small *c*. Is that how you would describe yourself?'

'I think so. Although for the record, I'm Catholic, big *C*, as well.'

She laughed gently. 'Well, I shan't hold that against you.'

I'd settled on German, although her inflections were decidedly different from those I'd encountered in Berlin. Perhaps she was from the countryside, or another city.

'I'm no longer practicing, for what it's worth.'

'Ah, a lapsed Catholic. That I find more to my taste.'

'Glad to oblige.'

'So, Mr Geist, the lapsed Catholic, you saw my advertisement. You are a Harvard student, I presume?'

To explain my exact status would have taken far too long. I said, mostly truthfully, 'Graduate student.'

'Yes? And what do you study?'

'Philsosophy.'

There was a tiny pause. 'Really. That is very interesting, Mr Geist. And what kind of a philosopher are you?'

Though tempted to puff myself up, I decided to proceed with caution.

'A catholic one,' I said. 'Small c.'

She laughed again. 'Perhaps I should ask instead your philosopher of choice.'

I couldn't possibly anticipate her tastes, so I said what I thought would best provoke and amuse: 'Myself, of course.' Except what I actually said was, '*Ich, natürlich.*'

'Oh, come now,' she said.

But I could hear her smiling.

'I shall be pleased to meet you, Mr Geist. Are you available at three o'clock?'

'Three o'clock – today?'

'Yes, three o'clock today.'

I almost said no. I didn't want to seem too needy. 'That should be fine.'

'Very good. Allow me to give you the address.'

I wrote it down. 'Thank you.'

'*Danke schön, Herr Geist.*'

Standing there, receiver in hand, it occurred to me that we had not set any terms. I didn't know how long she wanted to talk or what she wanted to talk about. Nobody had mentioned money, so I didn't know what, if anything, she intended to pay me. I didn't even know her name. The whole arrangement was incredibly bizarre, and I wondered if it was a scam after all. She sounded harmless enough, but.

The phone began to chirp. Distractedly, I depressed the hookswitch, fumbled out more change, and called information for the number of the local sperm bank.

CHAPTER 3

It may seem immature, not to mention impractical, for a thirty-year-old man to hold his breath and turn blue rather than go out and get a job like everyone else. I had far more at stake than pride, however. For years I had defined myself by my ideals. This had to be the case, because I had published nothing, received little recognition, beat back endless criticism of my choices. Everything I had achieved in more than a decade of study could be, and often was, dismissed as a waste of time. Certainly I hadn't made any money. So when I laid my head down, when I rose up in the morning, all that I had to sustain me was the knowledge that I had been faithful to a principle: to live by my mind, and my mind alone. What looks like laziness, the tantrum of a postmillennial slacker refusing to make concessions to the real world, was in fact an act of self-preservation. At the risk of sounding maudlin, I will say that it was a struggle for my very soul.

Why this should be so is best understood with a backward glance. The great chain of causality stretches far into the past, and only the cosmologist approaches the truth when he claims to begin

16

at the beginning. For the rest of us – shrieking as we tumble in medias res – an arbitrary starting point will have to do.

I was born in a small town between the coasts – flyover country, to those with less-than-perfect tact. The nearest city referred to itself as a suburb of a second, bigger city, making us the demographic equivalent of an asterisk to a footnote. We had two Dairy Queens, three diners, and an International House of Pancakes. Of sturdy German and Irish stock, sixty-five percent of us were registered Republicans. Firearms ownership was the rule, NRA membership common, atheism unheard-of. Our winters smothered; our summers drooped. On sharp October afternoons I would roam the woods behind our house, stomping leaves and startling the whitetails that came to nibble on my mother's flowerbeds. As a boy I could identify dozens of birds by call or sight, wearing out a copy of *Sibley* by fifth grade. Once I left home, all that knowledge bled away, and the deep sense of loss I felt whenever I went back was one of the reasons I never did.

My mother and father married young, enough so that her parents had to accompany them down to the court-house for the license. Needless to say, it was a shotgun wedding. My father was nineteen, estranged from his own family, a high-school dropout with little more than a muscle car to his name. My mother hardly knew him, her parents less still, and while I suppose that it's impossible to place a price

17

on respectability, I will always wonder whether everyone would've been better off counting to ten and taking a few deep breaths before doing anything rash. Is marriage so intrinsically valuable that it's worth sacrificing the happiness of all involved? This was 1970, after all. Single motherhood still carried a stigma, but the world was changing.

Of course, it's possible – however implausible – that my mother and her family were genuinely enthusiastic about the match. I'll never know, because I wouldn't show up for another seven years, and by the time I got old enough to ask questions, all the original intentions had long since vanished, the emotions dried up and blown away.

On April 23, six months before my older brother was born, President Richard Nixon signed Executive Order 11527, amending the selective service regulations and making it difficult for men to get draft deferments based on paternity. My father might have tried to appeal his conscription on the grounds that while not yet a father, he was soon to become one. Or he might have argued that the fetus had been conceived under the old law. As far as I know, he never did protest, on any grounds whatsoever, and neither did my mother or her family. The baby, a boy, arrived in October; in November my father shipped out to Nha Trang for the first of three tours of duty.

There is no need to discuss at length his experiences in combat.

Snapshots taken around the time of his

homecoming show him cutting into a cake; standing with other returned servicemen along the fifty-yard line at Stinton County High School stadium (last winning season: 1951–52), accepting a standing ovation from those present for the home opener; restraining his squirming son, now old enough to feel ashamed when held. In these photos, my father lacks the customary 'thousand-yard stare.' To the contrary: looking at them, one gets the sense that he can hardly contain himself, that keeping still requires an enormous effort on his part, and by the next frame he will have exploded all over the walls like a burst melon. The Polaroid is a poor medium for capturing a man who in life never stopped moving, whose defining quality was a physicality so animal, muscular, kinetic, and urgent that it sought any available escape route, however destructive.

Maybe it was Vietnam that brought this out in him. Maybe it was there all along. That's a question for a psychologist, not a philosopher, and anyway, not an answerable one. I understand this now. But when I was younger and still believed that lives could be read like stories, I strove to figure him out. Not by talking to him, of course. People seldom possess the self-awareness to describe themselves in detail, and even when they do, they're seldom inclined to, the confessional not being a form found in nature. Instead I looked at the effects he had on me and those around me, and – combining that with what I gathered second and thirdhand from my mother, my grandparents, my aunts and uncles – worked to reverse-engineer his soul.

Demanding, volatile, possessed of a blunt charisma, he's actually quite intelligent, albeit extremely concrete. It's probably for the best that he's never talked to me about my work. He wouldn't understand, and I wouldn't be able to explain it to him. (The flip side is that he can do things I can't, like run a business or fix a busted washer.) When he decides that someone is bad, they are irredeemable. When they are good, they can do no wrong – for a time, anyway. People like him are destined for torment, as they face the same two choices in judging themselves. That he should be funny, sometimes startlingly so, will come as no surprise, for the true face of humor is cruelty. My mother was not the last to be seduced by him. The checkout girl; my fourth-grade teacher – I remember them flirting with him, leaning toward him in a wet-lipped feline way. As far as I know he never had affairs, but who can say for certain? (By contrast, my mother's fidelity is unquestionable.) Many of these more pungent qualities have faded as he approaches old age, but back then he was a force to be reckoned with, and while I wouldn't call him a monster, I will say that he often did a very good impression of one.

Upon his return from Vietnam, he trained as a plumber, eventually becoming certified and going out on his own. He also moonlighted as a general handyman, evenings and weekends, which was good for everybody because it kept him active and occupied, and allowed him to sock away enough money to buy a three-bedroom tract home with aluminum siding and a gravel driveway. My mother did her best to humanize the place – planting the aforementioned flowers and a vegetable garden, hanging samplers along the staircase – but to my eyes it never looked like more than what it was: a failure of the American petit bourgeois imagination, an impression later reconfirmed with each visit home. Yet another reason why, once I'd left, I tended to stay away. It's not a place that holds happy memories.

A lot of men give up working with their hands once they control the payroll. My father did not, Continuing to come home every day reeking, famished, and, as people say round those parts, all swole up. I picture the veins in his right forearm, pulsing in a way that made the death's head tattooed there appear to clench and unclench its jaw. I remember him standing in the living room, stripping off his wet workshirt, his chest hair tangled; remember the way he bellowed for my mother if she wasn't there to greet him. I remember him kneeling, grabbing me, suffocating me in his testosterone stink. The constant exertion did little to drain off the furious energy roiling within him, and he sought to let it out in other ways. He did some amateur boxing. He was an avid hunter. Four or five nights a week, he drank heavily. And when all that failed to give him peace, he brutalized his family.

My mother got the worst of it, at least in the early

days. A lot of things about her make her the ideal target: an unwillingness to fight back, a tendency toward blubbery hysteria that breeds contempt and aggression in an already enraged man. She was a child when she married my father, and has always looked at him as more of an authority figure than a spouse. Three years raising a child on her own had not done much to give her backbone, as I gather that she had relied heavily on her own parents. Sometimes I think she saw him off expecting him never to come back. And would that have been so bad? My mother, elevated from junior class tramp to war widow; my grandparents, no longer burdened by the consequences of their prudishness and haste. Even my father might have preferred it that way. I have to consider the situation from his perspective. I'm sure he once had dreams, however modest, and I doubt very much that they included a wife and child. He might have seen death as a merciful out.

I'm being a little hard on them here, as most of the time our home was quiet, if not especially joyous. Indeed, it was the very unpredictability of my father's eruptions that made them so frightening. If there was a pattern, I missed it. Although this may reflect inattention on my part. As I said, I came on the scene somewhat late, and had hardly begun to make sense of the world around me when it imploded completely.

Like all younger brothers everywhere, I lived in hand-me-downs. Christopher was small enough that

I fit into his clothing three or four years after he had abandoned it, despite the nearly seven-year gap between us. When my father started to earn decent money, he decided that a young man ought to have a new church outfit no less than every two years, and he and Chris began making a biennial pilgrimage to Worth's Boys Town, where they invariably picked out the heaviest, itchiest suit imaginable, flannel straitjackets that later came to me trailing loose threads, the armpits discolored and stiff. Not that I cared. Expecting nothing more, I was content.

Compact and dark, Chris took after (in appearance, anyway) my quarter-Greek mother. Think 'Rebel Without a Cause' – not James Dean but his anxious sidekick, played by the young Sal Mineo. I, on the other hand, was gangly and marble-mouthed, constantly at the mercy of my expanding body: uncoordinated, incapable of throwing straight, prone to trip over my own shins. Always tall for my age, I didn't fill out until puberty, so as a young boy I looked broad from the front but ludicrously narrow in profile, like I'd been flattened in a hydraulic press.

In philosophical literature on free will, one sometimes encounters thought experiments in which a person is manipulated by an outside source, a demon or hypnotist or, most significantly, a mad neurosurgeon. The first time I came across this idea, I thought of my brother. That explained us: we were the result of a brain-swapping experiment gone awry. Why else should I look like my father and sound like my mother, and Chris the reverse?

There's no real reason for us to have behaved like the parent we resembled, but it would have made sense to me, satisfied my youthful craving for symmetry.

Of course, genetics is never quite as simple as all that. There are bits of my father in me, just as there were bits of my mother in Chris. And I never fully was the beast of burden that she was. Nevertheless, Fate played an ugly trick on Chris by loading our father's pugnacity into our mother's small frame, a meiotic shuffle whose tragic consequences began to manifest when I was about five years old and my father's fury turned away from his wife and went in search of a new target.

Though I can't blame Chris for being born to a violent drunk, in provoking the man, he did consistently display a remarkable lack of common sense. Disproportionate to his body, my brother had a loud baritone voice, and he matched my father decibel for decibel. Grades, money, perceived slights – any pretext would do, and supper became a regular battleground, the two of them squaring off like moose, plates rattling as my father pounded the table; Chris slouched, arms crossed smugly, smugly shaking his head; my mother, blanched and passive, hands clasped in front of her, lips moving in unconscious prayer. I, cringing behind my milk. What was wrong with them? It was obvious to me that they were fighting for fighting's sake, their posturing accomplishing nothing save to bring them closer to blows. Did anyone really want that? Even my father: did he really – and I mean *really* – want to hit his son?

I ask myself this a lot, not only because of all the terrible things I had to witness but because the question speaks directly to my scholarly interests. I have spent my entire career asking what it means to choose freely. Is it a choice if you're drunk? If you have been to hell and back? What about if your son is mocking you, calling you names, calling you an alcoholic? Is it a choice then? Further: at what point does that choice obtain? Is it a mental process? Or is the choice not a choice until you stand up and take off your belt? Until that belt makes contact with the back of your son's neck? Until he begins to bleed? Is that choice made now, or is it the culmination of a process that began years ago, when you knocked up a girl in the backseat of your 442? Has the violence of the present been living beneath the soil all these years, germinating, seething upward, so that what we see here and now is merely its emergence into the sun? If so, what makes your choices yours? And could you have stopped them?

Once things went from verbal to physical, and my father's size came into play, all bets were off. At his heaviest, he must've had seventy pounds on Chris, an advantage only fractionally compensated for by Chris's speed. My brother learned to anticipate the breaking point, quietly sliding his chair back from the table a few inches, enough room to get up and bolt before my father came lumbering after him. Truth be told, it was riveting to watch, the two of them careering all over the place, over-turning furniture, taking out lamps. When I think back on these episodes I see a speck of comedy glinting through the blackness – the *Tom and Jerry*esqueness of it all. But the house was small, with only so many places to hide. Eventually Chris would be cornered, and the actual and extremely unfunny business of child abuse would begin.

I was never hit, or rarely enough that it seemed like never. To be sure, I felt my father's scalding temper in other ways. One incident that sticks out in my mind took place when I was twelve, on a Sunday morning before we left for church. It was my responsibility to come downstairs when dressed, so that neither my father nor my mother would have to come fetch me. I had put on one of Chris's old suits and was sitting on my bed, my back against the wall, rubbing my itchy thigh and daydreaming. I have a tendency to get lost in thought, and I must have kept them waiting too long, for the door was kicked open and my father stepped in, sweating and bunched. He glanced at my hand, absentmindedly scratching at my leg, and said, 'Oh, are we uncomfortable?'

I started to sit up, and then to raise my arms as he came at me. He pushed them away and grabbed handfuls of jacket and shirtfront and raised me up off the bed, shaking me, shouting at me from six inches away, asking did I want to sit here all day picking my ass or did I want to come down and join my mother and him who bought me that suit and every other damn thing I had in the world after all they'd been waiting for me for only fifteen goddamned minutes and call him a jackass if this wasn't the last time he'd tolerate it, let me go ahead and try it again, just one more time, I'd have another thing coming.

I can still feel his spittle on my face.

Frankly, though, this kind of stuff was peanuts compared to what my brother endured.

With one exception, no bones were ever broken. (That was an accident: chasing after Chris, my father slipped on the steps, jamming his thumb into the wall and giving himself a hairline fracture.) The real trauma, of course, was emotional. As Chris entered his teens, his moods worsened, leading to more and more fighting, which in turn led to worse moods, and so on, a truly vicious circle. Adolescence is hard enough as it is; add to it everything that we had going on at home, and my brother's slide into depression seems a fait accompli.

The trouble compounded toward the end of his junior year, when he split up with his girlfriend. She was a year older, headed off to college, too much distance – all perfectly natural for that age. Chris took it hard, though. Much of the goodness in his life came from her, and when that went away, the change that overtook him was awful to behold, more so for its insidiousness. He stopped going out with friends. He quit the soccer team. He began cutting class to get high, alone, and the inevitable suspension when he got caught brought a new round of screaming matches, epithets, ultimata. I loved my brother, worshipped him, and seeing him disintegrate terrified me. Though far too young to understand what he needed, I did try to help in my own small ways. Which turned out to be not very helpful at all: he would respond to my meek solicitations by swearing at me and slamming his door. As the months wore on, and he grew more gaunt and peevish, I kept waiting for someone to do something, to recognize the problem and fix it. But who? Not my mother, who stood wringing her hands. And surely not my father, who kept telling me – not in words, but with his actions – to take notes, make sure that he never had to do the same to me.

In the past, Chris had spent his summers mowing lawns in Clayhill, the neighborhood over the river where our town's few rich families lived. The girl who'd dumped him lived in one of those houses, and so that year, the summer of 1987, he stayed up in his room, listening to The Cure, floating downstairs in a narcotic haze at midday, stretching out on the couch to channel-surf. He had lost so much weight by then that my mother had begun to fear that he had cancer. In a rare show of initiative, she dragged him to our pediatrician, who took one look at Chris, concluded that he had Crohn's disease, and promptly put him on steroids.

The drugs restored some of the fullness to his body. They also increased his irritability. He broke out horribly, and was too embarrassed to go back to school in the fall. Instead he tooled around town

28

on his bike, shoplifting and taking out car windows with his air gun. In November the cops brought him home in handcuffs. I remember him telling me that he'd asked to be taken to jail rather than go home.

All this had happened gradually, over years, and I can't say it got noticeably worse that winter. In fact, I believe the pendulum might have been swinging back toward center, due in large part to the intercession of our priest, Father Fred. Chris and I each had a long-standing friendship with him, having both served as altar boys, and when he got wind of what was happening, he began dropping by to get Chris out of the house. He took him bowling, took him to the movies, made every effort to draw my brother back out, so that by February, Chris had started to sound almost like himself again. My mother was so grateful that she went out and bought Father Fred a watch. He told her to return it and put the money toward a family therapist. Either he wasn't forceful enough or she ignored him, taking Chris's improved mood as proof that the problem was solved.

She can be foolish, my mother.

April Fools', 1988, a Friday afternoon. I was a few weeks shy of turning eleven. A freak snowstorm had shut everything down, keeping me home from school and trapping my father inside all day, where he paced, brooded, and drank. My brother and I sat watching sitcoms until four o'clock, when my father yelled for Chris to come help him shovel out the driveway. To my surprise, Chris said nothing, just got up, got dressed, and followed him outside. As the front door closed, and came the drum of their boots on the porch, I realized, with the painful slap of revelation, that the two of them were fundamentally alike – and fundamentally different from me, both of them embodying a vigorous masculinity that I lacked. I wouldn't have put it like that at that age, of course; I didn't understand it in words. I simply grasped, all at once, that they were two and I was one and it was these unseen tethers and gaps that made life so difficult. I understood, too, why my father never picked on me: I couldn't take it. I was soft. I was a sissy. They both knew how to mark territory and how to defend it. I did not.

Within minutes they began arguing. I heard it and went to the window to spy. Snow was flying everywhere like bloodspatter, the violence of their work a none-too-subtle stand-in for what they wanted to do to each other. By the time they came in for supper, things had gotten pretty heated up: my father flogging Chris for having no future, being a bum, being disrespectful, etc., and Chris making snide comments about my father's waist-line, his blackened fingernails, etc. My mother tried to change the subject to the Easter charity auction, for which Father Fred still needed volunteers. Maybe Chris wanted to help out?

'Fuck him,' said my brother.

Normally he would have scooted his chair back

in advance of this remark. That night he either forgot or had decided to hold his ground. He hardly had enough time to smirk before my father lunged across the table, belting him in the jaw hard enough to put him halfway into the living room.

'Up,' said my father.

'No,' said my mother.

'Up, you little shitbird.'

'No. Ronald, no.'

Chris screamed at the both of them. Fuck them; fuck them both. 'Fuck you, too,' he yelled at me, though I had done nothing but sit there and watch. Perhaps he saw my silence as complicity. If he expected me to take his side, he was deluded; I had no intention of getting smacked.

My father reached down and yanked, and instantly Chris was up on his feet, and with an astonishing display of brute strength my father wordlessly hauled him up the stairs, my brother writhing and screaming that my father had dislocated his arm. Over and over again my mother moaned. She hadn't moved at all, tears running down her chin and into her scalloped potatoes. I moved to the foot of the stairs and saw on the landing my father shoving Chris into his room, then going to the hallway closet and pulling out a small suitcase, which he threw against Chris's closed door.

I can't imagine that he really meant to kick my brother out. It was eight P.M. and freezing. Althought it occurs to me that this might be a problem of mine: I didn't believe Yasmina capable of it, either.

31

Alone in my own bedroom, lying on the floor, I listened to more yelling, cursing, flesh in contact with flesh and wood. Through the wall, the squeak of Chris's dresser. Around ten P.M. I heard footsteps headed downstairs and, a minute later, the truck starting up in the driveway.

We had two cars. My mother drove a 1974 Chrysler Town and Country station wagon, scab-brown with faux-wood paneling. My father owned a series of pickups, Chevys and Fords. The one Chris took that night was four years old, already bearing a hundred thousand miles. It was scratched and dented, salt-scarred and flaking, its GEIST PLUMBING CO. logo no longer legible, although I liked to trace my finger over the spot where my surname had been.

From my window I saw headlamps paint the front of the garage, briefly revealing the crooked, netless hoop where Chris and I shot around in more clement weather. Tires spun on snow, and as he backed out, I caught a glimpse of his arm, the one he'd claimed was dislocated, hanging from the driver's-side window, a cigarette dangling between two fingers.

I have vivid dreams, and at that age, I kept a journal, writing everything down before I got up to brush my teeth. My entry for that night is blank. I never made it to morning, waking sweaty and disoriented to the sound of a shriek from the kitchen below.

I followed two male voices – my father's, and

another, somber and unfamiliar – down to the living room. From there I could see into the kitchen, where stood a lanky man in green outerwear, a wool cap pulled down over his ears, his thumbs hooked through his belt loops in a poor attempt at nonchalance. He glanced at me. My father then leaned back into the doorway. Taking this as a sign of invitation, I started forward, stopping short when he ordered me back to bed. I had already come close enough to see my mother slumped at the breakfast table, her robe open like the prelude to a vivisection, nightgown sagging to reveal most of her left breast. She seemed not to notice me.

'Go,' barked my father.

Upstairs I tried to listen through the vents, to no avail. Around six A.M. the sky began to wash pale, and I went down to the kitchen to find the man and my parents replaced by my mother's best friend Rita. She put me in a chair and served me bacon and eggs. Three cups of coffee were still sitting out on the counter. It was obvious that Rita was trying not to cry, so I decided to take it easy on her and not say anything. Once I'd eaten, she moved the dishes to the sink and told me to go watch television. There was nothing of interest on – I never did like Saturday-morning cartoons – and I had to settle for a *Twilight Zone* marathon, which was what I was still watching, nine hours later, when my parents returned from identifying my brother's body.

CHAPTER 4

An eerie stillness then descended on our house. There was no more name-calling, no upended platters of green beans. Nevertheless, one would be hard-pressed to describe the atmosphere as peaceful. It was, to the contrary, extraordinarily tense, not because we expected another terrible turn of events but because the future seemed absolutely blank, holding no promise at all. We startled easily; we felt restless and unable to concentrate. Conversation faltered at the gate. My grades suffered, and I was reprimanded for repeated tardiness. Waking in the middle of the night, I would come downstairs for a glass of water and find my father sitting surrounded by crushed beer cans flickering like dull blue embers in the light of the muted TV. I would stand there, waiting for him to acknowledge me. Only once did he do anything more than nod, offering me a swig. It tasted like mildew; I gagged; he told me to go rinse my mouth out.

The change in my mother was even more profound. She stopped cooking, and for two months we ate donated casseroles. She abandoned her sewing circle. She neglected her garden; come springtime, where there had once been strawberries and tulips, the earth raised nothing but weeds. At times she looked catatonic. Migraines kept her in bed long past the start of school – hence my tardiness. Eventually Rita started coming by to pick me up on her way to work.

I changed, too. I had already figured out that I was different from the rest of my family, but how those differences would add up to a personality was, until then, still very much an open question. When Chris died, I began to answer it.

I had taught myself to read right around my fourth birthday. We had nothing on the shelves at home – come to think of it, we didn't have any dedicated bookcases, just places to stash disused crockery – and so I lived at the local library, becoming staff pet, volunteering there after school, pushing a cart up and down the aisles, restoring order. It has become cliché to say that knowledge is power, but as a young boy I came to understand the irruptive force of even a single new idea, not least with respect to one's self-image. I began to feel superior to my family, and contemptuous of them, developing a vocabulary and habits of speech that would've been odd anywhere, at any time, let alone there and then. My brother used to refer to me as 'the Alien,' and that pretty much summed up how everyone felt, including me. It wasn't people per se I had a problem with – I was friendly, if a bit shy – but these specific people, my immediate family, who valued the physical over the intellectual, the blatant over the oblique. I looked at the chaos around me and concluded that it was the result not of evil but of stupidity. Drinking yourself into a frenzy was stupid. Getting into fights over nothing was stupid, too. Resorting to violence when you ran out of logic was stupid, and so was spending your day moving around heavy objects, or rooting for a bunch of gorillas in uniforms, or believing that life held no higher purpose than the acquisition of a riding lawn mower. Stupid, all of it. My contempt soon became pity; pity, bewilderment. There had to be something better out there. There had to be a world grander than the one enclosed by Highway 77 and a muddy, unfishable river. I could see that, and I was a child. Why couldn't anyone else see it, too? But they couldn't, and since I had no hope of making them understand, I had to get away, or else risk becoming one of them.

If all this was true before Chris died, it became much more so after. Like many philosophers, I started out as a mystic, and like so many mystics, I ran first to the Church. I'm embarrassed to think of it now, although I take some comfort in counting myself among the ranks of luminaries who have flirted with zealotry, religious or otherwise. Until the age of sixteen, when I ceased to believe in God, I was a stalwart at Mass, the ace of my CCD class. In these pursuits I was encouraged by my mother, herself weepingly devout.

She considered my dropping by the rectory to hang out with Father Fred a welcome alternative to smoking dope on the auditorium roof.

These days a close, closed-door friendship between a priest and a young boy would be cause for alarm. Justifiably. But in our case it was innocent. Father Fred was (is) simply a decent man, and I credit him for keeping me sane.

He was young, not much older than my father, and despite having been born in our town, he'd gotten out, earning a BA from Columbia, an M.Div. from Yale, and ordination in Rome. Speaker of four languages (English, French, Latin, Italian), reader of two more (German, Spanish), music aficionado (he kept a mandolin on the wall of his office) – he was far too cosmopolitan for our little backwater, and as a teenager, I couldn't fathom why he'd ever returned.

'Eventually, life circles around. And when you arrive again at the starting point, it looks different, because you see it through the lens of accumulated wisdom. This is where I belong, Joseph. God was wise enough to put me here in the first place. In my ignorance, it took me fifteen years to grasp His intent.'

Unlike my parents, who called me Joey, Father Fred never referred to me by anything other than my full name, and it was thanks to him that I began to think of myself that way: as a complete person, rather than a childish summary of myself. With the onset of adolescence, the alienation I'd always felt from my family began to boil over into a more general hatred of humanity. I condemned everyone around me for sins real and imagined: their narrow goals; their lack of imagination; the false piety of their grief, girls who'd barely known Chris hugging one another and sobbing extravagantly at assembly. I was the prototypical Angry Young Man, my age-appropriate inner turmoil exacerbated by having endured something unspeakable. I was desperate for someone to take me seriously, and Father Fred was that person.

When I reread what I have written, I realize that it might make me sound overly clinical, even cold. This I consider an occupational hazard. People misjudge philosophers when they think us dispassionate. I was and am full of emotion. But I also believe that those emotions find their best expression in language, and that language ought not to be waved around like a loaded gun. Think. Deliberate. Examine. Question. Embrace ideas, and believe that they matter at least as much as possessions, for knowledge has value far beyond its instrumental use. Live awake, and you will have had a better life than the sleepwalker.

It was Father Fred who taught me these things. Through him I came to appreciate the thrill of rational dialogue, learning that even those who disagree can find wisdom in each other's positions. Argument could create, rather than destroy; it did not have to be loud or end in tears. He took the white light of my hostility and passed it through the prism of reason, separating my emotions, giving them vector and function. Most of all, he never condescended to me, never gave pat answers or tried to put a rosy spin on what was, to me, obviously a miserable, vain farce of an existence.

The Greeks, Avicenna, Descartes, Kant – he showed me how to read them and reach my own conclusions. Together we spent afternoons listening to Anita O'Day LPs and locked in discussion, all the old questions, the ones that have always driven philosophy: What is real? What can we know? And how ought we to act? No matter how many times we had hashed over a subject, there were always new angles to consider, always more to read. He coached me on my college applications, wrote me a letter of recommendation, and lobbied my parents to roll over the money from Chris's educational fund into mine, enabling me to aim higher than State. When I got into Harvard, he was the first person I called.

As the one to introduce me to Nietzsche, he readily appreciated the irony when I began to lose my faith. Still, he continued to treat me with respect. If anything, my atheism became a new and fruitful topic for discussion, because he wanted so badly to win me back. And though he never succeeded, he was proud of me for not having run from the confrontation. All he asked was that I continue to push myself. Philosophy, Plato has Socrates tell us, begins in wonder, and at that age I had much to wonder about, in contrast to my parents, for whom life had drawn the curtains.

Practically the only thing capable of rousing my mother from her torpor was the battle over what happened on the night Chris died. It took years for the case to be closed, although it was never truly resolved.

The facts were these. After leaving the house, Chris drove to a gas station, where he was denied cigarettes after failing to produce proper ID. He then asked for the bathroom key, informing the clerk upon reemergence that there was something wrong with the toilet. It is possible – although speculative – that while the clerk left the register to investigate, Chris reached over the counter and swiped a pack; by the time police got around to asking for the CCTV video, it had been taped over.

Sometime after eleven, he turned onto Riverfront, which runs east before curving north and becoming the Crawhorn Bridge. A patrolman parked at the corner of Riverfront and Delcorte reported seeing the truck go by; he noticed because the drivers window was open, one arm hanging out, never mind the cold.

Near the entrance to the bridge, along the right side of the road, the guardrail was partially down, having been mangled the day before by a snow-plow. According to the county, orange hazard cones marked the spot where the asphalt dropped away toward the water. No cones were ever found, however, not on-site or in the river, so either the wind had carried them a considerable distance or, as seems more likely, careless workmen had neglected to put them out.

Police later determined that Chris took the curve at upwards of sixty miles per hour, far too fast to make that turn on ice. The pickup slid clean off the road and tumbled down the embankment, flipping once before landing on its side in the partially frozen water. It took a while for the cab to become fully submerged, and, if conscious, he should have had more than enough time to crank open the window and climb out. But when they pulled everything up, they found him still wearing his seatbelt.

Initially, the coroner ruled Chris's death an accidental drowning. Four months later, this was revised to drowning resulting from a motor vehicle accident, with a probable indication of suicide. The general consensus was that the change came down from the county supervisor, who had taken heat in the local paper for his neglect of the guardrail and his failure to put out cones. Prior to that point, my parents hadn't considered taking legal action, even turning away an attorney who had approached them offering representation. Now, however, my mother was outraged. She went on the warpath, motivated less by greed than by a need to refute the county's unflattering judgment of my brother. Chris's behavior had been erratic, but that didn't make him suicidal. He was an inexperienced driver, and he might not have realized that he was going too fast. If he hadn't gotten out of the truck, that was because he was unconscious; one needed only to look at the bruises on his forehead where it had smashed against the steering wheel. If he'd intended to kill himself, why go to such elaborate lengths? We had guns in the basement. Moreover, the guardrail had come down less than thirty-six hours before the accident. How could he have known to drive there, of all places? It didn't add up. In another of her rare bold strokes, my mother called up the attorney and filed suit for wrongful death and negligence, thus beginning a six-year process that would eat up what scant reserves of spirit she had left.

Back then I sided with her, more out of loyalty than anything else. In years since, however, as I have devoted my attention to considering the ways in which people choose, I've grown leery of easy explanations. It's possible that Christopher both did and did not intend to drive off the bridge. I will never know. These days, more than ever, I understand that nothing is more inscrutable than the human heart, and that no act, great or small, righteous or wicked, can be so named by one who stands outside the actor's mind.

CHAPTER 5

Here is what Harvard looked like to the eighteen-year-old me: it looked like a giant redbrick treadmill. What I remember most of my first few semesters is a vague sense of panic, my big-fish-small-pond confidence crumbling as I sprint to catch up. Nobody from my hometown had ever gone to Harvard; indeed, reactions to my big news ranged from bafflement (as in, Harvard University?) to skepticism (they let you in?) to downright hostility (too big for yer britches?). And the gaps in my education were daunting. I came from a public school where my biology teacher, a born-again Christian, could refuse to teach us the theory of evolution, choosing instead to spend twice as much time on molecular biology. (On the plus side, I knew the Krebs cycle cold.) Compared to my new classmates, many of whom had gone to prep schools that offered classes on topics like post-structuralism and Jungian theory, I felt like an imposter. Just learning the lingo required an enormous outlay of mental energy. I became hyperaware of my accent, and although the odd girl seemed to find my colloquialisms cute, I nevertheless always felt self-conscious opening my mouth in section. No longer the smartest boy in the class, I was forced to revamp my self-image: hick-turned-autodidact.

Now I realize that a lot of this had to do with my own insecurities. It also had to do with the friends I chose, who like me were would-be intellectuals. There were plenty of non-snobs at Harvard. It's just that I shied away from them, and in doing so I made my lot considerably tougher than it needed to be.

Still, I loved it. For the first time I felt at home, surrounded by young people for whom a huge future was not only imaginable but expected. True story: my roommate spent an entire semester building a tiny, working MRI machine, which he then used to scan our hamster. I loved it. I loved the fact that the campus was older than the country in which it was located. I loved the traditions, loved the corny stories they trotted out on the campus tour. I collected Harvard: haunting its museums, investigating its architecture. I made pilgrimages to as many of its seventysomething libraries as I could. (The holdings in Washington, D.C., Chicago, and Tuscany would have to wait. I did, however, get to the New England Primate Research Center, an odyssey involving a borrowed station wagon and a missed exit on the pike.) I attended every formal, took every famous course by every famous professor, went to every Master's Tea. I soaked it all up, and when I spoke to my old high-school friends, pretended to sympathize with their minor-league yearnings, I knew at last that I was free.

Most people, should they ever chance to spare a thought for philosophers, picture a bunch of white-haired men in smoking jackets, or perhaps togas, pulling on pipes and expounding the meaning of life. Nothing could be further from the truth. In all the best departments in this country – places like Harvard, Princeton, or NYU – philosophy bears much more similarity to mathematics. This style, which predominates at English-speaking universities, is called Anglo-American or analytic philosophy, and it places heavy emphasis on formal logic and argumentative clarity. Once you've read papers with as many symbols as words, it comes as no surprise that most of the great analytic philosophers have had backgrounds in math or hard science: Frege, Russell, Wittgenstein, Gödel, Tarski, Quine, Carnap, Putnam.

Nowhere in that list are Nietzsche, Kierkegaard, Marx, Heidegger, Sartre, Foucault. There's a reason for that: at Harvard, we don't read them. Other departments do – comparative literature, women's studies. But citing one of those names during a philosophy class is the fastest way to get yourself laughed out of the room. They belong to contemporary philosophy's other major school, the Continentals, less a coherent group than a wild and woolly bunch of thinkers who refuse to play by the rules.

For many Continentals, the mechanics of an argument are secondary to its outcome. These writers tend to describe the world as they, as individuals, see it, and as a result they often (appear to?) eschew logic in favor of rhetoric, asserting as self-evident all sorts of ideas that an analytic philosopher would question. When, for example, Sartre posits that the essence of our humanity is freedom, he takes for granted that freedom exists. Not so fast, says the analytic philosopher. We're free? Prove it. Only then can we talk about whether freedom is important. To which Sartre replies: I don't have time for your petty *bullmerde*.

The animus on each side is considerable. I remember my sophomore tutorial leader outlining for us the rules of his favorite game: 'First I name a philosopher. Then you name a worse philosopher. We each take turns, naming worse and worse philosophers, until someone says Jacques Derrida. That person loses.'

I am sure that equally snide games take place in universities all across France.

In sum, Continental philosophers think that analytic philosophy misses the forest for the trees, and analtic philosophers think that Continental philosophers are unintelligible, egomaniacal morons.

Father Fred and I had read a lot of Kierkegaard and early Christian theology, as well as some existentialist fiction, works by Camus, Kafka, Dostoyevsky – which is to say, I'd mostly studied the morons, and was thus underprepared for what

I faced at Harvard, so grossly that I briefly considered abandoning the concentration for something more user-friendly, English or government. But I persevered, spurred on by the notion that I couldn't, and just as I taught myself not to drop my *r*'s or elongate my vowels, with practice I learned the system, coming to appreciate the crystalline beauty of the analytic style and winning several departmental prizes for my writing.

I had a dirty little secret, thought: all the while I'd been nursing a nasty addiction to existentialism. I couldn't get away from it, especially Nietzsche, whose ideas gripped me in a way I could not easily explain. People will always argue about what he really meant, but what stood out for me was his insistence that we are radically alone – and therefore bear ultimate responsibility for creating ourselves. His concept of the *Übermensch*, so often vilified as amoral, made perfect sense to me. I had done precisely that: I had overcome, rising up out of an unread cesspool, breaking myself down, reforming myself in a mold of my own making. As senior year rolled around, and I found my professors encouraging me to pursue a Ph.D., I could not help but believe that Fate had big plans for me. Or, more accurately, that I had big plans for Fate.

Thus it was that I enrolled in graduate school intending to write my dissertation on the one topic that meant most to me: free will. And damned if I wouldn't nail that puppy to the floor, melding

47

existentialist fervor with analytical precision, forging a new mode of expression that would not only reshape a three-thousand-year-old debate but clear a new path for philosophy going into the twenty-first century. Applause, please.

Such grandiosity was misplaced. To begin with, I'm not smart enough, although it has taken me years to come to grips with that. (If I even have.) More important, I was out of sync with the times. The bitter facts of contemporary American academia are thus: one writes not to change the shape of the world but to get one's degree; one gets a degree in order to get a job; one gets a job because one must live. If one is very talented and very lucky, one catches the attention of Oxford University Press; one sells three hundred copies, all to other philosophers, and toasts oneself with a bottle of mediocre merlot.

I was naive – not to mention arrogant – to expect an exemption. Yet all the great thinkers have that presumptuous streak, a sense of the universe waiting on them. I also had a notion that scaling back my goals would be an insult to the memory of my brother, who had, directly or indirectly, set my course.

My first graduate advisor was Sam Melitsky, a lion of the department best known for his work in the exquisitely misnamed field of ordinary language philosophy. As an undergraduate I had read several of his books, coming to admire his tortured, wordy prose. His author photo showed a craggily handsome man with a stiff thatch of dark gray hair and a prizefighter's nose, one that suggested he had gone to battle for his ideas. It was a photo more than four decades out of date when we first sat down to discuss my project. By then the rugged maverick had been replaced by a kindly, doddering fellow with gaudy sprays of ear hair. I counted my blessings, though: more than tolerating my pretensions, he encouraged them. I suppose that I misstepped in trusting a man of eighty-four. He had nothing to lose by backing me. In the unlikely event that I did turn out to be a genius, he would be vindicated in his old age. If I failed, he'd be dead too soon to give a damn.

In the end it didn't come down to that. Not exactly. What happened, rather, was this: two days after I handed in my first draft of my first chapter – a discursive, bloated thing more than one hundred seventy pages long – he had a stroke that left him unable to read or speak. The nasty but entirely predictable joke around the department had my shoddy editing as the culprit. In short order, Melitsky's daughters came to Cambridge and fetched him back to New York City, leaving me devastated and forlorn, even more so when I learned that the only person available to replace him was one Linda Neiman, logician par excellence and a legendary hard case. She loathed Sam, and me by extension. At our first meeting she shredded me, rattling off a long list of demands that would have to be met before we could have any hope of working together, starting with the requirement that I pick a new topic.

'I think I can make it work,' I stammered.

'You can't,' she said, and began the abuse anew. Three years passed in a deadlock. The more Linda denigrated my ideas, the more I overvalued them, and vice versa. She seemed to take my long-windedness and ceaseless requests for feedback as a personal attack – a fair interpretation, actually, as I was resisting her in the only way I knew how, with words, adding sentence after sentence after sentence in the hope that by piling on enough text I could get her to submit. This was a terrible strategy. She had power; I had none; the onus was on me to adapt, and my refusal to do so served only to confirm her low opinion of me. I was coddled, I was entitled, I needed a good spanking and then some. Giving her the benefit of the doubt, I'll say that her attitude toward me was corrective, at least in the beginning. Soon enough, though, it became punitive, and then plainly sadistic. She ignored my emails, restricted my teaching, blocked my grants, and poisoned my reputation. When I referred to her as my 'so-called advisor,' I wasn't being cheeky; the phrase was hers. 'As your so-called advisor . . .' she liked to begin, before drilling me yet another new one.

Several times I tried to replace her. I'd have the switch lined up, only to find the offer retracted at the last minute. The consistency with which this happened led me to believe that it was Linda herself who wanted me close at hand. Perhaps she wanted to make me an object lesson, a specimen in a jar she could take down and wave at other obstreperous students as a scare tactic.

And still I wrote. The highest praise you can give an analytic philosopher is that his work is perspicuous. By that measure even I could see what trouble I was in. I kept changing directions, reconsidering, restructuring. Every time I made a major revision, I saved the document as a new file, numbering these drafts successively. At one point I had forty-two versions of the introduction alone. I would cut a paragraph but refuse to let it go, moving it instead to a clippings file that eventually grew to twice the size of the manu-script – itself nothing to sneeze at. As the poem goes, a little learning is a dangerous thing. And ambition is a perverse master, lashing hardest those who bow down.

Aware that I was in way over my head, I never-theless couldn't stop, having staked so much of my self-worth on my success. Melitsky had once written, 'In large part, excellence consists of the willingness to stomach monotony.' I printed that out in letters four inches high and taped it to the wall of my carrel. When I felt discouraged, I looked at those words and thought of good old Sam. All around me, my peers were toeing the line, staking out some picayune corner of the field for themselves. I scorned them, telling myself that what I was doing was not pointless but brave, clinging to the existentialist idea that one must learn not to fear solitude but to embrace it. *They* wanted job security. *I* had the courage to venture forth into the unknown. Each additional page acted like so much swaddling, helping to shield me from the chill fact that I was getting nowhere. When Linda asked how *the book* was coming, I told her that Hegel didn't finish *The Phenomenology of Mind* until he was thirty-six. By that measure I still had eight years.

She replied that – speaking as my so-called advisor – if I wanted to read Hegel, she would gladly write me a letter of recommendation for the University of Texas.

It all came to a head one rainy day toward the end of my sixth year, when I went to Widener to do some writing and found my carrel cleaned out.

I looked back at the elevator. Had I gotten off on the wrong floor? No: there was the blue mark on the wall where I'd dropped a Sharpie. There was the deep scar that ran the length of the desktop; I had wasted hours, days, if you added them all up, tracing it with my fingertips. There was the chair in which I'd eaten, read, written, slept. This was my carrel – my home – and yet everything that identified it as mine – the Melitsky quote – all the books – not to mention the work that had gone into collecting those books – months spent poring over the catalog, cross-referencing, mining bibliographies – the tape flags and marginalia – *everything* – was gone.

For a moment I stood paralyzed. Then I rushed forward, as though to stanch the bleeding. There was nothing left to keep in. The sole remaining trace of me was a list of call numbers in my handwriting. I crumpled it into a ball, hurled it down the aisle, and stormed over to Emerson to confront my so-called advisor.

She was then in the first of a three-year stint as department chair, which meant that before I was allowed to see her, I had to contend with her idiot receptionist, Doug.

'One sec, please,' he said, simpering.

While he was gone, I stole all his pens.

'Joseph. What a nice surprise.'

Linda's office had been arranged to accommodate her wheelchair, all the furniture spaced a few inches wider than normal. Even when she was sitting, her personality was such that she could still seem to tower over me. I noticed, not for the first time, that her shoes were flawless – literally unused – whereas mine looked like they'd been fished out of the trash.

'I was just finishing up an email to you,' she said. 'Would you like to hear it?'

'I would.'

'My pleasure. Although if you don't mind, I'm going to make myself some coffee first.' She pushed her joystick, turning her back on me. By the window was a lacquered sideboard with a drip machine and several mugs. 'Sit down.'

I sat, dropping my bag as loudly as I could.

'You seem upset,' she said. 'Is there a problem?'

'The problem, Linda, is that my carrel has been emptied.'

'Really,' she said.

'Really.'

'Hm.'

'It didn't occur to you to warn me?'

'What makes you think I had anything to do with it?'

'Didn't you?'

'That wasn't my question,' she said, wheeling to her desk. 'The question of whether I had anything to do with your carrel being emptied is completely distinict from the question of whether you have any grounds to suggest that I did.'

'For God's sake, *did you* or *did you not*—'

She put up a hand. 'Calm down.'

'What did you do? Expunge me from the records?'

'Joseph—'

'I mean, wouldn't it've been easier to have me shot, or—'

'Joseph,' she said, leaning forward. 'Stop it right now.'

Though she spoke to me like I was a poodle, I instinctively shut up.

'Thank you. Now I'm going to read you that email, and I want you to listen very carefully. Can you manage that?'

'I'm listening.'

'Good.' She turned to her computer, moused something open, cleared her throat.

'"Dear Joseph,

'"It is my duty to inform you that, effective June fifth, your active student status will be suspended. Notice has been filed with GSAS and with the registrar.

'"I regret that the situation has come to this, and I hope that you will understand why the faculty has found it necessary to take such a measure.

'"We both know that your work has come to a standstill. Despite having been granted numerous extensions – extensions granted on condition that you submit work – you still have not given me, or anyone else, a single satisfactory dissertation chapter. This is unacceptable. Twice last year you failed to file applications for an academic extension. Additionally, you failed to file a tuition waiver. That in itself would constitute grounds for your removal. However, the faculty and I decided to give you one more chance, and to that end I have repeatedly sent you emails—"'

'But that's absurd,' I said. 'I never—'

'"—none of which you answered. I—"'

'But I never got any—'

'I'm not finished. "None of which you answered. I left a letter in your mailbox. This, too, went unanswered. I was therefore compelled to report to the faculty that you had grown noncompliant.

'"This decision will not preclude completion

of your doctorate. For the time being you may retain your email address, along with limited borrowing privileges. Provided you submit all outstanding coursework"' – a long stare – '"you may still qualify to graduate. However, your name will be removed from the department roster, and your active status suspended.

'"I doubt this change will affect you much, seeing as how you have already ceased to attend lectures, and have not taught in three semesters."'

'That's because you *told* me I couldn't teach anymore.'

'I'm not finished, please. 'I understand that you may wish to explain to me the cause of your dereliction, and to plead your case for yet another round of extensions. You are welcome to do so. You may also appeal to GSAS. However, be aware that, having consulted Dean Blevins prior to making this decision, the faculty are not alone in considering the burden of proof to rest on your shoulders rather than ours. Our patience is thinning.

'"On a more personal note, I wish you to be aware that while I respect Sam Melitsky, I cannot and will not permit his reputation to keep you in clover indefinitely.

'"Sincerely,

'"Linda Neiman."'

She put her manicured hands on the desk. 'Several of your cohorts are already assistant professors elsewhere. Gil Dickey is at Pittsburgh. Alexi Burgher is at Stanford. Nalini, as you know, is here. As we speak, both Hudi and Irit Greenboim are interviewing at Oxford. Everyone's moved forward – except you. How do you explain that? You can't, so don't even try.'

I said nothing.

'Listen,' she said, adopting what she must've thought of as a gentler tone; it only made her sound more patronizing. 'I'm simply saying what someone should have said to you years ago. This is not the right place for you. It never has been. I appreciate your commitment to your principles. But other people need the resources you're taking up. Just the other day I sat here with a student from Brown – with publications – looking to transfer here. What am I supposed to tell him? "Sorry, no can do, we're saving that spot for someone. No, hasn't produced anything of value in six years. But Sam thought he was the *Next Big Thing*!" I mean, honestly. When does it end?'

The mortification had gone on long enough. I stood up.

'My door is always open,' she said, right before it swung closed.

CHAPTER 6

A ll this carnage had one upside, and that was Yasmina.

By my penultimate year in grad school I'd run out of philosophy classes to take and had started picking my way through the rest of the course catalog, reasoning that I was doing myself a favor by broadening my horizons. I went first to our pet subjects, math and quantum physics. Nobody looked askance when I took an artificial-intelligence seminar. Nor did they take notice when I signed up for Greek. Film theory raised some eyebrows; but it was after I wangled a spot in an undergraduate photography studio that my so-called advisor not-so-politely suggested that I'd veered off course.

Chastened, I next semester enrolled in a political theory class given jointly with the law school. While meandering through the law library stacks I came across a pretty woman in a black cashmere coat, her brow furrowed in the unmistakable distress of a first-year. I asked what the problem was, and she showed me: the call numbers had switched mid-shelf. Having become something of an expert on the Harvard system, I escorted her to the right place, and she repaid me with a date.

We were halfway through dessert before she realized I wasn't a law student at all.

No, I wasn't.

'That's good. Lawyers are assholes.'

I pointed out that in three years' time, she would be a lawyer.

'Then I'll be an asshole,' she said.

She picked up the check.

At first blush, we made an odd couple. Yasmina came from Los Angeles, where her family was prominent in the Persian Jewish community. Back in Tehran, they had owned several carpet and furniture factories, amassing a minor fortune before the Islamic Revolution forced them to flee. Servants, a chauffeur, two vacation homes – this was a life known to Yasmina only in pictures, as she had been born in Rome, where her parents lived while awaiting U.S. visas.

Once in California, her father tried to stick to what he knew, opening a furniture store with borrowed money. But he'd learned his trade on the streets and in the souk, and Americans found his aggressive brand of salesmanship off-putting. The store floundered, and the family suffered through moves every three months, each apartment crummier than the last. Despondent, teetering on the verge of bankruptcy, he had a sign printed up that read going out of business – everything must go! He stuck it in the window and the inventory cleared within a week.

Now there were seven such stores, with seven such signs, scattered across the greater L.A. area, all of them going out of business continuously for the last twenty years. The Eshaghians once again lived in a big house, drove big cars, and lacked for nothing. Yet the fear of losing everything, instantaneously, clawed at them day and night. No place felt safe, no matter how democratic its elections or how free its markets. They obsessed over money: talking about it, equating it with moral worth, pestering their children to marry into it. They drove Yasmina bananas. In a sense, I owe them thanks, as it was their needling that drove her into the arms of a penniless Gentile philosopher.

But that's not giving either of us enough credit, because in fact we had more in common than met the eye. Both of us admitted to feeling like outsiders at Harvard. Having snuck past the bouncer, though, we both wanted to make the most of our time inside. We visited Walden Pond to see the leaves turn; we followed the Freedom Trail and sucked down clam chowder. On Saturday mornings we would take long walks through the leafy neighborhoods surrounding Radcliffe Quad, stopping in at open houses to pick up tear sheets, pretending to be a young couple in search of their first home. Yasmina liked to stand in these living rooms, remodeling them in her mind – but respectfully, with an eye toward preserving the details that gave them character. Afterward we would get coffee and donuts and sit by the river, watching the scullers:

pale young men moving in unison, bright boats against steely water. The Head of the Charles Regatta was by far our favorite weekend of the year. Standing there, cheering on the Crimson, we allowed ourselves the fantasy that our presence in the crowd signified more than high test scores and the need for demographic completeness; we shed our motley, inglorious pasts and became, briefly, full-fledged members of the American intellectual elite, part of a long line stretching back to John Harvard himself.

Plus, our sexual chemistry was fantastic. That explains a lot.

If not for her, I would have ended up homeless much sooner than I did. I was lucky enough to meet her right before losing my standing, and while the cynical might regard my decision to move in with her as one of expedience, at the time it felt like love.

In fairness, I never took her or her support for granted. The opposite: I felt indebted and strove to justify myself by assuming all the housework. I shopped for groceries. I picked up her dry cleaning. I went to the library, checked out *Joy of Cooking*, and read it cover to cover (knowledge whose application entailed considerable trial and error, and once triggered the hallway sprinklers). Yasmina loved to throw parties but was more or less hopeless in the kitchen, coming to rely on me and my ever-expanding culinary repertoire, which soon included Thai and Mexican, her favorites, as

61

well as a slew of Persian dishes: kebabs, crispy rice, unpronounceable stews.

Playing houseboy allowed me to ignore my professional collapse. More than that, though: I *liked* doing chores. Their simple physicality was weirdly freeing. It turns out that there is no one more mundane, no one more housewifely, than a thwarted academic. Funny – and unsettling, as I realized how easily I could have gone another route. Had I never left home, who knows what would've become of me? Office flunky, fertilizer salesman, account manager for the slaughterhouse. I began to sympathize with my mother, to understand what it's like to see one's world reduced to soups and saucepans. Martyrdom has its comforts.

And I didn't object to living in relative luxury. The fact that I paid no rent yet came home to a king-sized bed and walls filled with tasteful nautical-themed prints did not, to my mind, mean that I had sold out. I wasn't the one turning the hamster wheel. The bed, the art, the panini press – none of it belonged to me. All I had were my books, my clothes, my ideas, and half of Nietzsche. In this way, I justified becoming a yuppie.

Yasmina's disdain for her upbringing notwithstanding, at heart she's very traditional. She would roll her eyes at her family, mock their accents and their provincialism, but I knew she still loved them. (Here we have a neat demonstration of the difference between an annoying childhood and an abusive one.) Holding their conventional wisdom in inexplicably high regard, she never could manage to get over the idea that she had to be married by twenty-three or risk dying alone. Most of the women she knew, including her sisters, were, foremost, homemakers. She'd had to fight for permission to go to college out of state. Certainly nobody expected her to go beyond a bachelor's degree, and while her parents paid her law-school tuition, they refused to believe that she intended to work, viewing the pursuit of a career as a phase she'd grow out of once she met the right man.

I was not the right man.

I never met her family. I never spoke to them. As far as they knew, I didn't exist. Whenever a relative came to town, Yasmina would dig out an antique silver *hamsa* and hang it on the nail by the front door. That was my cue to pack an overnight bag and arrange a place to sleep. It was demeaning, the two of us running around trying to cover our tracks like naughty children. Banished to Drew's sofabed, I would fulminate as he threw darts and grunted sympathy.

Nor had Yasmina met my parents, who never visited me and whom I never went to visit. I'm not sure what she expected if we couldn't or wouldn't get everyone in the same metro area. That we loved each other was never in doubt. We made each other laugh; we fascinated each other with our Otherness. But we were destined to fail. We both knew it. To be honest I think we found the sense of inevitable doom rather romantic.

There was one more sticking point. Though she claimed to have fallen for my intellect, I always suspected that deep down, Yasmina had other plans for me. She sometimes referred to a nonspecific point in the future when I 'stopped,' the implication being that I would eventually own up to my shortcomings and find gainful employment. And if she wanted to remake me, I must confess that I sometimes felt the same way. She could be over-bearingly pragmatic. I wasn't sure I ever wanted to get married, and if I did, I wondered if it could be to someone who wasn't a philosopher.

The argument that led to her throwing me out began over something insignificant. I can't even remember what it was. Isn't that the way it always is, though? It starts with a dirty plate or the default orientation of the toilet seat, and before you know it you're at each other's throats. She accused me of being distant, citing my dissertation as proof that I couldn't commit. I replied that Hegel didn't finish *The Phenomenology of Mind* until he was thirty-six. By that measure I still had six years. For a fuller explanation of what ensued, the reader is referred to chapter one.

There are two Cambridges. There's the magical Cambridge, steeped in history and ripe with opportunity, the postcard of my undergraduate years and the first few years of grad school, before I fell from grace. Then there's the real Cambridge, the one where real people live, beyond the walls of the ancient cocoon. In the real Cambridge, there are no carrels. No grants. No deeply meaningful all-night discussions. Pride of membership is noticeably diminished. This second Cambridge can come as something of a shock to the system when you've spent a decade living in the first. All through my twenties I'd been hanging on for dear life, but as I slogged through the filthy slush, headed for a job interview with a stranger, I felt myself headed into hostile territory. Glancing back at Memorial Hall, I saw its bell tower giving me the finger.

It's a testament to the insularity of life in the academy that I could walk less than a mile off campus and find myself on a street hitherto unknown to me, a charming little cul-de-sac lined with white oaks and red maples. Cars lay buried under snow. A sidewalk in dire need of shoveling fronted a long row of clapboard Victorians – some high-gabled Gothic Revivals, others bracketed simply in the American folk style, all except the last converted to duplexes and triplexes. Number forty-nine's empty driveway revealed that the house ran quite far back. Soon enough I would discover what those depths held.

Down at the corner, a silent procession of pedestrians and taxis, spectral in the winter haze.

I could not blame my prospective employer for wanting to have her conversation delivered in. Getting to the end of the block would be night-marish for someone with bad hips or an arthritic knee.

One benefit to being so tucked away: it was quiet. Blissfully so. I grew aware of my own breathing, the fizz of my nylon jacket as I moved my arm to cover a cough. It occurred to me that this would be an ideal place to get some writing done.

I climbed the porch steps and knocked. The curtains in the bay window stirred. I looked over but not in time, and twenty seconds later the front door opened on darkness.

'Mr Geist. Do come in.'

I stood in the entry hall, my eyes adjusting.

'I would offer to take your coat, but you may want to keep it. I'm afraid the house is rather cold. Before we go any further, let me get a look at you.'

I did likewise. I put her at seventy-five, although it was still too dark to draw firm conclusions. What I could tell was that she had once been exceedingly beautiful, and that much of that beauty had lingered on into old age. Her face was heart-shaped, her eyes quick and moist. I squinted: were they green?

'You appear decent enough,' she said. 'You aren't going to rob me, are you?'

'I hadn't planned on it.'

'Then let us hope that your plans remain unchanged, eh?' She laughed. 'Come.'

Down a creaking hallway she went, trailing perfume. She was right about the temperature. New England homes tend to be suffocatingly overheated – anyone who has lived there will understand – and often I came in from the cold to start pouring sweat.

Now I zipped up my coat. She paused at the noise, turned with an apologetic smile.

'Ach. I must beg your pardon. My condition is provoked by heat. Bright light can be bothersome as well. I hope you shan't be too uncomfortable.'

We came to a delicately furnished room. A pair of pale pink sofas faced each other, perpendicular to the fireplace, which was accented by a hearth rug. In the middle of the room was a low glass table, atop it a half-empty china cup and saucer. The curtains were heavy enough to block out all sunlight; two brass floor lamps with chinoiserie shades provided the room's only illumination.

'You would like some tea, perhaps?'

'That'd be lovely, thanks.'

'Please sit down. I shan't be long.'

Watching her go, I wondered about this condition of hers. She seemed healthy enough. She walked slowly – not out of difficulty but with grace. It was the walk of someone accustomed to having others wait for her, the speed of dignity. She wore a long floral dress beneath a creamy cardigan, and from the back I saw her white hair tidily pulled into a bun, a pearl hairpin at twelve o'clock. Her sole concession to informality was a pair of slippers that slapped at her heels as she disappeared.

I got up to poke around. Aside from the entry hall, there were two ways out; the one she'd taken, leading, presumably, to the kitchen, and another opening into a still deeper darkness. The living room bowed out toward the front of the house, creating space for a dining-room set that gleamed through the dim.

Most striking was the lack of photographs. Who doesn't keep a portrait of mother and father over the mantel? Spouse? Children? Friends. Yet there was nothing except a ceramic clock. Indeed, the walls were almost bare. Near the doorway to the kitchen hung Audubon's famous lithograph of the Carolina parakeet – extinct in nature but alive in art, their greens and reds and yellows so vibrant that one could almost hear them screeching. Near the back hallway was an oil, a nighttime seascape, black sky and black ocean.

I heard her coming.

The sofa cushions gave up a faint breath of perfume as I sat.

She handed me my own cup and saucer. 'I don't know your preferences, so here are lemon and sugar. Should you want milk, I can fetch some.'

'That's perfect, thank you.'

'You are quite welcome.' She sat opposite me, her posture immaculate. 'I hope you found me easily?'

'Yes.'

'And you were not inconvenienced.'

'Not at all.'

'Excellent. I commend you on your punctuality, a virtue in regrettably short supply. *Der erste Eindruck zählt.*'

German gets a bad rap for being uniformly guttural and heavy. Her accent was airy, balletic;

I still couldn't pinpoint it. Her English *shall*s and *shan't*s seemed less an affectation than the product of upbringing, and I wondered if she had been raised with British tutors or studied abroad. If so, that would imply a wealthy background. Before I made too many assumptions, though—

'I don't mean to be rude,' I said, 'but I still don't know your name.'

She laughed. 'How extraordinary. I apologize again. My brain must be frozen. I am Alma Spielmann.'

'Nice to meet you, Ms Spielmann.'

'And the same to you again, Mr Geist. You must forgive my abruptness on the telephone. I regret that this is a bad habit of mine. I remember when even a brief call cost a fortune. When I was your age – ach. I don't want to be one of those old ladies whose stories begin, "When I was your age."'

I smiled. 'What would you like to talk about?'

'Oh, there are many places to begin. Yes? No subject is out of bounds to the philosopher.'

'Don't feel obliged to talk philosophy on my account.'

'I feel nothing of the sort,' she said. 'That was the reason I asked you here. I have known a number of philosophers over the years. You might say that I was a bit of a philosopher myself. But they are nowadays quite difficult to come by. Before you, I had calls from two filmmakers, three writers, a linguist, and someone studying forestry. All from Harvard, like you, although you are the first I have troubled to invite. I suppose that is my punishment for advertising in the student newspaper. I mistakenly believed that this would attract a more sophisticated element.'

'What was the problem?'

'They were all dreadfully stupid.'

'That's too bad,' I said.

'For them, yes, it is too bad. It is a terrible thing to be stupid, don't you think?'

'. . . yes.'

'You seem to disagree.'

'I don't disagree.'

'But you don't agree.'

I shrugged. 'I'm not sure it's my place—'

'Bah. Please, Mr Geist. I haven't asked you here so you could parrot my opinions back to me.'

'Well,' I said, 'some people would consider consciousness a kind of curse.'

'And do you?'

'Me? No. Not most of the time.'

'Some of the time, then.'

'I think we all have moments when we'd like to be able to shut off our minds.'

'That is what wine is for,' she said. 'Is that what you would like to do, Mr Geist? Shut off your mind?'

A lump of self-pity rose into my throat, and I almost started blubbering about Yasmina, about my rudderless career, about the fact that I was here singing for my supper. I shrugged again. 'You know. Angst.'

I'd been right in thinking her eyes green; but they

70

changed, or seemed to change, when she smiled. 'Very well, then. I don't mind that you are unhappy. It shall make you more interesting to talk to. That was the other problem with your predecessors. They all sounded so improbably cheery.'

I laughed. 'I'm sure they thought they were doing the right thing.'

'Yes. This is the American way, after all. But the Viennese do not believe in happy endings.'

'I was wondering.'

'About?'

'Your accent. I thought it might be Swiss.'

She looked offended. 'Mr Geist.'

I apologized – in German.

'Your own accent is good. Clean. I must ask where you learned to speak.'

'I lived in Berlin for six months.'

'Well. I shan't hold that against you, either.'

'I've never been to Vienna,' I said.

'Oh, you must go,' she said. 'It is the only real city in the world.' She smiled. 'Now. Let us discuss whether it is better to be happy or to be intelligent.'

It had been a long time since I'd had a conversation anything like the one I had with Alma that afternoon. We did not proceed methodically. Nor did we aim to produce a conclusion. To the contrary: ours was a sublimely haphazard cascade of ideas, metaphors, allusions. Neither of us staked out a firm position, remaining content to lob words back and forth, sometimes in support, sometimes to draw

71

contrast. I cited Mill. She quoted Schopenhauer. We argued over whether one could in fact claim to be happy without any grasp of truth. We talked about the concept of eudaimonia, which the Greeks used to describe both the state of being happy and the process of doing virtuous acts, and from there we moved to a debate about virtue ethics, systems of values that emphasize the development of character, as opposed to deontology, which emphasizes universal duties (e.g., 'Don't lie'), or consequentialism, which emphasizes utility, the happiness generated by an act.

It was the best conversation I'd had in a long time, precisely because it had no goal other than itself. Three facts about her emerged as we spoke: one, she was ferociously witty; two, she seemed to have read every major work of Continental philosophy published prior to the 1960s; and three, she enjoyed playing the provocateur. As such, we engaged not in a race but a dance, the two of us circling each other, every one of our ideas sprouting ten more. At last she drew up.

'It has been a delightful afternoon, Mr Geist. For today let us table the debate. Now, I must please ask you to wait.'

While she was gone, I glanced at the mantel clock, astonished to see that two hours had passed.

'For your trouble,' she said, handing me a check for one hundred dollars. 'I trust that is sufficient.'

Actually, I didn't think I deserved anything at all. Something about getting paid for a pleasurable activity feels wrong. Though in no position to argue – it would've been impolite, and I needed the money – I did think a bit of feigned reluctance was in order. 'It's too much.'

'Rubbish. I shall see you tomorrow? The same time?'

Without hesitation I agreed. She was so enchanting, so European, that I fought the urge to kiss her hand as she let me out.

'May I ask a question?' I said.

'Please.'

'I'm glad to have met you – very glad. I have to ask, though, how you knew you could trust me. I mean, I hope this isn't something you do often, open your door to strangers.'

'I find your concern touching, Mr Geist. You need not worry; I am a good judge of character, even over the telephone.' Her eyes changed. 'And naturally, I own a pistol.'

She winked at me and shut the door.

CHAPTER 7

'Once again I commend you on your punctuality, Mr Geist.'

This time my tea was waiting for me, but instead of putting out the entire sugar bowl, she had left a single cube – exactly what I'd used the day before – on the rim of my saucer. We took our same seats, and she folded her hands in her lap.

'So,' she said. 'What shall we talk about today?'

I reached into my pocket. 'I've taken the liberty of coming up with a list of topics I thought might interest you.'

She lowered her reading glasses, skimmed in silence. 'I see that you have a spiritual side to you. That must be a severe handicap in an American philosophy department.'

'It can be.'

'Perhaps you would care to share with me the focus of your studies. You must write a thesis, yes?'

'. . . that's right.'

She looked at me over the page. 'You are under no obligation to discuss it with me. I merely intended to give you free rein.'

I don't like to trumpet my failures – who

74

does? – and had it been anyone else asking, I would have changed the subject. It was, I think, the newness of our acquaintance that disarmed me. 'It's on hold at the moment,' I said.

'I see.'

'I'm taking some time to rethink. I mean, I'll get back to it soon.'

'Of course . . . May I ask what it concerned, formerly?'

'Everything,' I said, 'and therefore nothing.'

She smiled.

'It started out all right,' I said. 'It's just that it's gotten a little overgrown.'

'How much so?'

'In its current incarnation, it runs about eight hundred pages. I know,' I said, 'it's a disaster.'

'There is nothing wrong with writing a long book, provided one has much to say.'

'Right. But I don't.' I paused. 'It's actually a form of writer's block.'

She nodded faintly. 'And your professors? Have they given you no guidance?'

'I can't blame anyone else. It's my fault for letting it get to this point.'

'Take heart. You are a bright young man.'

'Tell that to my advisor. Or as she likes to call herself, my "so-called advisor."'

'This seems to me no point of pride. If one is an advisor, one ought to advise.'

'She wasn't my advisor originally. The man I used to work with was actually very good to me.'

She raised an eyebrow.

'He had a stroke,' I said.

'Oh,' she said. 'Pity.'

'Yes, well, I think I gave it to him. Anyway, with Linda, it's never been a happy marriage. She used to try to convince me that I'd be better off in another department.'

'Which one?'

'I don't think it matters, as long as it's not hers.'

'How perfectly awful.'

'I'm sure from her perspective it was totally justified. But no, she wasn't very nice about it. She's not a very nice person.'

'She sounds dreadful.'

'No argument here.'

'I should very much like to break her leg.'

'That seems redundant, considering that she's paraplegic.'

'Ah,' she said. 'In that case, I ought better to break her arm instead.'

I smiled.

'You did have a topic, once upon a time.'

I nodded. 'Free will.'

She cried delightedly, clapped her hands. 'Mr Geist. I must ask you to wait.'

She slipped down the darkened hallway leading toward the back of the house, returning shortly with a slim leather-bound book.

'My own modest efforts,' she said, handing it to me.

I rendered the title page from the German: *An*

A Priori Defense of Ontological Free Will. Below Alma's name it was noted that this document was in partial fulfillment of the doctorate, Department of Philosophy, the University of Freiburg, 23 März 1955.

'Alas, it was never submitted. Except for a few bibliographical notes, however, it is complete.'

Even had I possessed the skill to translate it on the spot, I would have felt out of order doing so. 'It looks fascinating.'

'Bah. You flatter an old lady.'

'I'd love to read it.'

'Well, perhaps one day you shall get your wish.' She smiled and held out her hand. I gave the book back to her, and she set it down on the sofa beside her.

'May I ask why it was never submitted?'

'You may ask,' she said. 'However, I shall not answer.'

'My apologies.'

'That is unnecessary, Mr Geist. Let it suffice for me to remark that you are not the first student to have difficulties with an advisor. Now. Let us talk about free will.'

The following afternoon, my knocks went unanswered. I tried to look through the front window, but the curtains were still drawn. I worried. Had I offended her with my nosiness? She hadn't specified the nature of her 'condition,' and my imagination immediately fixed on calamity: she was lying helpless on the living-room floor, her heart exploded, her hand stretched toward the door, feet scrabbling against the bare wood. The image made my own heart squeeze. I began to pound and call her name, then hurried around to the driveway, where four wooden steps led up to a side door. Through its small window I could make out the darkened interior of a service porch. All other windows within reach were shuttered. I pounded some more, then walked down the driveway toward the garage and backyard. Snow had softened the hedges, fleshing out the bare bones of a quince tree. I climbed onto the back porch, which was outfitted with a pair of rattan chairs, and knocked there.

Nothing.

I wondered if I ought to call 911. Then I remembered that I didn't have a working phone. I returned to the street and went up and down the block, ringing doorbells. Nobody was home. Of course not; it was three o'clock on a Wednesday; people had jobs. Standing on the sidewalk, shifting to keep warm, I reasoned with myself. The house was wide and deep and high, and if she was upstairs, napping, buried under blankets, she might not have heard me. To rouse the neighbors – to call for an ambulance – to batter down the front door – only to have Alma emerge in her nightgown . . . Surely I was overreacting. Aside from which, who did I think I was? I'd known her for two days.

I walked the mile back to the Science Center pay phones and dug out her number. The voice that came on the line was so weak that at first I thought I'd misdialed.

'I apologize,' she said. 'I am not quite myself today.'

'Do you need a doctor?'

'No, no. Please. I am fine.'

She didn't sound fine. But – again – I hardly knew her, and I didn't want to badger her. I asked if there was anything I could do.

'No, thank you. I must rest.'

'Should I come tomorrow?'

'Please do. Thank you, Mr Geist. You are too kind.'

She was waiting in the doorway the next day when I arrived. 'I must apologize again. I ought to have warned you that such a thing could happen. Unfortunately, my attacks are impossible to predict.'

I kicked the snow from my shoes. 'As long as you're okay.'

'Yes, thank you. Although painful, they are not dangerous.'

I nodded. I wanted to ask what the problem was, but it seemed overly familiar. Whatever had happened, she appeared to have recovered fully. I followed her into the living room and took my appointed seat.

'Naturally, I shall pay you for your time.'

I scoffed. 'I was here five, ten minutes, at most.'

'That isn't valuable to you?'

'It's no big deal.'

'Well, regardless, I have devised a system that

ought to spare you future worry. If I am feeling well, I shall turn on the porch light at a quarter to three. If I am unwell, then the light will be off, as it normally is. At a glance you shall know.'

'That's clever.'

'Yes, I thought so.' She smiled. 'Let it not be said that I am not resourceful. Now, let us proceed to more important matters.'

Looking back, I can appreciate how quickly we fell into a routine. I would come over every day at three o'clock. Finding the light on (as I did most of the time), I would knock and be admitted to the living room, where my tea would be waiting, prepared in exactly the right way. For two hours we would talk without pause, at which point she would utter her closing phrase: 'For today let us table the debate.' The *for today* part was what kept me going, because it reassured me that the conversation hadn't ended, would continue tomorrow – and possibly forever.

I could have made better money tutoring. Plenty of people I knew charged two hundred dollars an hour tutoring the SAT. I didn't care. I might not get rich talking to Alma Spielmann, but to me it was the perfect job: straight-forward, bracing, dignified. As I rode the elevator up to Drew's apartment, passed through his revolting kitchen, and sat on the pitted sofabed, I consoled myself with the knowledge that I would soon be able to afford my own room. Assuming Alma kept me on. I had to hope she did, as the alternatives were unthinkable.

A thousand dollars doesn't go terribly far in Cambridge. I could have found my own place in Roxbury or Southie, but I was reluctant to move across the river. Too far from Harvard – geographically and symbolically – and whatever I saved on rent, I'd lose in time spent getting to and from Alma's. In a moment of weakness I flirted with asking Yasmina to take me back. I had a job now, sort of, which would impress her. Sitting at Drew's desk, I went so far as to dial the first three numbers of her cell. That made me think about my own useless cell, which in turn revived my anger and pride. I put down the phone and went back to the computer to search the listings.

The apartment in Davis Square had looked decent enough, the Tufts seniors who occupied it a pleasant bonus. Their names were Jessica, Dorothy, and Kelly. All three were Asian-American and under five-foot-two. I expected them to slam the door in my face when they saw me, but they seemed unfazed, giggling to one another as they showed me the empty room. Its walls were off-white, thin enough to put my fist through. It looked out on the loading dock of the neighborhood CVS. There were foam ceiling tiles but no overhead light. One of the girls offered me her spare halogen.

I asked when I could move in. They appeared relieved. With the rent coming due, they were happy to have found a replacement for their last roommate. They neglected to mention why he'd left, and in my haste, I neglected to ask.

Soon enough I got my comeuppance. Jessica, Dorothy, and Kelly looked benign, and for the most part they were. Two (I forget which) were pre-med, and one was studying to become an actuary. They kept the bathroom cleaner than I had the right to expect. They asked courteous questions about my work, responding with girlish squeals when I described Alma. On the phone, they spoke to their parents in Korean or Vietnamese. Elfin, blithe, button-cute, they might have been summer camp counselors, save for the transformation that took place at dusk, when all three turned into braying nymphomaniacs.

I'm big. But the men they brought home were positively grotesque. They looked like Belgian Blue cattle. If I ran into one in the hallway I'd have to press myself up against the wall to allow him by. They doused themselves in Gold Bond; they urinated all over the toilet seat; they paraded around shamelessly in ratty boxer-briefs flecked with dried semen. One such behemoth, coming out of the bathroom to find me waiting in my bathrobe, shower caddy in hand, whispered, snickering,

'Damn, bro. Talk about a *screamer*.'

'Excuse me,' I said.

In daylight, the girls seemed so wholesome. What

did they say during those conversations in Vietnamese and Korean? *Dearest mother and father, I wish you to know that I crave a limitless supply of linebacker penis?* Already I'd paid a full month's rent, making it impossible for me to move out without either returning to Drew's or asking Alma for an advance – options foreclosed by both etiquette and common sense.

So instead I lay in my newly rented room, on my newly purchased air mattress, gripping my newly purchased cotton jersey sheets, stomach roiling as I listened to the earsplitting animal passion of my newly acquired roommates. What sleep I did get was unsatisfying, punctuated as it was by episodes of heart-stopping wakefulness when Jessica or Dorothy or Kelly found her joy. I tried earplugs, but the sensation unnerved me; it was like trying to fall asleep while drowning. Worse, once knowledge of what was happening a mere ten feet away had taken root in my brain, I started hearing their moans all the time, even when I knew the apartment to be unoccupied. Nightly the wail of bedsprings started up, and I prayed to the half-head on my windowsill for reprieve. What would Friedrich do?

Alma asked if I was ill.

'I don't wish to pry,' she said.

No doubt *ill* was her polite way of saying that I looked like roadkill. I hadn't had a decent night's sleep in three weeks. I was exhausted, my concentration slipping. And that morning I felt acutely uncomfortable in her presence, owing to a nightmare still steaming at the back of my mind.

It took place in the main reading room at Widener. Across from me sat a smiling Alma. *What shall we talk about today, Mr Geist?*

I told her that I had come unprepared.

Ach, she said. *In that case, let us table the debate.*

She took off her clothes and we began to make love.

The strangest part was that while her face looked the same, her body was that of a young woman. More precisely, I should say that she, her dream-presence, seemed to drift back and forth between old age and youth: skin going slack, then tight; strength surging and receding. Her perfume, which normally I thought of as matronly, now carried a raw, musky undertone. She began to moan, softly at first, then growing louder and louder, and making things shake, and bringing books crashing down from the shelves, and chairs rattling, and the entire room spinning, picking up momentum, bulging at the walls, spinning, spinning like a centrifuge until in one mind – cleaving instant it broke apart, flinging wood and paper and flesh off into the infinite emptiness, which echoed with her screams.

Now, sitting with the real Alma, I struggled to suppress that image.

I said only that my new roommates weren't ideal, and that I was looking for another apartment. She nodded, and that seemed to end the matter.

A week later, however, she asked how my search

was coming. I told her there was a shortage of vacancies. 'Maybe I'll have better luck when the semester ends.'

'That seems a long time to live in discomfort.'

'I don't really have a choice.'

'One always has a choice,' she said. 'If I may? Allow me to propose a solution.'

'I'm all ears.'

'Live here.'

'Beg pardon?'

'There is a room in the back,' she said. 'You may have it, if you wish.'

I smiled. 'That's very kind of you to offer.'

'Yes, it is.'

'Yes, but – and let me first say, thank you very, very much – but I couldn't do that.'

'Why not?'

'Because . . . I mean, I can't. That's incredibly kind of you. It really is. I appreciate it. But I can't just move in.'

'You certainly can.'

Back and forth we went for several minutes.

'Look, it's very tempting.' For some reason, I was doing my best to come up with objections. 'I mean, I couldn't afford a fair market rent.'

'Then you may live here free of charge.'

'Absolutely n—'

She raised a finger. 'Provided that you discharge certain duties.'

'. . . such as?'

'Continue our conversations. I may ask you to

85

carry out the occasional small task. To move something heavy, for instance. Should the need arise.'

'Ms Spielmann—'

'Mr Geist. Please. There's no need to stand on ceremony.'

I thought. 'I don't know. I mean – well. Look. What about your health.'

'As I've told you, my condition is painful but not dangerous. You may speak to my physician if you'd like; she will tell you the same. She comes bimonthly. My health shall be her concern, not yours.'

For all her assurances, I had a hard time believing that she wouldn't come to rely on me for more basic needs. I didn't want to become a maid. Then I wondered if I was being overly cynical. Could I not see authentic generosity for what it was?

'Naturally, you will still need pocket money. Let us say this: in addition to room and board, the fee for your services shall include a small stipend – say, two hundred dollars a week?'

Considering the cost of housing, I'd be getting a big raise, even without the cash. And I would be living in central Cambridge, rather than two T stops out. But what if Alma changed her mind, grew to dislike me? I'd find myself out on the street again, without any job at all. I said this to her.

'You must learn to hold yourself in higher regard, Mr Geist.'

I still couldn't bring myself to say yes. I kept seeing flashes of her, nude and writhing – not a dream I wanted to face ever again. I'm trained to be able to prove or disprove anything, and I felt myself stretching to build a case against her.

She said, 'You can't make a proper decision until you've had the full tour.' She stood up. 'Come.'

CHAPTER 8

hough I had been coming to Alma's nearly
every day for six weeks, I had never ventured
beyond the living room, using a powder
room off the entry hall as needed. The other four-
fifths of the house remained a mystery to me.

Thus it was that I followed her toward the kitchen
with a sense of high anticipation. Unreasonably
high. It was a kitchen, after all, not a dungeon or
a seraglio; although, unlike many Cambridge
kitchens, which have been out-fitted with stainless-
steel appliances and modern fixtures, Alma's hadn't
been touched in forty years. The oven was no bigger
than an average microwave and painted dark brown
to match the cabinets. As for an actual microwave,
there was none. On the stovetop sat a much-used
kettle, scorch marks licking up around its bottom
edge. I saw a breadbox, a toaster oven, a small
transistor radio, a chipped crock with four or five
utensils, and several bars of chocolate. A rotary telephone hung over the breakfast table.

'I confess that I am not much of a cook. The
market round the corner comes once a week.
Tomorrow is their day. Should you choose to accept,

I shall telephone them and add to my regular order the things you like to eat.' She unwrapped one of the chocolate bars and broke off a piece for me. 'My sole vice. I order it from Zurich.'

'Delicious,' I said. (It was.)

'The washing machine and dryer are through there. The housekeeper handles my laundry. She ought to be more than capable of handling yours as well.'

'You're making it harder and harder to say no.'

'My aim precisely,' she said.

We returned to the living room, crossing to the second door and arriving in a darkened corridor, where she paused at the foot of the stairs.

'My suite is on the second floor, along with the television room. Should you wish, I can purchase a set for your private use.'

'I don't think I'd need it.'

'Very well. I must make another confession: I *do* love certain programs. I hope you shan't judge me harshly for it.'

I smiled. 'No.'

'Perhaps I can induce you to join me, then.'

'I'll try anything once.'

She winked and beckoned me on.

We came first to a linen closet ('You may have it entirely'), then to a tall room, octagonal in shape. The curtains admitted a shaft of midafternoon sun, which alighted on a music stand displaying Sibelius's Humoresque No. 6 in G Minor. A violin case rested against a freestanding record player; a chickenwire cabinet housed LPs; over the arm of the loveseat was draped a large woolen blanket.

'My mother knitted that for me when I was a child,' she said. 'These days I find it oppressively hot. Nevertheless, it brings back pleasant memories.'

She went for the violin case. My first instinct was to get it for her. Then I decided that this would be a good test of whether she intended me to function as a home helper. I held my ground, pleased to see that she bent and stood up with ease, placing the case on the loveseat. Inside was a violin with an unusual finish, red approaching purple. This she set aside, opening a hidden compartment in the case and taking out a black-and-white photograph of a man with a Vandyke.

'My father,' she said.

Rough, square, he had none of Alma's delicacy. I found her, rather, in his enigmatic expression. Neither smile nor frown, it signaled that its bearer was about to pounce; in many hours of conversation, I had been its recipient (victim?) many times.

She looked at the photo a moment longer before putting it away. 'Onward.'

Ahead, the corridor forked. We went first to the left, coming to a pair of doors.

'Your bathroom,' she said.

The chief draw was the tub – clawfooted and deep. As a boy, I'd loved to read in the bath. I felt my resistance weakening.

'I must tell Daciana to clean,' Alma said. 'She

neglects this part of the house. My apologies. This would be your room.'

Two rooms, actually, a bedroom opening onto an office, neither one individually large, but taken together quite livable. Alma switched on the light and I saw a queen-sized bed, tightly made; a highboy; a nightstand with reading lamp. Typical of an old Victorian, the ceilings were low, with crown moldings. I stepped down into the office, which was wainscoted and furnished with a writing desk, matching chair, and slightly thread-bare chaise longue.

'There is no telephone here. I hope you shan't find it inconvenient to use the one in the kitchen.'

I nodded, taking it all in. The door that opened onto the back porch was inset with a leaded window. Most of the panes were clear, but one had been painted. I looked closer: a tiny hunting scene, a man and a dog watching a clearing in the forest, the forequarters and head of a buck visible through the foliage. Its whispers of craftsmanship, of history, enticed me. Through it I saw the pair of rattan chairs, the quince tree, the yard with its thin snow cover. My mind skipped ahead to warmer months; with her permission, I could put up a hammock . . . Most of all I relished the silence. I could hear the lightbulbs burning.

'I think a small portable heater might be in order,' she said. 'Otherwise I trust it meets your needs.'

I nodded again.

'Very well. Now, if you'll permit me, I should

like to show you one more thing.' She headed back into the hall. 'I do believe this shall seal your fate.'

As we moved down the other fork, the darkness seemed to congeal, and I touched the wall to steady myself. Up ahead I heard a key in a lock, and then came a gush of warm yellow light. I stepped into a room about thirty-five feet square. Only later would I realize that it had once been several rooms, whose combined space accounted for nearly half the house's footprint. At the time I was too dazzled by the abundance of riches: a spectacular herringboned floor; a bloodred Persian carpet; a cavernous fireplace outfitted with brass horsehead andirons; a grandfather clock; a globe; an antique rolltop secretary; lamps with brilliantly colored shades; foot-high sculptures in marble and bronze, Athena and Ulysses and others I could not identify; a pair of sumptuous easy chairs; between them, a round table with a leather top and brass nailheads – and above all, books. Thousands of books, the shelves jammed floor to ceiling, making up the most splendid jewel-box library I had ever seen.

'Do come in,' she said. I wandered about, dazed. Many of the spines had faded. Of those I could read, about half were in German, the rest a mix of English, French, Latin, and Greek. Philosophy, literature, music, science, architecture, history, the shelves labeled and numbered in a spidery hand. In the corner stood an old-fashioned card catalog.

This was the only part of the house that wasn't ice-cold – to protect the paper from drying out, I would learn – and its rich woods and plush fabrics and intimacy enwombed me instantly.

'The work took two years,' she said. 'These days I doubt I'd have the patience.'

I stood before the fireplace. The surrounding wall had been left free of shelving, lined instead with a green silk jacquard. The fabric was hardly visible, as most of the space above the mantel was taken up by a painting of a raven perched atop a skull perched atop a stack of books. A twig in its mouth, its head thrown back haughtily, the bird made a somber counterpoint to the lurid parakeets in the living room.

Around the painting hung several dozen photographs. Alma in a summer dress. With her father in a rowboat. Posing on a Viennese thoroughfare, blurry trams and women in high hats. Riding a bicycle. Among friends, six girls gathered around a pot of fondue, a pair of snowshoes hanging on the wall. Faces and places and laughter; a life, framed. I was spellbound. I wanted to ask about every one of them. All I managed to get out, though, was,

'Is that *Heidegger*?'

I didn't need to ask. The old potato-faced sour-puss: I knew it was him. Occupying the better part of a stone archway, hat in hand, and on his left, close enough for their arms to be touching, Alma.

'Indeed. That was a good time for him; he'd lost

93

weight.' She laughed. 'Martin never was one for exercise.'

Martin? Where was I? Who was this person? I looked at her, but she just smiled, Sphinx-like.

'So, now, Mr Geist, my case is made. Whether I have made it successfully is up to you.' She opened her arms. 'Do you need a moment to consider your decision?'

The girls were sad to see me go. I promised to let them know if I heard about anyone who needed a room (and, I added to myself, was deaf).

'Where are the rest of your things?' Alma asked.

'This is it.'

'Mr Geist. I hadn't realized you were a monk.'

'Kyrie eleison.'

'Small *c*, if you don't mind.'

On my bed she had laid out a pair of bath towels and a washcloth. 'I shall instruct Daciana to change your linens when she comes.'

'Thank you so much.'

'You are quite welcome.'

My clothing fit in the highboy with room to spare. This was a good thing, as the closet turned out to be unusable, taken up by file boxes. As I set up my computer, I realized that I hadn't bothered to consider whether she had an internet connection. Of course not. I almost asked if I could get one, then reconsidered. I'd wait until my tenancy was more secure before I started making special requests.

I suppose I should've felt uncomfortable with Alma watching me unpack. But it felt like the most natural thing in the world, the two of us together.

'Your dissertation,' she said.

'In all its splendor.' I opened the closet and stuck the manuscript on a high shelf.

'Perhaps I shall read it on the sly,' she said.

'At your own risk. Remember what happened to my first advisor.'

'I would look on that as a mark of skill,' she said. 'Rare is the writer who can bring his reader to the threshold of death.'

In response, I reached into the duffel and pulled out half-Nietzsche.

'Oh, Mr Geist. Oh, how marvelous. I know just the place for it.'

In the library, she cleared space in the center of the mantel.

'Naturally, I shan't presume. Perhaps you would prefer to keep it nearby.'

'It looks better here.'

'We are decided, then.' She stepped back and together we admired the bookend. 'You have impeccable taste. It is hideous.'

'Thank you.'

'Tomorrow I shall give you keys so that you may make copies for yourself. Now, if you will please excuse me, my programs are about to begin.' She paused. 'Unless you would care to join me.'

We went upstairs. I counted five doors off the landing, all closed except the last. It was there that

95

we went. I took a rocking chair, and Alma switched on the television set.

Theme music swelled. A title filled the screen.

ONE LIFE TO LIVE

She settled into her own chair, and, in a very dry voice, said, 'Suspend judgment, Mr Geist.'

I smiled, sat back, made myself at home.

CHAPTER 9

Soon after I arrived at number forty-nine, the snow began to melt and the house warmed a few degrees, allowing me to walk around without my parka on. I ended up using my space heater sparingly. It worked almost too well, and if I slept with it on, I had to crack the window a few inches to compensate.

Our schedule was simple. An early riser, Alma was always up before me, and by the time I bathed and dressed I would find her sitting at the kitchen table with toast and tea, the radio on softly, tuned to WCRB, Handel or Bizet. We would discuss the headlines or do the crossword together. Games and puzzles, she said, kept her sharp. Her favorites were cryptics, which I'd never done before but took to quickly.

Following breakfast I would head to the library and read for several hours. Some books for the first time and some for the dozenth. Many of them were too fragile to use – she had dozens of first editions, including *Thus Spake Zarathustra*, *Nausea*, and *Being and Time* – but merely being surrounded by them gave me a sense of peace.

97

This is why I will never own an e-reader: because a row of books is more than a compendium of information. It's a map of all the places your mind has been, a group of friends standing silently by to comfort you. Cocooned in books, protected by them, I felt safe, and all that had been plaguing me began to fade, my mind sloughing off the clutter of years. I read for the pleasure of reading, rather than to stripmine for facts. People sometimes describe meditation as 'relaxed wakefulness,' which phrase captures the feeling exactly. More often than not I stretched out across the carpet; that I could lie there without nodding off is proof of the quality of the holdings as well as the strength of Alma's tea.

The one book I could not find was her thesis. I was disappointed, but I had to remember that I'd hidden my own dissertatio from her; and with so many other wonderful options, it felt ungrateful to ask for anything more.

At noon I fixed us a simple lunch. Alma would quarter a chocolate bar and speak to me in German, to her the only medium suitable for capturing her youth. Prior to my moving in, we'd done plenty of talking, but always about philosophy, and I savored these pieces of biography, which over time I assembled into a coherent whole.

Born into a family of instrument makers, she had grown up in Vienna's ninth district, Alsergrund, a ten-minute walk from Freud's house. Every day her father would bicycle to Ottakring, near the Gürtel, where he oversaw thirty craftsmen in the making of pianos, harps, and harpsichords. Vividly she recalled for me her visits to his workshop: the close, heady smell of varnish; tools percussing; muscular men in shirtsleeves. Her father liked to tinker, and was constantly trying out designs that had nothing to do with his primary business. 'The violin in the music room he made for me when I was born,' she said. 'He and my mother were both very capable makers and appreciators of things, and theirs was a materialistic romance, highly sensuous in its own way. Accordingly, I distanced myself. It was my nature to be contrary. I suppose that I still am . . . Well, the violin came to me freighted with expectations. I think they hoped I would grow up to become a soloist. I never had the talent. Diligence, yes. But my teachers always said that I was excessively technical. I had to get old before I understood what they meant. My sister was far superior.'

'What does she play?'

'Did. The cello. My father built it for her, as well. It was never to be, as whatever small degree of ambition she possessed was quashed when she married.'

From an early age both girls had studied English and French. Alma, showing a gift for languages, had also received instruction in classics, leading to an early fascination with philosophy. In lush detail she described the *Gymnasium* where she took her qualifying exams, the *Kaffeehaus* where she went for pastry and conversation. It was a good time to be

99

young and curious in Vienna. You knew everyone, provided that you came from a certain class and had certain social credentials; the cast of characters she described read like roll call in nerd heaven.

'Have I told you about the time I met Wittgenstein?'

I shook my head.

'His brother Paul – he was a pianist, you know – well, after losing his arm in the War, he commissioned my father to make him a keyboard that would better cater to his impairment. That was the way they were, the Wittgensteins; they bought their way out of problems. He also had Ravel and Strauss write him left-handed concertos.

'Now, this keyboard was supposed to be bi-level, with the higher half of the register here, and the bass below, like so. I don't believe it was ever built. I do, however, remember Paul visiting our house to discuss the design. The first time he came, my father had me fetch them schnapps, and when I did, Paul pinched me on the cheek.

'On one of these occasions he brought a second man along with him. I was quite struck by this stranger, with his hair sticking up and his eyes spinning in his head. All throughout the meeting he kept getting up and leaving the study to walk around the foyer in circles, rubbing his temples, muttering to himself as though in a trance. I sat at the top of the steps, watching him. He did not seem to see me at all; then, suddenly, he looked in my direction and asked what I was learning in school. You may recall that Wittgenstein once worked as a country schoolmaster. He held rather strong opinions on education, and when I described my curriculum to him, he began to berate me for its incompleteness, as though I had chosen it.'

'How old were you?'

'Oh, no more than five or six. I thought him barbarous. He had no notion of how to talk to people. That was clear to me even then. His brother heard the commotion and came out of the study. "Damn it, Ludi," he shouted. "Leave the poor child alone." Well, that did it. Wittgenstein gave me a look – I'd never seen a look of such hate – and he slunk off to the kitchen, where he stayed for the duration of his visit.'

My jaw was hanging open. 'My God.'

'Yes,' said Alma. 'He was a queer man.'

'That's unbelievable.'

'Oh, it was quite real, I assure you.'

'No, I mean – I know people who would kill to experience that.'

'Then they are stupid. Among the few things worth killing for, let us not count the right to be harassed by an arrogant madman.'

She told me frankly, and without regret, that she had never married, ignoring the pleas of relatives and suitors and setting out to see the world, traveling by boat and propeller plane, jouncing along in decommissioned jeeps driven by toothless, tattooed, rifle-toting men. China, Russia, Egypt . . . all places a single woman traveling alone would have a difficult time these days. Back in the fifties? I could

101

scarcely imagine it. She had been shot at in Afghanistan. She had survived a derailment in Punjab. She had been threatened with imprisonment in Burma. She had been in Ghana on the day Nkrumah declared independence, missing the festivities due to a monthlong bout of malaria. 'Should you go,' she said, 'I urge you, in the strongest possible terms, to bring a mosquito net.'

Her journeys brought her, finally, to the United States, which she spent four years exploring. Among other adventures, she had ridden from New York to San Francisco on a motorcycle. Rarely did she stop in one place long enough to make friends. 'This is a country more interesting for what one fails to find than what one does find,' she said. In 1963 she came to Cambridge, taking a job teaching German at a private school. Though she had intended to stay no more than a year, somehow – she faltered when she said this – somehow, this place had become her home.

How she missed Vienna, though. The culture, the learning, the *life*. Everywhere you looked, there was music and art. It was all impossibly Romantic. She had once gone to a party at the home of a man who owned a dozen Klimts, one of which he kept in his kitchen, on the door to his icebox. During ball season the parties never stopped, orgies of booze and waltz that ran till five in the morning, when the dancehalls burst open, spilling everyone out, men staggering into lampposts and women running barefoot in their gowns. Those with sufficient strength and foresight would pick themselves up and go for *Katerfrühstück*, the morning-after breakfast, consisting of pickled herring and strong black coffee, guaranteed to stop a hangover dead.

All that was gone now. She hadn't been back since the eighties, finding it too depressing. Her Vienna – the real Vienna – existed only in her memories, and I understood that my job was to provide her a canvas on which to recreate them. I did my best. I listened with enthusiasm; I tried to ask intelligent questions. When she mentioned the impossibility of finding a decent *Sachertorte* in Boston, I went to the Science Center and downloaded several recipes, baking up one a day, every day for two weeks, until at last I managed to produce something she winkingly deemed 'an impressive fraud.' From then on I made it fresh every Monday.

Following lunch, we watched the soaps. Even in this she revealed herself as discriminating. Aside from *One Life to Live*, she enjoyed *As the World Turns* and *Guiding Light*. *General Hospital* she abhorred as 'inelegant'; *The Young and the Restless* and *The Bold and the Beautiful* were both 'implausible.' When she said that, I couldn't hold back a laugh. She started laughing, too. 'One must never abandon one's critical faculties,' she said.

If there was nothing on, I ran errands or read some more. At three o'clock she joined me in the library for our official conversation, and before dinner – which she ordered from the market, prepared in tins, and which we ate in the kitchen, never at the formal dining table – I went out for a long walk, my mind digesting everything it had taken in that day.

It was a wonderful way to live, at once relaxing and invigorating. If I had anything at all to complain about, it was the maid, a stout Romanian with loaf-like breasts and a three-dimensional birthmark on her upper lip. Once a week she pulled up at dawn in a blue Subaru station wagon, its headlights held on with duct tape. Letting herself in through the service porch, she under-took to wake me with her racket, galumphing around the house, humming to herself in a minor key as she dusted and swept, pausing only to shoot me spiteful glances as I stumbled out to brush my teeth. Her dislike for me was understandable (although no more pleasant for that). I added to her workload, and as I later learned, Alma paid her a flat fee, rather than by the hour. Before I showed up, she must have been making a killing. Now she had to contend with extra laundry – extra male laundry – and three extra rooms. She therefore went out of her way to disturb me, following me around the house, treading heavily, breathing heavily, and always *humming*. Every-thing she sang sounded like a funeral march. The Eastern Block must have been a sad place to grow up.

I don't think she knew my name, referring to me in the third person or, less often, as 'sir,' pronounced *seer* and dripping with sarcasm. I wonder who she thought I was. A young lover? A grandson? I decided to kill her with kindness. I thanked her for small favors. I complimented her voice. She started to make eye contact with me, and I thought I'd begun to bridge the gap, until the following week, when she barged into my bedroom at six A.M., vacuum roaring. I groggily ordered her to leave.

'Sorry, seer,' she said, slamming the door as she went.

Giving up, I begun spending those mornings out of the house, using them to catch up on email. That I could go a week at a stretch without withdrawal proved that I needed the outside world a lot less than I'd thought. It's amazing how much of what passes for communication is garbage. No phone, no internet – and no worse off. Other than Alma, there were few people I wanted to talk to, and doubtless Yasmina had been spreading propaganda, telling our friends her side of the story. I ignored Evites; I grew addicted to the delete button. My world was shrinking, and that suited me fine.

We each live to a rhythm, one that dictates the way we speak, move, and interact with our environment. Some people like to leave their mark. Enter a room after they've been in it and find the furniture displaced, the lampshades askew. Others, like me, live in the background. Throughout my adult life I'd had roommates, and in every case my rhythm clashed with that of those around me, Yasmina being the one exception. I had come to miss that kind of easy syncopation, and it was a joy to feel it once again. With Alma I felt both unalone and uncrowded. She gave off such quiet, steady vitality that I could sense her across the house. We kept in constant communication, trading witticisms from adjacent rooms, reassuring each other with our footsteps.

Comforting as it was to be near her, it was proportionally upsetting when she took ill. In my first five weeks of residence, she had four attacks. I'd know something was up the instant I exited the library to find a certain stillness hanging in the air, our rhythms decoupled. These episodes were unbearably random. One lasted an hour; another, all afternoon; and though she continued to insist that she was in no real danger – recovering by the next day – I had serious difficulty sitting on my hands. It was to my great relief that she told me her doctor was due for a visit. I came home from my walk on the designated afternoon and saw a green BMW parked in the driveway, a gaunt woman half into the driver's seat.

'You must be Joseph. Paulette Cargill.'

We shook hands. 'I didn't realize doctors still made housecalls.'

'I don't. Alma is exceptional.'

'That she is. I hope everything's okay?'

The doctor made a slightly helpless gesture. 'It's the same,' she said. She then gave me a mini-lecture on trigeminal neuralgia and the difficulties of case management. 'Surgery helped for a little while, that was back in oh-two, but the pain started to come back about eighteen months ago. We've discussed trying again, although in my opinion – and she agrees – it's the wrong choice. At her age, every additional year brings greater risk of complications. We could do more harm than good. The goal at this point is to get the pain to a more bearable level, not to cure it. I'm afraid that's simply not realistic.'

'She keeps saying she isn't in danger.'

'She's not. Actually, she made a point of telling me to reassure you. She says you're worrying yourself to death.'

'Yes, well, it's worrying.'

'In your position I'd feel the same way. Aside from the discomfort, though, she's in perfect health. With her bloodwork, she could live to be a hundred.'

A silence, as we both considered the implications of that statement.

'Will it get worse?' I asked.

'I don't know.'

'But it won't get better.'

Another silence.

'We're all doing the best we can,' she said.

I said nothing.

'That goes for you, too,' she said.

'I haven't done anything,' I said.

'But you have. Her mood is excellent.'

'I guess so.'

'Trust me. I've been caring for her for fifteen years. This is as good as it gets.'

I tried not to think about how bad it could get.

'Just keep doing exactly what you're doing. I've been bugging her for years to find someone to talk to. What she needs is to make the most of moments when she's pain-free.'

I nodded.

'Like I said, I don't make housecalls. Alma is . . .' The doctor touched her heart. 'Call me anytime.'

Inside, Alma was at the kitchen table, two plates and two forks and the remainder of that week's *Sachertorte* set out before her. She looked up when I entered, smiling her enigmatic smile. I saw it now as an expression of impenetrability, a hard veneer of sadness. Pain has long been a source of interest to philosophers as an experience that is both universal and incommunicable. There's a sense in which it's harder to watch someone else in pain than it is to endure that same pain yourself: we have no more potent reminder of our aloneness. It is pain that sets limits on empathy, drawing a bright line around what we can ever hope to know about another. At that moment I wanted badly to stand in Alma's place, and knowing that I could not made me ache twice over.

She picked up the cake knife, made to cut herself a largish piece. 'A little extra for me today. I believe I deserve it.'

We ate in silence. Or rather, I did; she in fact ate nothing at all, eroding the cake with her fork, prodding the little sachet of whipped cream until it deflated. I got up to rinse the plates and behind me heard her chair scrape the floor.

'I am very tired and should like to lie down. If I am not up for dinner, I assume you can fend for yourself.'

'Is there anything I can do?' I said.

Her face then passed through many phases, all of them obscure to me. 'I only hope that you shan't pity me.'

'Never,' I said. 'Never in a million years.'

She nodded, turned, disappeared.

I reminded myself what the doctor had told me; I tried to accept that this nothing, this shackled passivity, was as much as I could do. A bitter pill, for it was at that very moment, when she was too weak to talk, that I began to appreciate the depth of my debt to Alma. Whatever comfort I afforded her, she had already advanced me tenfold. For that I will forever be grateful, looking back on those early days as the happiest of my life, all the more so for how fleetingly they passed.

CHAPTER 10

'What it sounds like,' Drew said, 'is *Harold and Maude*.'

It was late March. I'd ventured out of the house in a feeble attempt to maintain the fiction that I still had a social life. To thank him for repeatedly putting me up, I bought us lunch at Darwin's: deli sandwiches and macaroons the size of trumpet mutes. We took our food to Harvard Yard, where we sat on the steps of University Hall and watched Japanese tourists snap photos of frazzled undergraduates.

Drew's real name was Zhongxue. A computer scientist by training, he came from Shanghai by way of Milwaukee. We'd met in the artificial-intelligence seminar and become fast friends. Like me, he was All but Dissertation; unlike me, he had stopped of his own volition, dropping out to play poker full-time. He now made his living shaking down bachelor parties at Foxwoods. His parents wept whenever he called.

'Please,' I said.

'All I'm saying, it's a strange way to talk about a lady old enough to be your grandmother.'

I said nothing. I couldn't think of how to describe my feelings for Alma. One deeply uncomfortable dream aside, I didn't find her attractive, not per se. Obviously not. If we'd met fifty years ago . . . But this was now, and given the circumstances, I could not reasonably look on her as an erotic subject.

But it wasn't quite friendship, either. These days, friendship is cheap and fungible; go on the internet and you can collect two thousand 'friends.' That kind of friendship is meaningless, and I considered it blasphemous to apply the term to Alma.

The closest fit I could come up with was Platonic love, not in the colloquial sense but according to its original definition: a spiritual love, one that transcends physicality, that goes beyond sex, beyond death. True Platonic love is the fusion of two minds.

'She's the most interesting person I know,' I said.

'I'll bet.' He growled, clawed the air.

'Idiot.'

'Seriously, I'm happy for you. I don't understand you, but I'm happy for you.'

'Stop it.'

'What.'

'Stop saying you're happy for me.'

'But I am.'

'I'm not *dating* her.'

'Uh-huh. Your old roommates sounded more my style. Introduce me?'

'You're about a hundred pounds underweight.'

111

'On it,' he said and stuffed half a macaroon in his mouth.

A tourist ran up to us and began photographing him.

'He thinks we're students,' I said.

Drew nodded, his mouth full of coconut.

'Just so you know, we're not students,' I said. 'I've been expelled, and he's a professional gambler.'

'Havad!' yelled the tourist.

'Okay,' Drew said, coughing out crumbs. 'Show's over.' He shooed the tourist away. Undeterred, the man positioned himself behind a tree, fitting on a zoom lens.

'These people,' said Drew. 'What's so appealing about pictures of complete strangers. Who cares?'

'Evidently, they do.'

'I should tell him to shoot my left side. That's the photogenic one. Hey, happy almost birthday.'

One of Drew's talents is a remarkable memory for dates and numbers. It's especially peculiar because he has a terrible time remembering anything else: to flush the toilet, for example.

'Thanks.'

'Are we going to party?'

'We?'

'I forgot,' he said. 'You don't like parties.'

'I don't mind parties, but I don't see why one's called for here.'

'Uh, because it's fun.'

'It's not a milestone.'

112

'It's your birthday. Think about it, at least.'

'I'll think about it.'

'Say the word. Crap, I almost forgot. Your mom called for you a few days ago.'

I was perplexed. 'How'd she get your number?'

'I guess she called Yasmina first. Anyway, call her back.'

'Did she say what it was she wanted?'

Drew shrugged. 'Probably calling to wish you a happy birthday.'

These days I heard from my parents only when they had bad news: the divorce of a cousin, the death of our family dog. If my mother had gone to the trouble of calling both Yasmina and Drew, then the news in question had to be of a far greater magnitude. I thought of my father. He wasn't yet sixty, but he had overworked his machinery, and his own father had died of a heart attack. Suddenly I had a vision of him, crouched beneath someone's kitchen sink, straining to loosen a U-bend – then an angry grunt, a mighty crash, a spilled can of Comet.

I stood, balling wax paper between my palms. 'I think I'm going to go.'

'Whoopsy. I didn't mean to freak you out.'

'It's all right.' I handed him the rest of my macaroon, wished him good luck at the tables, and walked to the Science Center to make a collect call.

'Joey,' said my mother. 'I've been trying you forever.'

113

I winced at the old nickname. 'Here I am.'

'Your girlfriend said you moved out.'

'I did.'

'What happened?'

'I moved out. That's all.' Having inferred from her tone that my father was still alive, I was ready to end the conversation. 'What's up.'

'Well, honey, I know you're busy out there, but I want you to think about coming home for a visit.'

I rubbed my forehead. 'I don't know, Mom.'

'You didn't hear me out yet. It's important.'

I waited. 'Yes?'

'Well, it's been twenty years.'

Twenty years, but never very far away, and with that mild invocation the memories poured over me with the force of an avalanche. I remembered an April snowstorm. I remembered the gagging sound of a truck starting in the cold, and a state trooper in our kitchen, and three cups of coffee left out on the counter overnight. I remembered all this and more as my mother began to ramble.

'We thought maybe we could have a little memorial service round bout Chrissy's birthday. Nothin fancy but Grandma's getting on and who knows. No time like the present. We could invite some of his old pals, you know Tommy Snell still lives in town, and so do a lot of the kids we used to have around. Course Tommy's all grown up, he has the shoe business like his dad, and wouldn't you know it but he's stone bald like him, too. Everybody's changed so much, Joey. You'd get a real kick, seen'm all. They weren't your own personal friends, I guess, but still and all . . . Anyhow, Rita said she'd ask Father Fred to say something, he's always so good with things like that. Not that I'd ever ask, but if people want to help, it's rude to turn'm down. But I wouldn't want to do it less you came. That wouldn't look right. I'd like to, though, and you know what, I think Dad would too if he came right out and said so. But he's not going to agree either, less you come. I know he won't. So it's up to you. You know we never put pressure on you to do one thing or the other, but I think it's the right thing to do.' A pause. 'Joey?'

'I'm here.'

'You hear me?'

'I heard you.'

The day of the funeral was my first and last time in a limousine, and I remember staring through the darkened glass as we pulled up to the grave-side, feeling awed by the immensity of the crowd. Next morning's paper would call it the biggest turnout since the town fire chief, who keeled over at a block party from an aortic aneurysm. Among the mourners I spotted Chris's soccer coach, a legendarily stony man, his face beet-red and wet. The limo idled and the door opened magically, like we had a ghost butler. Was this what fame felt like? My mother climbing out, hoisting herself up awkwardly on a pair of proffered arms. Next the swell of my father's behind, out of place in any-thing other than coveralls. And then me, in one of Chris's old flannel suits. It itched and the pants were too tight, and as I got out of the limo, I tripped. People lunged forward, grabbed me; someone called my father and he came back to take possession of me. With the coach flanking my other side, I felt like a prisoner being escorted to the gallows – a flight risk. In a sense, I was. It took me a few years to get my bearings, but as soon as I did, I ran.

On the phone, I heard my mother talking about plane tickets.

'Hang on,' I said. 'I haven't said I would come.'

In the ensuing silence I sensed her gearing up for one of her meltdowns. I said, to head her off, 'I'll do my best, but no promises. I can't leave whenever I want. When are we talking about?' She made a small, resentful noise. 'You forgot his birthday.'

'I didn't forget. It's October tenth. That's not what I'm asking. I'm asking how long you expect me to come for.'

'You'll have to spend the night, the last flight out's at five. I need to know, Joey. Rita said she'd get a big photo of Chrissy for people to sign. These things take time.'

'It doesn't take six months to have a photo blown up.'

'I don't want her to feel rushed.'

This was exactly the kind of irrational stuff that drove me nuts. The fact that she had already waited this long – twenty years, rather than five or ten – vitiated such stubborn urgency. Why now? It seemed so arbitrary. And yet it would be typical of my mother to stifle her needs until they could no longer be contained and frothed over in histrionics.

'Is something going on?'

'What do you mean. Nothing's going on.'

'Something must have happened to inspire this.'

'It's the anniversary.'

'So?'

'So, anniversaries are important.' And then: 'Father Fred's leaving.'

Whatever I expected her to say, it wasn't that. I considered Father Fred a lodestar, the single living fixture of my past by which to extrapolate my present position. Leaving? For what possible purpose? What about the whole speech on how God had brought him back home, and life moving in a circle, and so forth? All a bunch of empty moralizing, aimed at placating a restless teenager? It troubled me to think of him as that superficial, and I felt a throb of anxiety, followed by anger.

She said, 'Before he goes—'

'Wait a second. Where's he going?'

'He's moving to California.'

'When? Why?'

'You call him and ask him that. Meantime I want to make sure he's around, cause he was so important in Chrissy's life. Yours, too.'

I said nothing.

'So I need to know if you can come.'

'I don't know.'

'When'll you know.'

'I have to clear it with my employer.'

'When can you do that?'

'When I can. All right? For crissake, leave it al—'

'Don't get snotty with me,' she said. 'After every-thing I don't deser—'

Rather than yell, I hung up.

'Sorry I'm late,' I called. 'I lost track of time.'

Opening the library door, I stopped short on the threshold. Across from Alma, in my usual chair, sat a wiry man with the wispiest beard imaginable. His shirt looked five sizes too big, his shoes even shoddier than mine, their laces undone and their tongues coughed out, like they were vomiting up his ankles. Even with the strung-out aesthetic, he was undeniably handsome, quite the young buck, with a penetrating stare and Alma's heart-shaped face, which on him looked boyish, almost Grecian. They both wore the same conspiratorial half-smile, as though they'd been caught in flagrante. Queerly, this caused me to feel ashamed.

'Mr Geist, allow me to introduce my nephew. Eric, this is Mr Geist, my tenant and interlocutor.'

Eric tilted his chin back. 'Hey.'

I nodded hello.

'We were just discussing you,' said Alma. 'Is it three o'clock already?'

'Ten after,' I said.

'Goodness, so it is . . . I hope you don't mind if we table the debate for today. My nephew has been away and I have not seen him in too long.'

'. . . if that's what you want.'

'Yes, please.'

I wanted to snap my fingers at Eric, who was picking at a scab. '. . . all right.'

'We shall resume tomorrow, then? Very well.'

Thus dismissed, I crept away to my room, where I lay on the bed, reeling. She had never mentioned a nephew before. Here I'd thought we were growing close. We *were* growing close. How, then, to explain this? Had she known he was coming and kept it from me? Or had he shown up without warning, and had she accepted him without hesitation? The latter seemed to teach a crueler lesson: he needed to do nothing, prove nothing, to obtain her affection. By dint of birth, this person – and what kind of a lame name was that, Eric – had a bond with her that I never would, whether I'd lived with her for three months or thirty years. I thought of her face when I'd walked in on them, a private face, an outward expression of inner pleasure. It was not a face she'd ever shown me, and I resented her for it. Rationally, I understood how silly I was being. I had no right to jealousy. But the conversation with my mother had left me on edge, and the sudden appearance of a stranger who was not in fact a stranger but a threat (perceived or real, it didn't matter, it's all one to a mind ill at ease) brought panic. She was punishing me. For what? What had I done? Had I injured her pride by showing concern for her health? Is that what was going on here? They had been discussing me. Why? What was there to discuss? I had a right to know the context, didn't I? To my eye it hadn't looked like a discussion. It looked like mockery, and the message was clear enough: he had come to replace me. It was over. I would be out on the street. The beautiful dream, smashed. I gripped my sheets, clenched my jaw, wondered how long I had left before she ordered me to vacate. I should start packing now, leave quietly, spare everyone the indignity of a scene . . .

Standing in the hall, eavesdropping, I couldn't make out words, but I did hear laughter, and lots of it, and I burned. What in the world could someone like him possibly say to amuse someone like her, save something so unbearably asinine that she could not help but laugh at him? But no. She was laughing again, not at him but with him. He was laughing, too: easy, confident, triumphant. This had to be a punishment. I went back to my room to wait them out.

The clock ticked four, five, six.

At six-thirty I knocked on the library door and announced that I was stepping out.

'Pity,' said Alma. 'I had hoped we would all dine together.'

'I'm meeting someone. Sorry.'

'You didn't say so earlier.'

120

'It slipped my mind.'

She stared at me. I think she knew I was lying. 'Very well. Before you go . . .' She reached into her sweater pocket and took out her little blue pleather checkbook. Normally she kept it upstairs, in her room – never on her. What was going on? Had he asked her for money? I tried to glare at him, but he wasn't paying any attention to me.

'Mr Geist.' She waved the check at me, and of an instant I grasped the purpose of calling each other *Mr* and *Ms*. It wasn't affectionate, or a sly joke. She meant to establish a boundary. If I'd missed that, it was nobody's fault but mine.

I mumbled thanks and took my allowance.

'You are quite welcome,' said Alma. 'Enjoy your dinner.'

The evening was mild, and I stalked the brick canyons around Harvard Square, hoping that its crowds would work like white noise, drowning out the resentment that I felt guilt over feeling. A group of teenagers had gathered in front of the entrance to the T: the Pit Kids, suburban goth-punks with safety pins in their ears, their ragged outfits belied by years of expensive orthodonture. Inexplicably they reminded me of Eric – I think it was the bony elbows and the get-bent sneers – and I turned and made my way to the Common, where I slumped listlessly on a bench to watch a coed softball game. By then I felt more pathetic than angry. Really, I thought, grow up. The woman was almost eighty years old. She had earned the right to entertain whomever she chose, certainly a relative. Judging by the shape of his face, a blood relative. Alma's sister was older than her, making it hard to believe that he was actually her nephew. Great-nephew, more likely, which meant that in calling him 'nephew' she meant to express intimacy. Hadn't she that right? It wasn't up to me to decide on whom she chose to bestow affection. She could talk to him all day long if she wanted. It was none of my business. More to the point, nobody had said anything about kicking me out. My reaction reflected my own insecurities, nothing more.

That didn't excuse him, of course. Probably he had a drug problem. Who else dressed that way? I was no fashion plate, but at least I combed my hair. No, my dishevelment was artful; his the product of indifference. I kept thinking of the smug ease with which he occupied my chair – and wasn't that my right, after all this time, so many hours spent in it, to think of it as mine? – not to mention the way he'd eyed my check, the air of entitlement he carried . . .

Unable to face going home, I walked to the Science Center and stood at a computer kiosk. I hadn't checked my email in two weeks, and now I faced heaps of spam. Coming here had been a bad idea: I felt lonelier than ever.

Against my better judgment, I clicked COMPOSE and entered Yasmina's address. Then I erased it.

Then I typed it again. I repeated this process several times before moving the cursor to the body field.

Hi there. It's me. (Obviously.) Sorry to drop in unannounced (so to speak), but I was thinking of you and wanted to let you know. Don't worry. It's nothing malicious. I'm doing well. I have a new job and a terrific roommate. Your

BACKSPACE

I have a new job and an unbelievably cushy living situation. Nothing much to report besides. I haven't done any writing recently, but that's okay; I feel more focused than I have in a long time. I don't mean that as an insult, so please don't take it that way. Your decision was the right one – good for both of us. I wish it hadn't come to that; I wish there could have been another way. But you know me. I try to be philosophical about these things. (Ha, ha.) I want you to know that I will always think of you with great love

BACKSPACE

fondness

BACKSPACE

warmth, and that I am sorry I couldn't be the person you needed. He is out there somewhere, and the day you find him will be his luckiest.

Joseph

Halfway home, the catharsis I'd hoped for still hadn't come. Instead I felt like a bully, forcing my way into her inbox. I turned around and walked back to the computer kiosk, intending to write a new email, entitled READ FIRST and instructing her to disregard the previous email.
Too late.

hi
ive been trying to get in touch with you. Please if you can give me a call, i would like to talk.

y

124

CHAPTER 11

Getting Yasmina to meet me in person entailed an extensive negotiation; she wanted to keep it to a phone conversation. Left with no other choice, I played the birthday card. A cup of coffee: was that too much to ask? I upped the ante by suggesting an old haunt of ours, a café in the North End where they brewed espresso in a machine the size of a Sherman tank. She caved, as I knew she would. Her desire to keep me at arm's length could never outstrip her love of fancy hot beverages.

Upon arrival, we found the place shuttered. I tried not to take this as a sign. Yasmina let out a little cry of grief.

'When did this happen?' she said. 'I was here like two weeks ago.'

In the window was a letter dated March 23.

To all our dear customers, thank you for twenty wonderful years. We are sad to inform you that Ettore has passed away after a long battle with cancer. The café was his life and he loved everyone who came in. We will all miss him forever.

I shuddered to realize that Ettore (whose name I had never known) had opened his café right around the time my brother drove a truck into a river and drowned.

We walked under the expressway, settling for the Starbucks near Faneuil Hall. Yasmina tried to pay, but I stopped her. 'Give me the gift of self-respect.'

She smiled crookedly, bit her tongue.

'I've been calling you for weeks,' she said as we sat down. 'It rings and rings.'

'It's not my number anymore.'

'You switched it?'

'I don't have a phone.'

'Why don't you have a phone?'

'You canceled it.'

'You didn't get a new one?'

'No.'

'That wasn't – I mean, I waited one billing cycle. I figured you'd port the number over when you got a new phone.'

'I didn't get a new phone.'

'Oh. Well . . . Well, I'm sorry.'

'It's all right.'

'We didn't discuss it. We should have.'

'It's all right.'

'And I was mad.'

'I know.'

'But I should've told you first.'

126

'Forget about it. It's liberating, actually, not having a phone. You'd be amazed.'

'I'll bet.' She paused. 'So what brought that on.'

'Nothing in particular. I wanted to write to you, so I did.'

'. . . okay.'

'I didn't realize we had a moratorium on email,' I said.

'Don't get mad.'

'I'm not. I just don't see what the big deal is about me sending you an email.'

'It's not a big deal.'

'Then why are you getting upset.'

'I'm not upset. Please, Joseph. I'm – look, we're not *together* anymore, and—'

'I know. I'm well aware. Thanks for the reminder.'

'Can you not, please.'

I said nothing.

'I'm happy that you're doing well. I *want* to hear that. Tell me about this job.'

I thought. 'It's sort of like a research fellowship.'

'Like a . . . a think tank?'

'You could call it that.'

'That's great,' she said. 'That's perfect for you. Haven't I always said that? And a new place? I thought you were living with Drew.'

'For a while. Not anymore. Look.' All the small talk was beginning to derail me. 'I'm not sure how to say this.'

'Wait,' she said. 'Wait.'

'Let me—'

'Wait a minute. I know what you're going to say.'

'You don't—'

'I do.'

'Your family? Was that it? Because if that was the issue, then—'

'That wasn't the issue. That was never the issue.'

'Strictly for my own edification—'

'*Please* stop,' she said. 'We can't have this conversation here.'

'Then where can we—'

'Nowhere. We can't have it anywhere, at any time.'

'I'm trying to learn.'

'There's nothing *to* learn.'

'There's always something to learn,' I said. 'This isn't beyond me, Mina, I can und—'

'Please don't call me that,' she said.

Stung, I said, 'Why not.'

'Because I'm asking you not to.'

'But *why*.'

'Would you please, please, keep your voice down.'

People had begun to eye us over their lattes.

'Let's take a walk,' I said.

She shook her head.

'Why not?'

'I want to stay here.'

'Why.'

'It's neutral territory.'

'You don't trust me?'

'Of course I trust you—'

'Then let's go.'

'Do you want to argue, or do you want to talk?'

'We *aren't* talking,' I said. 'You won't let me.'

'Joseph.' She put her head in her hands. 'You're working yourself up.'

'I am merely—'

'Please,' she said, looking up. 'Please let me speak.'

For a moment I thought she might cry. I had seen it enough times to know. Her face takes on a greenish cast, as though she's going to be sick. I beat back the urge to reach out for her. She rubbed her eyes again, and this time when she came up, she looked perfectly sober.

'I'm engaged,' she said.

Now one of our neighbors, a girl with black plastic glasses, began to gawk openly. What entertainment! Better than *One Life to Live*! I glowered at her, and she went back to her Aphra Behn. Meanwhile, Yasmina was taking rapid sips, her eyes darting nervously.

'It's been five months,' I said.

'Six.'

'Not even. Five and a half.'

'So.'

'So that's – that's ridiculous.'

'Don't.'

'It is. It's *completely* ridiculous.'

'You're entitled to your opinion.'

'Who is he?'

'His name is Pete,' she said, 'and "*he*" is my *fiancé*, so if you don't mind—'

'Pete.'

'Yes.'

'That's his real name?'

'Of course it's his real name,' she said. 'What's that supposed to mean?'

'Does Pete have a last name?'

The tiniest silence. Then: 'Soleimani.'

'Ah,' I said.

'What's ah.'

'Nothing,'

'Nothing's ever nothing with you; tell me what you meant by that.'

'It's nothing,' I said. 'Just, that's what I thought.'

'*What's* what you thought.'

'Persian,' I said.

'Yes, in fact, he is.'

'So, that's what I thought.'

'Well, hooray for you. You were right. Bravo.'

'There's no need for sarcasm.'

'He's Persian. Is that all right with you, Your Highness?'

'Well, I don't think my opinion really changes—'

'No,' she said, 'it doesn't, but who cares? Who cares if we're talking about someone I love? It's not about me, or him, it's about *you*, it's always about you, so why don't you tell me exactly what you think. Get it all out on the table. Go ahead, it'll make you feel better.'

'Fine,' I said. 'Let's see: he lives in Los Angeles.'

130

'New York.'

'Okay, fine, New York. And he's forty-five and sells cars.'

'*Thirty*,' she said pointedly, 'and an investment banker. Are you done? Because I don't need this, so if you can't stop behaving like an infant, I'm going to leave. I don't need to tell you anything. I *wanted* to, as a courtesy, so you'd hear it from me first. That's why I've been calling. I'm trying to be nice, but you're making it very, very hard.'

A long silence.

'I'm sorry,' I said.

She said nothing.

'Mina.'

'Don't call me that.'

Another silence.

'Let's try that again,' I said. 'Tell me you're engaged.'

After a pause, she said, 'I'm engaged.'

'Congratulations. I'm happy for you. I couldn't be happier. Really, I couldn't be happier, not if—'

'Enough.'

I thought I'd been putting on a pretty good show. 'Where did you meet?'

'My sister set us up.'

'And . . . when's the big day.'

'We don't know yet. He's working on getting a transfer to the West Coast. I'm staying here next year, clerking for Judge Polonsky, so it won't happen for at least a year.'

'So that's how long I have to win you back.'

131

She rolled her eyes.

'Congratulations,' I said. 'I mean it.'

'Do you?'

'I'm trying to.'

Silence.

'Thank you,' she said.

Silence.

'I want to ask you something,' I said. 'But you can't get upset. Deal?'

'No.'

'All right, well, regardless . . . Is his name really Pete?'

I couldn't tell whether she was going to laugh or hit me.

'It's short for Pedram,' she said.

'Got it,' I said.

Silence.

'Thank you for not yelling at me,' I said.

The noise of steam and grinding.

'It's not what you think,' she said.

'What do I think.'

'He's a good guy. A really good guy. He's very thoughtful, and smart. He went to NYU.'

She sounded wistful, and I realized that if I needed to believe I still had a chance, she needed equally to prove – to herself, to me – that she hadn't sacrificed her ideals by trading me in for a snazzier model. Though I wanted desperately to refute her, all I said was, 'I expect nothing less.'

★ ★ ★

I couldn't sleep that night. At quarter to six Daciana's station wagon chugged into the driveway, and I rose and went to the kitchen, where Alma was unwrapping a fresh loaf of bread.

'Up early, Mr Geist.'

I smiled wanly. 'I'm not feeling my best.'

'I'm sorry to hear that. Perhaps we should once again table the debate.'

That would make twice in one week, and I felt my insecurities resurgent: she was trying to drive me away. Then I forced myself to calm down. I'd neglected to shave, and I looked a wreck. She was being considerate.

'I wouldn't dream of it,' I said. 'But thank you.'

'As you wish.' She handed me the bread to slice. 'I must apologize that I didn't warn you of my nephew's arrival. I would have, had I been given any notice myself.'

'There's no need to apologize.'

'Please, Mr Geist. Let us be honest with each other. Your irritation was plain.'

Knife moving, I shrugged.

'I must ask that you accept his presence here, for it is inevitable, and will inevitably recur.'

I put the bread in the toaster and reached for the whistling kettle. 'He's your sister's grandson.'

'The very same. The last remaining leaf on the tree, so to speak, and for that reason I choose to overlook his many flaws. While I consider a poor upbringing no excuse for lapses of character, much of the responsibility for that upbringing was mine.

133

He was orphaned at a young age, and for a time thereafter lived with me.' Before I could reply, she raised a hand. 'You doth protest too much, Mr Geist. I only tell you this in order that you should exercise patience with him and with me.'

'May I asked what happened?'

'A drunk ran down his parents.'

Now I really did feel guilty.

'Yes,' she said. 'It was very sad. As you might imagine, it was a rather uncontrollable boy that I received, though I no doubt contributed to these tendencies, or at least exacerbated them. Children frustrate me, as they give the appearance of possessing reason when they do not. That I failed to learn, time and again, is my fault alone.' She paused. 'Again I apologize. None of this concerns you. All I ask is that you not judge him too harshly.'

'It's you I'm worried about.'

'Allow me, then, to set your mind at rest. He tests me, it is true, but I am more than capable of handling him. I do, however, wish for you to be prepared. He has a habit of appearing out of the blue, and leaving just as abruptly. Before this week I had not heard from him in six months. We ought therefore to expect many visits in the coming days.'

I looked at her.

'He needs money,' she said.

'. . . I see.'

Somewhat tartly, she said, 'He is my only living relative, Mr Geist.'

'Of course. I didn't mean to pry.'

'My relations with my nephew always have been and always shall be effected through the exchange of funds. It is better that this should be so, in order that he remain interested in me and I avoid disappointment.'

But why, I wanted to ask, do you care whether he's interested in you? Why, when you have me? 'I understand,' I said.

Her point made, she sat back, far older than I had ever seen her. 'Ach. This has been going on for years. I am merely unaccustomed to a third party bearing witness.'

'He has no right to upset you.'

'He does all the same.'

'He doesn't have to.'

She smiled. 'No? You would murder him for me, then?'

'I can keep him outside the next time he shows up.'

'That is good of you, but I am afraid I couldn't accept. Though the burden be terrible, I bear it freely.'

Her weariness didn't seem to square with the laughter I'd heard from the other room. I knew as well as anyone, though, that love makes hypocrites of us all.

In the next room, the maid began to vacuum.

'Let us talk of happier things.' Alma reached into her sweater pocket and took out a check. 'For you.'

'You paid me yesterday.'

'Yes. This is for your birthday, which I believe is almost upon us.'

If I'd mentioned my birthday to her, I'd done so months ago; for her to have borne it in mind so long moved me. I was about to thank her when I looked down at the check and saw that it was for five hundred dollars.

'Ms Spielmann, please.'

'Please yourself, Mr Geist.'

'I can't accept this.'

'Rubbish. You must find yourself a decent pair of shoes. A scholar cannot go around in rags.'

I did need new shoes, but not five hundred dollars' worth. Think of all the books that would buy, I pointed out.

'There are other things a man should have, Mr Geist. You've plenty of books. Now, my tea, please. Let us attempt to restore order to the universe.'

CHAPTER 12

Despite Alma's blandishments, I still felt as though I had been relegated to second best in her eyes; added to the news about Father Fred, and the blow Yasmina had dealt me, it made for a triple whammy of disillusionment and rejection. Asking Drew to recruit people for a birthday party was, I suppose, a rather desperate attempt to reconstitute my ego. Considering the short notice, he did an impressive job, managing to fill two booths of a local cantina with an assortment of friends I had neither seen nor spoken to since moving in with Alma: colleagues from the department, other graduate students, a couple of lawyers, a couple of consultants. Wisely, he had gone with an all-male cast. Nobody asked how I was feeling. All they asked was if I wanted another Corona. Yes, I did.

Someone asked what happened when you turned thirty-one.

'It's the first year of your thirties.'

'Thirty is the first year of your thirties.'

'No, thirty is the last year of your twenties. It's like Y2K.'

A large chunk of the evening was devoted to resolving this question. I didn't have to talk very much, for which I was grateful. Because I kept quiet, I don't think anybody noticed how drunk I was until they made their excuses (work, wives, weeknight) and came over for a handshake and found themselves reeled in for a bear hug. Whoa, there. You all right? Yes, I was. In fact, I was ready for another.

By eleven-thirty only Drew remained.

'Yasmina's engaged,' I said.

He raised his eyebrows. 'Wowie.'

I drained my beer. 'Indeed.'

Outside he flagged a taxi.

'You know what,' I said. 'You go on. I'm going to take a walk.'

He knew better than to argue. He wished me happy birthday and left.

I staggered off across the Common, stumbling through the springtime mud and humming to myself, a dismal melody whose source I couldn't quite place. I hummed it again and then it came to me, Daciana, it was hers, some Gypsy song, one she liked to wake me up with, it put me in the mood for pierogi and suicide. Here's to you, comrade. Along Mass Ave, sodium lamps glowing orange gumdrops. The air smelled bleachy. Raw, excitable, I lurched, belching, toward Porter Square, ultimate destination unknown. I could keep going all the way to Davis Square. Why was every place around here a Square? City planner with

138

a quadrilateral fetish. But they weren't square, these Squares. Harvard Square was a triangle. Porter Square a trapezoid. Inman Square an intersection. I passed the building where I'd lived with Dorothy, Kelly, and Jessica, and I waved at their floor. I hoped they'd found a new roommate, a fourth to complete the square, what would her name be? Alison. Or – no. Myung. Her name would be Myung and she would be mmmpre-law, she'd be the loudest of all, her screams audible over a two-mile radius.

Outside a bar called the Thorn, a throng of people stood smoking. I was working my way through them when I felt a hand on my shoulder.

'Hey.'

I swiveled around loosely.

'Hey,' said the man again. His smile leaked smoke.

It was Eric.

Had I been in any other state, I would have kept walking, mortified to be caught out alone by him. As things stood, though, my mood was somewhat more expansive.

'Good evening,' I said, bowing deeply at the waist.

With him were two women, Boston Irish, blond and heavyset, their fingernails painted the same hair-raising purple. The only discernible difference between them was that one had a navel piercing and the other did not.

'Joe, right?'

I was embarrassed by how gratified I felt to learn that he knew my name – gratified enough not to correct him. His acknowledgment ought to've meant nothing to me. Yet it did. 'Indeed. And you're Eric. And you lovely ladies are.'

'Lindsay.' 'Debbie.'

I hadn't caught which name went with which girl, so in my mind they became Navel and Non-Navel. I bowed to both. 'It is an honor and a privilege,' I said.

They laughed throatily. One of them offered me a smoke. I declined.

'I must guard my health,' I said. 'It's my birthday.'

'Cool,' Non-Navel said. 'Happy birthday.'

I bowed again.

'Calls for a shot,' Eric said. He took Navel by the arm and they went inside. I looked at Non-Navel, who smiled and pulled me after them.

We cleared space in a corner, and Eric sent the girls for drinks. They seemed happy to do so, returning with a tray of overflowing glasses.

'Tequiiii*la*,' Navel said. She had a thick Boston accent.

Everyone salted and drank and bit. Then Eric told them to get beer chasers.

While they were gone, I asked if Navel was his girlfriend.

'Naw, I just met them.'

'Then why do they keep buying us drinks?' At my sloppiest, I could still find the hole in a situation's logic.

He shrugged, then winked. The similarity to Alma was so striking that I almost yelped.

I can recall snatches of what followed. There were drinks and more drinks. Jokes I knew I should not find funny but that made me sputter with delight. Then everyone got around to comparing tattoos. Non-Navel had a dolphin on her ankle. Navel turned around and lifted up her shirt to show a 'tribal' design across the small of her back. Eric had an AK-47 on one shoulder and a weirdly old-fashioned staghead on the other, as though he'd had the tattoo artist copy opposing pages out of *Field & Stream*. When I said that I didn't have a tattoo, the focus then became which tattoo I would get when (not if) I got one. Navel lobbied in favor of barbed wire around the biceps. Non-Navel seemed to think I was more of a Chinese character kind of guy.

'I'd get Nietzsche,' I yelled over the music.

They looked confused.

I explained that he was a nineteenth-century German philosopher. They still looked confused, so I added that I, too, was a philosopher.

'Oooh,' Non-Navel said. 'Say somethin deep.'

Later I tried to explain the Sorites Paradox to her.

'That don't make no sense,' she yelled.

She had come to be sitting in my lap.

'That's why it's a paradox,' I yelled. The flow of blood to my lower extremities was being severely restricted.

'What the fuck are you talking about?' yelled Navel.

'Sand,' yelled Non-Navel.

141

'What fuckin sand?'

'It's a metaphor,' I yelled.

Charisma is a mysterious and powerful thing. I have it in limited supply, and that which I do have functions under highly specialized conditions. A certain class of smart, strong-willed woman finds me endearing. In general, though, I'm not the type of person who wins people over in bars. Whatever Eric had working against him – that beard, for starters – he had a far more potent weapon coursing through his bloodstream, one unavailable to mere mortals like me. I've already mentioned that he was handsome in a predatory sort of way. When we'd first met he had been so sullen and uninterested in me that I had failed to credit him with anything more than a genetic hold on Alma. Under the influence of booze and despair, however, I now saw that I had been wrong: he was in fact preternaturally charming, oozing sexuality, and knowing instinctively what women wanted to hear and when they needed to hear it. It's hard for me to remember exactly what he said, but in truth the words themselves are unimportant; in seduction, as in all forms of marketing, form supersedes content. I do remember struggling to formulate questions that would reveal something of his character to me. I wanted to know who this person was, this confidence man who had the potential to replace me. What molten substance bubbled at his core? But he had a way of making me feel awkward when I asked a question he didn't want to answer.

He would pretend not to have heard me; he would invariably be looking in the other direction, nuzzling Navel, whispering in her ear, making her giggle. I watched her finger skip across the hollow of his chest and up to his cheek, then down to hook under the droopy neck of his T-shirt. I watched as the finger traced around the collar to the nape of his neck, dancing then down his back, coming to rest near the top of his buttocks, where the elastic of his underwear rose over his waistband. He did not react to this advance: he expected it and did not seem the slightest bit surprised. Non-Navel was watching them, too. She may have been in my arms, but it was his power keeping her there. Drunk as I was, I could tell from the way they responded to him, their bodies open and inclined, that he had both girls bridled. In this way, they looked familiar to me. They looked the way women used to look when they talked to my father.

I woke with my face squunched. Warm, stale air washed over my naked back. Itchy-eyed, cotton-mouthed, I lay there running my fingers over the surface below me, which I tentatively identified as an unsheeted futon.

I heard snorting, felt shifting, became aware of a body next to me. Rising up on my elbows turned a simple headache into pure evil, so I eased myself back down, lying motionless until the world stopped crackling. Then I slid out of bed and began hunting for my clothes. This was a real challenge, as the room was dark and covered in heaps of dirty laundry, and I kept having to pause to let nausea pass.

I'd collected both shoes, one sock, and my still-buttoned shirt when from the next room came a shout.

'Mothafucka.'

Startled, I dropped my shirt.

The body in the bed stirred, sat up. It was Non-Navel. 'Hey,' she said.

'Son of a bitch.'

'Jesus,' said Non-Navel. She rubbed her nose, watching as I excavated around her butterfly chair. 'What are you doing?'

'Mothafucka.'

'Simma down,' yelled Non-Navel. She told me to come back to bed.

I mumbled about needing to find my pants.

Outside, more ranting.

'Hey,' yelled Non-Navel. 'People are sleeping, y'inconsiderate cu—'

The door burst open. I, pantsless, dove for cover. Navel had no such qualms. In she marched, wearing nothing but a T-shirt, her makeup smeared into war paint. She planted herself in the middle of the room – arms akimbo, thighs aquiver – and bellowed:

'Youbastidwhethafucksmyshit.'

I seized a crusty dishtowel, tried gamely to cover myself with it.

'Get the hell outta my room,' yelled Non-Navel.

'Bastid.' Navel was striding toward me. 'Whez

my shit?' She wrapped her beefy arms around me and swung me toward the floor, my superior size mooted by hangover and the element of surprise. Down I went, noting as I did another tattoo she'd failed to mention, a cackling shamrock and the words ERIN-go-fuck-yaself inscribed on the inside of her left leg. I looked up to see her rearing back to strike me – and then Non-Navel came flying into the frame, tackling her, and the two of them went rolling across the room, caterwauling and yanking each other's hair.

'He took my shit! He took my shit!'

'You crazy bitch, shut the fuck up.'

'My shit!'

Briefly, I watched, transfixed. Then I came to, grabbed what I had, and ran.

The kitchen was littered with glasses and over-flowing ashtrays. My pants were splayed across the back of a folding chair. I had the presence of mind to check for my wallet and keys before step-ping sockless into my loafers.

'Motha*fucka*.' Navel was coming at me, arms out like a zombie, dragging Non-Navel, who had her by the leg. 'Mo. Tha. Fuck. A.'

Down a stairwell, skidding turns, slamming walls, daylight ahead; moving fast until a ghastly howl of pain brought me up short.

'Wait!' Non-Navel appeared, out of breath. 'Heah,' she said, pressing a piece of paper into my hand. 'Call me?'

★   ★   ★

145

With the help of a bus stop map, I determined that I was in Arlington, five miles northeast of Cambridge. I set out on foot, repeatedly glancing back in expectation of one or both women barreling down the sidewalk after me. Stores were open; it was long after nine, and I felt sick, having missed breakfast with Alma. I picked up the pace, jogging along until I found a cab.

I came in via the back porch and tiptoed to my bathroom. As I scrubbed away smoke and grime, I thought about Navel and her accusations. If anything had happened, Eric was surely to blame, although I suppose in her mind that made me guilty by association. What, exactly, had he stolen? Her purse? Phone? Drugs? Whatever it was, it had nothing to do with me. I groped indignantly for bits and pieces of the previous evening, feeling sick all over again when I got ahold of them. I saw a drinking game at the girls' apartment, everybody down to underwear; remembered grasping something sweaty and fleshy and not knowing to whom it belonged . . . Had we all been in the same room? Had it been that bad? I could never know for certain, but whatever had taken place could not be revoked; it would stand between us eternally. I wanted to vomit. I *was* guilty – not of theft but of lowering myself. I stood indicted in my own eyes: I'd done as he had done, I had made myself his equal, and I hated myself for it.

In the kitchen, Alma had put out a plate of herring and a mug of black coffee.

'Good morning, Mr Geist. I trust you had a nice party. I thought you might require this.'

Cheeks burning, I sat down to my *Katerfrühstück*.

CHAPTER 13

There are few places more beautiful than Cambridge in its blooming days, days all the lovelier for the preceding months of misery. For Alma, however, whose attacks were triggered by heat, the spring thaw meant a greater likelihood of being knocked flat by pain. Twice in three days she failed to come down for breakfast, and when it happened again a few days later, I dialed Dr Cargill. Her advice – wait it out – left me restless and dissatisfied, and to occupy my mind I set about making Alma some lunch, which I put on a tray and took upstairs. Her bedroom door was closed. Hearing nothing, I decided not to knock but to put the tray down, allowing her to take what she would whenever she was ready. I started downstairs again, then stopped and looked back. The tray was a few inches from the door. What if she came outside and stepped right into the food? Or worse: tripped and fell down the stairs? I nudged the tray back a few feet. But what if she was too exhausted to make it all the way over to the tray? I nudged it closer. But what if the food spoiled, sitting out here on the landing?

She might get salmonella. I picked up the tray; I would take it downstairs and leave it in the fridge. But what if she was hungry and needed food and couldn't call out to me? What if she did call out and I didn't hear her? Sandwiches didn't go bad, did they? I used to bring my lunch to school and keep it in my desk, where it sat all day long, fermenting. But I was a kid back then, I had a robust immune system, I never got sick. The elderly were especially susceptible to food poisoning. They could die. It was a curse, having these factoids at my disposal . . . But Alma was healthy. Sort of. But this. But that. Up went the tray; down it went; back it went, then forth. Finally I began to worry about waking her with all my futzing around, so I left the tray where it was, halfway between close and far, and went back down to the kitchen to call the doctor again. When I got there, though, I couldn't bring myself to do anything. I didn't want to cry wolf. I had to trust that her chosen course of action (i.e., inaction) was best. But she had said to call anytime.

But but but but but.

As I stood there, arguing with myself, my finger poised over the keypad, the doorbell rang. I hurried to answer it before the noise woke Alma.

Eric stood on the front porch, leering at me in a way that confirmed everything I'd feared. We were connected now, whether I consented or not.

'Hey,' he said. 'Is my aunt around?'

'She's not feeling well.'

'One of her . . .'

I nodded.

'That's too bad.'

I said nothing.

'Cause I was kind of hoping to see her.'

'She's not up for that.'

'Hm.' He smiled, as though it was my duty to move the conversation along.

'Was there something else I could help you with?'

'I need to see her,' he said. 'It's important.'

'She's resting.'

'No, I know. You know what, though, I think I'll wait for her.'

'It could be hours.'

'Right.'

'And,' I said, 'and she needs it quiet.'

'Okay.'

A silence.

'So you'd really be better off coming back.'

'Look, man, I'm not going to throw a party. It's hot as hell out here.' And he brushed past me, crossing the living room toward the kitchen. I followed.

'Can I get some water?' he asked.

'Help yourself.'

He started opening all the wrong cupboards.

Annoyed, I fetched him a glass.

'Hey, thanks.'

He drank, animal lapping sounds. When he faced me next his shirtfront was wet.

'Told you it was hot.' He tossed me the empty

glass. 'But it's always cold in here, right?' He laughed, then lifted the plastic cake cover, beneath which sat the remaining third of that week's *Sachertorte*.

'That looks fantastic. Lemme get some of that?'

With the thinnest composure, I handed him a plate and utensils.

'Nice,' he said, cutting a big slice. 'She loves her chocolate. She used to order it from Switzerland.'

I indicated the bars on the counter.

'Really? She still does that?'

'So it would seem.'

'Damn,' he said, shaking his head. 'Some things never change, huh.'

'I guess not.'

'You guess not.' He laughed again. 'You guess right.'

He bent to take in a forkful, knots of spine poking up beneath his T-shirt. I realized with repulsion that it was the very same shirt he'd worn that night in the bar. Whether it had been washed since, I could not tell.

Correctly made, *Sachertorte* is too dry to eat on its own; unsweetened whipped cream makes the traditional accompaniment. We had a bowl in the fridge, but I didn't mention it, leaning against the counter with my arms folded, advertising indifference.

The truth was otherwise. For although I hated the way he had barged in, disrupting my solitude, making me self-conscious by reminding me of our drunken escapade; hated his impertinence (*lemme get some of that*); hated what he stood for, the part

151

of Alma to which I had no access, the knowledge that I was a visitor here – while all that was true, it would be an oversimplification to say that I hated *him*, or wanted him gone. At many points I could have denied him entry. I could have refused to let him in the house. I could have ordered him to leave once he'd finished drinking or eating. I didn't, because another part of me still sensed in him an opportunity for information. And I admit that I am not immune to the purely chemical effects of charisma. I could no more deny it than pretend that the night in Arlington had never happened: I wanted him to like me.

He pushed the plate away, wiped his mouth on his wrist. 'You're a philosopher.'

I nodded.

'That's cool. She must love that. Huh?'

I shrugged.

'I mean . . .' He passed his hand over his head, laughed again. 'You know? I never did get any of that stuff.'

'Is that right.'

'Oh, sure, yeah. I have learning disabilities. I mean, she used to get really frustrated with me.'

I thought of something Alma had said during our first conversation. *It is a terrible thing to be stupid.*

'How long did you live with her?' I asked.

'Nine years.'

'Did you like it?'

He smiled. 'I was a kid. What was I supposed to do?'

'Has she always been sick?'

'Ever since I've known her.' He paused. 'She used to wake herself up. I'd hear her walking around upstairs, two, three in the morning. Sound familiar?'

I nodded.

'Must be rough,' he said. 'On you, I mean.'

I shrugged.

'Sometimes she would scream in her sleep. Does she still do that?'

Horrified, I shook my head.

'For a while she did it every couple of nights.' He toyed with the crumbs on his plate. 'The first time it happened, the neighbors called the cops. They thought someone was being stabbed to death.'

Silence.

'That sounds . . . difficult,' I said.

'It's messed up, is what it is.' He smiled. 'What can you do, though.'

I said nothing.

'So,' he said. 'You're in the back room. That used to be my room.'

Alma hadn't mentioned it. I stiffened. 'Is that so.'

'You know the thingamajig on the window? The painting or whatever you call it? The pattern on his hat matches the fur on the deer.'

'That's interesting,' I said.

'You ever notice that?'

I felt silly shaking my head.

'No?'

153

'I don't look at it that often,' I lied.

'Yeah,' he said. 'Check it out the next time. Or, you know what—'

He stood up and walked out.

I couldn't exactly yell at him to stop. I got up and went after him.

'See?'

Having entered my room without permission, he was now standing by the leaded window, gesturing like a game-show host. 'Check it out.'

I wanted to resist, but curiosity had gotten the better of me. I crossed the room. Lo and behold, the hunter's cap and the deerskin were both rendered in the same orange houndstooth.

'I always liked that,' he said.

I nodded.

We stood as one, admiring the art.

'Man, I used to hate it back here. She'd lock me in to punish me. But, hey.' He laughed. 'That's a long time ago.'

I said nothing.

'What about the gun?' he asked. 'You ever see that?'

I had always taken her crack about owning a pistol to be just that: a crack. I shook my head.

'Oh, you got to. Come on.'

He exited toward the library, never looking back to see if I would follow.

Growing up, my brother and I were under strict instructions not to go anywhere near the cabinet

154

in the basement. This led us to want nothing more, and left alone one evening, the first thing Chris and I did – after eating an entire coconut cream pie – was steal the key from our father's nightstand.

I was six, Chris not yet thirteen. Together we scrambled down the basement steps, far more frightened of what our father's reaction would be than of the guns themselves. My brother took down a hunting rifle and pointed it all over the place, making shooting noises. He offered it to me – forced it on me, really, as I had come along as an observer, not as a participant, and took it from him only after much goading. It was heavy, the stock warm from his armpit. I aimed at the far wall, sighting above a tall cardboard box labeled x-mas lights in my mother's neat, antiquated hand.

'Do it,' he said.

I didn't want to, but he made fun of me until, shaking, I pulled the trigger – to no effect. The safety was still on. Chris laughed at me, and I threw the rifle down and ran upstairs in tears.

That fall he began going out with my father for white-tail season, one of the few activities they could manage to do together peacefully. It was, perhaps, the situation's inherent deadliness that kept their tempers in check, spilt blood and torn flesh enough to remind them of the consequences of rash action. They would disappear before dawn, coming home after dark with flaking lips and ski-cap hair. These trips transformed them; for days afterward they communicated on a frequency neither I nor my mother could pick up. To be so blatantly excluded reinforced my growing sense that I did not belong.

Watching Eric pry a wooden box out from one of the library's top shelves, I had the same uneasy feeling as I'd had all those years ago, when I thought I was about to blow a hole in the basement wall.

'Here,' he said.

Made of a dark, burled maple, it could have held any number of things: butterflies, playing cards, a chemistry set. The latch gleamed.

'Open it.'

The interior was lined with green velvet, similar to that on the base of half-Nietzsche, but rather more fine and soft. The gun itself had a narrow barrel, protruding from the chamber like a bone from flesh. Stamped on the base of the grip was an insignia too worn to identify.

'I don't know if it still works,' he said. 'I mean, it's pretty old.'

I ran my fingers over the velvet, and then, with a transgressive thrill, lifted the gun out of the case.

We are *homo faber* – man, maker and user of tools – and every tool we make has an innate purpose. When a particular object's purpose is so clearly singular, one experiences an almost irresistible urge to use it toward its intended end. Just as books are for reading and cakes are for eating, guns are for shooting, and though it had been decades since I'd held one in my hand, the chill of the metal brought on a terrifying impulse to destroy something. Disquieted, I replaced the pistol and handed the case to Eric, stepping away from him and it.

'You see that?'

He was pointing to the insignia, tracing its shape. '*S*,' he said, '*S*.'

I looked at him.

'Her father was big in the Austrian army.'

'He was an instrument maker.'

'He was. He also made land mines.' He snorted. 'How do you think they got so rich? Pianos?'

I said nothing.

'Sorry to spoil it for you.'

'She didn't do anything,' I said. 'She was a child.'

'Yeah,' he said. 'Well, okay.'

A silence.

'Did you take something from those girls?' I asked.

He looked at me.

'The one you . . . the one with the . . .' I gestured to my abdomen. 'She was going on about you stealing something from her.'

He continued to stare at me, then walked to the bookshelf. To get the case back into place he had to go up on his toes. 'She said that, huh.'

'Yes.'

'What did she say I stole?'

'I don't know. She was pretty upset, though.'

He laughed. 'Oh yeah?'

'I'm serious. She almost broke my neck.'

'Well,' he said, turning around. 'I don't know nothin about that.'

I said nothing.

'Her room was a mess. Whatever she's looking for, it's probably on the floor.' He glanced at the grandfather clock. 'She's not coming down anytime soon, huh.'

I shook my head.

'Tell her I stopped by.'

I nodded.

'Don't worry about me,' he said. 'I know my way out.'

That night I dreamt of a clearing in the forest. Through glassy leaves I saw movement, and I felt afraid, not knowing if I was hunter or prey.

CHAPTER 14

Alma's reaction to the news of Eric's visit was dismayingly subdued.

'No doubt he came for his money,' she said. 'Thank you for keeping him at bay while I rested. In the future I shall leave a spare check with you. You can give it to him right away and thereby free yourself of any obligation to entertain him.'

'All I did was give him cake.'

'And now we do not have enough for afternoon tea. For shame, Mr Geist.'

'What do you mean?'

'See for yourself.'

I lifted up the plastic cover; the rest of the *Sachertorte* was gone. 'There was plenty yesterday.'

'Perhaps he took it when you weren't looking,' she said. 'That would be true to form.'

I gripped the empty plate in both hands. 'I can't believe this.'

'Patience, Mr Geist. An old lady can survive one day without her confections. Now, you had a request.'

I barely heard her; I was still fuming.

'Mr Geist.'

159

'Pardon?'

'You spoke of it a few days ago,' she said. 'We never pursued the matter.'

I remembered now: my mother's call. I told Alma about the trip, describing it as a family reunion and omitting the memorial. 'I said I had to ask you first.'

'Naturally you may go. Although I feel obliged to note that you do not seem overly enthusiastic about the prospect.'

'I'm not.'

'In that case, you may use me as an excuse, if you wish to beg off.'

I hesitated. 'I really should go.'

'Very well, then.'

'It'll only be for a couple of days.'

'Please, don't rush on my account. I can get along quite well without you.' She half-smiled. 'You've never spoken of your family.'

I shrugged.

'May I ask why?'

'It's nothing personal. There's nothing to talk about.'

'You are too modest.'

'I'm not. They never met Wittgenstein. They wouldn't even know who that is.'

'They produced you, Mr Geist.'

'I've never understood how.'

She waited for me to say more. I didn't, and she said, 'Of course, your business is your own.'

She sounded different then. Perhaps she was

160

annoyed at me for acting cagey when she had revealed so much about herself. Or maybe she meant what she said, and what I heard in her voice was concern. Either way, the moment passed, and we moved on to more mutually agreeable subjects.

Eric began turning up regularly for money. Alma's equanimity with this arrangement made me prickle, enough so that I began ducking out the back whenever I heard him climbing the front steps. If I didn't get out in time, I would be invited to sit with the two of them, the worst kind of torture. I would say nothing, counting the minutes, finally coming up with an excuse to go to my room, where I would clamp my pillow over my ears, stoking my own frustration by attempting to estimate how much she had given him over the years. Say, on average, a hundred dollars, once a week for . . . pick a number, say fifteen years . . . that came out to about eighty thousand dollars – an outrageous amount, considering he did nothing except stick out his hand. At least the maid and I earned our keep. What could he possibly need that much for, except to feed an addiction? This had to be stopped; it was not right; it was not good, not for him or her or anybody else. Then I berated myself: who was I to tell her how to spend her money, what nerve, what impudence. But then as someone who cared for her, I could not abide this rampant abuse of her generosity. If I didn't speak up at some point, would anyone?
And back and forth I went.

What really got to me was how Alma came alive in his presence, becoming, for a short while at least, positively coquettish. His flattery was so transparently phony that I couldn't understand how a woman of her intelligence and sophistication would fall for it. I found the process painful to behold. As weeks went on and I spent more time observing them, I began to understand why I couldn't draw a bead on Eric's personality: he had none. He responded only to immediate stimuli, and then only in pursuit of his own desires. He wanted money from Alma, and in order to get it, he rearranged himself as necessary. If she was feeling flirtatious, he flirted with her. If she appeared withdrawn, he was gentle and inquisitive. That he could so rapidly adjust his own mood to suit hers proved to me that he had no substance whatsoever. I couldn't possibly do the same. I was a real person, with an independent mind; I lacked his chameleon's gifts. But then how did he manage to fool her? Or, rather, why did she allow herself to be fooled? I tortured myself with this question. Endlessly I compared myself to him. I was the book; he was the movie. The more I turned the metaphor over in my mind, the more apt it felt. He was all surface, I had depth. He provided passive diversion, I required rigor and concentration. I was subtle where he was obvious, refined where he was crass, etc., etc., all manner of self-congratulatory sniping that did not improve my mood one whit. Because I could not deny the way

Alma looked at him. I could not wish him away, and reluctantly I came to the conclusion that I had once again overestimated my own importance, and underestimated people's capacity for self-deception. Sometimes, it seemed, a lady just wanted to go to the movies.

Far more troubling, however, was the correlation between his appearances and her attacks. Within a few hours of his departure, she would be struck down, retiring to her room for the remainder of the day. In the evenings I would creep upstairs to leave her a tray of food, which always went untouched but which I stubbornly went on preparing. I could see the harm he did her, and that was enough to make me want to bar him from coming inside. It was not my place, though, and so I stood by, grimacing, whenever he rang the bell, interrupting our conversation; when he joined us, uninvited, for dinner. They would laugh and nudge each other with private jokes, and I would stew silently until, unable to bear it any longer, I shuffled out of the room, inventing appointments. I walked for hours, muttering to myself, kicking divots in the turf along the banks of the Charles. Or else I would stalk to the Science Center, sit down at a computer and check repeatedly for emails that never came. I scoured the web for information on both Alma and Eric, believing that the more I knew about them, the more I could control them. A patently childish idea, and anyway neither of them had any presence in cyberspace. Alma, understandably. And Eric presumably because he had long ceased to participate in normal society. That I could not find his name anywhere told me that he hadn't finished school (if he had even started it). As far as I knew he didn't have a job, other than sponging off Alma and ruining my life.

Or I would stand outside Yasmina's building, my former home, picturing her inside, draining pasta as she chatted on the phone to her fiancé, letting my hatred of him overlap with that of Eric, twin jealousies intermingling, each boosting the other exponentially, my sense of aggrievement mounting, working myself into such a frenzy that by the time I got home I was in no state to do anything other than lie in my bed in the dark, snorting and staring at the ceiling.

'Patience, Mr Geist.'

Patience for what? What was I supposed to be waiting for? It was impossible for me not to hate Eric, especially as summer descended like a cloak and Alma's attacks grew in both frequency and severity. She needed *less* of him, not more. Yet he kept on coming, and she kept on seeing him in, only to be undone with pain after his departure, check in hand.

I basically ceased to call Dr Cargill, whose instructions were always the same: let Alma be, don't panic, it would pass. I began to doubt the wisdom of this approach. True, it might have been thus dozens of times before. But what if this was the one time the symptoms proved fatal? What if something else had happened, something un-expected, a stroke or a slip in the bath? Anything could happen.

June became July; July, August. Alma grew haggard, spending more time in her room than out of it, and leaving me free most of the day. I could have done whatever I wanted. I could have gone to day games at Fenway. I could have jogged around Fresh Pond. I could have watched the campus laze along, ogled the summer-school students. I could have acted my age, a regular young man in the prime of his life. But I denied myself. All day long I hung around the house, waiting for Alma to come out and ask me once again for conversation, longing to reclaim the rhythm I had so loved and which I felt fading, fading. I let all the blooming days pass me by unnoticed, and at night, when I was insomniac and I heard her above me, walking in circles, I wished that she could dial down her pride at least enough to let me come sit with her. In her pos-ition, I would not have wanted to be alone. Maybe that was my problem: I could imagine only what I would've wanted. For her, it was more import-ant never to be seen in a degraded state than to have company. I did my best to accept this truth. She did not want me to pity her, and I tried not to. I don't know how good a job I did, but I tried.

Eventually I couldn't help myself. I steamed open the envelope she had left with me, and was shocked to discover that Eric's check was not for a hundred dollars but five times that. Shocked – and furious. Because it added up to a fortune over the years, because he never failed to give the impression that he was on the brink of penury, because it was so much more than she paid me, as much as my birthday gift. It took tremendous restraint not to tear the check into bits on the spot. I didn't, because as good as it would have felt, to do so would have been a short-term response to a chronic problem. No, what we needed here was real action, lasting action. There would come a day – I fantasized about it often – when I would stand up to him. Sometimes these fantasies involved me giving him a righteous telling-off. Sometimes they grew violent: I cuffed him, grabbed him by the collar, and tossed him down the front steps, his rump imprinted with the tread of my shoe, like in a cartoon. Always they ended with Alma breaking down, acknowledging that I was right, she had to cut him off, once and for all, I was her protector, her guardian angel, she couldn't have done it without me, thank you, Mr Geist, thank you, thank you.

'Good timing,' said Eric.

I came up the front porch. I'd gone out for a walk while Daciana cleaned, and my shirt was damp from having crossed over the river to the Business School and back. The Subaru was no longer in the driveway.

166

'I've been knocking,' he said. 'I was about to give up.'

I told him to wait outside while I got his check, then went to the library, where I had tucked the envelope away on one of the shelves. Reaching for it, my eye was drawn by the glint of the latch on the gun case.

'Lemme ask you something.'

I hadn't heard him behind me; my scalp tightened, and I turned, the check pinched tightly between my fingers. 'What.'

'Is everything all right here?'

'What do you mean.'

'I mean here. With you and me.'

'Why wouldn't it be all right.'

'I dunno, man. I feel like you don't like me very much.'

'I don't know why you think that.'

'Because every time I come by you look like you want to skin me.' He smiled. 'Hey, I'm just messing. Look, I want to tell you something. I think it's fantastic, everything you do for my aunt. It's great that she has someone like you. I'd do it myself, if I could.'

I said nothing.

'Seriously, though, I want us to be cool. Are we cool?'

'Sure.'

'Oh, man,' he said. 'You're a shitty liar.'

I felt myself flush. 'I don't not like you.'

'I think that means you don't like me, either.'

'It, it doesn't mean that.'

'So you're saying you do like me.'

'I . . .' I looked at him evenly. 'I don't have an opinion.'

His eyes seemed to bug out. Then he laughed loudly, a curiously artificial sound, like a sitcom laugh track.

'Would you keep it down, please,' I said.

'You are funny. You know that? You're killing me, here.'

'Do you mind? She's sleeping.'

'Yeah,' he said, still laughing. 'Sorry.'

Silence. I held the check out to him.

'Hey, thanks.'

Now that he had gotten his treat, I expected him to go, but he remained there, grinning at me.

'Was there something else you needed,' I said.

'No, man. I'm good. But. Look. You hungry? Cause I'm starving. You want to get some lunch?'

I was in fact very hungry, but I wasn't about to tell him that. I shrugged.

'Come on. On me. Token of my appreciation.'

In the ten minutes it took to walk to Central Square, I must've asked myself what I was doing a hundred times. The answer I gave was: *for Alma*. For Alma I would bear sitting with him. For Alma I would get him away from the house.

'Here we go,' he said, holding open the door of an Irish pub.

At that hour the only other patrons reminded me of my father: working-class men, their hunched postures telling of lives whose sole consolation had been a Barcalounger. The stereo piped something screechy and aggressive; with the volume on low, the overall impression was that the singer wanted to tear apart society, tenderly.

We found a booth and ordered, and Eric took charge of the conversation, asking where I'd been born, how I'd come to Harvard, where I'd lived before I met Alma, how I'd met her, and so forth. Since he'd started coming around, I had done my best to avoid speaking to him. In a way I had set myself up for this lunch, because he could now ask me lots of questions without making it seem like an interrogation, questions that I could not refuse to answer without looking like a jerk. The combined effects of social conditioning and charisma make for a powerful truth serum: I knew what was happening, and still I found myself disclosing more than I knew to be appropriate. More than I had ever told Alma. We had not gotten to my brother's death when the food came, making me grateful for something to put in my mouth. I waited until he took a bite of his own burger, then attempted to grab the wheel.

'So what is it you do?' I asked.

He paused, mid-chew. 'Me?'

'Yes.'

'Well, what do you mean.'

'I mean what do you do.'

'Like a job, you mean?'

'If that's the answer.'

169

'All right,' he said. 'Well, you know. I have some things going on.'

'Like what kind of things.'

'Business opportunities,' he said. 'I can't really talk about it.'

'Sounds top secret,' I said.

'I don't want to jinx anything, you know? I do what I have to do. We all have to, right? You do what you need to do. I mean, look at you.'

I put down my burger. 'How's that.'

'I'm saying, you're right at home. You're where you belong.'

I said nothing.

'I'm glad you're around. Like I said, I'd be there myself if I could. It's not – you know. I've lived with her, it wasn't a good arrangement. But she needs someone around, and I gotta say, man: I'm glad it's you.'

'. . . thanks.'

'I mean, you really care about her, don't you.'

'Of course.'

'I can tell. It shows. I care about her, too. You know? I worry about her all the time, though. This thing she has . . . Don't tell me it doesn't worry you.'

I said nothing.

'Doesn't it?'

'It does.'

'There you go. Course it does, you care about her. I mean, you have to ask yourself if she's getting better.' He paused. 'What do you think?'

'About what.'

'Is she getting better or not.'

'. . . no.'

'Getting worse, actually.'

Silence.

'It's hard to tell,' I said.

'Well, you ask me, my opinion, lately it's a hell of a lot worse than I've ever seen, and I've known her a long time. Like, twice, three times a week now?'

'It's not always that bad.'

'But it is sometimes.'

I nodded.

'That's crazy, man. It was never like that when I lived with her.'

'I guess so.'

'I'm tellin you. Even from your end you must've seen enough to know she ain't improving.'

I conceded that she was not.

'Right,' he said. 'I mean, you and me probably know her better than anyone else at this point. So what do you think?'

'What do you think I think, I think it's awful.'

'Nnn. That's not what I mean. What I mean, in your opinion, is she happy?'

I wanted to blurt out yes, of course she was happy, of course. She had me, after all. But could I honestly make that claim?' I felt ashamed to realize that in all the time I'd known Alma, I'd never thought to ask myself that question. How does one measure happiness? Can one assign it a quantity? The

171

utilitarian attempt to do just that is now considered risible. Enumerate the soft signs, then: she still smiled when we talked (although, these days, how often did we talk?): still ate her chocolate (although how often did she feel hungry?). Did these behaviors mean anything? Were they artifacts? Where did the real proof lie? I thought back to our very first conversation, which had begun with the question of whether it is better to be happy or intelligent. At the time, setting those two concepts up in opposition had seemed eminently reasonable. Now, as I sat listening to the quiet fury on the stereo and the waitress telling the bartender to kiss her sweet ass and the men snorting into their beers, I wondered if the happiness I thought I'd given Alma was merely a wan projection of that which she gave me.

'I don't know,' I said.

'If you don't know,' he said, 'the answer's no.'

I said nothing.

'And, I mean, what if she gets worse. You must have thought about that.'

'I hope not.'

'Course not. I mean, sure, I wish I could stop it. That's make-believe, though. So, I dunno. If it's never going to get better, and if it's getting *worse*, like it looks like it *is*, then what do you do with that? I mean, what the hell does a person *do?*'

'I don't know.'

'Me neither. I just don't fucking know. Nobody does. You know? Maybe there is no answer.'

'Maybe not.'

'Yeah. Maybe.' He studied his fingernails. 'I can't say how you feel about this, but since you care about her, like I do, I bet that you think it, too. Sometimes I wonder if it'd be better if, I mean, better for her to just – *whhhp*. You know?'

I caught myself nodding and stopped. What, exactly, did he think I knew?

'For her sake,' he said.

What I read in his eyes froze my heart.

'You boys all set?' said the waitress.

Eric smiled at her. 'All set.'

'You want a beer, shout.'

'Will do.'

She left. When he spoke again, I heard him through static.

'Look,' he said. 'Whatever happens to her – and something's gotta happen at some point, and for her sake, you have to hope that it's sooner rather than later. She's in pain. Sooner rather than later, something's going to happen. It might be difficult to think about. It might make us uncomfortable. But it's a fact. Life is life.

'You see what I mean?

'I can tell what you're thinking. "Look at her. She's already – what. Seventy-eight? Seventy-nine? Even if we sit back and wait, how much longer can it go on?" And you'd be right to think that way, you would. So let me tell you something else, something you might *not* know, which is the family history. You're gonna have to trust me on this when I say that she could hang in there a long, long time. It runs in the family. Longer than anyone wants – her most of all. I mean, you're smart. Use your imagination for a second. What would it be like for her if this went on for another, I don't know, twenty years? All of a sudden it's not so simple anymore.

'Is it.

'So, day to day, for us, what does that mean? I think, and this is just my opinion, but I do think that it's one based on fact – I think that *we* meaning you and I and her, we have to focus on the present. What is happening *now*. What that leaves us with here, I think, is a balance of power. If you ask me, this is not a bad thing. It's the way it should be. You're there. You're with her. You're the one she sees every day. Something goes wrong, you're the one who can say what occurred. How the situation plays out has a lot to do with what you decide.

'That being the case, whatever happens next is really up to you.

'And I'll tell you something else. My grandma's gone, my mom and dad are gone. So for her, that's it, you know? Just me. What do I need a house for? I don't. I mean, something does happen, it goes down a certain way, fine, it's my house. Okay. But depending on what plays out, you could have it, if you wanted.

'But you know what, though. I can tell that it's not something you feel a hundred percent about. I can see that. That's okay. Of course not; this is something you probably never thought about much, and if you did, you thought about it only from one angle. So let me give you some other angles to consider. It's not a question of you or me. Look at it as a question of what's best for her. It's a question of dignity. You said it yourself: she's not getting any better. She is in pain. That's why I'm saying we have to look at this from her perspective. Is she happy? I mean – you said it yourself. No. She isn't. It's not natural. Is it? Tell me. Is it natural for someone to have to wake up every day and face that kind of pain? Of course not. I mean, it would be unnatural for anyone, but she's the kind of person, it's going to be hard on her, much harder than on your average person. I know that. *You* know it. You're not an average kind of person, either, so put yourself in her shoes for a second and ask yourself, "Is this really what I want?" And you tell me what the answer is going to be.' He sat back. 'You tell me.'

I said, 'Would you excuse me.'

He gestured *go ahead*.

I locked myself inside a bathroom stall and stood a long while massaging my chest. Had that really happened? Had he offered me the house? Conspired with me over cheese-burgers? Impossible. I knew what he had said. He'd said it and yet he hadn't.

What did he expect?

Did he expect me to do an accounting?

Did he expect that to come out in his favor?

The world was unreal, the floor tiles swimming, the toilet a grinning menace.

I slapped myself across the face.

The waitress had taken my seat in the booth. As I approached, she slid a piece of paper across the table to Eric and stood up, straightening her skirt.

'You take care,' she said.

'Will do,' he said. To me: 'All set?'

I started for the door.

'One sec,' he said.

He was holding up the bill.

Reflexively, I reached for my wallet and removed a twenty.

'Hey, thanks,' he said, snatching it from me and tossing it on the table. 'You didn't have to do that.'

Feeling numb, I pushed out into the blinding summer sun. I hadn't intended to pay for him, but somehow I had.

'You don't need to find me,' Eric said as we stood on the corner of Mass Ave and Prospect. 'I got some stuff to do but I'll be around. Meantime, you think it over, and the next time you see her hurting like that, you think about what I told you.' He smiled, clapped me on the shoulder, and walked toward the T. Through a shimmering cloud of exhaust, I watched him sink underground.

CHAPTER 15

I would never have wished an attack on Alma, of course, but I will admit that right then I was relieved not to have to see her. To sit and chat as though everything was the same – to look her in the eyes – I didn't think I could do it. For several hours I paced around the library, trying to make sense of what had just taken place.

Tell the police. That's the automatic first response. Tell them what, though? Eric hadn't asked me to do anything, not really. He'd described a set of circumstances – a sick old woman, a dangling fortune – and left me to reach my own conclusions. Though his intent was unambiguous, when I tried to pin him to anything explicit, I came up empty-handed. So much of what he'd said had been wordless, built into facial expressions, and pauses, and prosody; by talking around his point he made it far more forcefully than he ever could have by stating it outright. He was, I realized, a true Continental, his pitch a masterpiece of dramatic subtext.

Was it a crime to talk about such things? Did failing to report the conversation make me a party to whatever he did next? Was I legally responsible? Morally? I pictured someone like me walking into the station (in my mind, it looked like a public library, except with guns and thugs), approaching the front desk, and offering, unprompted, a confession. What would that look like to them? Very simply this: I had agreed to help Eric, then backed out. I didn't know why he had chosen me, but surely the police would think he had reason to do so; by offering myself up for scrutiny, I would become a suspect in a crime that hadn't been committed, that might never be committed, the idea of which might never be known to anyone except the two of us. He could easily claim that I had approached him, or that nothing had happened at all. I'd be crying wolf – about myself. No, the police were out. But whom did that leave? Alma? At best she would think me incoherent; more likely, delusional. One or both of the same two problems applied to telling the doctor or any of my friends. Perhaps that was Eric's insurance policy: the knowledge that if I sought help, I would either bring suspicion upon myself or else sound deranged. What came next, then? More cajoling. If that didn't work, threats. Physical intimidation. Or else he'd find another accomplice, and when he did, I would become the man who knew too much.

The next time you see her hurting like that, you think about what I told you.

What was it about me that suggested I would be willing to entertain such a notion? Did he think he could convince me? Did he think I didn't need convincing? I thought about all the times I'd sat beside him, watching him flirt with her. Had I given him the go-ahead? The wrong kind of look? Had he smiled and nodded at me, and had I smiled and nodded back? What could I have done to bring this on? How long had he been planning this? Since we met? Since our night in Arlington? Had he planned that, too? Were the girls in on it? Was the scene the next morning calculated to achieve some end? But now I really did sound delusional.

Worst of all was the way he had framed the idea, as an act of mercy. An arrow aimed at my soft spots, or did he truly see it that way? Had he had to work on himself, or had it been easy for him? Did the idea drip like cave water, dissolving the bedrock of his conscience? Or had there never been a conscience in the first place?

What about me?

Did he know what he was doing when he put the idea in my head?

We all have thoughts we'd rather not have. While I could not conceive of ever seeing things Eric's way, I did think about what he'd said. How could I not? I couldn't delete the concept. It was, perversely, to the contrary. The more tightly I muzzled it, the more insistently it barked. I thought about it, all right: I thought about it that night, when I heard her hobbling around, and I wanted to go to her, and restrained myself for fear of offending her.

179

I thought about it throughout the following week, when the temperature soared and she got worse and I had to call the doctor once again, and was once again told that there was nothing we could do. So of course I thought about it; like an earworm, it had eaten its way into my consciousness, and I thought about it again when the doorbell rang and he stood on the porch, winking; thought about it as I handed him the envelope with his check; thought about it as I slammed the door and ran to the library to hide myself in a book.

I began to think about it all the time.

Because you couldn't claim that the idea had no upside whatsoever. There was something to be said for alleviating suffering, wasn't there? That was what doctors did, after all: they made people 'more comfortable.' They adminstered drugs that divorced the mind from reality, painkillers that gradually shut down the body. A slower kind of death, but was it all that different? Not that I was a doctor. Not that I had a mandate to act one way or the other. But when someone was in extremis – as Alma clearly was – did the distinction between what morphine did and what Eric wanted me to do mean anything at all? Was it a question of scale? Of semantics? Say that she had asked me to help her commit suicide. Illegal, perhaps. But immoral? Whom did it help, keeping her alive if she no longer wanted to be alive? Nietzsche tells us that one should die proudly when it is no longer possible to live proudly, and

180

Alma was nothing if not proud. She had told me never to pity her, but given the present state of affairs, that was all I could manage to do. So if – let me say that again: *if* – if she had asked me to help her end her own life, I would not have hesitated. In fact, I would have felt morally obliged to help her. Now, obviously, that situation would be different from one in which I acted preemptively. By asking, she became the actor instead of the acted-upon, the agent instead of the victim. And, crucially, she had not asked. The whole thing was theoretical, the very thought absurd. But as Bertrand Russell wrote, 'Whoever wishes to become a philosopher must learn not to be frightened of absurdities.'

So when, a few weeks later, she stopped watching her soaps, complaining that the whine of the television nauseated her, I thought about it.

When I heard her vomiting up my *Sachertorte*, I thought about it some more.

I thought and thought and thought.

It was possible (scarcely so, but that will suffice) that that was what she *did* want, if only she weren't too proud to ask for help. Everything I knew about her (and I knew her well, didn't I, knew her better than anyone else) told me that she would not readily confess to weakness. She never called the doctor; I did. She never asked for me to bring food up to her room; I did that on my own, knowing she was too tired to do it herself. She never asked for these things – she never would have; they were beneath her – but she was grateful when I did them for her. This is love: anticipating another's needs, providing what they cannot or will not ask for.

Another thought experiment: eventually she would die of one cause or another, and if I was still around when that happened, in one or five or twenty years, I would be out on the street. (Twenty years? Did I really intend to stick around that long? But this was all theoretical.) At that point, Eric would have no motivation to give me the house, not when he could sell it for profit and I had done nothing for him. On the other hand, if she left the house to him, and he gave the house to me . . . it was repellent, of course, but the thought was there. I had a flexible mind, and though I would never – *never* – put these theories into practice, it was in my nature to ask questions, probe the abstract, conceive of possible worlds. One could make an argument – an anemic argument but an argument nonetheless – that by acting now, I was simply securing my future, allowing myself to one day return to my writing in peace and quiet – something Alma herself had encouraged me to do. She believed in me. She told me all the time. In a certain sense, I would be carrying out her wishes. I could live in the house until I completed my dissertation – or beyond – or I could sell it and find a place of my own . . . I'd never owned property. I didn't know anything about titles and deeds. How did it work? Could Eric simply gift me a house? Wouldn't that look suspicious? Of course it would; we'd have to let some time pass before I took possession, in the meantime I could rent it out, it'd be easy enough to find tenants, they could pay in cash.

And but so now these once-harmless thoughts had grown terrifyingly specific, terrifyingly concrete, and though I'd done nothing – nothing at all except treat her well and think – I felt guilty, I felt sick, I tormented and lacerated myself, I lost my appetite, I had heartburn, I had palpitations, my head hurt, my liver hurt, I could not sleep. And while these terrifyingly specific and concrete thoughts were bad enough as themselves, they seemed factorially worse when I realized what they said about the kind of person I'd become. Not only was I the kind of person who would marshal arguments in favor of murdering someone who had done nothing but good for him – someone he loved – but I would do so solely for material gain. It was this that frightened me most. I had grown fat and happy, drunk on comfort. I had come to take for granted that I should have food and shelter and books and beautiful objects; I had come to possess these things in my mind, so that they were not luxuries to be wary of but necessities to plan around. It was not a chair that I sat on: it was *my chair*, and, if not willing to kill for it, I was willing to allow the thought of its loss to serve as a premise for the vilest fantasies. I was impure. I was a merchant in the temple. And so I afflicted myself: I fasted.

I read until the text blurred and my eyes burned. I brushed my teeth until I spat blood. I did calisthenics to exhaustion. I slept on the floor without a pillow. I took no pleasure in these exertions, like a man wallowing in a toothache. I wanted to be free. But my lust, once provoked, could not be undone: I desired.

I had hardly seen any of my friends since the night of my birthday. Now I began frantically calling people, making plans, meeting for cocktails, going to movies, engaging in all manner of trifling chatter, drinking myself stupid; that is what wine is for. Still I had no peace, and as Indian summer arrived, I again took to the streets, rambling over miles, sweating through my sportcoat, smothered by heat and dust, abused by the racket of jack-hammers and the clang of construction, tripping over piles of bricks laid out across the brick sidewalk, Eric's grinning face blooming in shop windows and on strangers; and I turned and fled into the bosom of the crowds, hounded by guilt, haunted by the awareness of my own power, the knowledge that I had the capacity to do evil, even if I chose not to exercise it. One cannot fire the gun until one recognizes it exists and that it is clutched in one's own two hands. When that happens, one wants to fire it, because that is what guns are for.

And I felt guilty for feeling guilty, because I had no right to dismember myself for something I hadn't done. All I'd done was think. What's wrong with thinking? Was anyone ever hurt by a thought? I had no control over which images my brain chose to present to me, did I? One must distinguish theory from practice. I repeated to myself G. E. Moore's famous proof of the existence of an external reality. 'Here is a hand,' he said, holding out one palm, 'and here is another.' I held my hands out. They were clean.

But I could not do anything to prevent it when, at night, in my dreams, I really did kill Alma. Was that my fault? I could not stop the thoughts from coming. I dreamt of strangling her. Bludgeoning her. Stabbing her with a kitchen knife. I dreamt of riding a horse, a red-eyed horse, across her body, trampling her to death. The horse was large and fiery; its nostrils shot steam; its hooves crushed her bones to jelly. I halved her skull with an axe, spattered her brains across the carpet, wiped my hands on my shirt. I crammed pieces of paper down her throat, filling her throat with paper, her smile widening as the light left her eyes, her lips mouthing *Thank you*, Mr Geist.

'Hot as hell,' said Eric.

'Is that my nephew?' called Alma. 'Tell him to come in.'

I stood aside to allow him into the entry hall, then went to my room and closed the door. I lay down on the bed and tried to nap, but I was trembling so violently that it was impossible, and anyway their voices from the library kept me awake. I was about to leave the house when Alma knocked and asked if I would be so kind as to heat up dinner.

I rose to my duties, then sat at the kitchen table, pretending to work the crossword.

'What's up.'

He stood before me, his lean body curved against the doorframe.

'She's taking a bath,' he said. 'She'll be down soon.'

I said nothing.

'Gimme a clue,' he said.

Still I didn't answer, and he sat down across from me.

'Hey, I'm making conversation. Isn't that what you do?' He sat back, laced his fingers behind his head. 'Come on, let me try one.'

I said nothing.

'You think about what I told you?'

I said nothing.

'You must've thought about it a little.'

I said nothing.

He said, 'I don't know what you're so worked up about.'

'I'm not worked up.'

Silence.

'I'm no good at those things, anyway,' he said.

I said nothing.

'You know, I really think we should talk it over.'

'There's nothing to talk about.'

'Sure there is.'

I said nothing.

'Let's talk,' he said.

I said, 'I told the police.'

For a moment he paled. Then the smile. 'Oh, yeah?'

I nodded.

'What did you tell them.'

'Everything you said to me.'

'What did I say to you.'

'You know what you said.'

'No, I don't.'

'Then there's nothing I can tell you.'

He smiled again. 'Didn't I say you're a shitty liar?'

'I'm not lying.'

'Okay,' he said. 'Well, then, I guess we'll have to wait and see.'

'I guess so.'

'You guess right. Maybe you did, maybe you didn't. Either way, it's okay. I mean, you can tell them whatever you want. I mean, it was your idea.'

I looked at him.

'Sure,' he said. 'I mean, you're the one came to me. Right? Of course you did. You're the one asked me to make a deal. You asked for the house. So, I mean, if they're going to come talk to me about anything, I'm going to have to tell them the truth. And the truth is that I love my auntie. I thought you did, too. But, look, man. If they ask me what happened, I'm going to have to tell them what you said.'

Though I had tried to prepare myself for this

moment, I still felt completely upended. 'Tell them what.'

'Lots of things.'

'Like what.'

'Oh, you know.'

'No. I don't.'

'Think,' he said. 'It'll come to you.'

A silence.

I said, 'Do you expect this to change my mind?'

'I don't know, man. Maybe. I do know that you're a shitty liar, though. So, really, you can consider this me giving you a second chance.'

I said nothing.

'Up to you,' he said. 'Just remember, if I feel worried, I might have to go to the police myself, first. I don't want to have to do that, but look. It's one way or the other. Hey, here comes the bride.'

'Good evening,' Alma said. Her hair was damp. 'Shall we eat?'

'For sure,' Eric said. 'I'm starved.'

'He exhausts me.'

Alma groaned as she sank into the sofa. I was standing near the entry hall, having just closed the door on Eric. He had winked at me again on the way out, and my mind was still spasming.

Tell her.

It would be so easy.

Speak up.

Use words.

'You have disobeyed me,' she said.

I looked at her.

'Your shoes.'

I looked down at my loafers, much the worse for wear.

'For shame, Mr Geist. One thing I ask of you before I die. I gave you that money for a specific purpose; did you think I would forget?'

'I'm . . .'

Tell her.

'I'm still looking for the right pair.'

'Well, do find them, or else I shall think you ungrateful.' She shifted with discomfort. 'Forgive me for noting that you seem a tad anxious today.'

Tell her.

I shrugged.

'I imagine that it has to do with your imminent return home.'

I'd forgotten all about my trip.

'I don't have to go,' I said. 'I can cancel.'

She raised her eyebrows.

Tell her.

'I don't want to go,' I said. 'It's going to be depressing.'

'A little angst is good for the soul.'

'But,' I said. 'But who's going to look after you?'

'As I have said, I managed very well without you for years, and I shall continue to do so in your temporary absence. Dr Cargill is due Monday. I expect that I shall survive until then.'

Tell her.

189

'But what if something happens to you?'

'What in the world would happen to me?'

Tell her now.

'Anything could happen,' I said.

'You would shield me from the Apocalypse, then?'

'I—'

'You are expecting a typhoon.'

'I can't leave when you're . . . like this.'

She frowned. 'I shall elect to let that pass without rejoinder.'

'Don't. Let's be honest. Isn't that what you want from me? Honesty? Well, I'm being honest, and honestly, I'm worried about you. You're not well.'

'Surely you do not believe this to be a new development.'

'You know what. I'm going to call and cancel. It's far, and I'm not in the mood to get on a plane . . . I'm going to call her right now.'

'You will do no such thing.'

'It's really fine.'

'It may be fine with you,' she said, 'but it is not fine with me.'

Tell her.

'But I don't want to go.'

'Rubbish.'

'Ms Spielmann—'

'Mr Geist. Whence this obstinacy?'

'I'm *worried.*'

'Unreasonably.'

'You don't know that.' This was not some logical

exercise, a point of debate to be won or lost. This was real, with real consequences, and I felt myself beginning to lose my head, heard my voice beginning to rise. 'You don't know what's reasonable or not.'

'Until I am more convincingly dissuaded, I shall rely upon my own critical apparatus, thank you very much.'

'But, no. Look. Look: you don't know.'

'What, may I ask, is there to know?'

Tell her.

'I – I can't explain it.'

'Try.'

'I can't.'

'Then I cannot see how you shall win this argument.'

We volleyed a while longer, with me growing progressively more strident, until finally I spit it all out, everything Eric had said to me in the bar. I stammered throughout and was panting by the time I finished, waiting for her to react with appropriate horror. But all she said was,

'Ah.'

'That's it?'

'Mr Geist, I am moved by your concern. And I can appreciate that you have been under a good deal of strain. However, I cannot see why any of this bears upon your travel plans. Were my nephew truly capable of such a thing—'

'I'm telling you what he said.'

'You misunderstand me.' She smiled. 'Morally,

191

he may be capable. But he is far too incompetent to bring it off.'

'This isn't a joke.'

'You needn't worry, Mr Geist. I shall arm myself.'

'This is *serious*.'

'Oh, quite.'

The more agitated I got, the less seriously she seemed to take me. That I could seem to express myself only in the form of impotent anger frustrated me immensely, making me even more petulant and angry in turn. 'For God's sake—'

'Suppose you are correct. What, then, do you propose I do?'

'Call the police.'

'Ach, Mr Geist, be reasonable.'

'*You* be reasonable.'

'Allow me to point out that if in fact Eric does mean to harm me, he would be unwise to do so now, having shown you his hand. Were I him, I would gnash my teeth and regret that I had mistakenly chosen an accomplice who turned out, against all odds, to have scruples.' She smiled again. 'One of my nephew's profoundest limitations is that he sees himself in everyone.'

I couldn't understand why she was so calm. 'I'm not leaving unless you call the police. Even then I might not.'

'Then what do I stand to gain by complying?'

'You can't stop me from calling them.'

'I can. It is my house, and my telephone.'

'Then I'll call from somewhere else.'

'You will not. My nephew needs no more bother from the police—'

'"No *more?*"'

'—certainly not when—'

'What does that mean, "no more"?'

'Merely that I have no desire to see him interrogated over a matter which shall inevitably prove to be so much sound and fury.'

'This is your safety we're talking about.'

'I assure you that your fears are ungrounded.'

'You don't kn—'

'I do,' she said, 'and it shall offend me greatly if you disobey me. Eric can be difficult, but he poses no danger to me.'

'I'm not going.'

'You would stay inside for the remainder of your life?'

'If I have to.'

'Mr Geist.'

'Ms Spielmann.'

'You shall go, Mr Geist.'

'I w—'

'You shall, because if you continue to argue with me, I shall sack you.'

'With all due respect—'

'Enough,' she said. 'You *will* leave, and you *will* cease to argue with me this instant, or else I shall call the police and have them take *you* away.'

Silence.

'Is that clear?'

I was too startled to do anything but nod.

'The matter is settled,' she said. She put her hand on her forehead; her body seemed to shrink a tiny bit. I could see how much the argument had taken out of her, and I felt awful for raising my voice. I started to apologize, but she shook her head. 'I beg you, no more. I am tired and I should like to go upstairs, please.'

This was her way of asking for help. I took her arm, and we walked to the stairs. It was slow going.

'Are you all right?'

'Come, now, Mr Geist. Don't make me answer that.'

As we climbed the first three steps, I felt her weakening, relying more and more on me to stay up. Midway up, she paused, breathing hard. 'Perhaps I ought to remain here for a short while,' she said.

With some hesitation, I said, 'May I?'

She looked away. Then, to my surprise, she nodded.

Her body felt like straw, and as I picked her up, one arm under her knees and the other around her shoulders, her head lolled against me, and her hair came loose, veiling her face. Beyond the perfume I smelled her, all eight decades of her, the commingled scents of a lifetime of activity and thought and movement and sorrow and joy and then, on the end, the bitterest finish. I feel no shame in saying that I wished she would fade away right then and there.

I had never been in her bedroom. As I brought

her over the threshold, I was enveloped by a more concentrated version of that scent. I carried her to the bed, removed her shoes, and drew the blanket over her.

'Thank you.' She sounded like ten percent of herself. 'You are a good boy.'

I told her I would be downstairs if she needed anything.

'Joseph . . .'

'Yes, Ms Spielmann?'

She didn't respond; she was already asleep. She had never used my Christian name before, and I stayed there for some time, watching over her.

CHAPTER 16

In the end I went. What choice did I have? I was afraid of what Eric would say to the police, and Alma's vehemence, however puzzling, was irrefutable. I had to trust that she was right, that I was being paranoid, and that if I wasn't, Eric would not be so stupid as to act now. One seldom truly believes that the worst will happen.

Before I left I apologized again.

She winked forgiveness. 'Friends must be honest with each other, mustn't they?'

I told her I would call her once I touched down.

'Do not concern yourself with me,' she said. 'Put me out of your mind.'

'You know I won't be able to do that.'

'Do your best, Mr Geist. Enjoy yourself. As the saying goes, we have only one life to live.'

Father Fred was at the baggage claim to greet me.

'Welcome home,' he said.

In the years since I had last seen him he had fallen straight into middle age: his face seamed, his eyebrows the color of Spanish moss. We embraced, and through his coat I felt bone.

196

'I was going to take a taxi.'

'Your mother told me. That's why I'm here.'

I'd forgotten what a crazy driver he was. We hit the interstate going ninety, giving us three quarters of an hour to talk. I asked after the church, after people close to him. When we got around to discussing the memorial, he employed his usual tact, never a bad word, although it was clear my mother had run him ragged.

'It's a blessing,' he said, 'if for no other reason than it's brought you back. I was afraid I wouldn't get to see you before I left.'

'So,' I said. 'California.'

He nodded.

'What's in California.'

'This time next year, a lovely Catholic school near Santa Barbara will be in need of a principal. I'll be doing some teaching, too. They have an olive grove on the grounds. I went for a visit, and I'm pleased to report that the climate reminded me of Rome.'

'. . . sounds wonderful.'

'Joseph,' he drawled, 'you never were much of a liar.'

Whatever ill will I'd felt upon getting the news from my mother had long since dissipated, certainly after I'd come through the revolving door to find him waiting for me. My urge to fix him in place was selfish, not to mention futile, and I wanted very much to be happy for him. I worked to muster more enthusiasm. 'It won't be the same without you,' I said.

'Oh, I don't know about that. One thing I've learned over the years is that it's impossible for a clergyman to overstate his own insignificance.'

'And Mater Dei?'

'Father Martin's taking over. You've met him, I assume.'

The other priest had freckles and blunted critical thinking skills. 'Once or twice.'

'He's extremely popular, as I'm sure you're aware. Almost every parish around here has been going downhill over the last five years. Ours is one of the few exceptions, and he gets all the credit for that. He has a background in computers. He made us a website, if you can believe it. I have an email address now.'

'I didn't know. I would have written.'

'I've always had a phone.'

'Mea culpa.'

'At any rate, I'm very comfortable leaving the community in his hands. For all intents and purposes, it's already in them. What the Church needs now is new blood, people who can restore some of the trust that's been lost. I've had many good years here, and now things have changed. All part of His plan. I know you don't think there is a plan, but someday you'll see.'

'You think?'

'I do. But either way, I believe God appreciates the fact that you've given Him a good deal of thought.' He smiled, flicked on his turn signal. 'Even if you came out wrong in the end.'

As we left the interstate and headed along Riverfront, a light rain began to fall. We came to the place where my brother drove off the road, and Father Fred pulled over and cut the engine. Wet shadows streaked the interior of the car.

'I come here to reflect sometimes,' he said.

'It's not very scenic.'

'No. But it helps me remember.'

I said nothing.

'I'll miss this place,' he said.

'I never have,' I said.

'You will.' He started the car. 'Someday.'

The memorial took place that afternoon in the church social hall. The aforementioned photo of Chris sat out on a stand near the entrance. Taken his freshman year of high school, it captured him in all his fresh-faced glory. There was a guestbook. I sat toward the front, where I wouldn't have to talk to people as they entered.

The turnout was much larger than I'd expected, close to forty, wives and children accompanying men my brother had grown up with. Father Fred spoke first, warmly recalling Chris's service. Then came the school friends, telling stories about the teenager they remembered and the good times they'd had – stories intended to be funny but that for the most part came across as elegies to adolescence. As per my mother's description, everyone had changed, few for the better. Tommy Snell was indeed as bald as his father; so was Kevin Connar, plus he had a gut the size and shape of a compost heap. I overheard someone whisper that he was getting the gastric bypass.

My mother's friend Rita Green recited a selection from Housman's 'To an Athlete Dying Young.' I was impressed by this until I realized that Father Fred had chosen the readings. She then presented, on behalf of the ladies' sewing circle, a check in support of Children's Hospital, and a wall hanging of a lighthouse, which, she explained, symbolized the presence of lost loved ones in our lives.

I glanced at my father. He, too, had aged. No longer the ox-like tyrant of my memory, but loose, soft, inert. He'd barely spoken to me since I'd gotten home, barely spoken at all. I wondered what he made of the people standing before him, evoking his dead son, singing of what had been and what would never be. If he heard an indictment, he did not show it. Sometimes I envied him: his was an unexamined life, and therefore a more peaceful one than I could ever have.

The ceremony ended, and I told my mother I'd see her back at the house. I asked Father Fred to drive me to the cemetery, where I could pay my respects in private, with words of my own, or in silence if I so chose.

Standing in the kitchen, my ear plugged to block out the noise of the reception, I phoned Alma several times that evening. Nobody ever answered, and each time I returned to the living room feeling incrementally more tense. By nine o'clock a handful of people remained, circling the crudités and a skinned-over bowl of onion dip. Tommy Snell did his best to engage me in a conversation about insoles. I told him it was good to see him and again made my way to the phone, sitting down alone at the breakfast table and trying to think of what I could possibly do for her from this far away. Most likely she wasn't picking up because she was in the throes of an attack – which, while upsetting to imagine, was far better than the alternative. I considered calling Drew, asking him to drop by. But she didn't know him, and more-over, if she was resting, she wouldn't answer the door any more than the phone.

'I'll be seeing you.'

Father Fred was in the doorway, one hand up.

As I walked him out, we passed through the living room – empty now except for my mother, who was stacking paper plates and stuffing them into a trash bag. Father Fred kissed her on the cheek.

'It was a beautiful ceremony,' she said. 'Thank you.'

'Thank you for suggesting it,' he said.

She smiled tremulously. 'I never do stop thinking about him.'

'That's all right,' Father Fred said. 'You think as much as you want.'

The katydids had begun their nightly riot. Father Fred regretted that a morning meeting kept him from driving me to the airport. I thanked him and wished him luck.

'I have email now,' he said. 'No excuses.'

I watched him peel out, debating whether I ought to try Alma one last time. It was close to ten P.M., eleven in Cambridge. I had left my parents' number with her – all but irrelevant if anything had gone seriously wrong. I told myself I was getting lathered up over nothing, and had just begun to believe it when a crash from inside the house brought me hurrying up the front walk.

My mother was standing in the center of the living room. Her face was dry, and the only way to tell she was crying was by looking at her stomach, which convulsed as she watched my father try to tip over the china cabinet. He'd had greater success with a glass end table, which now consisted of a circular faux-brass frame and a sea of shards. The cabinet didn't give in quite so easily. A good eight feet tall and loaded down with plates, it would raise up a few inches before my father lost his grip and the whole thing slammed back down, narrowly missing his toes. That this was such a tiresome and involved process spoke to the passage of time; in his prime, he would have already dealt with the cabinet and moved on to something else. Now, though, he was sweating, bent over and putting his back into it, grunting swinishly.

And laughing. He was laughing like a maniac. That wicked sense of humor of his was intimately connected to his physical vitality. Both had attenuated with age, and watching him heave and oink and giggle, I realized what it was he was trying to achieve: resurrection through an act of destruction.

'Dad,' I said. He ignored me. My mother looked at me beseechingly, though I did not know whether she wanted me to go on or to shut up.

'Dad. Stop it.'

He grunted, slipped, almost fell, steadied himself, began again to push.

I took him by the arm; he flung my hand away and turned on me, smiling cockeyed, stink rising off him in great brown waves.

'Joey,' my mother said.

'Go to bed,' I said.

'Let's dance,' my father said.

He pitched forward into my arms. The smell was even worse from up close.

'Oh, how we danced,' he sang.

I tried to hold him still.

'Dance, you little shitbird.'

'I'm not little,' I said.

'Oh God,' my mother said. Her hands were curled at her mouth.

'"Let's twist again. Like we did last summer."'

'Come on. Upstairs.'

'Oh my God.'

'". . . like we did last yeeeaaar."'

'Move it,' I said, wrestling with him.

'I'm not done,' my father said.

'You're done, all right.'

'Shitbird.'

Though I had been taller than him for years, this was the first real-world application of our strength differential. He had no choice but to stumble along with me as I walked him to the stairs.

'I'm gonna kick your ass,' he said to me.

'All right,' I said.

'Think you can lip off to me.'

I pinned his arms to his sides as we toddled down the hall.

'Goddammit. Let me go.'

'Almost there.'

'Let me the fuck go.'

We reached the base of the stairs. I released him and he fell down, moaning and holding his head.

'I can't carry you up the stairs,' I said.

He stopped moaning, looked at me, grinned. 'I know.'

I didn't know what he meant by that, but it unnerved and insulted me, and I felt my neck growing hot. 'Do what you want,' I said. 'I don't care.'

'You look like my father,' he said.

I'd never met my paternal grandfather – never seen him, not even a picture – so I could not vouch for the truth of this statement. I braced myself for what came next. A secret of some sort, a key piece of family history that would, if not justify, at least explain how it was we had all come to this point.

'He was a piece of shit,' said my father.

I turned my back on him and walked away.

My mother was on her knees in the living room, picking glass out of the carpet, her hands spotted with blood. I told her I was leaving.

'Your flight's not till morning,' she said.

I shrugged.

'You're going to sleep at the airport?'

'I guess so.'

Silence.

'What about me?' she asked.

I looked at her. 'I can't answer that.'

She made a broken noise, then went back to work.

I ordered a cab, gathered my things, and left without saying goodbye.

I boarded the first leg of my flight sore from sleeping in a hard plastic chair. There were no working pay phones in the terminal, though I did manage to call Alma's house during my layover in Cincinnati. No one answered. While dialing Drew's number, I heard the boarding announcement for my second flight and had to hang up.

Normally I would have taken the T, but I felt antsy enough to spring for a second cab. Down through the Ted Williams, along Storrow, under the irrelevant graffito bemoaning the Curse. What would happen to Sox fans now that they had nothing to complain about, the driver asked.

'They'll think of somethin to complain about,' he said. 'People always do.'

In no mood to chat, I overtipped him, taking the front steps in a single bound, calling her name as I entered.

Silence.

Her bedroom door was closed. I resisted the urge to knock by telling myself that if I needed to see her, it was mainly for my own gratification. To distract myself I did laundry. On my way back through the kitchen, I stopped to cut myself a piece of *Sachertorte*, finding it close to stale, all the whipped cream gone, I made a note to go out and get fresh supplies. I rinsed my plate, dried it. It seemed impossible that only twenty minutes had elapsed since I'd gotten home. I waited until the wash was done, then transferred my clothes to the dryer and went out for a walk, returning ninety minutes later with groceries in hand, utterly beside myself. I dropped the bags in the entry hall and went upstairs. I knocked. Silence. I knocked again, turned the handle. Her room was pitch black and the shades down and the air rank and I saw her bent shape in the bed, touched by a sliver of hallway light. She was lying oddly, one arm propped up by the pillow and jutting like a mast or a branch, her face angled away so that she showed me the back of her head, strands of white silk limp and dry and I knew that it was all wrong and I ran in, barking my shin against the bedframe, an injury I did not notice until later that night, or I should say rather the next morning, when I would see that I had gashed the flesh wide open. That was all later. Now I turned her over. Her nightgown was scaled with dried vomit and her lips parted as though she was breathing but she was not and I found her wrist and then said to myself call an ambulance, you are not equipped to make decisions. I called the ambulance. I sat on the floor, holding her hand, and though my mind became aware of the approaching siren and the ringing bell I could not stand or move, and believe it or not they broke down the front door, two nice young men in blue uniforms who sent me downstairs while they confirmed what I already knew to be true.

My dear Joseph,

I apologize for the trouble I will have no doubt caused you. To spare you any additional burden, I have sent a letter to my attorney, who shall make all the necessary arrangements.

For your amusement, herewith a copy of my thesis. It is of no value whatsoever except perhaps as a jeu d'esprit. Read it with a kind eye.

Know that what I do, I do freely. You above all ought to understand.

With everlasting fondness,
Alma

CHAPTER 17

I can't say, like people sometimes do, that what happened next was a blur. The opposite: time slowed way way *way* down, every second stretched out like taffy, and thus my memory of the ensuing hours is sharp, painfully so. Perhaps that's what 'it was all a blur' really means, for I have a hard time going back to that night without feeling overloaded, as though my brain cannot handle the amount of information packed into a single frame and wants to capitulate and shut down. Clarity requires the ability to filter out extraneous information. When I think back on the first part of that night, I see not a smooth series of events but thousands upon thousands of jump cuts: an amoebic smudge on the living-room table, the interval of the ambulance's lights' pulse, the jerk of the minute hand on the mantel clock whenever time, officially, advanced. I see the house empty and then instantly full of people. I hear myself spoken to, asked questions, told to relax, told to be patient, juggled from room to room. Cell phones ringing. Croaky three A.M. laughter. The startling blue of a flashbulb. Water in a cup, in my hand, down my dry throat. My leg, bleeding; do I need to go to the hospital? No, thank you.

Eventually I landed in the library, in one of the easy chairs, sitting across from a uniformed patrolman – a disorienting sight, as I had grown accustomed to seeing Alma in that very spot. He said nothing and I said nothing and we sat there like a couple of gargoyles until the library door opened and a man with a beagleish face appeared. He took one step into the room before reacting visibly to its contents.

'Jesus Maria,' he said, goggling. Then, remembering himself, he cleared his throat and told the patrolman he'd take it from here.

'Detective Zitelli,' he said, sitting down. 'I understand you're pretty shaken up.'

I said nothing.

'You don't want to go to the hospital?'

I shook my head.

'What about your leg.'

I looked down at the bloodstain.

'Looks bad,' he said.

'I'm fine.'

He studied me. 'All right,' he said, flipping open his notebook. 'Let's begin at the beginning.'

Pressured by a sense of duty, and by his authority, I willed myself to answer his questions, and as I did, my brain started to regain its normal operating speed. This was not a good thing. Psychological shock serves an important purpose, cushioning the psyche from a reality it is not ready to face, a process analogous to an injured joint filling up with fluid. It might look frightening when someone's knee balloons to twice its normal size, but that's the body's way of preventing further damage. In the wake of Alma's death, my mind had behaved similarly, and to have the swelling forcibly reduced – to have my emotions iced – was singularly horrible.

'So you're a caretaker.'

'. . . sort of.'

'Sort of how.'

I told him about the ad.

'She must have felt pretty comfortable with you, letting you live here.'

'We were close.'

'Close in what way.'

I looked at him.

'Was your relationship of a sexual nature?'

'. . . excuse me?'

'Did you and Ms Spielmann hav—'

'No. No. Of course not.'

'All right.'

'I can't believe you'd even think to ask that.'

'It's a question,' he said. 'That's all. You answered it, and now that's that.'

Silence.

'Did she ever talk about harming herself?' the detective asked.

I shook my head.

'Was she depressed?'

Silence.

'I think so,' I said. I paused. 'I don't know.'

'You said she was sick, thought.'

'She was in terrible pain. Talk to her doctor, she can tell you more than I can. Paulette Cargill. The number's in the kitchen.'

He was scribbling. 'Take me through what happened when you got here.'

I did.

'Did you read the note?'

I nodded.

He flipped back a few pages. '"Know that what I do, I do freely. You above all ought to understand."'

Silence.

'It's something we talked about,' I said.

'Suicide?'

'Free will.'

'Uh-huh,' he said.

Silence.

He said, 'Is there something else you want to tell me?'

'How come you didn't call the police before?'

'He said he would tell them it was my idea.'

'Was it?'

I recoiled. 'No.'

'All right.'

'Absolutely not.'

'Hold up, now.'

'And frankly, I find it offensive—'

'Hold up.'

'I took *care* of her. I made her food, I spent hours—'

'They're just questions.'

'Okay, well, I don't like what your questions imply.'

'They don't imply anything,' he said. 'I'm just asking.'

'And I'm answering, aren't I?'

'Excellent,' he said. 'Then we're both doing our jobs.'

Silence.

'Keep going,' he said.

Silence.

'Alma didn't want me to say anything, either.'

'Why not?'

'I don't know. To protect him, I think.'

'From . . .'

'He's had trouble with the police before.'

'That seems like a good reason to let someone know.'

'That's exactly what I told her.'

'But . . .'

'She didn't think he was serious.'

'But you did.'

I paused. 'It was hard to tell.'

The policeman raised his eyebrows.

'If you heard him, you'd understand.'

'Tell me again what you were doing out of town.'

'I was home for a family event. I told you. You can call anyone; there were fifty people there. Call the church. Father Fred Hammond. Call my parents.'

'Mm-hm.'

'Look, he's the one you need to talk to. Him. Eric. Not me. If anyone did anything to her, he's the one responsible.'

'Is that what you think? Someone did something to her?'

'I don't know. How should I know? I don't know. I'm saying *if*.'

'Okay, fine. So, you don't know if something happened. But if it did, then you didn't do it. Right?'

'Right.'

'And it wasn't your idea, this thing that may or may not have happened.'

'Correct.'

'Okay, well. Glad we've cleared that up.' Zitelli rubbed his nose. 'Now, let's go over this for a second. Cause first I come in here, you're telling me she's in pain—'

'She was.'

'She's in pain, she's depressed, she leaves a note. Fine. But then you want me to think he killed her—'

'I don't want you to think one way or the other, I—'

'So which is it?'

'I don't know.'

'Well, but you must have an opinion.'

'I don't. I'm speaking hypothetically. I'm – please, this is hard enough as it is.'

He held up his hands. 'I'm just repeating back what you said.'

'That's not what I said. I said to look into it. Look: I'm trying to help.'

'I appreciate that, I do. Now, let's say I do talk to him—'

'Are you?'

'Am I what.'

'Going to talk to him.'

'That depends.'

'On?'

'Lots of things. But let's say I do talk to him. What's he going to tell me?'

'. . . that it was my idea.'

'What was.'

'Whatever happened.'

'But you don't know what happened.'

'Isn't that the whole point of this process? To find out what actually happened?'

The detective stared at me. 'It sounds pretty important to you.'

'I—'

'You seem pretty wound up.'

'It is important to me. Of course it's important to me. I care about her. And no, I'm not wound up. I mean, I'm wound up, I'm just, I'm not, *wound up*.'

'. . . all right.'

'I mean, you'd be like this, too, if you had to endure this.'

'Endure what.'

'Being interrogated.'

'Is that what you think this is?'

'Isn't it?'

'Let's say this,' he said. 'Let's say, for argument's sake, something *didn't* happen . . .'

Around and around we went, two hours' worth of dizzying ontological games, until I put my head in my hands.

'Can I take a break, please.'

'No problem.' He walked around the room, browsing. 'Nice stuff,' he said.

Something occurred to me then.

'What happened to the thesis?'

'Come again?'

'Her thesis. She left it on the bed for me. It was with the note.'

'Oh, that thing. I'm gonna have to take a look at it.'

I sat up sharply. 'Why.'

'I'd like to give it a look-see.'

'She left it for me.'

'Don't worry, you'll get it back.'

'When?'

'When we're done with it.'

'It's a philosophy paper,' I said. 'That's all it is.'

'Then I should be able to give it back to you soon,' he said.

By continuing to argue with him, I would only draw attention to myself; still, I found it preposterous that they would impound a fifty-year-old piece of academic writing as evidence. 'But it's in German,' I said.

He shrugged, strolled around the room until he came to the mantel. There he paused.

'Is that Nietzsche?'

When at last I was alone again, I went upstairs. They had left her bedroom in disarray. The rising sun showed the shape of her body, still visible in the sheets.

CHAPTER 18

Now the blur set in.

For days I did nothing. I didn't clean up. I didn't read. What little I ate came out of cans. Pockmarked nights yielded to mornings clotted with dreadful silence, an hour or more of which would pass before I could get myself out of bed. The bags of groceries sat untouched in the entry hall, right where I'd left them, until the smell overwhelmed the living room and I put them out for collection. I avoided the library, avoided most of the house, including the entire second floor, spending all day in my room, unwashed, unfocused, pacing, waiting for her to call me to conversation, the memory of the weekend playing on infinite loop, damning me. Never have I suffered under the weight of ignorance as acutely as I did in those hours. I didn't know what had happened to her body, where she would be buried, when it would take place. I didn't know if I would have to move out. I didn't know how to keep the power on, pay the water bill; didn't know what to do with the mail. I didn't know if the police were treating Alma's death as a suicide or a homicide; I didn't know whether they had talked to Eric, and if so, what his reaction had been. I kept taking out Zitelli's card, its corners rounded from my worrying. I resisted calling him, knowing that anything I said had the potential to incriminate me, that anxiety would be misinterpreted as guilt, that my eagerness to see justice done would come off as blame-shifting. It behooved me to hold my peace as long as I could, and so I was stuck doing nothing, with no one to talk to, facing the silence, prosecuted by it. Whatever the official ruling, wasn't the ultimate cause of death my absence? On some level, had I not allowed this to happen – willed it to happen? There were many things I could have done – stayed back, called Drew, called 911 – but I had done nothing, an omission tantamount, in my fevered brain, to action. I'd left her alone, and she'd died.

What I do, I do freely.

The existentialists considered suicide the single greatest philosophical problem. If a person is free, by what right do we stop him from taking his own life? Camus, Sartre, Nietzsche – they all give answers, all of which seemed useless just then.

You above all ought to understand.

Perhaps she had intended to soothe my conscience. If so, she miscalculated; it was impossible for me not to see myself as the audience, indeed the engine, for her final proof.

★　★　★

I awoke, too early, to a tremendous racket.

In the hallway, Daciana rocked back and forth, vacuuming.

'Excuse me.'

She didn't respond.

I pulled the plug out of the wall.

'Seer, why, I need clean.'

As patiently as I could, I explained what had happened. She seemed not to understand, so I repeated myself. Dead, I said.

Now she got it. Her hands flapped, her face arraying itself in Slavic anguish. I wanted to slap her. I had my own grief to deal with; hers by comparison seemed vulgar and theatrical.

'Mees Alma,' she keened. 'Ooohhh.'

I stood there in my pajamas.

'Ooohhh. Ooohhh.'

'I'm sorry,' I said.

'Ooohhh.'

'It's terrible, I know. Look—'

Abruptly she stopped crying and looked at me. 'I clean you.'

'Me? No. No, I—'

'Please, only to work.'

'I can't—'

Hands flung heavenward. 'Seer. Ohhhh. Seer.'

'I can't have you working here. I can't pay you.'

'Yes, okay.'

'You're not understanding me.'

'Very good job.'

'I'm sure that's true, but—'

'Three year,' she said. 'One, two, three.'

'Be that as it may—'

She stuck the plug back into the wall, switched the vacuum on.

'Turn that off, please.'

Humming.

'Turn it off. Will you pl—goddammit.' I pulled the plug out again.

Undaunted, she hustled down the hall, headed for the kitchen.

'Wait a second. Wait.'

She was washing the dirty dishes I'd neglected. I looked around: fruit flies, crumbs, open jars, the countertop gritty and desquamated. A real horror show.

'I'll make you a deal,' I said. 'You can work today, but that's it.'

'Yes, I work.'

'Fine. But listen. Stop – turn off the water, please. Please? Thank you. First of all, I'm not going to be here much longer. You want to work, you can take that up with whoever moves in next. So, today, fine. But that's it. No more. Okay?'

She nodded and hummed.

'And I want you to leave her bedroom alone. Don't go in there. Do you understand me? No bedroom.'

'Yes, seer.'

'The upstairs bedroom. Don't go in there.'

'Yes, I clean.'

'*No.*' I took her by the wrist and escorted her upstairs. 'No clean.'

Daciana seemed puzzled.

'No,' I said. 'Okay?'

'You boss.'

I went back to bed and covered my head with a pillow.

At the end of five hours she came to me.

'Finish, seer.'

'You didn't touch the upstairs bedroom, did you?'

'Yes, seer, no.'

Not knowing what that meant, I pointed upstairs. 'Yes?'

'No.'

'No?'

'No,' she confirmed.

'No. Okay. All right. Good. Now. What did she pay you?' I paused. '*Money*. How much money?'

She looked away, scratching her neck. 'One hundred.'

'That's what she paid you.'

'Okay, eighty-five.'

Now I understood: she was giving herself a raise.

'Forty-five,' I said.

'Eighty.'

'Fifty.'

'Seventy-five.'

'Fifty-five.'

She made a mournful, Wookiee sound.

I opened my wallet, removed three twenties, and held them out. After a brief pause, she snatched the bills and shoved them into her brassiere.

In her smirk I saw a bulging hatred – or was it respect? Maybe I had impressed her with my mettle.

'I come next week,' she said.

'No. No more. That's it.'

She bent to pick up her basket. 'See you soon.'

The caller identified herself as assistant to one Charles Palatine, Alma's attorney. Mr Palatine wished to speak to me in person, the following day, if possible. I made an appointment for two P.M. and went to pick out an outfit. As I fully expected this meeting to conclude with an order of eviction, I hoped that, properly dressed, I might be able to plead for an extension. Unfortunately, thus it was, as ever before: the best I could do was a pair of ink-stained khakis and a blazer. I don't know why I had expected my wardrobe to spontaneously improve. I laid the items out on the bed, then contemplated my shoes. *For shame, Mr Geist. One thing I ask of you before I die.* I remembered the twinkle in her eye, the teasing cadence. She had been having a joke with herself at my expense, I realized. She'd known what was coming. Of course she would have. She had planned around my trip, insisting that I go home, insisting that Eric posed no danger. And why would he? He couldn't do anything to her if she did it first.

The question, then, was whether she had.

I showered, dressed, and set out to go shopping.

Along Brattle Street was an upscale menswear store I had passed many times without entering. Now I stopped to peer in the window. Headless mannequins wrapped in tweed heralded the new semester. The back wall displayed shoes, glossy blacks and chewy browns, set out like pastries. A bell rang as I opened the door, and a white-haired salesman in a trim glen plaid suit came out to greet me.

He measured my feet and brought out several boxes.

'These will last a lifetime,' he assured me.

The leather was stiff, new, unforgiving. I asked if he had something less formal.

He took down a softer-looking shoe. 'Mephistos. Wonderful. One pair and you're loyal for life. Let me see if I have your size.'

Left alone, I began to feel uneasy. I no longer had a steady source of income, and new shoes seemed less important than, say, a place to live. I had to assume that Alma would not have objected to my reappropriating the birthday funds in order to stave off homelessness. And the notion that buying myself a gift would somehow honor her . . . It was beyond crass. Before the salesman could return, I put on my loafers and slipped out.

The sky was gathering as I stopped at the corner market to buy fresh supplies. I walked the last block to number forty-nine through a full-blown monsoon, stepping into the entry hall, where I paused, dripping, to await her ghost.

Silence.

In the kitchen I switched on the radio and – still in my wet clothes – went to work on a fresh *Sachertorte*. Shivering, my teeth clacking out a violent and irregular tempo, I worked frantically, automatically, making a god-awful mess, caking myself in cocoa and sugar and flour, rattling the whisk against the side of the bowl, banging the jar of apricot jam down on the counter, slamming cabinets and slamming drawers and slamming the refrigerator door. Anything to escape the silence. It was not enough, though, and so I found a station playing loud rock music, screamed along though I did not know the words. And still there was silence, leaking through the spaces between notes, running like dirty undammed water across the floor, rising past my ankles, up to my knees, rising until I was waist-deep, chest-deep, drowning in silence; and I turned the volume all the way up, twisting the dial to yield a deafening tide of nothingness. I let the faucet run at full blast. I opened the oven and shoved the cake in roughly, batter sloshing over the edge of the pan, hissing as it touched the hot metal walls. I took a dishtowel and rubbed my rain-drenched hair, rubbed my cheeks raw, stuffed the cloth into my ears, trying to fill the silence with silence and noise, breathing in the bittersweet scent of burnt chocolate.

Palatine & Palatine LLC occupied the top floor of a high-rise on Batterymarch Street. Arriving early, I was shown into an office defined by a mammoth leather desk. Behind it was a mammoth leather chair, and behind that a picture window spreading a magnificent view of Boston Harbor, home to everything from plastic bottles to bodies to leftover particles of the famous two-hundred-year-old tea. If Jesus had walked on its waters, nobody would have blinked.

Everything on the walls and in the display cases spoke of wealth and taste, and I was beginning to regret having tried to dress up, a feeling that spiked nastily when the lawyer himself entered in a bespoke suit. Fleshy, humpbacked, stertorous as an outboard motor, he hobbled in and hopped up into the giant chair, combing one liver-spotted hand through the sparse remains of a crew cut as he looked me up and down.

'The famous Joseph Geist,' he said.

I tried to smile. 'Famous to whom.'

He didn't answer. He reached for the topmost of a stack of folders, opened it, took out a stapled document, unfolded a pair of reading glasses, and stared at the text in silence until I began to feel like I was on trial.

'What's happening with her funeral?' I asked.

He peered at me over his glasses.

'I'm sorry, I'm – I'm not familiar with what's supposed to happen next.'

Palatine closed the folder. 'There isn't going to be a funeral.'

'Beg pardon?'

'Her instructions were clear: no service, no clergy.'

'Is she going to be buried?'

'As soon as the autopsy is complete.'

'When—'

'I don't know. The ME is backed up to the rafters, not to mention incompetent. It could take months.'

Disturbed, I said, 'So she's just . . . lying there?'

'For the time being.'

'Okay, well . . . When the burial does happen, I'd like to be there.'

He pursed his lips. 'I'll have Nancy contact you.'

'I appreciate it.'

He went back to reading. 'I told her it wasn't proper, not having any sort of ceremony. I told her several times. Not that she ever listened to anything I said.'

I said nothing.

'She could be very stubborn.' He looked up at me. 'But I'm sure already you knew that.'

I said nothing.

'After thirty years, I know better than to argue. That always was a losing game with her. When she told me about you, for instance. To be honest, I thought it was a lousy idea.' He smiled at me. 'You don't even have a credit rating.'

I opened my mouth but said nothing.

He leaned back in his chair. 'Tell me: what did you two talk about, during your little philosophical discussions.'

Silence.

I said, 'Free will, mostly.'

'What about it.'

'Whether it exists.'

'And what did you conclude.'

'We didn't conclude anything,' I said. 'It wasn't that kind of conversation.'

'What kind of conversation.'

'The kind that concludes.'

He snorted. 'Well,' he said, 'it's over now.'

I said nothing.

He sighed, rubbed his face. 'I'm sorry,' he said. 'This is all such a rotten business.'

I nodded.

'Normally, I'd have done this by mail, but given the nature of her instructions, I thought it'd be better to meet in person.'

He pushed the folder across the table.

'Have a look.'

I opened it. Inside was Alma's will. I looked at him.

'Go on.'

The first sections were technical, invalidating previous wills and codicils, ordering the payments of taxes, and so forth. The distribution of the estate began with various donations to charities promoting literacy, as well as an Austrian cultural center. Doctor Cargill was to choose a piece of jewelry from the upstairs vanity. The middle paragraphs referred to several preexisting trusts, the beneficiary of which was Eric Alan Banks, and each of which was given to him on conditions that I deemed more or less impracticable. One of the trusts hung – absurdly, I thought – upon his completing a college degree. Another held the funds for tuition. Just about the only fund I could ever imagine him gaining access to was the one that provided the money for a defense attorney in the event that he was charged with a crime carrying a potential prison sentence of five years or more. I almost felt bad for him; reading the will, one got the sense that Alma was mocking him. Still, none of it had anything to do with me until, all at once, it did.

SECTION IX.

A. To Joseph Geist, who has been a most suitable and pleasant companion to me, I leave my home, its contents, and all assets not otherwise specified in the preceding paragraphs, provided he meet the following conditions:

    (1) he shall complete his doctoral dissertation;

    (2) that dissertation shall be submitted to and accepted by the department of philosophy, Harvard University;

    (3) he shall graduate from Harvard University with a doctoral degree in philosophy;

(4) the foregoing three conditions shall be met within twenty-four months of the date of my death, during which time he shall be permitted to live in the house and to draw upon monies specified in section IX, paragraph E.

B. Upon fulfillment of these conditions, ownership of the assets specified in section IX, paragraph A, shall pass into his hands immediately.

C. Should he fail to meet any of the conditions specified in section IX, paragraph A, or fail to do so within the period of time specified in section IX, paragraph A, part 4, the assets specified in section IX, paragraph A, shall revert in equal parts to the parties specified in section VI, paragraphs C-K.

She'd left me a budget of twenty thousand dollars.

A long, foggy silence.

I said, 'Does Eric know about this?'

'Not yet.'

'When is he going to find out?'

'I wanted him to be here today,' said Palatine, 'but he's indisposed.'

'Where.'

'I can't tell you that.'

'Is he in jail?'

Palatine said nothing.

In the distance, a tugboat honked.

He said, 'I'll have you know that I did my best to dissuade her. Games like this never lead to anything but strife.'

I said nothing.

'Nancy will have copies of everything sent to your attorney.'

'I don't have an attorney,' I said.

'Then you'd better get one.' He stood. 'Have a good day.'

I must have looked like some harried clerk out of Kafka, struggling to keep my huge stack of papers neat as the train lurched and swerved. In addition to the will, I had been given a slew of other documents, a fiduciary and probate surety bond, a military affidavit, and, most significantly, a year's worth of statements from fifteen different banks in the United States, Austria, and Switzerland. I paged through them rapidly, totting it all up: in addition to the real estate and the collectibles, she had left me two million dollars in stocks, bonds, and cash.

I was so addled that I almost missed my stop, leaping up as the tone sounded. My foot got caught on the edge of the platform, and I tripped, sending everything flying. I fell to the concrete, lunging and grabbing for pages, aware of people giving me a wide berth as they passed.

I stopped at a drugstore and asked for plastic bags. The weight of all the paper caused the bag handles to cut into my palms, and my fingertips were purple and numb by the time I arrived at Drew's.

I buzzed.

'Hello?'

'It's me.'

'What's up.'

'Let me in, please.'

He was blessedly accepting, asking nothing as I came in and sat down on his couch, where I stayed, bags of paper piled at my feet, until the late afternoon.

'I'm gonna hop in the shower,' he said.

'Alma's dead.'

He blinked. 'Oh, shit.'

'She left me everything.' I looked at him. 'She left me the house.'

'You're kidding.'

I shook my head.

'. . . wowie.'

I said nothing.

'What happened?' he said.

I said nothing.

'Are you okay?'

'I can't go back there.'

'Why not?'

'Because I can't.'

'Joseph—'

'*No.*'

'Okay. Okay. Sorry.'

Silence.

He stood. 'I have to go to work.'

I said nothing.

'There's stir-fry in the freezer.'

I nodded.

'Are you going to be okay?'

I said, 'I don't know.'

After a beat, he left the room. I heard water running. I put my head back and closed my eyes.

Over the next few days I moped around the apartment, cleaning, an exercise in futility if ever there was one. No sooner had I finished wiping down countertops and alphabetizing DVDs than Drew would come home, compliment me on my achievement, and then undo it, five hours' work gone in five minutes. Interestingly, he would put everything back where I'd found it, this particular tea-stained mug on that particular chair, the half-roll of duct tape kicked under the desk. Even he had a system, it seemed.

I can't say that his grief-counseling skills were very nuanced, but he did make an effort to cheer me up.

'Have you ever considered,' he said to me one evening as he sat as his computer, fingers flying, 'that one of the few places in the world where you can't order from Amazon is in the heart of the Amazon itself?'

I said nothing.

'You know, at some point you're going to have to accept that this is what she wanted.'

I rolled over on the sofabed.

'Fine,' he said. 'Just – stop cleaning up, okay?'

I hoped Alma was getting a big laugh out of this. I hoped she thought this was totally hilarious. If she had wanted to reward me for my companionship, if she'd thought she could spur me to work, there had to be a better way. I had before me the possibility of what every struggling intellectual longs for – financial freedom – and what I felt was not relief or gratitude but guilt and helplessness.

Twenty thousand dollars might sound like a lot, but until then I hadn't been paying for food or utilities. If I had to get a job, that would in effect negate my twenty-four months of supposed free time . . . Why twenty-four? From her perspective, all I needed was a kick-start. One year would not have been enough, while three would only encourage more of the same . . . Two years, then, which meant I should aim to get a draft done by June, so that I could spend the coming summer revising and the second academic year finishing up everything I needed to get done in order to submit, defend, graduate . . . My head hurt with all the variables. The lawyer was right. No good could come of this, especially not after Eric found out. How much of that twenty thousand would I have to spend to make myself feel secure? I'd have to put in an alarm. I'd have to redo the locks, secure the windows . . . It added up.

Now, it would have been easy to disentangle myself. All I had to do was fail to meet Alma's conditions and the estate would pass right out of my hands, leaving me the same as before. But that didn't feel right, either. Because Drew had a point. People could do whatever they wanted with their money. Could I, in good conscience, deny her last wishes?

One thing I ask of you before I die.

I left a thank-you note, gathered up the papers, and walked over to the house.

The house?

My house.

Assuming, of course, that I did my work.

The concept of ownership is totally bizarre. I recognize that it's fundamental to society and so forth, but when one examines it closely, it starts to look a lot like voodoo. Political philosophers have spilled a lot of ink trying to determine what makes a person's things his. To cite one famous example: Locke writes that we acquire property when we mix our labor with it – by cultivating a piece of land, say. (Leading Robert Nozick to ask, three hundred years later, 'If I own a can of tomato juice and spill it in the sea so that its molecules mingle evenly throughout the sea, do I thereby come to own the sea, or have I foolishly dissipated my tomato juice?') Of all the explanations for what creates ownership – general consensus, political or physical might, a receipt, etc – none seemed to address the present situation. The house, its contents, and all assets not otherwise specified had been thrust into my domain without my asking for them, paying for them, or giving my consent.

Afraid of going inside, I set the bags down on the sidewalk and stood trying to bend my mind around the notion that this thing, so large, so Victorian, so goddamned quaint, was – would be – could be – mine.

My house.

An awkward phrase, an ill-fitting phrase, a suit five sizes too big. I tried again, out loud.

'My house.'

Oh, Eric would be angry, all right.

But it wasn't up to him.

It was her choice. What she did, she did freely. For her sake, I had an obligation to her to get over myself. To refuse to try would be the height of disrespect.

'My house.'

Why did I feel so guilty, anyway? I knew why: because I had imagined this very outcome. I had driven myself mad imagining it. In its original incarnation, the fantasy entailed that I harm her, which thought gave rise to guilt. But I hadn't actually harmed her. There is a world of difference between an omission and an action. It wasn't logical, the way I'd been persecuting myself. Alma had lived for the relentless pursuit of truth, and the truth was that having bad dreams didn't make me culpable for anything. What she did, she did freely.

'My house.'

Better. Easier. Still far from perfect, though, and so I said it again and again, cinching it up

236

here, straightening it there, embroidering it with various inflections, making conversation with myself. 'My house has shingles.' 'My house has gables.' 'My house is white.' 'My house is a hundred years old.' Repetition soon turned the words familiar and then meaningless and then almost comical. 'My house,' I said. 'Mine.' Did the concept fit? Not yet. Not perfectly. Not remotely. But I could feel myself growing, and it shrinking. Look up there: there it was: *my house*. My house had a front yard and a porch and cement pavers and a weather-beaten trellis and a mailbox and the thingy that holds a flagpole, whatever it's called, painted white to match. It was my house, and these were its components. How many times had Alma teased me for my aversion to life's finer things? I dressed like a hobo, my greatest personal indulgence was scrambled eggs and toast at a diner, and with her last act she sought to change my mind. Did I not owe it to her to give it my best effort? It was puerile, was it not, to throw a tantrum. All around me, the country was falling apart, good hardworking people losing their homes left and right, and I had the audacity to say thanks but no thanks; I can't take a *house*. What was wrong with me? It was a house, for God's sake. *A house. Mine. My house.* And not just *my house* but everything inside, too. For the first time in my life, I owned *stuff*, lots of stuff. *My house, its contents, and all assets not otherwise speci-fied.* Money. Antiques. Furniture. I was to be rich.

A most suitable and pleasant companion, that's what I had been. She wanted me to have it all. Could I disobey her? Of course not. I might feel guilty, yes, but I would feel guiltier about letting her down, and when I thought about it that way, it occurred to me that not only was Eric not entitled to anything, but I had an ethical obligation to keep her property, which is to say my property, out of his hands. She was wiser than I had ever given her credit for. This was her way of administering justice. This was her way of teaching him a lesson. She had seen him for what he was, a leech, and she would let him know. He had taken advantage of her in her lifetime, never realizing that by doing so he forfeited a far greater future bounty. Hence I was *duty-bound* to take hold of the place, to make it mine, and to shut him out. And in order to do that I had to stitch up any guilt, stash it someplace never to be looked at, be a man and accept what was mine, and thus it was with proud pounding heart and hot swimming head that I climbed up *my stairs* to *my porch* and unlocked *my door* and dropped *my bags* containing *my documents* in *my entry hall* and stood admiring as never before *my living room* and *my mantel clock* and *my pale pink sofas*. There were no ghosts here. Just *my Carolina parakeets* screeching, *my seascape* rolling. It didn't take long to adjust to this, did it? No, it did not. My desire, conceived in agony months before, now quickened, conctacted, came fully into the world, bawling for my undivided

238

attention. *Mine*. Mine, I chanted to myself as I walked down *my hallway* to *my room* – they were all *my rooms* now – and grabbed a pen and a piece of paper, both *mine*, from *my desk* and began to write down everything I could see. *My leaded window* with *my tiny hunting scene. My back porch. My wicker chairs. My yard* with *my grass, my quince* dying its yearly death. *My pillows* and *my blankets* and *my bed*, not just a bed that I slept in that belonged to someone else but a bed actually *mine*. I wrote it all down and then I went on to *my music room*, where I enumerated *my vases* and *my record player* and *my wooden music stand* holding *my copy of Sibelius's* Humoresque No. 6 in G Minor. Over the arm of *my loveseat* hung *my large woolen blanket*, and on this floor sat *my violin* and *my record player* and in *my chickenwire cabinet my extensive collection of classical LPs*. Linens and cedar hangers and mothballs and shower curtains and dishes and glasses and the fridge and the oven and I hadn't even taken into account the library. *Mine*. And I walked the length and breadth of my kingdom, opening the shutters, letting in the forgotten sun, thinking about me before and me now and what had changed. Because I did not feel the same anymore. Does change happen all at once, at the cusp, or is it the sum of an infinite series of events, each individually tiny but, taken together, unstoppable? Who sets the billiard balls in motion? And I thought about her shape in the sheets, a shape that matched the rent in my heart. I thought of how I had wept for her, not having done so for anyone since my brother, and I had been good to her; she had called me a good boy; she had used my name. And if they were to be mine, truly mine, this house, its contents, and all assets not otherwise specified in the preceding paragraphs, then I could not be afraid of a room. There were no ghosts here. I asked myself what she would do and I knew the answer, and so I took a box of trash bags from underneath the kitchen sink – mine, both of them – and went upstairs to her bedroom, *my bedroom*. She didn't live here anymore; I did. These were the facts. Accept them. I had her example to follow. So: no sentimentality: no self-indulgent beating of the breast: but *truth*, what we had always sought, the two of us together on our private journey. And what was the truth? The truth was that I could sleep in that big bed if I wanted. I could and I would. I would move in and make it mine. No longer stuck in the back of the house like a tenant. I flipped on the lights and lifted the blinds. The room reeked. But there were no ghosts here. I tore off the blanket, stripped the linens, piled them at the foot of the bed. Ocher stains had worked their way through to the mattress pad – more vomit? Blood? Urine? *Mine*, too. *Mine* feel disgust at and to want to be rid of, *mine* to dispose of if I saw fit. There was dust everywhere. I stripped the pad as well. I emptied the closets and dumped out the chest of drawers: sweaters, skirts, socks, slacks, blouses, a humiliating multitude of undergarments. I made great heaps, pushed it all into the trash bags, carried everything down to the service porch. I couldn't decide whether to wash it or put it out by the curb. I left it there for the time being. As per my proprietary right. Because there were no ghosts here. And if there were, they belonged to me.

I took my house key and locked my front door and walked down my front walk, unaware of where my feet were carrying me but willing to let them lead.

'Good timing,' said the salesman. 'They just went on sale.'

I sat on a low velvet bench. He measured me once again and brought out two boxes. 'Basic black is your best bet, although the oxblood's lovely, as well. You can't go wrong with them for casual wear. Of course, you don't have to choose just one.'

I looked at the price tags: three hundred ninety dollars a pair, plus tax. An exorbitant amount for shoes.

But she had given me instructions. And I was a millionaire.

'Autograph, please . . . Thank you very much.' He handed me my bags. 'You're a Mephisto man now.'

CHAPTER 19

I chose my lawyer because his office was within walking distance. Also, Davis Solomon was one of those people with two first names or two last names, depending on how you look at it, which sort of thing appeals to me, in the way that logical para- doxes or figure-ground illusions do. He charged four hundred twenty-five dollars for an initial consult- ation, during which he advised me, with no trace of irony, not to start blowing through my savings. Under the best of circumstances, Middlesex County South probate court moved at a crawl.

I asked what would happen if Eric contested the will.

'He'd have to show that you exercised undue influence over Ms Spielmann, i.e., both that she was capable of being manipulated and that you did in fact manipulate her. It's tough to prove. In the past, people have tried to point to suicide itself as evidence that the decedent was, by definition, not thinking clearly. But the burden of proof is on them. Bear in mind, that doesn't prevent him from being a pain in the neck. You get the ones who drag it out – women, mostly. Side of caution,

I'd say you're looking at a year, once all the conditions are met.'

I'd been envisioning something along the lines of the Publishers Clearing House, Charles Palatine ringing the doorbell and presenting me with a four-foot cardboard check. 'There's nothing we can do to speed it up?'

Solomon shrugged. He had huge shoulders, golem shoulders, and the act suggested a mountain uprooting itself. 'If you want to feel productive, you can round up some evidence of your relationship with her. That might be useful, in the event he does sue. Photographs of the two of you, or letters. That sort of thing. Something to show that it was genuine, and not mercenary.'

He seemed to think that Alma and I had taken road trips together.

'I don't have any photographs.'

'Someone who knew the both of you and could testify that you were close.'

The only person I could come up with was Dr Cargill.

'There you go. Otherwise we wait and see what happens. Meantime, you might want to get started on that paper.'

The next morning, I awoke to humming.

'Goddammit,' I said, emerging onto the landing. 'Didn't I say n—'

Daciana screamed and dropped her vacuum and ran into the TV room, locking herself inside.

I realized that I hadn't warned her about moving into the master suite.

'Open up.' I pounded. 'Daciana.'

Moaning, keening.

'Open up.'

'Oh no, oh no.'

It took a good ten minutes to persuade her that I was not a phantom. When she finally did come out, I said, 'Listen, I told you the last t—'

'Okay seer,' she said, rushing past me and commencing to vacuum.

I watched her for a minute, then gave up and went downstairs.

My intention was to go through my existing dissertation, salvaging as much of it as possible. What point was there in starting from scratch when I already had so much text? Belly filled with tea, I fetched down all eight hundred pages and sequestered myself in the library, where I spent that entire day reading. (Save an hour when Daciana kicked me out in order to 'clean book.') Having not touched the manuscript in almost a year, I could come to it with newfound objectivity, and what I found disturbed me. It was as though I had been sent back in time, forced to confront my earlier self, a self whose vanity, immaturity, and impatience shone through on every page. I used four words where one would do. I indulged in extratextual references. Large swaths did not cohere, consisting entirely of tangents, all sprung from a higher-level tangent . . . itself emerging from a third cluster of tangents . . . *Finnegans Wake* with a bibliography.

'Finish, seer.'

Through dry eyes I saw her standing in the doorway, her blouse shadowed with sweat.

I set down the manuscript, tugged out my wallet, counted off sixty dollars.

'This is the last time,' I said. 'Do you understand?'

'Okay, seer.' She stuffed the money into her brassiere, then bent to pick up her basket of cleaning supplies. 'See you soon.'

Nobody knew better than I how quickly two years could slip away. As I began anew to wrestle with writer's block – razing in the afternoon that which I had built in the morning – I felt the first tickles of what would soon become a constant, low-grade panic. Rereading the manuscript had demoralized me, tightening the spigot until nothing at all would come. Instead I busied myself with false preliminaries. I compiled a new reading list. I went out and bought a large whiteboard, upon which I began to draw elaborate 'idea maps,' conceptual networks that depicted, more than anything else, the cobwebs in my own brain. Telling myself that I needed access to more current resources, I called up the phone company and had an internet connection put in, which of course achieved nothing except to make me more distractible. Frighteningly, I seemed to have lost my capacity to concentrate for more than a few minutes at a time. I would type a bit, get up, stretch, walk around, get a glass of water, read a couple of paragraphs from some irrelevant book, sit down, type a bit more, fret, delete everything I'd written, check the headlines, check the weather . . . Eventually I'd end up at the Wikipedia entry for the Pointer Sisters, having somehow bounced there from the page on Kripke models. Desperate for inspiration, I thought back on my conversations with Alma. All those long, wonderful hours of talk – they flitted teasingly at the periphery of my memory, vanishing when I turned to reach for them. If I'd only kept a tape recorder in the room . . . And when I did get my fingers around an idea, I found it useless, barely flapping, almost dead, a delicate thing I had crushed in my haste. The same discursiveness that had made our conversations so pleasurable made it impossible to fashion them into a workable argument. We didn't have that kind of conversation, the kind that concludes. That would have defeated our purpose, which was to think, to explore, to feel unconfined. And yet now she demanded that I yoke myself to a deadline. Madness! Depravity! I felt furious at her; then I felt sorry and ungrateful; then paralyzed and depressed . . . But none of this was helping me write.

I had an excuse, though, a really good one. The dissertation was only one of two obstacles. The other was Eric. Perhaps that was what was causing me to lose focus: I was preoccupied by the thought of a lawsuit. The probate citation would have to be published in the newspaper, circulated to interested parties, and returned to the court – at which point he would lose the right to object. Until then, I decided, I couldn't expect to have the presence of mind necessary for creative work.

Thus it was that I arrived at November with nothing to show for myself.

'You know what you should do,' Drew said. He stood in the middle of the library, arms up like a signalman. 'You should throw a party.'

I scoffed.

'For real. This is a great party house. I'm serious, it's got a very classy vibe.' He sank into one of the armchairs, moaned. 'That's what I'm talking about . . . How come you never had me over before?'

'She liked it quiet,' I said – a partial lie. Alma had never forbidden guests; I simply hadn't asked, wanting to keep her to myself. Now that she was gone, I felt compelled to reveal where it was I'd been hiding. And, I must admit, to brag.

'Do like a wine and cheese,' he said. 'Or you know what? Poker night. Whiskey, cigars . . . We could use that big table out front.'

'That's the dining-room table.'

'And therefore.'

'It's an antique.'

'And therefore.'

'It's not a card table.'

'It's the perfect size. All you need is a felt.'

'No.'

'Well,' he said, spinning the globe. 'If you change your mind, let me know.'

Down the hall, Daciana passed, humming. Drew looked at me.

'The maid,' I said.

'Moving on up, my friend.'

'Please.'

'Like the Jeffersons.'

'You don't understand,' I said. 'I told her to stop coming. She keeps showing up anyway.'

'That's . . . I don't know what it is. Weird.'

'Indeed.'

'Why don't you fire her?'

'You say that like I haven't tried.'

He laughed.

'It's not funny. She's driving me insane.'

'How hard is it to fire someone?'

'You have no idea how persistent she is.'

'Don't pay her.'

'I tried that.'

'And?'

'She started crying.'

We paused to listen to her hum.

'At least she has a nice voice,' Drew said.

'It's not worth sixty dollars a week.'

We listened again.

'Thirty,' he said. 'Tops.'

'If I had a party, do you think Yasmina would come? A regular party, not a poker party.'

'You understand that the goal of a party is to meet other women.'

'I don't know any other women.'

'I do.'

248

'I think she'd like to see the house.'

'Look, if you're still obsessed—'

'I'm not obsessed.'

'—just ask her to come by. You don't need an excuse.'

'It's not an excuse. She'll find it less threatening if you ask.'

He shrugged. 'I can try.'

'I haven't agreed to anything. I'm speaking theoretically.'

'Yeah, well, that's your problem,' he said. 'You're all talk.'

Eight weeks had passed since Alma's death, and I was beginning to suspect that Palatine had 'forgotten' to invite me to the burial. When his secretary did call, she told me twice that no guests were permitted.

Mount Auburn Cemetery, misty and still. I stood alone on one side of the grave. Across from me, Dr Cargill clutched her husband's arm; next to them, a stolid Charles Palatine leaned on a walking stick. Eric was nowhere in sight.

Because of the cemetery's historical significance, there was no heavy machinery allowed on-site, and it took thirty minutes for four men, armed with shovels, to get the job done. Nobody spoke. I found the whole episode profoundly anticlimactic, not to mention socially unnavigable. Not wanting to ogle the casket (too brazen) or the other mourners (too creepy), I let my gaze stray across silvery lawns crowded with headstones, whole families of Boston Brahmins mossed over and forgotten. A group of birdwatchers came over the rise, binoculars trained on some distant branch, pausing to confer before departing in unison, flocklike, down a wet path sheeted with orange and yellow leaves. Palatine shifted. He seemed to have a cold, the skin around his nostrils raw with repeated blowing. I kept thinking of my brother's memorial service, both the original and the more recent one. A lighthouse symbolizing the presence of lost loved ones in our lives: how sick, sick and predictable. And mawkish. But what about this? Was this better? This damp banality of a morning? I looked across the grave at Dr Cargill and saw her eyes flick away. She had been staring at me? It made me squirm in my new shoes. This was the first occasion I'd had to wear them in public. The morning rain had given me pause, and I'd almost swapped them out for my old loafers. But Alma had made one request of me before she died, and I decided to continue to honor her wishes, going with the black, a choice I imagined she would have approved of, as they were in keeping with the solemnity of the occasion and moreover matched beautifully the new sportcoat I'd bought in her honor as well.

The last spadeful of earth fell. Palatine hobbled away.

I came around to extend Dr Cargill my condolences. Her mouth pinched slightly as I approached.

'I'm sorry for your loss,' I said.

She nodded. 'Yours, too.'

There was a small pause; then her husband put out a hand. 'Ron Cargill.'

I introduced myself. 'Beautiful place,' I said. 'It's kind of a shame she didn't want a ceremony.'

'That's what she wanted,' Dr Cargill said.

'Yes . . . Still, it would have been nice to be able to say something.'

She nodded, tucked away her handkerchief. 'Well, take care.'

'Thanks. You, too. But, uh. I'm not sure if you're aware, but she left you a piece of jewelry.'

Silence.

'So I'm told.'

'Oh,' I said. 'I take it you've seen the, the—'

'I have.'

Immediately I felt like an idiot. I hadn't meant to gloat, but how else could she take it? Here I was, lolling atop a fortune, while fifteen years of house-calls had earned her a bauble. Still, I thought her iciness uncalled-for. Alma had made the decision, not me.

'Was there one piece in particular that you admired?' I said.

Silence.

'I can't say I've given it much thought.'

'There's all sorts of things.' I knew I ought to shut up, but I kept digging, digging, talking and digging. 'Come by anytime, you can pick one out. Or, I mean, do you want to have a look?'

251

She stared at me. 'Now?'

'No no no, of course not, of course not now. At your convenience.'

Silence.

'You know what,' she said. 'Let's just get it over with.'

The drive back to the house was atrociously long.

'Number forty-nine,' I said to her husband. 'It's at the end of the block.'

'He knows where it is,' Dr Cargill said.

Upstairs, she froze on the threshold to the master bedroom. I knew right away what she was thinking: I had eradicated all traces of Alma.

'This way,' I said, striding overeagerly toward the vanity.

There were rings, bracelets, whisper-fine neck-laces in gold and platinum; sapphire earrings and a matching pendant; South Sea pearls; a ruby brooch in the shape of a parrot – none of which I had ever seen Alma wear. As Dr Cargill ran her fingers over the offerings, I found myself mentally urging her toward the cheaper-looking things. Whatever she left would be mine to sell, after all, and I had decided that twenty thousand simply wouldn't cut it. I had bills to pay; I had research costs. I was thinking of getting a new computer, a desktop. Hunching over a tiny screen was all well and good when you had to be prepared to move at a moment's notice, but it didn't suit a home-owner. These things didn't grow on trees, did they?

At the same time, I felt badly about the way I'd

comported myself in the cemetery. I might need to call on the doctor as a character witness.

'Feel free to take more than one piece,' I said.

Her lips pinched again. 'Thanks.'

'Would you like a drink?'

'I'm fine.'

'Do you think your husband would?'

We'd left Ron Cargill down in the living room. 'He'll be fine.'

'All right,' I said, watching, relieved, as she set down a weighty gold cuff. 'I don't know much about jewelry.'

She looked at me.

'Why would you?' she said.

At once a frightening thought came to me: the change that I'd felt come over me on the day of my homecoming, when I took possession of my house – she could see it on me, it had spread across my body like a rash. I tried to speak, could not.

The doctor returned to browsing, holding a pair of earrings up to look in the mirror. 'I got a call from the police.'

'. . . did you.'

She nodded. 'They asked me about your relationship with Alma.'

Silence.

'Hm,' I said.

Silence.

'I said that you cared a great deal about each other,' she said.

'. . . we did.'

She put the earrings down. 'Obviously.' She stepped back, crossed her arms. 'I don't want any of this.'

'Is something wrong?'

'Nothing's wrong, I just don't want anything.'

'Well. But. Okay, but, be that as it may, she wanted you to have something.'

'That doesn't mean I have to accept.'

'I understand, but . . . Here.' I seized the parrot brooch. 'What about this. Or – or – okay, but, but it doesn't have to be a piece of jewelry.' I heard myself, I sounded crazed. 'Strictly speaking, okay, yes, it should come from here, that's what she specified. But if there's a book, or a piece of art, I'm fine with you going and having a look . . . I mean, she wanted you to have something. She was grateful to you, and she wanted you to have something. It's totally up to you, of course, but in the spirit of the bequest, it seems appropriate, I think, for you to . . . I mean. There isn't anything you want?'

Silence.

She said, 'Why don't you pick something out and send it to me.'

'I – uh. I guess I can do that. I mean, did you have a pref—'

'No.'

'Okay. Okay, well. If you're sure—'

'I'm sure.'

'All right. Okay. Although, like I said, ha ha, I don't know much about jewelry, so it's not my fault if you don't like what I choose.'

254

'I don't really care,' she said. 'I just don't want to think about it anymore.'

'Well,' I said. 'All right.'

She thumbed at the door. 'I'd better go.'

Downstairs, her husband was examining the Audubon. 'All set?'

'All set.'

Listening to them drive away, I made up my mind to send her more than one item. Two or three nice pieces, half a dozen of the cheaper ones . . . Naturally she was upset. We both were: the image of Alma going into the ground was fresh in our minds. I considered, as well, the shock of losing someone to suicide after devoting so many years to healing her. I was angry, too, and I'd known Alma less than one-fifteenth as long. But I had gotten over my squeamishness, and so would Dr Cargill. She would like what I would send her. She would, it was beautiful stuff, all in the best taste.

On some level I did worry that she would see my gift for what it was: a bribe. I couldn't take back the clumsy things I'd said, though, and I needed her on my side. She of all people could best attest that I had loved Alma. That I had to prove so – to a court or to the police or to anyone at all – was degrading. But I reminded myself that none of this had to do with love anymore. It had to do with money, and I couldn't trust anyone, not anymore.

CHAPTER 20

The first snow came early, two days after Thanksgiving, though it didn't stick, running from the roofs in gray streamlets. Down by the corner, a gutter clogged, flooding the street and making the trip to the market a filthy, muddy chore. Alone with my thoughts, exhausted, I rubbed my eyes and stared at my computer screen. Is there any abyss deeper than the blank page? Anything more ominous than a winking cursor, its slow beat a death march?

The doorbell provided a welcome distraction. I inched back the front curtain and saw Eric standing on the porch, shifting from foot to foot. His lips were blue, his coat alive with vibration, and I took a shameful degree of pleasure in noting that the universe had not been treating him well of late. He looked shaggy, malnourished, sapped of confidence, his Adam's apple prominent, his hand darting to touch a deep, unhealed cut that glistened above his left eye. If my meeting with Palatine had left me with any doubts as to Eric's recent whereabouts, they were now dispelled: it seemed fair to assume that he had been in jail, fair also to assume that he deserved whatever rough treatment he'd gotten there. The change in him was profound, and I smiled as I watched him struggle to keep warm.

It then occurred to me that I had not seen him since the day he had threatened to report me to the police. If he had been locked up shortly thereafter, he could not have killed Alma. There was no reason to assume this to be the case. He might have been free until recently. But if in fact he had been away the entire two months – and I suspected he had; how else to explain his total absence? – then that would make Alma's suicide just that: a suicide. It seemed that Eric had missed his chance, probably not for the first time in his life. It had taken her initiative and my neglect to realize his dreams. And thinking of my neglect made me feel implicated, and guilty, and angry all over again. These were feelings I thought I'd gotten past. I didn't deserve to feel them again; I had more important things on my mind. I put the chain on, cracked the door.

'Hey,' he said. 'I need to talk to you.'

'Go ahead.'

'Come on, man, lemme in. It's like twenty below out here.'

I, nice and comfy inside my inheritance, while he stood there like a pauper . . . I stilled my hand, moving unconsciously toward the chain. 'What is it,' I said.

'I can't come in.'

I shook my head.

'Why not.'

'Because I don't want you to.'

'Listen, man, you don't need to be like this.'

'Be happy I'm talking to you at all,' I said. 'You should be speaking to my lawyer.'

'Jesus Christ, would you chill out?'

'I'm going to go now.'

'Wait.'

I waited.

'Just let me in for like five minutes,' he said.

'Goodbye,' I said, and closed the door.

Moments later he was at the side door, banging. When that failed he went around to the back. Finally the phone began to ring.

I picked up. 'Knock it off or I'm calling the police.'

'Hey, hey, hey. Calm down. I just want to talk to you, all right?'

'There's nothing to talk about.'

'Sure there is. Come on. I'm dying out here. It's important.'

'If it's so important then stop wasting time and get on with it.'

'What do you think I'm going to do, shoot you?'

'How should I know?'

'Come on, man. Are you kidding me?'

I said nothing.

'Well, shit.' He sniffled. 'Can I at least get some coffee or something.'

'I don't have any coffee.'

'Tea's good.'

'Goodbye, Eric.'

'Wait, wait, wait wait . . . All right, look. I'll show you, okay? Come to the front.'

He hung up.

I could all too easily imagine opening the door to a flashing muzzle. Instead I went upstairs, to the TV room, which overlooked the porch below. He had struck a pose of expectancy, the pockets of his coat turned out.

I raised the window, causing him to glance up.

He wiggled the linings. 'See?'

'Take off your coat,' I said.

'It's *cold*, man.'

'Take it off or I'm calling the cops.'

He muttered inaudibly.

'What was that?'

'Nothing. Nothing. Here.' He took the coat off, flapped it around. 'See? Come on, now.'

I told him to take off his shirt.

'Aw, for fuck's sake, enough already.'

'Do it.'

He gritted his teeth and complied. He was emaciated, his skin waxy white. He spun around like a fashion model – I saw the tattoos: the buck and the assault rifle – then grabbed himself for warmth, shivering violently.

'Fuck, dude, I'm gonna freeze to death.'

Part of me wanted to shut the window and walk away. Let him bang: I would ignore him. Let him learn who he was dealing with. I was not a man to be trifled with, no ho ho, I was a man of means, and of greater patience than he. I was wiser, and stronger, and better, and he could learn to fend for himself for once. Another part of me, though – I can admit this now – another part of me was enjoying humiliating him. After everything he had done, he deserved to be humbled.

I said, 'Your pants.'

He turned out the pockets.

'Take them off.'

'What?'

'Take off your pants.'

'Here? What the hell, man.'

'Fine.' I shut the window and stepped out of view.

Below, he began to yell. I counted to ten, then stepped back to the window.

'Fine,' he said. 'You win. Okay?'

He undid his fly and let his pants fall to his ankles, revealing old boxer shorts in a camouflage pattern. His legs were hairless, and though I was too far away to tell for certain, they appeared to be dappled with tiny black spots.

'Now open the fucking door,' he yelled.

I closed the window and went downstairs. He stumbled across the porch, pulling on his clothing, crying out in surprise when the door bounced back on the chain.

'The *fuck*, dude.' He kicked the doorframe. 'You said you'd let me in.'

'I never said that.'

He started at me hatefully. 'You're a fuckin asshole, you know that?'

I started to close the door.

'*Wait.*'

Silence.

'Apologize,' I said.

Silence.

'I apologize,' he said.

'Now say your piece and leave me alone.'

His jaw bulged as he got control of himself. 'All right . . . all right, look. I've been thinking it over. I want to make a deal.' He paused. 'What do you think?'

'I don't have an opinion. You haven't said anything yet.'

'Okay, so, fine, so, I'm getting to that. Now, I've been spending a lot of time on this. Like I told you before, I don't need the house. As far as I'm concerned, you take it.'

'I already own the house. I don't need you to give it to me.'

'I know. All right, I know. But – I mean. I'm telling you, it's fine with me. I don't want it. I'm not even going to try to ask for it.'

'Terrific.'

'Okay, so, but if you get the house, then I should get something, too. Fair is fair.'

I said nothing.

'Right?'

'What do you want, Eric?'

'So if you get the house, and – let's not forget,

261

it's a big house. Tons of stuff. So, I mean, it's only fair I should get the money.'

'The money.'

He nodded.

'As in all of it,' I said.

He nodded again.

Now I really did laugh. 'You're out of your mind.'

'It's only fair,' he said.

'And how do you figure that.'

'The house, that's like a couple million right there. All her stuff. The books, I don't even know what they're worth.'

'I'm not selling the books.'

'Yeah, but you could if you wanted to.'

'I don't want to.'

'Well that's up to you,' he said. 'That's your choice.'

'It sure is.'

'But I mean there's other stuff, I know that for a fact. So, bottom line, you'll be fine, and anyway you don't need it like I do. Or – look. I'm willing to deal. How bout we say this. Ready? Okay, look. Let's say I give you half.'

'*You* give *me* half.'

'That's totally fair,' he said.

'No, it isn't. It isn't even remotely fair. Let's get something straight: it's not yours to give away. The money's mine, Eric. That's your starting point for negotiations.'

'So what. I get nothing? That's what you're telling me, I get nothing.'

'She did leave you something. It's in the will. Have you read it?'

'How'm I supposed to do all that stuff she wants me to do? I can't, man, you know that.'

'That's really too bad, then.'

'I have *learning* disabilities.'

'You've said.'

'Yeah, so, help me out here. This isn't fair and you know it.'

'She thought it was.'

'You have no idea, do you.' He sounded weary; his face softened to match. It was a command performance. 'She made my life hell.'

'I suppose she smacked you around.'

'She did.'

'I don't believe you.'

'She—'

'And even if I did, it's got nothing to do with me, or the house, or the money.'

'I'm broke.'

'Sorry to hear it.'

'That doesn't mean anything to you?'

'It means you should have spent what she gave you a little more prudently.'

'Why are you doing this to me? What did I ever do to you?'

'What am I doing, Eric.'

'You're taking *everything*.'

'I'm not *taking* anything. She gave it to me. And frankly, after what *you* tried to do, coming back here and asking for handouts is unbelievable.'

'I don't know what the fuck you're talking about.'

'You know what you did.'

'No,' he said. 'I don't know.'

'Then that's your problem.'

Silence.

'Stay warm,' I said. I started to close the door.

He said, 'How's the writing coming.'

I shut the door and bolted it.

How was it coming? Not well, of course, not that afternoon or the next. I had three pages of a new outline, which I was rereading when the phone rang. I let it go a dozen times. It stopped. There was a brief silence. Then it began to ring again. I closed my computer and went to the kitchen.

'Hello?'

Silence.

I hung up.

I started back down the hall to my office.

The phone rang.

I returned to the kitchen.

'Eric?'

Silence.

'Go to hell,' I said and hung up.

When it happened a third time, I disconnected the receiver.

This went on for the next several days. I had to credit him with tenacity: no sooner would I plug the phone back in than it would begin to ring. I rarely picked up, and when I did there was nothing

264

on the other end. It was hard to understand what he hoped to achieve; my failure to finish didn't entitle him to anything. I suppose spite was motivation enough.

I called the phone company. Someone in Bangalore told me that it was impossible to block a specific caller, suggesting rather that I get a new, unlisted number. I did, and immediately the calls stopped.

In their place, however, came something for more unsettling. I began to have the feeling that I was being watched.

How I knew this, I can't say. I never saw Eric, or anyone else, for that matter. Tiny, niggling, liable to crop up at the most unlikely moments – when I was in the shower, or standing at the counter with the jeweler while he appraised the contents of Alma's vanity – the sensation would not leave me. I went around the house closing the shades, restoring the sepulchral atmosphere that she had maintained. Still I felt it: a quivering, invisible eye. I went to the post office to mail the doctor her gifts, and as I stepped out onto the sidewalk, I felt it again. Like a madman I spun in place, arms flying, nearly knocking over a bicyclist. There was nobody, nothing wrong, but I walked home briskly, then faster, it could be behind me, hovering, jellylike, bloodshot, obscene, all-seeing, all-knowing, and I was sprinting, my new shoes sliding on the sidewalk. Before I went inside I checked the perimeter of the house, and once in the kitchen I poured myself a tall drink.

Feelings ought to mean nothing in the face of facts. I gave myself a shake, drank again, and set about to cook for my party.

I didn't know what to call it. Christmas was still ten days away. Drew said who cared, as long as there was booze. I spent the evening running around, refilling glasses, thanking people for their house-warming gifts, making light conversation, and agreeing that yes, it had been far too long since I'd seen anybody.

'Sounds like you found your soulmate,' they said when I described Alma.

I smiled.

'It must have been wonderful to have someone like that in your life.'

It was.

'You *made* this cake?'

Indeed I had.

Yasmina never showed, and as the clock ran down, and the other guests – whom I considered filler – began to trickle out, I wrote the entire evening off.

'I told you,' said Drew on his way out. 'Classy.'

Dejected, I went into the kitchen, turned on the radio, rolled up my sleeves, and plunged my arms into hot, soapy water. Terrible idea, this party. I felt annoyed at Drew for talking me into it. As I scrubbed hard at dried jam, it occurred to me that he might not have invited Yasmina at all, taking it upon himself to liberate me. I crushed the sponge; suds ran down my wrist and onto the floor. No more socializing, then. I would retreat into privacy and get the job done, then take my fortune and start a new life, one that had nothing to do with Harvard or any of these people . . . So immersed in self-pity was I that I almost missed the doorbell. Expecting someone come back for forgotten mittens, I dried my hands and went to the entry hall. It was Yasmina.

Silence.

'Can I come in?' she said. 'It's kind of cold.'

I took her coat and led her to the kitchen, where I cut her a piece of *Sachertorte*.

'Thank you,' she said.

'Do I get to meet Pete?'

'He's in New York.'

'Another time, then.'

She nodded. 'Nice shoes.'

'They're oxblood,' I said.

'What happened to your loafers?'

'I threw them out.'

'Well, Joseph Geist. I never.'

I watched her chew. 'I didn't think you were coming.'

'Yeah, well. Neither did I.' She licked whipped cream from her thumb. 'I hear you're landed gentry now.'

'So it seems.'

'Congratulations.'

I nodded.

'So,' she said. 'Do I get a tour or what?'

★   ★   ★

267

'Her father mode this violin.'

'Wow. Really?'

'He was an instrument maker.'

'It's beautiful . . . Why do you have all the curtains closed? Isn't it kind of dark?'

'It's nighttime.'

'Still . . . See? Much better.'

I dragged the curtain back into place. 'I like it better this way.'

'You would.'

In the office, she spotted my manuscript, piled sloppily and bristling with useless tape flags. 'Are you writing again?'

'You could say that.'

'I'm glad to hear it.'

'Thanks . . . Look: the pattern on his hat matches the pattern in the trees.'

She let out a little squeal.

'You like,' I said.

'I love. This is so my style.'

'I know,' I said.

'Every time I go home to do wedding stuff, my mom wants to drag me around to open houses. All these Persian palaces.' She shuddered. 'You know. *Pillars.*'

I smiled faintly.

'Well,' she said, 'it's pretty fantastic. Gloomy and haunted – perfect for you. Although I hope you'll take my advice and let some light in.'

'There's one more thing you have to see.'

'She left you a car.'
'Better.'

Yasmina's reaction to the library made me aware of something I'd forgotten about her: her earnestness, the child inside the sophisticate. It had been a long time since I had seen her so rapt, oohing and aahing as she touched everything with her delicate fingers.

'Oh my God,' she kept saying. 'Oh my God. Joseph. This is crazy. I mean, do you even realize how crazy this is?'

'I've been here long enough that it seems normal.'

'It isn't. Oh my God. Is that a real Tiffany?' She bent to inspect the lamp. 'Do you have any idea what this is worth? Oh my God. What else is here?'

I showed her some of the first editions. For a moment she remained gauzy-eyed. Then, businesslike: 'You should hire an appraiser.'

'I'm not selling anything.'

'You should still know what it's worth. For insurance purposes.' She stood before the wall of photographs. 'That's her? With the ribbons?'

'Yes.'

'Oh my God, she was so pretty. Look at that *dress*. Did she own a horse?'

'It wouldn't surprise me. Her family was well-off.'

'Uh, *yeah*. And. Oh. Of course.' She picked up

half-Nietzsche. 'I knew you'd find a way to ruin a perfectly lovely room.'

'Alma liked it there. It was her idea.'

'Oh, I don't believe that.'

'She said so.'

She put the bookend back. 'When are you going to learn that women say all kinds of things.'

I smiled.

'You must miss her,' she said.

I nodded. 'I wish you'd met her.'

'I would have liked that.'

Silence. She greened.

'What's wrong?'

She shook her head, moved across the room.

'Mina.' The nickname came out unthinkingly, and I braced myself for the blowback. None came.

'This is a beautiful carpet,' she said. She crouched to run her hand over it. 'It's probably worth a fortune. What happens if there's a fire? Have you ever considered that?'

'I—'

'You need to learn about these things. You have to take care of what you have.'

'Yasmina. What's the matter?'

'Nothing, all right? Stop it. Nothing's the matter. I'm stressed.'

'About.'

'Lots of things. Weddings are stressful.' She stood up and headed toward an armchair, then reconsidered, sitting cross-legged on the floor, dipping

270

her fingers into the thick pile. 'It really is a nice carpet. Believe me, I can tell.'

I said nothing.

She said, 'It's all who wants *this*, who wants *that*. Who won't eat this, who'll only eat that. My mom – oh my God. And his mom is even worse. Put the two of them together . . .' She mimed an explosion.

Silence.

'Tell me,' I said.

'You don't want to know.'

'I do.' I paused. 'Tell me.'

Silence.

'All right,' she said.

Among the gory details were: an argument over whose family rabbi would preside; the bridesmaid controversy (Pedram's sisters refused to wear the strapless dress Yasmina had picked out); the lingering question of the main, chicken or beef or a duet.

'It sounds crazy when I talk about it,' she said.

'No.'

'It does. It is crazy. It's *insane*. I want a nice wedding, too, but I haven't even had my second fitting and already everything's out of control. I don't care who you are. There is no reason in the world to get this invested in a single day.'

'I take it you've set a date.'

'June twenty-third.'

'That's sooner than you expected.'

She nodded.

'Well,' I said. 'I hope it all works out.'

'Could you be less convincing.'

'There's always Las Vegas.'

'You don't get it, do you. It's a community event. It has nothing to do with me. And Pedram loves the idea of a big wedding. He's like the craziest of all. Groomzilla. Do people say that? They should.'

'Sure,' I said.

'What's that supposed to mean?'

'All I said was, "Sure."'

'Don't get high and mighty.'

'Mina—'

'Like you knew all along this would happen to me.'

'I never said that. I never even thought it.'

'You did.'

'All I want is for you to be happy,' I said.

'Well I'm not,' she said. 'There you go. I'm not happy. Happy now?'

'I—'

'I can't deal with it anymore. Them or any of it. I want to get on a plane. Oh, shit. I need a tissue, please.'

I fetched the box from the nailhead table and knelt before her.

'This is so embarrassing.'

'There's nothing to be embarrassed about.'

She laughed, wiped her eyes. 'Okay.' With a second tissue she enfolded the first. 'My parents have already put down seventy thousand dollars in deposits. I don't even want to know what it'll cost by the time it's over. The guest list is over three hundred so far, and that's just our side . . . I don't know what to do. I don't know what I *can* do.'

'It's your life.'

'It's not. It's mine, and his, and my parents', and his parents', and grandparents . . . Everyone is pouring everything they have into this. It's like the highlight of my mother's existence. I can't do anything about it now.'

'You always have a choice,' I said.

'You're doing it again.'

'What.'

'Talking in aphorisms.'

'This is your wedding. It's marriage. It's not a pair of shoes.'

She shook her head. 'I wish I could send you to talk to them.'

'I will if you want me to. Give me the number.'

'They'll just yell at you in Farsi. "Who eez dees? Vhot are you dooing?"' She laughed wetly. 'Anyway. At least one of us is happy.'

'You should be, too.'

'I'll deal.'

'You deserve more than that. You deserve to be happy in every respect. You—'

She started crying again.

I apologized.

'Never mind,' she said. She wiped her face. Then, with only the briefest hesitation, she reached out for me.

★ ★ ★

273

If I considered the library a sacred space – and I did – then I ought to've felt ashamed defiling it. I didn't. I felt terrific. I felt at peace, enjoying the softness of the carpet against my bare back. Yasmina lay bunched against me. Her makeup was smudged, her hair a black tangle, and the feeling of her there brought to mind quiet Sunday mornings past, when I woke early, her skin moist and darkly radiant among the pure white sheets, one neat lacquered hand darting out again and again to slap the snooze button, a quiet comedy that could last the better part of an hour. She spent a lot of time fretting over body hair, bleaching and epilating, the base of her neck, her forearms, the small of her back. In all honesty I preferred her the way she was. She always felt to me like a feral thing I had managed to tame.

Now she sat up and began gathering her clothes.

'Mina.'

She faced away to put on her bra.

'Mina. Talk to me.'

'What do you want me to say? I'm getting married.'

'Are you?'

She ignored me.

'Mina—'

'Please stop. I feel bad enough as it is.'

'Wait.' I sat up. 'Let's have a conversation.'

'I'm engaged.'

'To someone you don't love.'

'It's still wrong.'

'What can I do to convince you?' I asked.

'You can't,' she said. 'Not even you.'

She wouldn't let me walk her home, so I called a cab and we went out on the front porch to wait. It was cold out, the moon in hiding. Behind me I sensed the heft of the house, my house. Watching Yasmina take pleasure in it had given me untold joy.

'It's going to snow soon,' she said.

Her car turned the corner.

'It's up to you,' I said. 'Remember that.'

'Okay, Confucius.'

I stayed on the front porch, willing her to turn around. But it was two in the morning, and she had to get up for work. She had decisions to make. Not even I could convince her. I'd made my case as best I could, and now all I could do was wait. I stood up to go inside.

Fifty feet away, across the street, the darkness moved. A bright orange spot pierced the oily black – cigarette – and then disappeared.

CHAPTER 21

Cambridge emptied out for the holidays. Drew left for a poker tournament in Reno. Yasmina flew to Los Angeles, where her family was throwing her and Pedram a second engagement party. I stayed indoors, ordering food from the market, surfing the internet, typing and deleting, inching forward, sliding back. Realizing that I would have to take more drastic measures, I called Detective Zitelli.

'Not really,' he said, when I asked if he could tell me what was happening.

'The autopsy must be finished,' I said. 'They released the body.'

'It's finished.'

The verdict was cardiac arrest, caused by an overdose of a combination of medications, self-inflicted.

'What about Eric?'

'What about him.'

'You didn't talk to him?'

'Listen up,' he said. 'I'm driving the bus here. Not you. Now, you can be an asset or you can be a liability. Your call.'

I apologized.

'You're going to have to take my word on this, all right? But based on the information we have so far, it's pretty clear that Ms Spielmann took her own life.'

I said nothing, thinking of her last, lonely hours on earth.

'I know it's not an easy thing to accept,' he said. 'For what it's worth, I can tell you cared about her a lot.'

His tone, just shy of sincere, raised my antennae. I wanted to get off the phone, but I hadn't yet asked my second question. In trying to make the segue sound natural, I ended up stuttering like a ham actor. 'Uh – thank you, I app – thanks, but – detective? One more – sorry. One thing, about her thesis, the thesis. Do you think I might be able to get that back anytime soon?' I paused. 'I need it, you see, for research purposes.'

A brief silence.

'I'm working as fast as I can,' he said.

'Of course. Only that it's rather important, and if the case is closed—'

'I didn't say that.'

'Well, but you said it's clear what happened.'

'I said it's pretty clear.'

I had to hand it to the man: he knew how to split a hair. 'A ballpark estimate, then,' I said.

A longer silence.

'It mostly depends on when I get it back from the translator,' he said.

'. . . you're having it translated.'

'My German's a little rusty.'

I pressed my fist against my forehead. 'I see. Well . . . well, I could help you out with that, if you wanted.'

'That's nice of you to offer, but we got it covered.'

'Anything I can do to help.'

'Duly noted,' he said. 'Happy holidays.'

The next day I went back to the menswear store. The salesman recognized me, shook my hand, made conversation. With his guidance, I selected a set of gold cufflinks as a Christmas present to myself, one that entailed the purchase of a new shirt with French cuffs. I can't say that either of them brought me to any substantial philosophical insight, but they did look quite dashing, and standing in front of the three-way mirror, I felt a sense of accomplishment, as though I had sewn the shirt myself. Consumption can serve as a proxy for production, can it not? I entered the store with nothing and emerged laden with goods: the shirt and the cufflinks, yes, and some matching slacks, and a tan shoulder bag made of a magnificently buttery lambskin. And a second shirt as well. To complement his two pairs of shoes, the well-dressed man requires, at minimum, one shirt in white and one in blue. Plus a third in pink. I always did like pink.

So agreeable was I that I stopped at a women's boutique to buy Yasmina a gift. Of everything on offer, a ruby pendant set in yellow gold was the clear favorite. I balked momentarily when I saw the price tag – twenty-six hundred dollars – but I reminded myself that I had to strike while the iron was hot, and worst-case scenario I could always raid the vanity again for more things to sell. I had the pendant gift-wrapped, signed the note *with love from Confucius*, and shipped it to her parents' house.

On December 24, after making the requisite call home, I transferred my dinner from tins to plates, poured myself a large glass of champagne, and carried everything on a tray to the dining-room table, which I had set for myself for the first time, a gesture I thought appropriately festive.

On December 27, Yasmina called.

'What do you think you're doing.'

'Beg pardon?'

'You can't do this.'

'Happy Hanukkah,' I said.

'You can't, Joseph.'

'If you don't like it, I can take it back.'

'Whether I like it or not is beside the point.'

'Do you?'

'Seriously. What am I supposed to do with this?'

'Wear it.'

'Oh, please.'

'Consider it a gesture of friendship.'

'Oh *please*.'

'You think it's an unfriendly gesture?'

'I think I'm *engaged*.'

'That's a start,' I said. 'Before you were certain.'

'Uch, will you please, please stop.'

'I'm trying to woo you with brazen displays of largesse,' I said. 'I don't know, I feel like it's working.'

'It's not.'

'So you don't like it.'

'Of course I like it. It's gorgeous.'

'Then it's working.'

'Joseph . . .' Her voice dropped. 'Shit. I have to go.'

'Wait.'

'I'll call you later.'

'Mina—'

She hung up. I smiled, then opened the refrigerator door and reached for the remaining champagne.

That night I dreamt of Alma.

We were walking in a giant emporium, like Wal-Mart but far larger, with shelving so high it seemed to bow inward, stocked to the edges with colorful items of all types, sporting equipment, cleaning products, children's toys, all outsize and nuclear bright. The two of us were pushing a rattling shopping cart twice my height, grabbing item after item down off the shelf. The cart would not fill up; we kept reaching for more; and the rattling grew louder and lower, a monstrous gastrointestinal sound like a demolition derby. I asked her to wait; I needed a break; I couldn't bear it any longer. She kept on going without me, though, and I screamed at her to stop, one second of quiet and rest; on she pushed, headed for the end of the aisle, and I knew that if I didn't catch her soon, I never would. I felt around for something to throw, not at her but near enough to get her attention and make her realize that I'd fallen behind. I came up with a china saucer but hesitated, throwing a saucer is wrong, you can't go around destroying perfectly good saucers. Up ahead she had begun to make the turn; it was now or never; and I coiled up and let loose. Away the saucer sailed, careening off the shelves, touching off chaos wherever it struck, boxes and products flying everywhere, plastic and cardboard in traffic-cone orange and coolant green, everything raining down, burying me, blacking out my last sight of her.

Five thirty-three A.M. and breaking glass.

Eyes open. Chest prickling with perspiration. Outside, charcoal morning: the backyard, the quince tree peeled bare, the fence open, and there, something else, light knifing across the grass, its origin a downstairs room, its origin the library. Someone was in the house, I knew who it was, he was here.

I reached for my bathrobe, took a poker from the fireplace, and crept downstairs. An icy draft led me to the back room, my old room, where I saw the leaded panel with the hunting scene smashed clean out. I reached down, touched one of the larger shards. The hunter's cap. Or was it the deerskin? I could not tell. Now they were indistinguishable, beauty become trash. I turned on my haunches, trembling with rage.

I expected him to jump up as I came into the library, but he sat there placidly, in the middle of the carpet, surrounded by crumpled paper, bent covers, loose ripped spines, looking like some deranged scholar. He had pulled down, and destroyed, the better part of a dozen shelves.

'Get up,' I said.

His hand moved beneath a splayed facedown book and came up holding Alma's pistol.

'No,' he said. 'You sit down.'

It is interesting how many calculations your brain performs in a moment like that. The distance to him; the distance to the door; the weight of the poker in my hand; the probability that the gun was loaded, multiplied by the probability that it still worked. The numbers clanked and whirred, but no solution came. I sat in one of the easy chairs.

'Put it on the floor.'

I put the poker down.

'Give it here.'

I did.

'Good,' he said. 'Now we can have a conversation.'

I said nothing.

'I can't find the checkbook.'

'I threw it out,' I said.

He frowned. 'Why'd you do that.'

'It's worthless,' I said. 'They're in her name.'

He stared at me. 'Why'd I come here, then.'

I didn't think that merited an answer.

'Well,' he said, 'that sucks.'

I said nothing.

'It's really cold out there, you know.'

I said nothing.

'Really cold,' he said again. 'She always liked it

to be like a freezer in here. I used to walk around in fifteen layers. Can you imagine? She didn't care, though.'

I said nothing.

'I know it was for her thing and blah blah. But a little human decency, you know? That's the problem with people like you.'

I said nothing.

He said, 'Take off your clothes.'

I did not move.

He pointed the gun at my chest.

I stood up and removed my robe.

Silence.

He was waiting for me.

I took off my pajama bottoms.

'You're not done yet.'

I stood naked before him.

'Are you cold?'

I said nothing.

He looked at my genitals. 'You look cold.' He laughed. 'Sit down.'

'You can have the jewelry,' I said.

'And you can go fuck yourself,' he said.

Silence.

I sat. Against my skin the upholstery felt like sand.

'So, come on. Let's talk about something.'

Silence.

I said, 'What do you want to talk about?'

'Oh, I don't know. Let's see.' He thought. 'Okay. How bout this. Did you ever think about her when you jacked off?'

I said nothing.

'Did you?'

'You're disgusting.'

He laughed.

'You were an embarrassment to her,' I said.

'Maybe,' he said.

'You're a failure.'

'Maybe. But I don't know, man. I mean, look at us. Which one of us would you say is the failure?'

I said nothing.

'Say, "You're right, Eric."'

I said nothing.

'Say it.'

'You're right.'

'"You're right, Eric."'

'You're right, Eric.'

'"You're right, sir."'

'You're right, sir.'

'Say, "I'm a piece of shit."'

'. . . I'm a piece of shit.'

'Louder, please.'

'I'm a piece of shit.'

'Say, "I'm a douchebag."'

'I'm a douchebag.'

'"Who thinks about dead old women when he jacks off."'

I said nothing.

'Aw, you were doing so well.'

I said nothing, and he came at me and jammed the barrel of the gun under my chin, causing me to gag.

'*Speak.*'

I could not. He pushed and I gagged again, and he smiled and as he did his head went back a few degrees, like Alma's used to do when she was tickled by something, and I felt the gun loosen and my body rose up out of the chair and I crashed down on top of him, naked and burning and slick with sweat, I the bigger man, twice his size, he seemed to disappear beneath me, spraying hot spittle and his arms against my chest like power lines snapped and writhing in the road. Click I heard, click click click like a broken type-writer. He had miscalculated and so instead he slammed it, the gun, he slammed it twice and twice more against the side of my head and the world sucked out like the retreating tide and foamed in like the advancing tide and he broke atop of me, beating me about the face as I groped for the poker, my fingers closing around paper, crushing it by the handful and came the butt of the gun hard against my spine, a hollow sound of metal on skin on bone. He was going to kill me. I recognized this. My brain said it. It said *He is going to kill you.* Then it added *unless you get up.* I got up. He was swinging wildly at me then, and it is in part due to his imprecision that I was able to make it to my feet, skating blurrily away from him through the pile of books, sliding through torn paper. He ran at me. I reached out with my long country boy's limbs and took him by the arm and used his own momentum to swing him toward the

285

mantel. He was so thin and light that I imagined (for it must have been my imagination, it could not have really happened) that his feet left the ground and for an instant he became a graceful thing, a thing in flight. His head came whipping round after his body and cracked against the plaster and I released him, he wobbled on his feet, he looked drunk like we had both been that night in the bar, the two of us together. We had nothing in common. We really could not be more different I thought as I took hold of the nearest object which was the half-head of Nietzsche.

You're probably seen Nietzsche before. If you haven't, let me describe him for you. The only part of him that matters, of course, is his moustache, which in early photos looks like a standard nineteenth-century version of a moustache, cigar-thick and smoke-black and vaguely pubic. A normal person might have stopped there, tending and grooming and restricting it to within the bounds of convention, but Nietzsche was of course anything but normal, and so he continued to let the moustache go and by middle age it had begun to turn up at the ends like wings, or some kind of alien punctuation mark. Everyone claims to understand Nietzsche but few do. I have always thought that one could correlate the loosening of his mind with the growth of his moustache. A good subject for a paper, not for a philosopher perhaps but for an intellectual historian with a sense of humor. Nietzsche had a mental collapse at the age of forty-five, no one knows exactly what brought it on but legend has it that he saw a man whipping a horse and lost his mind. This story is almost certainly apocryphal. He spent the last eleven years of his life confined to an institution. In the final two years he did not speak at all. During that time the moustache – by then a fearsome thing – took over his face completely, and we may choose to regard it (unruly, impenetrable) as the most precise expression of his lattermost thoughts. It's something to behold, Nietzsche's moustache, and one renders it in iron as a half a mushroom cap. Halved, this half-cap becomes a quarter cap, sharp at the end, like a tomahawk. Eric said nothing when I hit him with it. There was an eggshell sound and then he fell down. I thought of him threatening Alma and threatening me and maligning me and sickening her and barging into my house and interfering with my life and making me feel scared and breaking my window and taking away my words and replacing them with his own which were stupid and foul and unintelligent; correction: I didn't think these things but I saw them swarming before me and I swung at them to clear the air, I cleared my mind of twenty years. There was no need for words. He had long stopped making any noise at all and so had his skull, which was soft and forgiving when I struck it one more time.

CHAPTER 21

You could claim self-defense but look. Look at the carpet, the floor around the fireplace. Look at the books. You need not look at the thing itself, inert; at the face no longer a face; greasy hair dripping at the ends. You need not see them to know what has taken place here. The room itself tells the story. Look at what has taken place – the vivid, tribal slashes of color – the way your hands tremble: in horror, yes, but also in exultation – and you can see it as well as anyone. You had all the reason in the world to do as you did. And so ask yourself, ask: who will believe you?

What became of you in those moments amazes you. You call yourself a thinker, but for a brief time you were altogether physical, your strength and fury as shocking as they were manifest. Having read widely, you know in a physiological sense what took place: the glands that contracted and the hormones that spurted and the twittering neural circuitry governing fight/flight; know, in the abstract, of analogous cultural phenomena, Norse berserkers and Bacchic revelry and Aztec orgies of violence and Pentecostal glossolalia to cite but a few examples of spiritual madness whose practitioners claim to be privy in their frenzy to flashes of godliness and superhumanity, phenomena well documented and thoroughly dissected in the annals of sociology, psychology, history, archaeology, anthropology, and the comparative study of religion, reams of serious-minded scholarly prose demonstrating when and why and how people excite themselves into such a state, and moreover drawing inferences for the broader implications of such behavior vis-à-vis human nature, nurture, culture, et al. You've read. You have mapped these ideas on paper but never in three dimensions; and now that you have, you are entirely present, brimming with sensation, so awake and alert and sensitive to reality that it's excruciating just to stand there, alive. The yellow of the lamps is the yellowest imaginable. The air tangy and viscous like seawater. Your belly roars with a hunger akin to sexual ecstasy. You are present; you have acted. Who will believe you, when you do not believe it yourself?

Torn open all over, you feel no pain. Gather your clothes, an old molted skin. Books are everywhere, everywhere destroyed. He has done this. You turn toward him in hatred and see again what has become of him, the gray crater staring eyeless at the fireplace, and your stomach kicks and you rush to the toilet jackknifed just in time. When it is over the silence fills up with a high-pitched whine

289

that drives your head between your knees, and you remain there a long time, first deciding what needs to be done and then girding yourself to do it and you stand wiping thick slime from your upper lip and when the water stops running you hear it: a mournful gypsy melody, a song of love and death. She is on time, as usual, headed for the library, where she now begins her workday, on your orders, so as not to wake you up upstairs.

Step into the hallway and through the open door see: the heaving bosom and the birthmark and the drab denim skirt and the permanently soiled apron and the blouse cut far too low for a woman her age. In her hair a comb, plastic colored to look like tortoiseshell. She is framed by the breaking day, a light with thickness and texture and unique refractive properties, making her appear as though set in glass, suspended like a trinket inside a paperweight, staring at the floor and the mess you've made, she's never seen such a mess in her life. From her cowy mouth comes an unearthly sound, starting low and ascending smoothly until it hits a certain pitch and begins, to hitch, hitch, hitch like a chuffing piston, hovering in a weird vocalic triangle between *u* and *o* and *e*, approximating what would technically be called the open-mid central rounded vowel, a term you know because you have taken several courses in linguistics. *Ueoww*, waving her fat hands in front of her fat stupid face. *Ueohh ueohh ueooowww.* Though appalling, the noise serves a clear purpose, awakening you to what is happening now, in this instant, here, in this place.

You say her name.

She looks at you, and her face seems to push into itself. Hers is a consummate disgust. This is America. She thought you was nice man. She say you boss. But what are you now except a filthy streaked savage with a good vocabulary? And she won't stop making that noise. You say her name again and take a step toward her, and now she lets out an honest-to-goodness scream, an extended twelve-tone aria of pure terror. Before this you've never really understood what's meant by 'blood-curdling.' Because the sound she makes really does cause you to feel your insides congealing, and for a third time you say her name but she is not to be reasoned with, screaming as she comes jousting at you with the hook end of the poker. Back you go, tangling with her abandoned vacuum and landing hard on your tailbone, grabbing at her ankle as she rumbles past. It's eighteen long and short feet down the hall and all you need is for her to stop screaming long enough for you to explain, you chase her into the living room saying her name. The poker swings at you and you catch it with reflexes you didn't know you had and yank hard and she is near and your arm catches her around the waist spinning waltz-like and down you both go rolling around together on the living-room floor, along the way kneecapping one of two brass lamps. She smells like detergent and chamomile. What must this look like, you wonder. In a way, it must be quite funny. If only she'd be quiet. That's all you really need. What will the neighbors think? You can explain exactly what happened and why, but first she has to *shut up*. You pry the poker out of her hands and fling it away, trying to hold her shoulders so that you can look her in the eye and order her to calm down, but she isn't listening to you anymore, no sir, she's got her own agenda now and she won't quiet down long enough for you to get your point across, and when you put your hand over her mouth not to hurt her but to briefly stopper the noise driving you mad with fear, she bites your hand eye-wateringly hard, blunt nails scratching your face; for God's sake she's trying to claw out your eyes. What is wrong with her. This doesn't involve her, none of it does, and you don't need her to get involved, you just need her to stop screaming right now, it is a need larger than the sun. Grab her arms and pin them down and hang on to her like she is a steer. Her advantage is viciousness, she'll try anything, every dirty crafty trick in the book. Your advantage is size. This is something you have always had: mass. One knee on her chest and then the other and she is subdued, thrashing weakly, her heels kicking back against the floor. Listen to me. You are trying to explain, trying to win her over with words, listen to me, listen. Listen. But look at her now. She makes a face. Some part of you recognizes that you must be hurting her. Is it a decision or something that happens? Is it something you do or something that is done? Who is the agent; what is the verb? Because you aren't moving at all, you're staying right where you are, and her eyes grow large and you understand what is happening to her – or did you understand already, when you chose to remain there, in place, your knees bearing down, twin anvils on her fifty-year-old heart. She makes a noise like an iron releasing steam and her stare is all white and her head falls back, exposing her throat, and you stay there until you stand up and face the silence anew, an additional problem on your hands.

This, now?

It is absurd.

It cannot be real.

But here is a hand.

And here is another.

Whatever excuses you might have had before are gone now. The choice is binary.

Go on.

Or stop.

You are so afraid.

Look back and the past telescopes to this very moment; look forward and the future is clear. You are not ready to ask yourself questions. You will need to lay out context, to provide a theoretical framework; and that will have to wait, as the abstract now yields to the very concrete.

★ ★ ★

The strain of dragging her back to the library causes your back to seize up, and it is through sheer force of will that you manage to get her the rest of the way. You set her down on the carpet next to him, shaking out your limbs to loosen up.

Gather what you need. She has left the rest of her supplies in the entry hall. Bottle of ammonia, can of solvent. In the kitchen hang a sloshing bucket in the crook of your elbow. Tuck a mop under your arm. Peel off trash bags. Take sponges.

Aside from the books, the carpet has caught the worst of it. The stains have dried rapidly, forming lots of hard little specks and a few puck-sized patches, black fibers gummed together as though cauterized. Paper towels dissolve, useless. What you need is a good old-fashioned rag. You take off your robe. It stinks of exertion and fear and you dip its hem into the bucket, by now warm and scummy, afloat with all manner of unidentifiable black bits. The urge to vomit comes and goes. Your throat hurts from retching. Your solar plexus aches. Your eyes want to go to the faceless face, and to prevent this you look down, only down. Squeeze the excess out of the robe and back to work, scrubbing. It isn't really working, is it. You can't tell. Your vision is blurry, blink that away. It occurs to you that the stains may have gone all the way through to the floor. With trepidation you lift the corner and run your hand over the herringbone. Clean. Dry. Remember that this is a nice carpet, really nice, fine quality, the pile thick enough to absorb your sins. Lay the corner down and put your back into it.

Oh but the books. Many cannot be saved. You try to wipe them clean but of course that doesn't work; it has soaked through the old paper, passing deep into the text. Blotches on the frontispiece echo through the third chapter. To see this twists your heart up like a wire. Some you have read; others you have pledged to read. Still others you have never considered opening, and it is only now, when you must let them go, that you appreciate their worth. Bravely you reinsert pages, restore torn corners, fill the body bags.

The green silk looks unscathed, which is a good thing, because you doubt anything would ever come out of that; and damage to a few square inches would have necessitated removal of an entire panel, of which there are four, two on either side of the fireplace running from floor to ceiling and one covering the area above the mantel. You might have had to throw it all out and repaint.

The lamp that might or might not be a Tiffany is intact.

The bluejays cry *stop stop thief thief thief.*

You spend several minutes scrutinizing the easy chairs. The upholstery is dark enough that you might be able to get away with leaving them be. Better safe than sorry. You bend to pull up the cushions, catching, as you do, a glimpse of the face, not a face.

And again, on your knees, over the bucket. Some time later the feeling passes and you stand, exhausted and at the edge of yourself. Without looking at him, you drape a trash bag over his upper half.

You vacuum.

You carry everything to the service porch, empty the bucket into the large plastic basin sink, strip down, putting your ruined clothes in a trash bag.

Upstairs, you stand beneath the hot water. The runoff is pink. You rub yourself raw with a washcloth, turn the temperature up until the gashes in your flesh are bleached clean. Then you cut the water and stand in a column of steam, tingling with purpose, making plans.

Dry, anoint, and dress. Aside from the cuts to your body, which sting but are of no real concern, she has left her mark on your face, three jagged trenches dug deep into the flesh below your right eye. You reach for a box of bandages, then reconsider. Which is less conspicuous: the injury or the dressing? You wish you had some makeup. But whatever she kept in the vanity you have long thrown away. It's your vanity, isn't it, and what use does a grown man have for makeup? You never need anything until you need it. Isn't that the truth. You put the bandages on and go downstairs.

The situation calls for tea, which you make with two teabags and heaping spoonfuls of sugar plus the juice of an entire lemon. You make a list, check it several times. Today, you are setting out on a journey – you have already lost sight of the shore – and the fear of having not taken into account some undoing detail dogs you.

Go on.

Go.

Her keys are in the pocket of her apron.

To your surprise, the station wagon starts beautifully. You ease down the driveway. It has been a long time since you've been behind the wheel, any wheel, and Boston drivers are notoriously aggressive. A college friend who grew up around here told you once that he learned to parallel park by backing up until he hit the bumper of the car behind him. He called it 'kissing.' To him this was perfectly normal. You think about this now as you cruise the neighborhood in a widening spiral, looking for a parking spot that isn't metered, insanely tight, or restricted by permit. Maybe you ought to put the car in a pay lot. But that's no good: they'll have a record of you coming in and out. You can't have that. Keep looking until a mile away, you find a space that suits your needs. You read the signs and go, praying to a God you haven't believed in in years.

Your first stop is the ATM. There you withdraw several hundred dollars in cash. You don't feel too good about this; it is one of the many potential flaws in your plan, which is, of necessity, ad hoc. You try to avoid looking at the camera set behind the tiny one-way mirror, wondering then if avoiding the camera actually appears more suspicious than gazing directly at it or, better yet, trying to seem as though you haven't given any consideration at all to being caught on camera. To appear relaxed, you whistle. Do ATM cameras capture sound? The machine is taking forever, making an exasperated noise, as though it has to print the money from scratch, and suddenly you become aware of the bandages on your face. You can feel the glue holding them there. This should be impossible, because the bandages are static, and the only way you ought to be able to feel anything is if they were moving against your skin; but their weight is there, it's like a giant leech. You want to rip them off but of course you can't and it's hell, keeping still. Take your cash and your receipt and go, peeling off the bandages and casting them into the gutter, sickened by your own foolishness.

Next a hardware store. You buy a shovel. It costs twenty-four dollars and ninety-seven cents plus tax. You are tempted to buy other items as well but you have decided that the thing to do is spread your activity over a wide area. The cashier, a pretty girl named. Greta, says it looks like snow. You smile and nod but say nothing because you don't want to lodge in her memory. Then you worry that by not answering you will look like a creepy mute, thus lodging in her memory, so you say something to the effect of what a surprise. And though you did not intend to be funny she laughs in a distinctly flirtatious way. You follow her eyes with your eyes but she never glances in the direction of the gashes on your face and you feel better. Maybe you look more normal than you think. It might be that they are not as prominent as you

298

think; perhaps you are suffering from a distortion in self-perception, the kind that causes anorexics to see themselves as fat or teenagers to believe that the zit on their chin, no bigger than a period, has swallowed their entire head. Or maybe, though, she's simply being polite; after all, it's rude to stare. Maybe her eyes went straight there (seeking out imperfection, as eyes tend to do) before moving away as her social training kicked in; although if such a thing had occurred, and she *did* see the cuts, and this *had* given her pause, could she really be smiling and joking with you in such a perfectly casual way etc, all this emotional yoyoing being quite hard on your heart, which has to keep shifting gears. You pay and thank her and walk out.

You don't want to be seen carrying a shovel, which in urban Cambridge looks like a stage prop, so you go home, stopping along the way to purchase concealer. You leave the shovel in the library, then stand in the bathroom, dabbing makeup below your right eye. It stings as it goes on. It's not a professional job but it will do for now.

Near the cantina where you had your birthday party, there's a shop that specializes in travel books. It is hilariously comprehensive. The only time you actually purchased anything here was before your trip to Germany. The choice you faced then was paralyzing: all manner of guidebooks, designed for travelers of every cultural and socioeconomic stripe. Hip pseudonarratives for backpackers. Upscale guides to East Berlin couture. You went low-budget, buying one of a series written by local students and updated every year by a fresh round of unsuspecting field agents who vow never to do that again after a hostel in Croatia leaves them with what their pediatrician back home calls without a doubt the nastiest case of scabies he's ever seen. You know this because you used to teach these students and they used to tell you. You had frank and open relationships with them. You held your office hours in a café and always someone came, if not to ask questions, then to shoot the breeze. Sophomores had crushes. Your sections were coveted. For three years you TFed introductory logic, as well as Kant and the Enlightenment Ideal; once you applied to teach a seminar on indecision. That was the title you proposed: On Indecisiveness. Your so called advisor turned you down, proposing that what you really wanted to do was work out your own hang-ups in front of a captive audience. Maps of New England shingle a wire rack. You find one that unfolds to the size of a picnic table, detailing roads all the way to the Canadian border. You pay your thirteen ninety-five plus tax and yes, please, a bag would be good.

The office-supply store sells three-cubic-foot cardboard boxes for two twenty-nine apiece plus tax. You estimate the station wagon's cargo area and settle on six. They're an ordeal to carry, six flattened boxes along with a roll of clear packing tape and a black permanent market. The only way to do it is to pin the boxes to your flanks as you walk, taking short, shuffling steps so as not to lose your grip on the slippery cardboard, the surface of which seems to have been finished with a kind of wax. It takes you a while to get home. Plus you've got the map (in a high-quality paper bag with twisted paper handles and the artfully weathered logo of the store imprinted on the side) to contend with. All the cash transactions have left your pockets swinging heavily with change. You arrive home winded, your mood black. But you must go on.

Catch the bus across the river, where you enter a store that sells camping equipment. Along the back wall is a supernumerary array of hiking boots. A lanky boy comes over to dispense wisdom. Hardcore, he says when you tell him you're taking a winter backpacking trip. He sells you your third pair of new footgear this year, as well as down-filled nylon pants and high-tech gloves and a parka and a rugged backpack and a box of plastic packets that produce heat when twisted. They go inside your gloves, he explains.

The total comes to about thirteen hundred dollars. You hand him your credit card but it comes back. You have exceeded your limit. You exceeded it when you bought new shirts and new pants and cufflinks and a ruby pendant, and so you ask the boy to hold your purchases and go off in search of another ATM.

The first one you come across doesn't allow you

to take out more than five hundred dollars at a time. All right, then, you'll do it three times. Again the machine stops you in your tracks: you have reached your limit for the day. You tingle unpleasantly. Does 'limit for the day' mean the calendar day, meaning midnight, or a twenty-four-hour period, in which case you're going to have to wait until morning? Either way, you can't wait that long. You're going to have to make an unscheduled stop at the bank.

The lady behind the desk at a nail salon directs you to a branch five blocks away. You hightail it there and get into what feels like a conga line at an old-age home. Only one window is open. You hold back bleats of impatience and when you finally do make it up to the window, the teller asks if you want that as a cashier's check and you say cash, please, twenties. This causes her to stare at you in a harrowing way, and you wonder if she's going to call the police or hit the button for the silent alarm. Then you realize that she's annoyed at having to count it all out. Which is highly inappropriate: they're a bank, giving out money is their job. If you were of a different state of mind and less pressed for time, you'd ask to see the manager.

Back at the camping store, the boy has got everything all packed up and ready to go, which seems to you a remarkable act of faith on his part. You tell him that upon further consideration, you don't need those hand warmers after all. They work great, he says. You're sure they do, but no, thanks.

He shrugs and fishes them from the bottom of the bag, saving you sixteen dollars and ninety cents. Every little bit counts. When you lay out the stack of bills, he goggles.

Near the building where you lived briefly with nymphomaniacs is a purveyor of cheap housewares. The salesman encourages you to go for something heavier than the lightweight duvets you have chosen. They won't really keep a body warm, he says. That's all right, you say.

Your final errand run takes you to a second drugstore. You fill a basket with the following: lighter fluid, matches, a box of latex exam gloves, ten rolls of duct tape, trash bags, a jumbo package of baby wipes, and a large bottle of double-caffeinated soda. For appearances' sake, you have also thrown in a fishing magazine. The total comes to sixty-one eighty-five plus tax. You'd like to pay with some of your abundant loose change but that's not a way to remain inconspicuous, making people count nickels.

Outside, it has begun to snow, big flakes like nonpareils.

At home you stand in the entry hall, brushing yourself off. You close your eyes and dream up contingencies. The vanity of this soon dawns on you: there are an infinite number of them. You could make them up all day long. You might as well accept that something could go wrong, because if you're not willing to accept that, then you're not really willing to go on. And you must go on. It is four o'clock in the afternoon. You go upstairs and close the blinds and set your alarm for seven P.M. You lie down fully clothed and fall into a dreamless sleep.

Wake ravenous. You haven't eaten since breakfast, and that was tea. Now you go down to the kitchen and eat everything you can find. You make a fresh cup of tea, fortifying yourself for what comes next.

The air in the library has grown fetid. (Is this possible? Does it happen so fast?) Begin by taking everything out of their pockets. He has a single house key and a bent promotional postcard for a rock band and a state ID with an address in Quincy and a parole card and a phone and a small amount of cash. Her cellular phone is lipstick-red and chipped. You set it aside, adding her thirty-one dollars to his sixteen, folding the bills into your back pocket. Every little bit counts. Her wallet contains coupons, a driver's license, a library card, which last amazes you. Unduly: for why should she not read? (Because you cannot allow yourself to conceive of her as anything other than an object.) She lives, lived, in Roxbury. You never knew. You will yourself to unknow it.

Her skirt peels up as you drag her out of the way. Thighs the color of suet, convenience-store briefs, a sparse gray fringe protruding. Once she's moved, you make her decent again.

You spread out one of the duvets. Being thinner, he moves more easily, although in the process the

304

trash bag slips off, exposing what you still cannot bear to see; and you have a moment where you can't go on. But you must. You position him parallel to the short end of the duvet, roughly four-fifths of the way down its length. Crouch down, head averted and mouth tightly shut, and fold over the edge of the duvet, covering him. Roll him over. It's difficult. He is noncompliant, dead weight ha ha ha. The smell is impossible to describe, don't even try. Curse yourself for having forgotten to purchase a surgical mask. You're going to need another shower by the time this is done. Over and over he goes, on a bias, so that instead of a neat, even burrito you've formed a kind of cone. Back up and start again. And once more. There. That ought to do.

Now you duct tape like it's going out of style, resulting in something that resembles a silver cocoon or, more accurately, a chrysalis.

You unpack the second duvet and repeat the process with her.

She is noticeably larger. The lack of symmetry bothers you. Nevertheless you regard your chrysalises as things of beauty. A vision comes to you: they erupt, two new creatures formed from the soup of what used to be him and what used to be her, winged, magnificent, ethereal, flapping off into the sky, taking your troubles away.

While you linger in this fantasy, her phone goes off with a mighty blast of trumpets. Scrape yourself off the ceiling and look at the screen: andrei.

Her husband? Son? Pimp? Who knows. You wait until it stops ringing, then check the missed calls.

There are six.

This concerns you. Has she mentioned the name of the man who pays her sixty dollars to clean house? (Does she even know your name?) Does she keep her schedule written down? In an accessible place? As you cannot answer the questions, nor hope to alter the actualities underlying those answers, you set them aside and concentrate on what you can control. You turn their phones off.

Ten thirty-two P.M., and you're behind schedule. It's a good thing you slept three hours instead of four or five. You've needed the extra time. Constant activity has prevented you from confronting what you have done; nor have you given much consideration to the alternative, which now stands before you as you go to the kitchen to start assembling cardboard boxes: the phone. Look at it. It is still possible to pick it up and dial. But is it? No. Not anymore. Or perhaps they would understand, if you explained to them the expression on his face, the pressure of the gun against your throat. The gun wasn't loaded, but he could have jumped you from behind and strangled you or – or – or what about this: he could have hit *you* with the bookend. Or the poker. Anything was possible, and you can talk, you have always been able to talk; pick up the phone; it would be so easy, wouldn't it; would obviate all this effort, free you of so many burdens. If you do not, your night has only just begun.

Go on.

Two by two you carry the assembled boxes to the library, where you fill each with ruined books, not all the way to the top but enough so that they won't go flying everywhere or feel unnaturally light, should anyone want to pick them up – not that that will happen. Why would it? You must believe it won't. Sealing the boxes with packing tape, you label each one either BOOKS LIVING ROOM or BOOKS MASTER BEDROOM.

You jog through the streets, through the gentle snow.

Her car is right where you left it and your heart stops: a parking ticket. How is that possible? You checked the signs. *You read for content*. Then you see that it isn't a ticket but a leaflet advertising a two-for-one tapas brunch. Angrily you tear it into bits, resolving to never, ever eat at that restaurant.

For someone who cleans for a living, her car is a hellacious mess. Standing beneath a gas station over-hang, surrounded by curtains of snow, you rid it of everything belonging to her: unopened soda cans, smeared newspapers. A bit of jiggering gets the second row of seats down, leaving the cargo area empty and flat. You pay for your gas and ask for two tree-shaped air fresheners, both in Royal Pine.

Despite your bang-up mummification job, the stench in the library seems to have worsened. You gag as you crouch down beside her. Slip your hands under her. It's hard to get purchase, because the tape is so taut and smooth. It's your own fault for being thorough. What you need is a handle; and so you use duct tape to fashion one, drawing inspiration from the bookstore bag's twisted paper handles. Gingerly you raise her up – she bends a little, but less than you expected – and give her a test jounce. Solid.

Go.

Deep breath and open the library door and drag her down the hall and into the living room and down the hall again and across the kitchen and into the service porch, the linoleum helping you along, outside and thudding down the frosted wooden steps and drop her in the snow with a powdery *whup*. Butterfingered, you fumble out the keys to the station wagon and raise the rear hatch. Sit on the bumper, then bend over and pick up the handle and row backward, scooting yourself into the cargo area with your neck and body bent over sideways, you're too damned tall but you do it, you get her mostly up, and when she is half in and stable, you climb carefully out the passenger door and hurry around to the back and push her the rest of the way in. You would never have guessed how awkward this is. She won't move like you want her to; she is heavy and stiff. You lower the hatch without closing it and go back for round two.

With him everything's chugalugging along dandily until you get to the top of the exterior steps and the handle rips loose and you go tail over tea-kettle into the snow. There's no time to fix it; scramble back up and pull him bodily until he's on the ground, then squat down and slip your arms underneath him and the cold burns and your lower back yodels and you get up, staggering around. The hatch is closed. Why couldn't you have *left it up*. And so you have to drop him again. When the hatch is open, you squat and lift again, ignoring the pain. You get him in semi-straight but this isn't the time to be concerned about aesthetics; you're out there in the open and you glance at the windows of the neighboring house, miraculously still unlit. Run back to the library and grab the third duvet. It hides them both with room to spare, although to your eye it's more than obvious what's underneath. To solve this problem you go back into the house and collect the pillows from the downstairs bedroom. They do nicely to fill in the gaps, smoothing the two lumps into a solid mass, sort of like an air mattress. Why you would be transporting an air mattress, you have no idea. If pressed, you would use the excuse that you needed padding to cushion the boxes of books that you intend to put on top of them, or else the boxes would bounce around, damaging their contents. In your head you practice delivering this explanation.

The first box fits, though you have to wedge it in, and you realize that if you fill up the entire cargo area, you'll have obstructed your rearview mirror. Under normal circumstances that's bad enough; in this case, it might be a fatal error. Recalibrating feverishly, you go inside and collect all the plastic bags from your long day of shopping. Indian-style on the kitchen floor, you use a chef's knife to slice open all your nice, neat boxes, transferring the ruined books from the boxes to the bags, tying the bag handles twice so the contents won't spill out. You use up all nineteen bags – exclusive of the paper bag from the bookstore, which still holds the map – and take them outside to place them atop the duvet. Now you're talking. Now it looks like an amateur moving job, the exact impression you're shooting for. You give yourself a mental high-five.

You're still going to have to do something about the ruined carpet.

But not right now. The stove clock says one ten in the morning. You shower again, don your new cold-weather gear, and pack your (her) duffel with a change of clothes, including one pair of new shoes still in their soft drawstring bag.

The shovel. The bag with the map, to which you add their phones and both sets of identification. Lighter fluid and matches. Trash bags. Backpack. Soda. Fishing magazine. (Why not?) A flashlight. The knife, seems like a good idea. Put on your eleventh pair of latex gloves for the day and load up the car. The wind throws down snow from the branches. You zip up your parka. The shovel goes under the edge of the duvet, the garbage in back, everything else on the floor in front of the passenger seat. Road trip ready, you get behind the wheel and head north.

★ ★ ★

Early on you glance at the speedometer and are surprised to see the needle touching eighty. This is idiotic, given the road conditions. Not to mention the danger of getting pulled over. So you police yourself (hahaha) closely, with the result that the trip drags. Radio stations surface, then sink, all holiday favorites. A cassette sticks halfway out of the tape deck. With some hesitation you push it in, but what pours from the speakers stands your hair on end, a tune you've heard her singing before. You eject the tape and throw it out the window. You will have to live with silence. You've done it enough.

The rubbery beat of the windshield wipers.

Tiny explosions of snow.

It seems that the air fresheners are making the stench worse, calling attention to what they are intended to conceal. You toss them out, too. But you can't drive with the smell building up like that, so you lower one of the rear windows an inch. Cold air rushes in behind you, a noise like a pursuing tornado. It keeps you alert, and the smell dwindles to a tolerable level.

At least the car has four-wheel drive – something you didn't think about in advance. Luck or fate has saved you there.

I-95 runs all the way to New Brunswick, but you don't go nearly that far, stopping north of Portland for food and fuel. The gas station is strung with tinsel. In the bathroom you remove the battery from his cell phone, dropping the phone itself in the trash. The battery you pocket.

The clerk wears a floppy Santa hat and a look of existential despair. You buy another green soda. So much caffeine must be unhealthy. It sure feels bad. Try not to look jittery as you take out more twenties. Gas alone will cost you several hundred dollars over the course of this trip, and it occurs to you that criminals, just like everyone else, must be feeling the recent increases at the pump. Everybody hurts during tough times, even the wicked. You almost giggle, right there in the middle of the mini-mart, to imagine mafiosi complaining of shrinking profit margins.

Before leaving town, you place the trash bags in an alley.

Alone on the road, with nothing to do but stare into the surging snow, you bury or shed or at least suspend the klaxon thought that you, too, are among the wicked.

For a while you hug the shoreline, running a string of quaint towns whose wreathed wooden homes evoke visions of ruddy-faced lobstermen and plump, jolly wives, everyone gathered round the fire, glugging eggnog, swapping presents, intoxicated with good cheer. Turning inland, you pass a sign for Kennebec County, population 117, 114. In the last two hours you've seen three other cars, all going in the opposite direction. You toss his cell phone battery clattering onto the blacktop.

North again, a narrow road unspooling through the forest. The sun has started to send up shoots; iced-over ponds glimmer. That's okay.

You anticipated this. Your goal is a location remote enough that you won't have to worry about operating in broad daylight. Consulting the map, another westward turn. The forest closes around you like a hand. Stop the car and get out and stand on the shoulder, playing the flashlight through the trees, your breath rising in great white balloons.

The snow is deep and inviting.

You should have sprung for the hand warmers.

Strap the shovel to your new backpack, tighten the laces on your boots. Put the high-tech gloves over your latex gloves. Open the hatch and push aside the books.

You have your doubts about the strength of her handle. On the fly, you decide to use the duvet as a kind of stretcher or sling by which to drag her.

This idea fails, spectacularly. After crashing down the embankment (much steeper than it looked; plus you land awkwardly on the shovel handle) you have to spend time digging her out and repositioning her. Even then, she won't keep straight. The duvet grows heavy, starts to tear. This will never work. You overestimated yourself. You scramble up the embankment with the ruined duvet and exchange it for the knife.

She has sunk into the powder. You kneel beside her, cutting slits in the tape wide enough to work your gloved fingers into. Lean back and pull and walk backward. She comes. Slowly, but she comes.

Okay. Good. Now we're getting somewhere. Your fingers hurt and your back hurts, but you are moving, and that's enough to power you on through the trees, smearing a trail that anyone could follow. Fifty feet. Your nylon pants make a swishing sound. A hundred feet. Owls low. Hundred fifty. Complexly woven branches render the sky a vast gray rosace. Smell the evergreens, dense stands of eastern white pine. Much better than your air fresheners. You wish you could chop down one of these tall soldiers and hang him from the rearview mirror. There's less snow on the ground now, most of it clumped in needles over-head, like cotton bolls. Brown needles on the ground. Patches of ice; you slip and right yourself and pull on. Swish swish. Two hundred feet. That's what they call Maine, isn't it? 'The Pine Tree State.' Your fifth-grade teacher Mrs Yawkey made your social studies class memorize the state capitals and flowers and so forth. To keep your mind off the difficulty of the task at hand, you run through nick-names. Massachusetts: the Bay State. Vermont: the Green Mountain State. Swish swish. Three hundred feet; four. The only state without 'state' in its nickname is New Mexico: Land of Enchant-ment. Focus on warm places. Florida: the Sunshine State. California: the Golden State. Hawaii: the Aloha State. Five. After Arizona: the Grand Canyon State, you set her down and catch your breath (it comes sharp and clean and electric), unstrap your shovel, and bend to dig.

Except you can't. The earth is frozen. You strike at what feels like solid rock, and for the first time all day and night and day, frustration wells up to the point where you cannot contain it. With an animal howl you slam the shovel into the ground, the mud cracking into poker chips. You do this again and again, but nothing. It would take hours to clear even a few feet. What you need is a pickax, and since you don't have one, you're going to have to leave her here or else bring her all the way back through the forest, back through the snow, back up the embankment, the thought of which makes you want to surrender. You cast about for salvation and it comes, literally, in a ray of light: there: a hollow log. Go to it. You test it by getting down and crawling halfway in. Yes, it will work. You drag her to it, then cut off the duct tape, heeding the (unsubstantiated but intuitive) notion that she will decay faster this way. You unroll the duvet and out she comes, not reshaped and winged but the same as before, perhaps a little grayer.

You're well past the urge to vomit but slipping your arms under her armpits does give you a bad moment. You wrestle her toward the log, smelling the deadness on her, feeling her clay through your gloves. On second thought you might not be totally done with vomiting yet. You get her head inside and then push her by her legs, bit by bit, her knees bending rustily, so slowly it's going, so slow until at last you get her in up to her waist and that's enough, enough already, *enough*, piling bark and twigs and pinecones and rocks and snow over the rest of her and pray that some scavenger gets to her soon, run.

Run, hobbled, sinking, wanting nothing but to get away from her. Ice in your socks and down your sleeves to your armpits cold and shocking but still you run, run, claw your way up the embankment and fall in the car seizing with terror and cold, calm down. You're fine. Calm down. You're hot, is what you are. Your fingers disobey you as you try to unzip your jacket, which is covered in dirt that might be from the ground or might be from someplace on her, you smell like her deadness. She is clinging to you, you must take off your jacket. Get it off. Get it off. Calm down. Your T-shirt is soaked. You can hardly see the road. The windshield is fogged. You cannot see. Calm down. Calm down. Look at the clock. Look. It's seven in the morning. You've a whole lot left to do. Calm down. Calm down. Calm down and start the car. Start the car. Go on, start the car. Do it. Do it now, do it right now. Start the car. Drive. Go. Move.

Move.

Ninety miles short of the Canadian border, a sign for a diner appears. Semis crowd the lot. Despite making what you assume to be a grubby impression, you don't draw more than casual glances upon entry. Looking around at the clientele, you can see why: it's all mountain men and long-haul truckers. Other than waitstaff, there is a single woman – fairly robust, as far as women go – eating alone at the counter, her tensed shoulders indicating an awareness that around here, she is not much more than Something to Look At. You're the only one in the place without facial hair. Has anyone else here read the complete works of Plato? With confidence, you claim that title for yourself.

The menu is in English and French. You order, then open the fishing magazine on the table in front of you, reading up on the Seven Secrets to Steelhead Success as you sip your coffee. You eat eggs and bacon and toast, and drink yet more coffee, finally rising to move your bowels in a filthy, frigid stall. On the way out of the bathroom you drop her cell phone in the trash, taking the battery with you.

A landscape flat, windless, and lunar. The sun low on the horizon. The road badly paved, icy, running northwest-southeast; as far as you can tell, it's not even on the map. To the south, a frozen meadow; beyond it, the undulant treeline.

The snow covering the meadow has turned to ice, a mixed blessing. On the one hand, he slides. On the other hand so do you, your feet skittering Chaplinesquely. Dig your heels in. What good are these boots? You need crampons. Oversight. Keep going. You pull. The station wagon starts to shrink in the distance. How far have you gone? Not far enough. The hard part is almost over. You should be fine. You will be fine. Go on. Move. Put your back into it. Swish swish go your pants, a steady 4/4. You've been working on the railroad, all the live-long day. You've been working on the railroad, just to pass the time away. Who would work on a railroad just to pass the time away? What kind of hobby is railroad work? It's not like needlepoint or tennis, something you pick up out of boredom. Countless people died laying the first Transcontinental Railroad, many of them imported Chinese laborers, done in by brutal winters or accidental explosions. It's no laughing matter. All those old songs make no sense. Why should you care if Jimmy crack corn? Why should anyone? Keep going. You once audited a course about folk songs and their relation to the unconscious. It's taught by some imbecile. You should have gone to law school. The trees are close now. Keep pulling. The slits in the tape widen; pull any harder and they risk splitting open. Slow and steady wins the race. That's nonsense, too, isn't it? Just like the notion that cheaters never prosper. If this isn't prosperity, you don't know what is. Hahahahaha. Twenty-four hours ago he wasn't this heavy. Your fingers are blistered. The tendons in the back of your hands are ready to snap. Nobody can endure what you're enduring. You are the overman. You think of Nietzsche and his injunction to remake the world in one's own image. You think of his moustache. He would have fit right in back at that diner, hahaha. Keep going. Swish swish. Davyyyyyyy, Davy Crockett. King of the wild frontier.

Once you reach the trees you keep walking backward until the light changes and changes again and you look up and see that you have come to a clearing. Above you the treetops rise like a crown, like the walls of a bottomless pit. You have seen this place before. You have seen it in your dreams, seen it painted on a piece of glass. It is unconcealed to you, now, aletheia. Look around and wonder.

Where is the deer?

Where is the hunter?

Which one are you?

You set him on fire.

Smoke rises through the trees.

Your relief is instantaneous. The pilgrimage is done, the offering elevated, and you would strip naked and run through the snow singing hymns.

But it's never as simple as that, is it?

Because he burns for a few minutes and then, in an instant, he goes out.

The aroma is of grossly overdone pork, and you hold your breath as you douse him once again in lighter fluid. To speed the process you add handfuls of dry branches and leaves. You drop a match and away he goes.

This time he burns a little longer before going out.

The third try uses up the rest of the can and goes for fifteen minutes. You consider abandoning him there and then you hear a sound of approaching.

No point in running. You take down the shovel

and grip it, waiting. Whoever it is, he or she has erred in deciding to walk in the woods this afternoon. Silence. Silence. And you move in a semicircle around the source of the noise, bringing into view, one hundred feet away, a lone, malnourished wolf.

He grins shaggily at you.

Hello, he says.

You take the crumpled duvet and back away. In the distance you see him slink out of the underbrush and crawl toward the smoking pile, sniffing interestedly at the remains.

And in the silence that follows? You are alone in the darkness and snow. And in that silence? When all that remains is nine hours of road and white noise? You do what you have successfully avoided doing until now: you think. Your thoughts have been held back long enough; they're not waiting any longer. They're impatient and want to come in, they'll take the door off the hinges. Think about his staved skull. Think about her death song. Think about what you automatically did – the way you knew what to do. Who are you? It is you who have metamorphosed, you who have burst from the chrysalis. And if that is the case – if today a process reached its apex – then it must be true that that process began some time ago.

Halfway home you stop at a fast-food restaurant. Your clothes reek of smoke, with a base note of burnt hair. People stare. You rush through your sandwich, then put her cell phone battery in the trash along with your untouched fries.

Near the state line you pull into a rest stop. A concrete arcade shelters four vending machines. You go around back, where the ground is littered with wrappers and cans, and throw the shovel as far as you can into the black.

At eleven-thirty p.m. you pull into the parking lot of a mall in Candia, New Hampshire, a suburb of Manchester. You drive around until you find what you're looking for: a loading dock with several Dumpsters. A sign forbids un- authorized persons from dumping trash. Violators will be prosecuted. You lift the lid on one of the Dumpsters and pour in the contents of all nineteen bags of books, wadding up the empty bags and putting them, along with the duvets, in the adjacent Dumpster.

At one-fifteen a.m. you arrive in Roxbury, parking in an alleyway about a mile from her home. Normally you'd be nervous – this is one of the most dangerous neighborhoods in Boston – but tonight you feel dreamily impervious. You take out the duffel with clean clothes and everything else that belongs to you, which at this point fits into the back-pack. You swab the interior of the car with baby wipes. It takes a while, but it's better

321

than thinking. You restore the second row of seats and lock the keys inside the car.

A quarter-mile away you find a gas station with an exterior bathroom. You change out of your smoke-scented clothing, stuffing it into the duffel. You take the duffel and the backpack and walk out with them, wandering up a residential street where people have set their trash out for collection. Drop the duffel in a can at the end of the block. Go another few streets and do the same to the backpack. Pat yourself down. All you have on you are your house keys, your wallet, and the high-tech gloves. Take them off. Take off the latex gloves underneath. Throw these away, one at a time, while walking north, toward the river, toward the bridge. There are no cabs. The T has stopped running. Walk three and a half miles to Cambridge. It's four-thirty A.M. Step up your front porch. The neighborhood is quiet. Windows are dark. You've been awake for almost forty-eight hours, not counting your nap. Go inside. Shut the door. Welcome home.

CHAPTER 22

I woke the next morning with something akin to a hangover, which is understandable, given that both alcohol and caffeine cause dehydration, and the enormous quantity of the latter I'd ingested had made it difficult for me to fall asleep, even after the most exhausting two days of my life. What sleep I had gotten had been patchy and ruined by nightmares. In some of these I was doing the same things I had just done: driving in the darkness, or walking through thigh-deep snow. For the most part, though, the dreams didn't describe any particularly upsetting activity. Nor did they possess any definite narrative shape. They consisted, rather, of static images, or brief sequences in which no other living thing appeared – soundless, fractured dreams, at once ordinary and menacing. I stood in a classroom filled with dozens of unoccupied desks. A foul wind stirred. Stacks of paper whirled around me, and I could not see, and when my vision cleared I stood at my high-school locker, looking at the photos taped to the inside of the door. I had the distinct sensation of being late for class, but before I went anywhere I wanted to see these photos.

I couldn't: they were too blurry. I kept squinting harder and leaning closer, all the while knowing that I was wasting time, making myself even later, and I began to flail about and I was then transformed; I was an infant, squirming against the cold linoleum, naked, silently shrieking, beetred, my toothless mouth a wet open hole, and I woke myself with my own very much audible cries, arched, panting, the sheets pulled off at the corners and my pillow skinned, mind sodden with dread – a feeling that persisted much longer than such feelings tend to, every surface filmed with unreality. To reground myself, I tried getting up and walking around, forcing myself to focus on the solidity of the floor beneath my bare feet, but I got dizzy, ending up huddled under a blanket at the foot of the bed, rocking myself as I counted down to daylight.

My first look at the library was sobering: long smears of blood were still visible around the mantel. Bare shelves told of the missing books. Several of the photos hung askew, and one had been cracked clean up the middle. To my eye the carpet presented the biggest challenge, given that I no longer had a car. I took down the cracked photo (Alma and her sister on the beach), my unease redoubling by the second. Had I really been this sloppy? While away, I'd told myself that if someone should happen to enter the library, he would see – at worst – the remains of a raucous party. If I'd been so blind as to miss what was right in front of my face, what other, less noticeable, problems had I ignored? How

324

many details neglected? The air stank of death, and I wanted to go back to bed. That was, I thought, the only answer: to sleep, to keep on sleeping until I woke up and found myself in another land, a hundred years hence. There was simply too much to worry about, disaster hovering over me in perpetuity, and all at once I saw, with a kind of prophecy, what I would soon come to appreciate firsthand: that life as I knew it was over, and that as long as I was conscious, I would have no peace.

Opening the window helped dissipate the smell, and I appreciated the bracing cold as I gathered a new arsenal of cleaning supplies. I cut up several of Alma's old bath towels, and got down to scrubbing, going over the exposed wood in tight circles, sweat collecting at my hairline and following the bridge of my nose to dangle itchily at the tip before falling free and splattering below. Every time I thought I had eliminated one of the bloodstains I would bring my face down close and squint and see it still there, a ghostly pink watermark or thin crimson stripes outlining the junctions between the floorboards, hardly visible to the naked eye but in my mind bold as neon. Would I have to refinish the flooring? Rip it up? A chilling image came to me – blood, acid-like, eating its way down to the foundations, leaving me no choice but to demolish the entire library . . . And if that wasn't enough? If the earth itself retained vestiges of what had happened above? What then? Plow it over? Drop napalm? Cover it in fifteen feet of concrete? What could I do to make myself feel safe, once and for all?

As I twisted around to dunk my rag in the bucket, I placed my free hand atop something scabby. I looked down at a large bloodstain, from whose center sprouted a bristly bouquet of human hairs.

I rose, walked calmly to the bathroom, and vomited.

At two P.M. I carried three sagging trash bags to the service porch.

Though the Science Center was deserted, everyone gone for winter break, I still felt rather reckless that afternoon, standing at a computer kiosk, Googling 'bloodstains carpet removal.' (I'd read a few too many articles about men whose wives disappear and whose browser histories are later found to contain searches for 'untraceable poison' or 'getting rid of a body' to consider doing this at home.) Suggestions ranged from professional crime-scene cleanup to my eventual choice, a recipe calling for water, salt, and hydrogen peroxide.

It worked better than I could have imagined. The blood lifted out, taking a small amount of color with it. One had to admire the collective wisdom of billions of people, so many of them individually stupid. Worked so well, in fact, that I began to wonder if I really did need to get rid of the carpet after all. It was so beautiful, and you couldn't really tell what had happened to cause the fading. Could you? Then again, I'd driven off thinking the rest of the library looked fine.

My backache flared up again as I pushed all the furniture to the margins of the room. The globe, the easy chairs, one leg of the secretary lifted to free an edge. Perspiring heavily, I opened the window another six inches and rolled up the carpet, securing it with duct tape and lugging it into the hallway. All that plush pile adds up: it must have weighed close to a hundred pounds. Thus denuded, the library felt strangely empty, and I realized that I would have to find a replacement. The music-room carpet was far too small. Nor could I take the living room's, as removing that would likewise result in a glaring blank space. The decision made for me, I went upstairs to my bedroom.

I'll spare you the acrobatics of single-handedly extracting a Persian carpet from beneath a queen-sized bed. It took longer than I could have imagined and brought my back to full boycott. And when I finally kicked the new carpet out in the library, it didn't look right, its intense blues and purples clashing with the green silk around the mantel, the red of the wood. Perturbed, I dragged the ruined carpet into my office, where I shoved it partway under the bed, pending disposal; then, stooped with agony, I hauled the library furniture back into place, closed the window, and went to take some ibuprofen.

And for days I worked. I abandoned Daciana's vacuum cleaner in an alley. I left the broken floor lamp in a supermarket parking lot. I scoured the hallways, the kitchen, the service porch; I used buckets of water, gallons of soap. In the living room I squatted with a tube of joint filler, fretting over a dent in the plaster caused by the thrown fireplace poker. I laundered the bathmats, stocked the refrigerator with food I could not stomach. Many businesses were closed for the holidays: I had to go all the way out to Brookline to find an open framer, where I dropped off the cracked photo to be repaired. I called in an upholsterer who offered to redo both easy chairs in a fabric similar to the old one at a cost of thirteen hundred dollars. I agreed, and he took them away. I measured the space left by the missing books, then went to Blackbird Used, where they sold by the yard, and asked the clerk for everything they had in German. The glazier who came out to replace the smashed windowpane said he could not reproduce the miniature painting. No one could; that kind of thing was one of a kind, a real work of art. Once destroyed, it was gone forever.

These tasks, however onerous, expensive, and time-consuming, were to me a lifeline. Without them I surely would have had a complete breakdown. The more I occupied myself with minutiae, the easier it was not to think about what I had done, or what might next happen to me. Better to make lists.

It's not quite accurate to say that I was plagued by fear, as neither word accurately captures the turmoil of those first few days. Not 'plagued,' as that implies suddenness, a devastation whose power

328

lies at least partially in its acuteness. Whereas mine gathered slowly: a rumbling, bowelly feeling that crept steadily upward, promising to worsen, and worsen, and worsen . . . and not 'fear,' either, because what I felt was more a cluster of various emotions, each one coloring and shaping the others, much in the way symptoms constitute a single disease. There was a sense of detachment, and something else I can best describe as mental nausea. The threat of an inappropriate outburst was ever-present, the desire to scream or laugh throwing itself against the gate of my mind as I stood impatiently before a cashier, watching him miscount my change. Often I felt not in my own body, and would find myself staring at my own hand, wondering how it got there, then wondering what would make me behave this way, then wondering about *that* wonder – i.e., whether I was seeing anything clearly, or whether I was losing my mind . . . and so forth and so on . . . an enervating and recursive self-analysis that got me nowhere except deeper into my own head, which was exactly the place I needed to escape from most. Everywhere I went I was aware of the impression I made: spacey, shifty, quick to startle, unnecessarily brusque. And knowing this about myself increased my sensitivity to people's reactions, making me shiftier and brusquer still. I felt them staring at me, everyone staring at my eyes, bloodshot from cleaning fumes; at my hands, wrinkled and chapped and trembling. Staring at my wounded right cheek: an announcement that I was guilty, guilty, my very own mark of Cain. I began putting on a heavy layer of concealer first thing in the morning, in case someone came by. I wasn't expecting anyone, but better safe than sorry. The makeup irritated the wounds, causing me to rub at them, reopening them . . . leading me to feel self-conscious of how I looked . . . leading me to hurry home to reapply more concealer before someone else could see me, suspect me, report me.

Can one live like this? Unhinged by every inter-action – tethered by the thinnest of threads, and that fraying – can one live like this and not go mad?

I leapt from my bed at the first sign of dawn, fleeing indescribable dreams.

Six days after I returned from killing two people and dumping their bodies in the New England woods, my doorbell rang. I went to the bathroom to check my face, added a little extra concealer, straightened my shirt out, and opened the front door on a smiling Detective Zitelli. Behind him stood another man, by his carriage and mien also a police officer. Pasty, with corkscrews of red hair and a button nose, he was prototypically Boston Irish, although his extreme height – he had at least three inches on me – suggested a Scandinavian grandparent. He fixed his gaze on me in the most unsettling way, his eyes lingering on the cakey spot on my right cheekbone.

'Sorry to disturb you like this,' Zitelli said. From his coat pocket jutted a rolled-up manila envelope, ominously thick. 'This is Detective Connearney. This an okay time?'

I found my voice. 'Uh, yes. Please. Come in.'

They stood in the living room like two cops would. I offered them something to eat.

Zitelli thwacked the envelope against his open palm. 'Coffee would be killer.'

Not having made the offer in earnest, I now had to explain that I did not own a coffee machine. Perhaps some tea instead? Zitelli waved *no, thanks,* but Connearney said, 'Sure,' still holding that stare on me, as though I owed him money. I told them to make themselves comfortable and walked from the room as slowly as I could.

With slick hands I opened a kitchen cabinet and grabbed at a mug – knocking it to the floor, where it shattered. I knelt, hurriedly sweeping shards into my bare hand. A warrant. That's what was in that envelope. The end of me spelled out on paper. Certainly, but there had to be more, much more, to make up that thickness. A series of statements, perhaps, taken from Charles Palatine and Dr Cargill, attesting to my low moral worth, my avarice and superficiality. Or perhaps eyewitness accounts of every purchase made on December 28 and 29, from the hiking boots to the duvets to the pile of cigarette-ash-laced scrambled eggs at the Luncheonette Jean-Luc. Surveillance photos showing me white-knuckling up 1–95, hunched and scooping leaves over her, touching matches to the smoking hem of his shirt. DNA reports on the skin underneath her fingernails, my skin, zested off during the struggle. In the living room the two policemen were talking. Talking about me, of course, speculating about how I would react when they moved to arrest me, planning to overwhelm me, should I resist. Who would hold my arms, who my legs. Who would read me my rights. Would they hog-tie me? Or would it be civilized, with light refreshments and witty banter before we all went down to central booking? I had made their job easy, hadn't I, being so careless. I looked toward the service porch: I could slip out the side door. Take off running, run until I was free of this freezing-cold hell. I could start my life over again in a small town. I could go – maybe not home but someplace close enough, get a minimum-wage job and change my name. But where? And how? I didn't belong to an underground network. I didn't have 'contacts.' Everything I had done until that moment had been improvisational, its substance and rationale drawn from movies. In real life it didn't work that way. In real life the police found you. No doubt they had anticipated me, setting up a barricade at the end of the driveway . . . I couldn't go, not now. I would have to face them. But that, too, seemed equally inconceivable. These two men represented the first genuine human contact I'd had in more than a week, and knowing what I knew, I did not think I could contain myself in their presence. They were the Law. I felt my guilt tattooed across my face; it *was* tattooed across my face. I needed concealer. I heard Zitelli laugh and choked on my own breath, startled by what seemed to me an abrupt spike in the ambient temperature. I was thinking that I must stop thinking. Must to act. The longer I weighed my options, the fewer options I had. The stovetop clock ticked unbelievably loudly, an inordinate amount of time passing; I had to get the water going. They were waiting; they would suspect me; nobody takes this long to make a cup of tea. I set the kettle on the stove and stood over it, imploring it to boil.

'You know there's a saying about that.'

Connearney stood in the doorway, his head grazing the lintel.

'So what are my options,' he said.

I said, 'Uhm.'

He stepped past me, reaching for the ziggurat of tea boxes on the counter, plucking off the topmost. '"Elderberry Explosion."' He looked at me, soliciting comment.

'Fruity,' I said.

He put down the box. 'You don't recognize me, do you.'

I indicated that I did not.

'How about a hint,' he said. 'Ready? Here goes: it is not sufficient to do that which should be morally good that it conform to the law; it must be done for the sake of the law.' He smiled. 'Any guesses?'

Zitelli appeared. 'Party's been moved in here, I see.'

I said, 'Uh—'

'Final answer?' Connearney asked.

I shook my head.

'Kant and the Enlightenment Ideal.' He pointed at me. 'You were my TF.' To Zitelli: 'He was my TF.'

'What's a TF?' Zitelli asked.

'It's what you people call a TA.'

'We people?'

'The great unwashed,' Connearney said.

'This guy . . . Seventeen years in law enforcement, I've never met a cockier bastard.'

'Ha ha,' I said.

'No bells ringing,' Connearney asked me.

'Wh – uh. When—'

'My first semester senior year. So that's fall of oh-two.'

'I. I'm sorry. I've had a lot of students over the years, and—'

'No worries,' Zitelli said. 'It's not like he's particularly memorable, giant redheaded Irishman with a tiny penis.'

Connearney laughed.

'Ha ha ha,' I said.

'Was he a good teacher?' Zitelli asked.

'Oh, yeah,' Connearney said. 'He was great. The whole class was great. It's sad what happened to Melitsky, you know?'

'Yes,' I said. Then, sensing that more was expected: 'You were a philosophy concentrator.'

'Social studies.'

'Isn't that like where you look at maps?' Zitelli asked.

'Not at Harvard.'

'Well,' Zitelli said, 'excuuuse me.'

'Ha,' I said. 'Ha ha.'

Zitelli asked Connearney if I'd given him an A.

'B-plus,' Connearney said.

He smiled at me.

The kettle screamed.

Back in the living room, Zitelli offered me the manila envelope. For a moment I did not move, as though by refusing to accept it I could refute whatever its contents held in store for me. I took it and lifted the flap. Inside was a photocopy of Alma's thesis.

'I'll have the original back to you soon as I can,' Zitelli said. 'I thought you could use this in the meantime.'

'. . . thank you.'

'My pleasure. I apologize again for showing up like this. We were in the neighborhood, and I know how it's going to sound, but I was wondering, if it's not too great an inconvenience, maybe you could give my friend here a tour of the library. He's into that kind of thing. Do you mind? Just for a few minutes.'

'Right this way,' I said.

I had gone over every square inch at least a dozen times. I had no real reason to believe that the two men were there for anything other than to gawk. I strove – successfully, I think – to project ownerly insouciance. And yet I have never felt so terrified as I did during those twenty-five minutes. Oddly, what made the situation so nerve-wracking was also what enabled me to maintain a veneer of calm: the incongruity of two homicide detectives prancing around a room that had so recently served as a makeshift morgue was, in its own way, incredibly funny, and I kept having to swallow back the church giggles.

'Jesus,' Connearney said, his big foot on the spot where Daciana's head had lain.

I stood near the globe, spinning it idly. 'It's a nice thing to have.'

'No shit.'

Zitelli looked at me as if to say *You believe this guy?*

I smiled back, waiting for him to comment on the swapped carpet, the missing chairs—

'What happened to your friend?' he said.

The floor dropped out. Game over. Touring the library had been a pretext, after all; here came the axe. *Your friend.* Ha ha ha. Connearney was still pretending to browse, but I knew that he'd tackle me if I tried to bolt. It would happen here and it would happen now and I could do nothing but relent. 'Friend,' I said.

'You know.' Zitelli laid his index finger across his upper lip.

Silence.

I said, 'My girlfriend asked me to move him. He creeps her out.'

'What are we talking about?' Connearney asked.

'Nietzsche,' I murmured.

'Aha.' He closed his eyes. '"Pity in a man of knowledge seems almost ludicrous, like sensitive hands on a cyclops."'

Zitelli grinned. 'You Harvard guys,' he said. 'You're all dickheads.'

As I saw them out, they thanked me profusely, swearing never to bother me again – a chip I doubted I'd be able to cash in.

I fetched half-Nietzsche from behind the file boxes in my office closet, where I'd left him. Upon return I'd been too distraught to deal with cleaning him, and in the intervening days the blood had turned to pinpricks of rust. One large patch cataracted his single eye. I scraped at it and my fingernail came away orange. The green velvet lining the base was dyed black. I tugged it off, crumpled it up, flushed it down the toilet.

Google's preferred method for removing rust from cast iron involved dish detergent and a potato. These I obtained at the corner market. Sitting at the kitchen table, I cut open one of the potatoes, dripped soap on the exposed face, and used it to rub at the bookend until the flesh turned black, the rust slowly coming away. I sliced off the dirty layer and began anew. The police had come and gone and said nary a word. But I wouldn't be fooled. Something was up. It had to be. Once you begin to believe that the world could end you, you not only accommodate yourself to that belief but learn to feed off it. You gorge on your own fear. And when it is gone, you churn more, and gorge yourself again. I cut off another blackened slice. My friend, the policeman had called him. My friend was looking good.

CHAPTER 23

Between the background noise and Yasmina's sobbing, I could scarcely make out a word she was saying.

'Where are you calling from?' I asked. 'Are you calling from the airport?'

'I'm on the red-eye. I get in at five forty.'

'I thought you weren't coming back until Wednesday.'

'I changed my flight. It's over. I told Pedram about us.'

If she was expecting me to let out a victory whoop, she was to be disappointed. All I could get out was, 'Really?'

'I had to. I couldn't stand it anymore.' Still crying, she described the engagement party, guests packed up to the rafters of a Beverly Hills steakhouse; glistening platters of melon, crystal vases brimming with grapes; Pedram digging his fingers into her shoulder, making her feel like a naughty girl being kept close at hand. When it came time for her future husband to speak, she listened as he said nothing of her education, nothing of her as an individual, referring only to her sterling upbringing and her pristine family history and, above all, her beauty.

She blew her nose. 'My sister found me freaking out in the bathroom.'

I sat at the kitchen table, fingering my wounded cheek. The area around it was tender, warm to the touch. 'I don't know what to say.'

'You don't know what to *say*?'

'Well—'

'Say you're sorry.'

'I'm s—'

'Say you're *happy*.'

'I – I am, I'm just, I'm a little surprised.'

'For God's sake, I didn't *plan* it this way,' she said, her voice rising above the blare of a boarding announcement.

'I know—'

'It's not like this has been a whole lot of fun for me.'

'I know. I'm sorry.'

'Shit . . .'

'I'm sorry.'

She was crying again.

'Mina—'

'I thought you'd be happy.'

'I am.'

'You don't sound happy.'

'It's surprise. That's what you're hearing. But, but – but a good kind of surprise.' My right temple had begun to hammer, the room to effervesce. I shook my head hard to clear it. 'Think of it like this, it's like someone jumping out of your birthday cake. It's surprising, but you're happy to be surprised, once the, the' – pain; spinning; I shook my head again – 'the *initial* shock wears off. See? Listen: I'm happy. Don't I sound happy?'

'No.'

'This is the sound of me happy. Really, really happy.'

Silence.

'Hello?' I said.

'Yeah.' She blew her nose again. 'My mother already knew something was up when she saw the necklace.'

I felt equally queasy and pleased. 'You wore it.'

'Of course I didn't wear it. She was going through my drawers.'

'You're joking.'

'Nope.'

'That's absurd.'

'Yup.'

'You're a grown woman.'

'That's never stopped her before. Why are you surprised by this; I've told you how it works.'

Woozily snapping my head back and forth. '. . . I guess.'

'Anyway, she was right, wasn't she? I had something to hide, and she found it.'

Somewhere in there, I could sense an accusation: I had set her up. And yet here she was, crying on my shoulder. The whole scene was very Yasmina, and far too fraught for me to work through on the spot, what with ninety-eight percent of my brain busy chasing other paranoias. I heard her talking about her parents.

I said, 'I'm sure if you explain—'

She made an impatient noise. 'Did you hear what I said?'

'. . . uhhy—'

'I'm out of the family. Okay? Do you get it now? Do you see?'

'I, I'm sure that isn't true.'

'It doesn't matter whether it's true. What matters is that she said it.'

Silence.

A scratchy voice called for group three to Boston.

'That's me,' she said.

'You'll feel better when you've slept,' I said, as much to myself as to her.

She sniffled. 'Whatever.'

Silence.

'Okay, then,' I said. 'Get some rest, I'll see you soon.'

'Wait . . . Joseph?'

Silence.

She said, 'Can I come stay with you?'

Impossible. I couldn't have her here, not with so much left to clean up. Not when I had policemen dropping round for tea. Not with a bloody carpet rolled up and tucked in the corner of my office. No, it was impossible; the only question was how to tell her that without setting her off.

'Please,' she said. 'I can't be alone.'

'Of course,' I mumbled.

'Thank you,' she said. 'Thank you so much.'

I offered to meet her at Logan.

'It's too early. I'll take a cab.'

'You remember where it is.'

'I think so.'

'Number forty-nine. It's the last one on the block.'

'I remember.'

'I'll leave the porch light on.'

'Okay,' she said. 'Thank you.'

I said nothing.

'I'm sorry it's so early,' she said.

'I'll be awake,' I said.

She never was a light traveler, Yasmina, and I tried not to let on how much my back hurt as I humped up the front porch with her bags. I had reinjured myself the previous evening. Stuck without a car – all the rental agencies in Boston close at nine P.M., along with everything else – I'd gone on foot, a hundred awkward, floppy pounds' worth of library carpet laid across my neck, staggering along through the twenty-degree weather, losing my footing and falling and righting myself and staggering on. I'd managed to make it about two miles, arriving at a vacant lot near the Museum of Science, where I unburdened myself and limped homeward, soaked and freezing and aching from stem to stern, my sole consolation that the late hour had made for few witnesses.

'I'm sorry,' Yasmina kept saying.

We stood in the entry hall, wiping our feet.

I told her to stop apologizing.

'I am.'

'It's fine.'

'I'm such a mess.'

'No.'

'I'm sorry.'

'It's fine.'

'I am.'

'It's fine, Yasmina.'

I settled her bags on the landing. When I turned toward her she was coming toward me, one hand out.

'Did you get in a fight?'

'Ha ha,' I said, ducking away. 'Please. I tripped.'

'It looks like it hurts.'

'I'm fine. You must be hungry.'

In the kitchen she sat warming her hands over a mug of tea.

'Would you mind closing the window?' she asked.

I complied.

'Thank you . . . Aren't you cold with it open?'

'It tends to get stuffy in here.'

'I can see my breath,' she said.

Actually, I still felt overheated, but I wanted to make her comfortable enough to mask the fact that I was supremely uncomfortable having her there. I offered her toast.

'This is fine, thanks.'

'Say the word.'

'Thank you.'

I started to fix myself breakfast. I wasn't hungry, but it had to be done.

'My mother left me a voicemail,' she said.

'And?'

'They're cutting me off.'

Silence.

'That's abominable,' I said.

'I'm going to have to give up my apartment.'

Silence, pregnant.

I smiled sickly, opened my arms in invitation.

'Are you sure?'

'. . . of course.'

'Thank you.' Her face greened. 'So much.'

I pulled her chair close and held her against me, shushing her. For some reason her crying was making me very agitated.

'I mean it. It'd be so easy for you to laugh at me. You're such a good person.'

'Shhh.'

'I'll pay you rent.'

'Don't be ridiculous.'

'I mean it. I'll do the cooking. I'll learn to cook.'

'Stop it. Please.'

'I'll find another place as soon as I can. I'll start looking next week . . .'

I stroked her head, trying to soothe her, but she kept on talking nonsense, making promises she could never keep, crying all the while. She recalled the cruel things her aunt had said to her. She talked about Pedram: poor, guileless Pedram, whom she never wanted to hurt but who – her sister told her – hadn't eaten in days, he was so depressed. She had humiliated herself, disgraced her family name. I didn't know, couldn't know, what it was like, the way people talked, the rumors, the importance of reputation. Nobody would ever forget, not after that scene, the threats and imprecations. She would be a laughing-stock. She could never go home again. I wanted to be sympathetic, I did. I knew she needed me. But I couldn't bear the sound of her just then, and I would have given anything for her to be quiet. I told her everything would be fine. Still she wept; still she talked. Hush, I said, hush. But she wouldn't, no matter what I said or did, and finally I had to kiss her. Truth be told, I wasn't feeling up to it, but it was the best way – the only way, really – to get her to stop making noise.

The free-will problem is as old as philosophy itself, the debate around it just as fierce as it was two thousand years ago. More so, perhaps, for as our world grows increasingly known, quantified, mechanized, and constrained – technology gripping us tighter every day, science daily smoothing the contours of reality – people seem to feel correspondingly eager to prove that human beings are the exception to the rule, that we are not preprogrammed but free.

Broadly speaking, two things must be true for us to be free in a meaningful way. We must be the originators of our own actions (i.e., we cannot merely be the next in a series of falling dominos). And the future must be 'open' (i.e., we must be able to affect its outcome in a significant way).

It turns out that these conditions are related, and rather difficult to fulfill. They butt up, hard, against the concept of determinism, which is (again, broadly speaking) the idea that there can be only one physically possible future. Why this should be so is not simple to explain, but suffice it here to state that the question has taken many forms over the years, and is vexed in the extreme. The obvious contradiction between an omniscient deity and man's freedom to obey or disobey him, for example, has driven many from the Church, or at least to the rear pews. In their modern incarnation, deterministic theories tend to rely on the laws of nature as the determinant – these being a more comfortable topic of conversation than God for philosophers, who are, as a general rule, an impious bunch.

Why is it important for us to be free? Picture a world in which there is no free will. In such a world, is anyone truly culpable for anything? If I am not the cause of my actions, it is irrational to hold me responsible for their consequences. From that, it would seem to follow that two of our most cherished concepts – right and wrong – are illusory, and that the main thing keeping us from a stupendously ugly existence, a chaotic and violent hell on earth, is a flimsy bit of self-delusion.

In response, some declare that we are not in fact free, and ought to abandon the idea entirely. Nietzsche, for example, labels metaphysical free will the province of the 'half-educated.' But this kind of hard determinism is rare. Most moral philosophers are in fact compatibilists, acknowledging the strength of determinism but unwilling to relinquish the notion that we can be free. They want to eat their cake etc., and their proposed solutions in pursuit of this end run the gamut from hardheaded and rigorous to obscure and positively finger-wiggling. Lots of semantic games get played; lots of tinkering gets done with the meaning of 'free,' 'determined,' 'choose,' 'cause.' One detects in the compatibilist literature a kind of desperation, borne of the fear that our own powers of reason have condemned us to a world in which morality cannot be stably grounded.

Whether free will is real or incoherent, though, one point is beyond dispute: we *feel* free. The sensation of acting freely is integral to our consciousness. Fire off every objection in the book and it still won't die. I raise my arm and I feel as though I am the author of this movement. I write these words, and they seem to come from deep within me. By extension, we cannot help but view others as responsible, logic be damned. This is the position of the British philosopher P.F. Strawson. Imputing responsibility, he argues, is as much part of our humanness as walking upright, and we'd be foolish to deny it. Whether we are *actually* free

347

is less important than whether we can step outside the house without getting stabbed to death. Strawson's theory is considered an important one in the history of the free-will debate, revolutionary at the time of its publication, in 1962, and still compellingly practical. It does, however, feel like a bit of an avoidance tactic, in that it dismisses the fundamental ontological question of whether free will exists by saying, 'Who cares?' The premise of the entire philosophical inquiry is that such questions bear asking – indeed, demand it.

It was at this point that my new dissertation took up the reins.

In the three days between my visit from the police and Yasmina's return to Cambridge, I was able to produce thirty pages of material, almost the entire introduction. With progress that rapid, it didn't matter to me that my argument was a bit outmoded. (How could it not be? After all, the first draft dated to 1955 – remarkably, seven years before Strawson himself.) What mattered was that I could be done by springtime. I even had a title – *An A Priori Defense of Ontological Free Will* – though I was thinking of shortening it, as it came off a little ungainly in translation from the German.

Those were trying days. It was hard enough acting normal around Yasmina without having to wonder if she would come barging into my office and catch me in the act, Alma's thesis open on the desk and my German-English dictionary in my lap. Since

I was sleeping so poorly anyway, I began dragging myself out of bed at two in the morning, knees jellied, mind roaring like a fireplace; I would crash downstairs to the office and type away until I heard creaking overhead, Yasmina performing her morning ablutions. Then I would close up shop, make breakfast, and twiddle my thumbs until she had left for work. I would pass the rest of the day napping, working, and forcing down food, at six o'clock rising to greet her return with false cheer and reheated market suppers.

I knew that she knew that something was wrong. I barely spent any time in bed; I was tetchy and curt; I yawned constantly and looked more cadaverous by the day. The scratches below my eye had begun to throb all the time, such that I ceased to notice, the rhythm becoming as imperceptible to me as my own heartbeat. I sponged the site and applied concealer; it took four bandages to cover the length of the wounds. Still I sensed her studying me fretfully, wearily, much as one regards another's misbehaving child, held in check by etiquette but nevertheless wishing to make one's disapproval known; and I got in the habit of angling my face away from her when she entered the room. Once she started to ask was I sure I was all right, and I snapped back at her that of course I was, I was extremely busy, I was preoccupied, I had a lot on my mind, didn't I? From her shocked expression I could tell that I had responded with disproportionate force, and

I began making a conscious effort to monitor the level of my voice, to proofread my thoughts before they came out of my mouth. It didn't matter, though, because from there on out she said nothing more, at least with respect to prodding me about my health. I suppose she assumed I was on a hot streak – I was, sort of – and that some degree of moodiness had to be excused. Great minds cannot be expected to abide by social convention, everyone knows that. So she resumed speaking only of herself, perhaps aiming to divert me from whatever it was that was so evidently troubling me. Either that or she found her own problems too absorbing to devote further thought to mine. I could only hope that she would continue to let me be. It frightened me to imagine what I'd say if pressed. As it was, I could barely keep myself in check. The urge to confess clawed at me always, the words roiling in my gut, climbing up the back of my throat, ready to vomit out at the slightest provocation. I did not trust myself and would have felt much safer alone.

But she was there, seemingly to stay. Within days of moving in, she began negotiating her way out of her lease, and a week later, we borrowed Drew's car and used it to move over the bulk of her possessions, everything save the large pieces of furniture. The house, my house, once so beautifully spare, so perfectly balanced, filled up with her things. Her art occupied the television room. Her clothes invaded my closet. In the kitchen went her stage-V espresso machine, along with the pots and pans that had once been the tools of my trade. Though she assured me that she would get rid of anything I didn't want, all signs indicated otherwise. I girded myself for an onslaught of redecorating.

'Can I ask you a question?'

I hurriedly turned the thesis facedown, swiveled around in my office chair. 'Yes?'

'I seem to remember a carpet in the upstairs bedroom.'

'. . . right.'

'Did you do something with it?'

I paused. 'I moved it to the library.'

'That's what I thought. Cause the one in there isn't the one I remember, either.'

'That one, I had to get rid of it.'

'What? Why?'

'It . . . it got a cigarette burn. It had a hole in it.'

'When did that happen?'

'During the party. Also a wine stain.' I spread my hands to show her how big.

'I don't remember that.'

'You're probably just not remembering.'

'Okay, but I still don't see why you had to throw it away. Those are fixable problems, and it was a beautiful carpet. Wasn't there a pair of chairs, too?'

'I didn't want to deal with the hassle. And I didn't throw it away, I sold it.'

'The chairs, too?'

'Those, they're being cleaned.'

'I don't understand why you would bother with one but not the—'

'Look,' I said, 'I'm in the middle of work.'

'Oh. Sorry.' She shut the door.

A few nights later she buttonholed me on my way to the kitchen.

'Can I talk to you about something for a minute?'

'. . . all right.'

She led me to the living room. 'It's the curtains.'

'Curtains.'

'I told you before that the front of the house needs more light. I mean, honestly. You can't prefer it the way it is.'

'It doesn't bother me.'

'It's like a crypt. The eyestrain alone is going to kill me.'

'I don't know what to tell you,' I said. 'Read someplace else.'

'Where?'

'The kitchen. Upstairs. I don't know. Buy a lamp. I'll buy you one.'

'The light's not the only thing, it's like arctic in here. Look at this,' she said, tugging at her scarf. 'This is indoors.'

'That's why I put the heater in the TV room.'

'I can't spend all my time up there.'

'I really don't know what to tell you. The system is old; it was like this when I moved in here.'

'Can I at least get someone to give us an estimate?'

'It's not something I want to spend money on.'

'It doesn't cost anything to get an estimate.'

'There's no point in getting an estimate if I know—'

'But you don't know,' she said. 'That's why you need an estimate.'

'I *know*—'

'Please don't get upset.'

'I'm not getting upset.'

'Okay,' she said. 'But, I mean.'

Silence.

'What,' I said.

'Can we finish talking about the curtains?'

'I thought we were finished.'

'Just, hear me out. That's not going to cost more than a couple hundred dollars. Think about it: wouldn't it be nicer than the blackouts? Restoration Hardware makes a toile, it's kind of creamy—'

'Will you please leave it alone.'

'I can't understand what you're—'

'I don't want people looking in.'

'Who would be looking in?'

'Anyone.'

'Joseph. Seriously, you really . . . but – but – wait. You're getting upset again.'

'I'm not getting upset.'

'I can see you getting upset.'

'Mina.' I pressed my fist against my mouth, and a vein of fire coursed up the side of my face. 'I don't w – I can't deal with this right now. I've got work to do, I'm not feeling my best—'

'What's wrong?'

'Nothing. Nothing's wrong. Would you please excuse me, please.'

'Joseph—'

I locked my door and sat motionless at my desk, listening for the sound of her retreat upstairs.

What was she getting at? Why that line of questioning? Why so many questions about the chairs, the carpet? Did she know something? Was she trying to smoke me out? I told myself to be rational: she wanted to put her stamp on the place. Still, if she kept it up I'd surely crack. I'd never been good at what most people consider small talk, and now it felt deadly. If she kept harping . . . For a moment I considered ending things with her. But how could I? After so many months, I had earned her back. That was what I had wanted. I was supposed to be happy. And grateful. And she had supported me for two years, no questions asked. And yet there I was, contemplating throwing her into the street. After what she had just been through, what she had sacrificed – for me.

On balance, I thought, it would be easier on both of us if she just went away.

In the window I saw my reflection. The area under my eye was florid, shiny, like I'd slept too long in one position.

CHAPTER 24

'Welcome back,' said Linda Neiman.

'Thanks.'

She made no attempt at tact, ogling my face for a good three or four seconds before inviting me to sit and wheeling over to her drink station.

'Coffee?'

'Please.'

While her back was turned, I loosened my shirt collar (overwarm again) and felt to make sure that the gauze hadn't slipped. It was still there, which meant that either she was staring at the dressing itself or the redness had spread beyond its edges, which I doubted could have happened in the hour since I'd put it on. Either way, I thought it took remarkable gall of her to stare. She'd probably been stared at her whole life. I didn't tell her that, though. I wanted to, but I didn't. I smiled and said whole milk would be fine, thanks.

As she fixed our drinks, we chatted about happenings in the department. It struck me that once upon a time I'd been sitting in this exact chair, getting spit-roasted by the same woman who now set out two mugs emblazoned with the Harvard seal, passed me a tin of almond-fennel seed biscotti, and asked if I knew about the upcoming Anscombe colloquium.

'Technically, of course, you're still not enrolled. But I suppose I wouldn't feel obliged to call campus police.'

'You're too kind.'

'That's something I've never been accused of.' She smiled and laid her hand atop a stack of printed pages.

'Right. Let's talk turkey. This is really you?'

'Indeed,' I said.

'Because reading it, I can't help but wonder if someone came and replaced the Joseph I know with a robot who looks and sounds like him but is a halfway decent and efficient writer.'

Trying to capture Alma's voice had been a challenge. It had a lightness to it, a musicality and playfulness befitting her voice in life, quite in contrast to the turbid stuff I'd spent years churning out. In doing the translation I also had to overcome a pervasive fogginess, one I could drive out for only a few minutes at a time, and then with fierce concentration. I was doing the same now, trying to appear alert and nonchalant rather than drained and anxious.

'People change,' I said.

'Well, let me be the first to say it: I may have misjudged you.'

I made a conciliatory gesture.

'I will say that parts of the argument feel anti-quated to me, such as the section on action theory. A lot has happened since mid-century. Still, I'm interested in seeing where you go from here.'

Though I had already finished translating most of the second chapter while waiting for her to read the first, I didn't want to give the impression that my new work was coming to me too easily. I said I could get her the next section by mid-February.

'I look forward to it,' she said.

I asked if I could still qualify to graduate in the spring.

'Let's not get ahead of ourselves. One page at a time, mm?' She smiled, raised her mug to me. 'For now it's enough for me to feel gratified that there are still some things about the universe I don't fully understand.'

My relative good mood was dashed that afternoon when I came home to find a stranger standing on my front porch.

Heavyset, with smooth, sallow skin and heavy bags under his eyes, he presented with a peculiar combination of youth and age. A dingy brown scarf overflowed the collar of his oversized nylon jacket; on his belt he wore a beeper.

'Can I help you?' I said.

He stared at me for an interminably long time before asking to speak to Ms Spielmann. His tone was robotic, an impression bolstered by the color of his eyes – bluish-gray, what people call gunmetal.

'She's passed away.' I paused. 'I live here now.'
He nodded once.

The wad of gauze on my face felt gigantic; it was difficult not to turn away.

'Was there something I could do for you?' I said.

He came down off the porch, a photograph in his hand.

It was a snapshot of Daciana, faded and badly creased. I was startled to see that in her younger days, she had not been entirely unattractive. A tad horsey around the mouth, but far from the meaty fortress I had known. I set down my lambskin bag, pretending to examine the photo for much longer than I needed to but not nearly long enough for me to explore every branch of a rapidly expanding decision tree. On the one hand, I could say that I was new here and had therefore never known Daciana. This would seem to nip any problem in the bud, but it also had the potential to backfire severely. If, for example, she had talked about her new employer. Getting caught in a preemptive lie could raise all sorts of questions that might otherwise go unasked. On the other hand, I could allow that I did in fact know Daciana, but had (a) not seen her in a long time (a lie somehow less damning than claiming to have never known her in the first place) or (b) had seen her on the day she showed up to work and had paid her as usual and sent her along on her merry way. The advantage of (b) was that it accounted for the possibility that someone had seen her car in the driveway;

the disadvantage was, obviously, that it linked me to her in time and place. On the other hand, I might not have anything to be concerned about at all. It wasn't the police at my door but a stranger. Her son, I assumed. He seemed about the right age. Andrei? And I understood then that if he was her son, then she was his mother; together they made a family, one that I had destroyed. Families were not abstractions, they were made of real people; but that did not factor, it could not factor, in the present calculus, and so I wrenched myself back toward a more constructive line of thinking. Whoever this person was, he was clearly not the police. Come to think of it, it was possible he hadn't yet reported her missing. Perhaps he didn't live with her, and had come home only recently to discover her gone. How old was he, exactly? Old enough to have moved out? I couldn't refine my initial impression of him any further without looking up from the photo, which I didn't want to do because I could feel him waiting for me to speak. Even assuming the worst – that he did live with her, and that he'd known of her absence since that very morning – would a young man really know his mother's work schedule, down to the hour? What child pays that kind of attention to his parents? (And how hard had she worked to give him a life here? And how many toilets scrubbed? And how many loads of laundry washed, dried, fluffed, folded?) Moreover, that it was specifically him standing here *and not* the police could mean that he *had* talked to them but that they did not consider me a person of interest; therefore, I had nothing to be afraid of. On the other hand, that might just reflect ineptitude on their part, a slow or lazy investigator. Neither the police nor her son (if that was in fact who he was) had any reason to suspect me at all, and if they or he somehow discerned that I was lying, that might rouse them or him to full attention. On the other hand, why in the world would I ever want to hurt Daciana? What did I stand to gain? She was a housekeeper. (A hardworking lady with a library card, the modern embodiment of the American dream.) On the other hand, if it emerged that Eric was missing as well, that lit a fire under the idea that people had a tendency to disappear around me. On the other hand, nobody had contacted me about Eric, which might mean that his disappearance had gone unnoticed – which made sense, given the kind of person he was, the kind of circles he probably ran in. On the other hand, I had to assume that he had at least a couple of friends, other losers or girls he'd picked up and dropped much in the way he had that awful night that I couldn't bear to think about now. No man is an island, I thought, and then I thought about my first Harvard roommate, a gay theater junkie named Norman Slepian who liked to tell people that he was an island, as in 'Norman is an island,' and though it was outrageous and inexplicable to be thinking of him then, I couldn't help but wonder what had happened to him. We had gone our separate ways after freshman year. And but back to the present: Eric was gone. Someone would know. When they could not find him, would they assume that he had skipped town? Would they call the police? It was a giant leap to assume that anyone could/would connect Eric with me, and me with Daciana; what happened happened rather more out of serendipity than due to any planning on my part. On the other hand, I still had so many other hands to consider, and this boy – this man-boy – he was waiting for an answer, and I was operating in a complete vacuum, right out on the brink of plausibility, all of these pluses and minuses racking up in my white-hot brain in the space of twenty long seconds. I had to say something.

'Right,' I said. I flapped the photo, handed it back to him. 'My housekeeper.'

'It's my mother,' he said.

The decision tree began to collapse.

'Ah,' I said. 'It took me a second. How old's that picture?'

'She hasn't been home in three weeks,' he said.

Another branch collapsed.

'Oh, no,' I said. 'I hope everything's all right.'

He licked his lips. They were horrendously chapped. 'Did she come to work that week?'

'When are we talking about?'

'About three weeks ago.'

A third branch.

'Gosh. Well, I – I hate to say it, but I actually

had to let her go a little while back. I was sorry I had to do it, but—'

'How long ago.'

'Beg pardon?'

'How long ago did you fire her.'

'Well, I wouldn't exactly say that I *fi* – it wasn't like that, it's more a question of cost, the economy being how it is right now, but, uhhhh. Maybe six, seven weeks?'

'So she wasn't here.'

'When are we talking about, again.'

'Three weeks ago.'

'Well, then, I suppose not, no, I don't think so.'

Silence.

'Is everything okay?' I said.

'They found her car,' he said.

A fourth.

'Oh, no. Oh, that's, that's . . . So you've called the police, I assume.'

'They're looking for her.'

'I see. But you don't know where she could've gone.'

'No,' he said. 'Do you?'

My right eye socket pulsed. 'I don't know why I would.'

'Maybe she said something to you the last time she came to work.'

'I don't think so,' I said. 'If she did, I'd've forgotten by now.'

'Okay,' he said.

Silence.

362

His face shimmered and danced before me.

'She was a very nice lady,' I said.

'She might still be alive.'

'Well, yes. I'm sure she is. I mean, hope so.'

He said nothing.

'I'm sorry,' I said. 'I didn't mean – I'm sorry. It's upsetting to hear, is all. I hope she's fine. I'm sure she'll turn up. You don't know anything else?'

'No.'

'Well. Please, do let me know if there's anything I can do.'

'Can I get your number?' he asked.

'Well—uh, sure. Sure.' I reached into my pocket, found an old grocery store receipt. 'I, uh, I don't seem to have a—'

He held out a pen.

'Thanks.' I used my leg as a desk. 'Please do let me know what happens.'

He said nothing.

I gave him the receipt, raised a hand. 'Take care.'

'My pen,' he said.

It was a cheap ballpoint, not the kind of thing people are particular about getting back. His asking for it made me nervous. As he took it from me, the briefest flicker of a smile passed across his face. It left as quickly as it had come, and he walked away without looking back.

'That sounds like it went well.'

'Hm?'

'I said it sounds like it went well.'

'What does.'

Yasmina glanced at me over her shoulder. 'Your meeting with Linda?'

'Right,' I said. My mind was still replaying that little smile of his, the way it blinked on and was gone, like a blown lightbulb. 'I guess it went pretty well.'

'Don't get too excited, now. It's only your entire academic future.' She gave the pot a stir, covered it, reduced the heat. 'This has to simmer for a half-hour.'

'. . . okay.'

'If you're hungry in the meantime, I picked up some hummus.'

'. . . thanks.'

She faced me, her hands working in a dishtowel. 'Honey?'

'Mm.'

'Is everything okay.'

No.

'Yes.'

'Okay. Are you sure?'

'Sure I'm sure.' I paused. 'I'm thinking about everything I have to do.'

'You've been working so hard. You must be tired.'

'I'm a little tired.'

'Maybe . . .' she said.

I looked at her. She was biting her lip.

'What,' I said.

'Maybe you should see a doctor.'

Silence.

'What for,' I said.

'I don't know, maybe they could give you something to help you sleep.'

'I sleep fine.'

'Last night you were thrashing around so much I had to wake you up.'

I said nothing.

'Were you having a bad dream?'

Silence.

'I don't remember.'

'Well, it must have been bad.' She reached for a package of couscous. 'You were mumbling.'

'. . . oh?'

She nodded, reading the back of the box.

'What did I say.'

'Nothing, per se. Mumbling's not really the right word. More like humming.'

The room bowed inward, as though the surface of reality had been depressed by a giant finger.

'Was I,' I said.

'Mm-hm.'

'What was I humming.'

'I couldn't tell.' One corner of her mouth went up. 'It was pretty off-key.'

'. . I'm sorry.'

'Oh, I don't care. I have my earplugs. But you always used to sleep like a log.'

I said, 'I guess I'm stressed.'

'I'm sorry. Is there something I can do?'

I shook my head, which in movement felt large and dense and graceless and above all suffused with heat. The room – my visual field – they were still rippling, and I began to sway drunkenly.

'I'm going to sit in the living room,' I said.

She looked at me.

'It's the stovetop,' I said. 'It's making the whole room stuffy.'

Without waiting for her response, I got up and left the room and took a seat on the sofa, staring at the empty fireplace. It might as well have been going full bore; the small of my back felt humid and so did my armpits and I untucked my shirt. My feet, too, seemed swole up, too big for my shoes, which I kicked off, flexing my toes in discomfort. The drunkenness was intensifying, and along with it came a truly unnerving sensation of my mind slowly migrating outside my skull, so that my thought process was happening a foot in front of me, and that when I turned my head my awareness followed on a delay, drifting like a buoy . . . To release the heat building up under my shirt, I undid the top button, rolled up the sleeves, and finally pulled it off, and that was when I became conscious of Yasmina, watching me from the doorway.

An aura surrounded her, golden and lambent.

'Honey?'

I stared at her, fascinated.

'Honey, you . . .' She did not sound like her usual self. 'Do you want a drink?'

'I'm not thirsty.' I said it but then realized that I was thirsty; very thirsty, in fact, thirstier than I had

366

ever been. But I didn't want to ask her for anything or do anything to alarm her further. I wanted to be left alone, to keep very still until the room slowed down.

'You should check on the stew,' I said. My words had a close echo, like I was speaking into a paint can. 'You don't want it to boil over.'

'What's going on with you,' she said.

'Of course I'm okay,' I said.

Silence.

'That's not what I asked,' she said.

I said nothing.

'You look . . .' she said.

'I look what.'

'Nothing,' she said.

Silence.

'I think you should go to the doctor,' she said.

'I'm not going to the doctor.'

'It doesn't look like it's getting any better.' Timidly, she approached. 'It looks infected.'

'You're not a doctor,' I said. I gathered my mind, made a bulwark against this attack of hers.

'That's why I want you to go see one.'

'I don't have any coverage.'

'Go to UHS.'

'I'm not a Harvard student.'

'I thought Linda said she would reinstate you.'

'She said she'd think about it.'

'You can't just ignore it.'

'I'm not ignoring it. I'm letting it heal.'

'But it's not healing.'

She was standing close to me now, and I could feel her body radiating heat. I edged away from her, toward the end of the sofa. 'Will you leave it alone? Please? Leave it alone.'

'There's a free clinic a mile and a half from here.'

'Yasmina—'

'Or go to the emergency room. They have to take you. It's the law. Here,' she said, bending toward me, 'let me have a look.'

She plucked at the gauze and it was a faceful of nettles and I seized away from her and flew back over the arm of the sofa as though jerked by a harness; I landed on my arm and got up, reeling down the hallway.

'*Goddammit.*'

'Shit. Oh, shit. I'm so sorry.'

'I told you to leave it *alone.*'

'Are you okay?'

'No, I'm not okay, that *hurt.*'

'I didn't mean to—'

I slammed the bathroom door. My face in the mirror was glossy with sweat. I hadn't taken the gauze off in several days, and as I peeled back one corner I saw a thumb-sized patch of flesh, hysterically swollen and red, so sensitive that I had to bite down to prevent myself from crying out as I removed the rest of the dressing.

'Joseph?'

'Hang on a minute.'

I tried to trim myself a new piece of gauze, but I couldn't hold the scissors straight and I was afraid of stabbing myself in the wrist. I let the scissors drop to the floor and tore off a ragged strip, good enough.

'Can I come in?'

The tape got stuck to itself. I wrung it in frustration; it twisted into rope.

'Are you okay?'

'Just – hang on.'

As I put the new dressing in place, I indaverently pressed down on the hot spot, sending a spike through the entire right half of my head. Everything capsized, but I stayed up, gripping the sink.

The door started to open. 'Joseph—'

'*Not now.*'

Silence.

The door closed.

Six ibuprofen, dry-swallowed: they caught in my throat, it was like scraping asphalt all the way down, and as I cupped sink water I saw my palms blotchy. My arms, too. And my chest, and my neck; all of me, I was speckled pink and white. I drank. The heat was back within seconds, and, shutting the medicine cabinet, I saw not me but him, his little smile.

Hello.

And I lurched down the hall to my office, where I lay on the bed, sweating into the duvet, until it began to feel like lava against my back, and I got up and threw open the window, letting the cold night air stream over me like mercy itself. I began to plan, ignoring Yasmina's voice calling me for dinner until I heard her coming down the hall, heard my name, heard her pause at the threshold.

'What are you doing,' she said.

'Working,' I said.

'Joseph,' she said. 'Come away from there.'

'I like it here.'

'You're going to get sick.'

The horizon canted; I righted myself against the sash. Brother, was it ever hot in here. 'I'm working, Yasmina.' It appeared that I was stuttering. It's my teeth, I thought, they're chattering. That they should chatter when I felt so hot was strange. Everything was strange. Why was she looking at me in that way. I lunged toward the doorway, causing her to cringe and leap back.

'Wait—'

I shut the door, locked it, leaned against it, listening to my blood. She was knocking, the rat-a-tat of her knuckles against the door rapid and insistent and telltale. I unbuttoned my pants and kicked them off. God, it was so intolerably awfully hot, hottern two mice humpin in a wool sock. Even the outside air wasn't helping anymore, and so I tugged off my drawers. Still no relief. I was on fire. My face was on fire. My face hurt. Pressure behind my right eye, I wanted to gouge it out. She was talking, it was driving me mad. Why wouldn't she leave me alone? I had worries to worry, plans to plan. I walked in circles. Why did he come here, he had to have a reason. We have reasons for what we do: reasons are what make us different from other animals, they're the core of decisions, which are the core of our ability to choose, and hence our freedom. Without reasons we are machines. Was he a machine, he looked like a machine. Maybe he was a machine? But he had a photograph. She was his mother, she gave birth to him, machines didn't reproduce that way. Maybe she was a machine, too. Maybe we all were. I was a robot who looked and sounded exactly like myself but who was a halfway decent writer. He was analyzing me with his camera eyes: he had built-in apparatuses. I thought of his smile and then I thought of the pen, of course: *the pen*. He took the pen because it had my fingerprints on it. He was goofing on me, getting me to write down my phone number: he didn't need my number; he had it already; my number was his and it was up. Well I'd show him. I knew what I would do, it was foolproof. I would wait for him. I would follow him, study him until I learned his patterns and habits, better than he knew them himself, I would educate myself. I would find the right moment and then I would act to quiet him, thereby reducing the total overall risk I faced. Life is full of risk, one can never be risk-free, but one can certainly mitigate the forces acting against one, and that was what I would do. I would act to protect myself. Somewhere in a small, dark room there were small, dark men laying small, dark plots against me, I would not be their plaything. There

371

existed the possibility that they already had the pen in their possession, but that problem was not insurmountable, because fingerprints are made of skin and skin can be removed. I put my hands against the woolen blanket and began to sand away, I would do this one thin layer at a time. It didn't seem to be working, though, and I searched the room on my hands and knees for something rough with which to exonerate myself. Underneath the bed near the baseboard I found a leftover piece of glass, a fragment painted in orange houndstooth, and with its longest edge I began systematically to shave the soft pad of my left thumb, one thin layer at a time. It wasn't working, was it? I scrutinized. My thumb was red but the ridges and whorls were still very much intact, so I investigated the possibility of perhaps slicing off a layer parallel to my thumb. All it did was bleed, though. I felt nothing, the nerves wired for pain were all jammed with signals from my face, so I sat there grinning at my own blood, watching as it trickled down my wrist and into the crook of my elbow and pooled on the floor. I was thinking I had so much planning to do. I wanted to plan as far ahead as possible, but it was impossible to concentrate with her making noise like that. Listen to her. Honey. Please. What's going on here? Please open up. I'm scared. You're scaring me. Please. I love you. I know you love me. I don't know what's going. Let me know you're okay. I'll leave you alone if you say something.

Don't do this to me. Please. I want it to be better. You're going to be okay. Everything is. I promise. I can help you. Let me help you. Please open up. Please don't stay locked in there all night. And on and on and on and on and you only wish she would stop talking. Shut up. Shut up. You can't stand it anymore, just shut up and let it be, shut up. Listen to how scared she sounds. It's nothing compared to what you feel, though. You feel capable of anything. You need silence so you can think. Put down the glass and stand up and walk again in circles, covering your ears to wall her out. Shut up. The anger inside you has teeth; is it its own living thing, independent of you. You are merely a host to it. Shut up, please shut up. If she doesn't shut up, you might have to do something about it. Please shut up. You might have to bash her brains in. You wouldn't enjoy it, but it's all you can think about right now. Once upon a time you loved her but now there is nothing but fear, fear and heat and pain and the pressure of a billion vises, and standing at the closet, you reach for your good old friend, cold and heavy, the coolness of it feels wonderful pressed against your molten skin, hug him close. Things don't work out, do they. *Shut up.* Things are what they are until they aren't any longer. You have changed and changed again, you are a creature constantly evolving. Who can say when these transformations occur? Think about your brother. Was that fair? Think about the house and the money and the jewelry, was that fair? Sometimes the inequity lists in your favor; sometimes not. The universe moves and it moves you, the future pulling with inexorable gravity. You wonder if it is true, if you might actually harm her, and then you are small and curled and shaking, babbling to yourself as she pounds at the door, holding your friend by the neck, willing her to leave you be. You stay there until she gives up with an angry kick and you release him and he falls languidly to the floor and you fall, too, right there. Where you remain, and in some infinitely small time you dream

dream of a horse being whipped to death

waking to the moonlight streaming lucid through the open window and you are unclothed with a fist in your chest and your groin dripping and above all pain, obliterating the right half of the world, your brain a champagne bottle shook up ready to pop and as you move howling to the bathroom vertigo sends you crashing into the door. Your face is thick. Your cheek explodes every second. Get it off. It hurts. You must get it off. You cannot hear her, she is so far away, but she's calling your name as you grope for the lightswitch. See your reflection through a one-dimensional haze.

'Oh God.'

In the doorway, her hands at her throat, looking at you. Nothing can conceal it, not anymore. Red and turgid, the inflamed rump of an animal in heat. Along your neck below your bulging jaw a bloody thumbprint where you earlier left evidence of yourself.

'Oh God. Oh my God. I'm calling an ambulance. Where are you going. Joseph. You can't go out like that. Wait. *Wait.*'

Outside stroll naked through the snow. You expect it to be cold underfoot but it's not so bad. In fact, it feels warm, with a pleasant beachy crunch. You dip your hands in the snow to see if it will remove the texture of your finger-prints, but to no avail, oh, well, keep on going, go on, walk.

Some distance away your name is being called.

Ignore it.

Maybe the brick of the sidewalk will work? But no. Your hands are bleeding again. This isn't going to work. You need professional help. They can do amazing things with surgery.

Your name again, farther away.

A siren whines.

You're almost there.

The tall hospital winks a thousand white eyeblinks.

They all blur together into one.

A sliding door, a wet rubber mat, a room full of people, good evening ladies and gentlemen, may I have your attention, please.

The woman at the desk sees you and coming out of her chair breathlessly says the name of the Lord God.

★　★　★

375

'—Fever under control first.'

'Okay.'

'Quite honestly it should never have been allowed to get to this stage.'

'I had no idea – oh. Oh, no. Joseph.'

Head up.

'Relax.'

'Sit back, honey. You have to sit back.'

'Relax.'

Relax.

DAYS AND NIGHTS.

Dreams.

Daylight. TV Nattering.

The world looks funny.

Flat.

'Joseph.'

Why's that like that.

'You're okay. You're fine, now.'

Touch your face.

'Don't fiddle with it, please. They just changed the dressing.'

Try again.

'Please leave it alone. Please.'

'Knock knock.'

'Come on in. He's up.'

'Oh good. Joseph? Hi there.'

A floating shape nearby. A voice familiar.

'Take it easy, there . . . There. Isn't that more comfortable?'

'He's still pretty out of it.'

'Mm.'

'Thanks for coming by again.'

'It's not a problem. Don't you worry, they'll take good care of him. It's good you came in when you did. It could have been much worse. You know, you look pretty tired yourself. Why don't you go home for a bit.'

'I don't want to leave.'

'Sometimes the best thing is to get out for a little while. Get a bite to eat. Take a shower. Don't worry about him. He's not going anywhere.'

' . . . thank you, Dr Cargill.'

'You rest up now.'

'Joseph? Did you hear that?'

'You know what, let him rest.'

'Take care. Thank you.'

Later:

'It's nice of her to stop in. She's not even your doctor. She just saw your name on the board.'

Later:

'Drew called. He's in Atlantic City. He'll be back tomorrow.'

Later:

'You could have died. Do you realize that? You're such an asshole sometimes, you're so fucking *stubborn*.'

Later:

'Please stop touching it. The nurse is getting mad. She said the next time she's going to tie your wrists down.'

Later:

'Are you happy now?'

Later:

'I'm going to get some coffee. Do you want anything? Do you want me to change the channel? All right.'

Alone, free yourself and stand looking through a lens smoky and partially occluded.

A blue bulb flutters above the bathroom mirror. Lean in. The upper-right quadrant of your head mummified; with your hands (you still have fingerprints, it seems, you will have to file a complaint) find the joint and start to unwrap, unconcealing. It hurts. The gauze sticks to itself. Yellow crust. Red crust. The light ever more penetrating until: cold dry air on sutured skin, your face no longer yours, changed, the eye's curtains drawn shut and sewn up tight and the space beneath vacant, you can scream now, that's fine, it's all over now, go on, go ahead, scream.

CHAPTER 25

Hardly anyone comes to see me these days. Even my cellmate, a convicted rapist, gets more people dropping by. In fairness, his brother lives in Marlborough, a short drive away; whereas I entail a plane ticket. Still. It gets lonely.

I do get letters. Four-fifths of them come from women, many of whom have read the true crime book about me or seen the half-hour basic cable show that aired last spring. An astonishingly large number of my correspondents believe that I am innocent. It's hard to understand. I pled guilty. The videotape of my confession was excerpted for TV. And yet they write, these women, that they can see goodness in me, that I could never have done as I did unless driven by extraordinary circumstances. Perhaps I confessed falsely, compelled by fear. A man will say anything when he's afraid. A generous mistake they make, these women: they fail to grasp what a relief it was to confess.

At first, nobody believed me, not Yasmina or the nurses. They thought I was still delirious, or stewed on morphine. They had me forcibly sedated, and several days passed before I was calm enough, and trusted sufficiently, to make a phone call. I asked for Zitelli, and when he was not in, for Connearney.

My first interview with him is the one that everyone saw. At the start, I am bent over, barely audible, the words dribbling out of me, and one can easily understand why people might believe me to have been coerced: I lose the thread, back up, contradict myself. My second, third, and fourth interviews – done to dispel the notion that I might be confabulating – were taped, as well, though never aired. Had they been, I think viewers would have gotten a much different impression of me. In them I'm sitting up straight, speaking soberly and with a practiced air. The judge who sentenced me called them chilling, and I'll be the first to admit that he's right. The lesson being that you should never, ever believe anything you see on television.

I spent the last third of my hospital stay in a private room, handcuffed to the bed, an officer stationed in the corner, lest I attempt to harm myself or escape. When the time came to change my dressing or empty the bedpan, he would stand up, poised to spring into action if I tried to do anything to the nurse. Other than that, our inter-action was minimal. He wouldn't say more than a few words at a time, and he avoided making eye contact with me, giving me the first taste of that blend of pity and revulsion now so familiar to me.

I am told that Yasmina's assessment was correct: I could have died. Orbital cellulitis is no joke, and by failing to clean the wounds properly, and continually reapplying makeup, I had done a superb job of first culturing, then aggravating, the infection. It took my eye; it could have easily spread to my brain; and I wonder now if on some level I did not recognize this possibility. No doubt there are more efficient ways to commit suicide. I know better than most, though, that such decisions are rarely, if ever, discrete.

The case against me was straightforward enough. Even so, it did not go to trial for eight months. My attorney argued that I first needed to recuperate. Plus, they had to find the bodies. This took a while, as I could give them only the most general directions. Thanks to my exemplary willingness to cooperate, I was released on bond, confined to house arrest, and fitted with an ankle monitoring bracelet. I didn't mind. I used my remaining time to finish my dissertation, emailing Linda Neiman a final draft at the end of April.

At that point there still hadn't been any press coverage of the case. Her reply thus threw me for a loop. They wouldn't graduate me, she said, not now or ever.

'We can't condone plagiarism,' she said.

Apparently, my confession had renewed Detective Zitelli's interest in the contents of Alma's thesis. Fed up with his first translator, who found the paper's arcane terminology a bit much to contend with, he contacted the Harvard Department of Germanic Languages and Literatures. They referred him to the director of graduate studies, who referred him to Philosophy. Somewhere along the line my name must have come up, as in short order, the original landed on Linda's desk. She took one look at its opening lines before phoning the detective to let him know that a full English text already existed.

The remaining fifth of my mail comes from a motley bunch of folks. Christians pray for my soul. Screenwriters offer to collaborate. After women, the second largest demographic slice is teenage boys intoxicated by the notion that I intended to make with my actions some sort of broader philosophical point. Where they got this idea is beyond me. Certainly I didn't say anything to that effect, either during the trial or since. Nevertheless, these boys write me long, intimate letters. They pour their blackness out onto the page, spinning violent fantasies – if such are the ones I receive, I can only guess at what the prison censor removes – and insisting that I'm being self-deprecating when I say mine was a simple case of greed gone awry.
  Nor would the media accept this explanation. Looking for something fleshy to sink their teeth into, they made my résumé their feast, so that when my name appears in print (it still happens, and when it does, one of my fans will usually mail me a clipping) the phrase ex-Harvard

professor and convicted murderer' is often appended to it. The first few times this happened, I wrote to the publication in question, asking that they run a correction. Nobody acknowledged receipt, and eventually I stopped trying. A Harvard professor I shall be, then. I can't begin to imagine how severely this must irritate Linda.

We don't have access to computers here, but a young man in Walla Walla took the time to print out thirty pages' worth of material from his website, on which I feature prominently. Among its other subjects are Leopold and Loeb, the Preppy Killer, Theodore Kaczynski, and Robert McNamara, who I suppose might take a certain degree of umbrage at being inducted into our little fraternity.

Most puzzling are the proposals, of which I have had five. I am imprisoned for life, with no chance of release. I have expressed no interest in marriage. I am disfigured, not forbiddingly so but enough that I likely wouldn't qualify for an all-prison beauty contest. Maybe these women think the eyepatch gives me a kind of piratical swagger. Who knows? I've given up trying to understand what makes people want one thing versus another.

One would think that such letters would be written exclusively by lunatics. Not so. Of all my prospective brides, three sounded frightfully sane. One even included a photo of herself in a mortarboard and gown.

Sinead from Colorado: you seem very nice, and I wish you the best of luck.

I never reply to anyone. It doesn't matter. People keep on writing. The truth is they're lonely, too, and I make the perfect receptacle for their own fears and frustrations, no different from a fictional character, a figure out of myth.

My cellmate's name is William. Six years ago, he raped an eighty-two-year-old woman, who died as a result of her injuries. When I first met him, he was withdrawn, basically mute. Months went by before we had any conversation lasting more than two or three exchanges. His skittishness awakened me to the idea that my scarred face and imposing height made for a kind of insurance policy. William himself is about five-foot-five.

At some point he decided that I posed no danger, and the words started coming, first cautiously, then torrentially, a disjointed autobiography that I have managed to reassemble after hearing it four or five times. His parents were both alcoholics, at whose hands he suffered constant sexual and physical abuse; he has been in and out of the prison system regularly since the age of twelve, when he stole a car. In recounting his crimes he sounds less remorseful than inconvenienced, to the extent that I wonder if he has any real grasp on why he's here.

He once told me that we're all bad, deep down.

My instinct was to reply that that was nonsense, there had to be good people out there. I stopped myself. Whatever gives him solace – even if it's believing he's a regular joe who happened to get caught – what right do I have to deny him that?

Among William's many impairments is a crippling dyslexia. Most everyone in prison reads a great deal, in one form or another. In my first six months alone, I went through more than a hundred books, whereas in all that time, I never saw him with so much as the funnies. Sometimes he'd pick up whatever I had just finished, glaring at the cover in an intimidated way.

On one such occasion – the book in question was *The Trial*, which I hadn't read since high school – he asked me in an offhand way what the story was about. I related it to him, in brief, and as I did his face took on an enraptured glaze. He interrupted me, prodded me for details, asked questions about the lives of the characters that I could not answer. His curiosity made me smile and, without thinking, I suggested that he read it himself, if he was so interested.

The words were not out of my mouth before I regretted them, and I sat back, ready for a violent reaction.

Instead, he asked me for help.

Have you ever taught someone to read? If so, it was almost certainly a child, whose mind was plastic, voracious. We tend to take for granted our ability to extract meaning from a page of writing, but it is in fact nothing short of miraculous, and if we did not learn to employ it at an age when we still believed in magic, few would.

William was forty-seven years old when I began teaching him to read. We didn't have to start at the very beginning. He could sign his name, and he knew the alphabet. He could not, however, assemble those letters into words. I put a lot of thought into how to approach the problem, but every technique I tried failed, no matter how cutting-edge the pedagogy behind it. In the end we had to resort to brute force: I spent long hours drilling him with flashcards, helping him commit to memory the shapes of individual words, such that *bird* became a single unit, *apple* another, and so forth. In effect, we made English into a pictographic language, akin to Chinese. It's notoriously difficult for Westerners to learn such systems, because we're trained to think of words as divisible. In a sense, then, William's knowing the alphabet was more a hindrance than a help.

We worked together for close to two years, and on my thirty-fourth birthday, he made to me a gift of a letter he had written, without my help or knowledge. It described our cell. Though its style was repetitive, and its subject matter a little too close for comfort (shades of Nabokov's ape), it did possess a kind of crude poetry, and more to the point, it was spelled perfectly. I hung it near the window. It's the first thing I look at when I wake up in the morning.

My chief occupation is running the prison library. Officially, there's a state employee in charge, but it's not a job with a good retention rate, and thus far I have had to train three new initiates, the latest of whom is a newly minted Harvard graduate. His name is Adam, and he holds a bachelor's degree in Yiddish literature. Like me, he hails from flyover country, and despite my best efforts to the contrary – one swiftly learns to eschew sentimentality – we have developed a rapport. He has never hidden his true motivation for working here: he's collecting material for a book. Recently he asked me to take a look at his letter to literary agents. It was well written, if a bit cerebral. He cited Foucault and referred to 'the interiority of prison as a social space.' I told him that that was all well and good, but in my opinion, he'd be better off taking a more narrative tack. Sell yourself, I said. He told me he'd think about it.

It was he who first suggested that I teach a class, although it took him a good while to convince me. Aside from my (quite reasonable) skepticism – why would a bunch of felons want to talk about philosophy? – I had a much more elementary cause for concern. At that point I still hadn't made any friends. I knew I was thought of as aloof. From there it's a short trip to becoming an object of ridicule, and thence an even shorter trip to becoming a target.

But boredom is a potent catalyst. If it can get us to do things like bungee-jump and shoot heroin, it's surely enough to get me in front of a classroom. I decided to begin with a general introduction: what is philosophy, and why is it important? I typed up a sheet with sources, Adam put up a sign in the library, and together we hoped for the best.

As expected, the initial response was tepid: three people, two of whom had the idea that I might pass out dirty pictures, and who left when I did not. Something must have taken root, though, because I tripled attendance over the course of the next lecture, a two-parter covering the early Greeks. Heraclitus's statement that 'character is destiny' triggered some mild debate, but what really got the conversation going were Zeno's paradoxes, which made intuitive sense to a bunch of men staring down infinity. By the time I got to Aristotle, I was pulling in seven regulars, and the lecture on Descartes brought us to ten, at which point the warden capped enrollment, citing safety concerns. We've established a waiting list.

In retrospect it seems obvious that the class should have succeeded. People in prison have nothing to do but think, and their confinement tangibly demonstrates the power of abstractions: love, hate, desire, vengeance, justice, punishment, freedom, hope. They might not have all the jargon down, but they have more than enough energy and fervor to fill an hour every other week. They are, I believe, the perfect students.

With Adam's help, too, I have begun a correspondence course. It took a fair bit of digging to find an accredited Ph.D. program. I wrote to Linda to see if she'd arrange to send a transcript, enabling me to skip some of the prerequisites. She never replied. It's just as well. I'm starting from scratch, however you look at it.

I hear from Drew that Yasmina's wedding was an affair to remember. She and Pedram live in Los Angeles, where he works for her father. She's due next spring.

There has been considerable legal wrangling over Alma's estate. Citing health problems, Palatine recused himself as executor, throwing a major kink into the process. Taxes needed paying; my lawyers (I now have several) needed paying. Andrei has brought a civil suit. And so forth, everyone grabbing for their piece of the pie.

Leaping into the fray is a certain nonprofit organization that pursues compensation for victims of the Holocaust. Eric knew whereof he spoke when he said that Alma's family had worked for the Third Reich. It's unclear whether the estate will be forced to pay, less clear how much, still less which creditor takes precedence. What about the money held in trust? What about interest?

I don't keep close tabs on the various motions and maneuverings. It's a mess for other people to sort out. Even if anything is left for me, I'll never get to use it. Which is fine by me.

In this way, prison becomes me. I have a roof over my head. I have three meals a day. I have books, and students, and time. Nobody is looking over my shoulder. Here, my opinions carry weight. I am respected. Once I believed that I stood above the judgment of the world, and while that continues to feel less true every day, I do take some small satisfaction in knowing that I've found a home. Alma once suggested to me that freedom obtains when we think of it. If this is true, then I ought to be the freest man on earth. And who's to say I'm not? When I am outside, walking the yard, I look up at the great gray walls, at rows of tiny portals and curls of barbed wire and cameras and floodlights and towers presided over by shadows – I look at these instruments of control, and I know that none of them can penetrate my mind. I picture the teeming mass held in by those walls; I consider my place among that mass; and I think: *my ivory tower.*

The one thing I miss is the bookend. The police took it away as evidence, and anyway, I'd never be allowed to keep such a sharp, heavy object in my cell. I don't know where it is. In a storage locker, perhaps, in a box. My friend. I wish him well.

Dear Joseph—

I apologize that it has taken me so long to reply to you. I've struggled to find the right words, repeatedly discarding earlier drafts. Language seems wholly inadequate to the task. My emotions change, even as I set them down on paper, and they will have changed again by the time I put this in the mailbox.

California has been lovely. The students are a good bunch, the faculty, a genuine boon. And I would be remiss not to mention the weather. It is no small thing to wake up everyday to perfection. Whether such abundant pleasantness is good for the sould I leave up to you to decide.

This isn't to say that it feels like home. I had always thought that I would finish out my days near the place of my birth, and to have been called away at my age still amazes me. Perhaps some are meant to live in exile. I suppose that's true regardless of where one lives, however long one lives there. All earthly homes are temporary. One does not need to be a believer to appreciate the truth of this.

To answer your question: I have been in contact with your parents. I will ask them again to visit you. I can't say whether they'll listen to me, of course. These terrible events have been hard on all of us but, understandably, hardest on them. No matter what

you say, they will continue to fault them-
selves, and they resent being made to feel
guilty. They are angry at you, very angry.
As am I. I wish I could say otherwise. My
office demands otherwise. But you and I don't
have that kind of relationship, do we?

You didn't ask to be forgiven, which leads me
to believe you're not seeking an easy out. Good.
There are none. You've done a grievous wrong.
I am sorry if it sounds cruel of me to say so.
Having always regarded you as a seeker of truth,
I expect that you will not flinch to face it.

Peace unto you.
Father Fred

As for remorse: yes, I feel it. Of course I do. I
took two lives, wrecked at least one family, brought
shame and grief to myself and those I love. Of
course I wish things had turned out differently.
Sometimes, when I am in the mood, I imagine
other possible worlds, worlds in which I am not
this person but another. I think about Alma. I
think about my brother. I weave together past and
present, meditating on the foregone. It's a silly
game, giving reasons, pointing fingers, and I ought
to know better by now. But I can't help myself.
It's in my nature to wonder. It's who I am.